THE ROMANCE OF MY LIFE... NO WAY!

THE ROMANCE OF MY LIFE ... NO WAY!

Farah Anah

WARM PUBLISHING

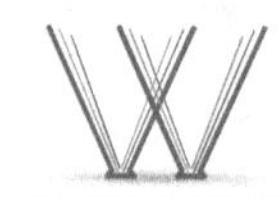

WARM PUBLISHING
El Paso, Texas
www.warmpublishing.com

Original title: *La romance de ma vie... tu parles!*
published by Black Ink Édition
La Jarne, France

Interior design by Warm Publishing
Cover design by Angela Haddon
Art by Scarlett Lovell
Translated from French by Iris Clark
Proofreading by Claire Ashgrove

ISBN: 978-1-958447-29-1

To my maple syrup muse

CHAPTER 1

Damn blank page!

Blank. Blank. Blank. Blank. Blank. Blank. Blank. Blank. Blank. Blank. Blank. Blank. Blank. Blank. Blank.

Fuck, I'm losing my mind!

If I ever manage to start this story, I swear my heroine's name will be Blanche!

My fingers brush the keyboard, trembling. As I start typing the first letters, my stomach tightens. It's impossible to write anything… Immediately, I delete my words, take a deep breath, and erase the unpleasant memories that impose themselves on me.

Midnight. Cold sweat runs down my spine. Vampyr comes to purr on my desk, stationed next to my laptop. Petting his dark fur relaxes me. My baby…

"Don't you want to help me a little, you dirty creature? You must have known one or two horny cats in the neighborhood, right?"

He looks at me with his silver eyes, yawns, and ignores me, a clear sign he doesn't care about my distress.

Okay, Alizee, close this window. Open Bloody Stars, *your super gory thriller, and come up with the best excuse in the world for the best romance editor in publishing.*

In the meantime, engrossed in this delightfully grim story, I let the text numb my unease and only shut my laptop down at dawn.

***

"Write, write, write! You're the one who told me it's not complicated! You have to write every day," exclaims Gala, my best friend, who doesn't understand a thing.

She's bustling around my apartment, hands on her hips, making her long golden hair dance on her bare shoulders. What an idea to wear a tank top in October, seriously… I can't help but suspect her of having a radiator in her butt; it's impossible otherwise!

"Oh! Zee, are you listening to me?"

I lift my eyes to her, clearly showing that she's getting on my nerves big time.

"I do write every day," I retort, dipping my lips into my chicory drink.

"Yeah, creepy and twisted stuff. I'm talking about writing romance!"

"My *creepy and twisted stuff* is really well-crafted, you know. You should read them someday!"

"No way," she says, as usual. Galati only reads and writes feel-good and chick lit.

Of course, my best friend writes. On the side. As a hobby. Her sales job is her true passion.

"We both know your biggest sales are in romance! Besides, I'm craving your stories, doll," she whines, flopping onto my couch. "You haven't published a romance in two years!"

Yes, *doll*, because according to her, with my prominent cheekbones, my little upturned nose, my almond-shaped green eyes, my little plump lips and my golden hair, I look like a doll.

"Yeah, well, why don't you write one then? It's not something you can just command. You should understand that pretty well," I say.

She knows me, and the aggression in my tone doesn't offend her at all. She just doesn't realize how much her arguments are bothering me.

"I'm just afraid that Alan might end up forgetting you, and your privileges might go away as well."

Yeah, right! My publisher is on my ass every week, begging

me to deliver a new manuscript. I'm his golden goose. I'm his biggest moneymaker, and given his thirst for money, he's not ready to let me go anytime soon.

Except I can't do it anymore. Sometimes, I try to do some steamy scenes, just to kickstart the process. Nothing works. For the past two years, when it comes to romance, it's been a blank page.

Well, I did try… They all ended up as bloody thrillers with a murderous heroine and pieces of the hero scattered here and there in the final lines.

As noise from the hallway catches my attention, Gala glances at me wide-eyed.

"Have you seen the specimen moving in next door?" The sparkle in her golden-brown irises

warns of trouble.

"Unless I've been sleepwalking, no."

I'm aware that it's already noon, but as a famous author's schedule requires, I've just gotten up…

The naughty girl bites her lower lip in a smile. "He's not at all unattractive," she says.

On our scale, it's worth a, *He's hot as hell.*

"Glad to hear it." I yawn, finishing the rest of my cup.

She sips her coffee, lost in her thoughts.

Galati Stravis and I met in middle school, but we lost touch after that. As an absolute fan, she contacted me one day through my author profile, and then I recognized her. I went to see her at a book fair for her book release. Since then, our friendship has grown considerably stronger.

Rather reserved, she keeps her hopes to herself. Just like me, she's gearing up for her thirties. However, being single at this age weighs on her. Flourishing in all aspects of her life, she dreams of love, while I don't expect anything from it, despite my career.

I'm a workaholic. I empty myself, excel in my field by expelling all the darkness that lies within me, all the light that refuses to shine. All the life I no longer live. That I run away from. That I loathe.

Vampyr hisses as a knock sounds from the door. My heart jumps, and so does my friend.

"Do you think it's the neighbor?" she whispers as if he could hear her.

I roll my eyes, shrug, and raise my pinky finger, pretending to listen for her answer.

Of course, there are only two apartments on the fourth floor.

"Oh, open it and admire!" she retorts.

I put on my fluffy robe, stuff my feet in my woolen sneakers, and drag myself to the entrance.

Fuck, she's right. My new neighbor is quite good-looking!

"Can I help you?" I mutter with an awkward smile.

Tall. Handsome. Rich brown hair. No ridiculous goatee. Deep, dark, piercing eyes. Rangy and muscular. I have to tilt my head up to make eye contact. He seems intrigued, his smile more genuine than mine.

"Hello, I'm from the apartment next door. I was wondering if you have any coffee, by any chance?"

Wow, he's cute! Wow, he's nice! Maybe he could have introduced himself, though.

"Just a minute."

Unable to be more friendly, I disappear behind the open kitchen while my friend eagerly chats up with Handsome Neighbor. From the corner of my eye, I watch her smile, fidget, flirt...

Despite her blond mane, Gala doesn't exactly fit society's beauty standards. She's a few inches taller than me at five foot five, and has the same small breasts as me, but she's not burdened by the massive rear end that sticks to me. Nevertheless, she exudes a powerful natural charm, a femininity that attracts a category of men that doesn't necessarily enchant her. A category above fifty. For an almost thirty-year-old, it's not always engaging!

When my charitable soul puts an end to her banter with a cup of coffee, my friend starts swaying in a daze.

Starting today, her visits are likely to increase—I'd bet my nails on it. Well, let's stay cautious and not bet my hand...

***

Like every Tuesday, I put on warm clothes, and we brave the outdoors, walking the streets of Montmartre, France. A lump weighs in my stomach. The images of Gala and *Milo*, my new neighbor, haunt me. I mentally delete them, just like I do the sentences of my non-romance novel.

As usual, Gala and I do some shopping before distributing toys and clothes to the Vanille-Chocolat orphanage. My good deed of the week. I have to make up for all the bad things I say all the time. Compensate for all those screaming children that I scare with my murderous glare when their parents aren't looking.

Show empathy for their cause, since I'm familiar with it.

***

With my bowl of popcorn filled to the top and Vampyr on my lap, I open my laptop and take a deep breath.

My flow is complicated tonight. I need more food, more focus.

Suddenly, muffled cries ring out. I frown, trying to decipher what they are.

My heart races. It's coming from next door. Intrigued, I hold my breath for better perception. When I still can't place the sounds, I stand and press my ear against the wall.

Moans! Feminine ones!

Stunned, I step back and rush to my seat, plagued by the need to create more distance between my desk and the lovemaking happening at the neighbor's.

It's not working! Seriously, though? And the high-pitched feminine voice is unbearable!

She keeps going, going, going. *Oh, yes, please. Take my ass, beautiful stallion! Make me come for you!*

My irritation matches my mocking smile. *Make me come for you? Seriously?* All right, but he better hurry.

Unable to concentrate on writing, I stand there, arms crossed, brows furrowed, fuming while enduring their little fuck.

My heart rate picks up. The scent of coconut-scented incense can't blur the distinct images forming in my brain. The guy from this afternoon in action with a hottie. And yet, my fingers refuse to put the scene on the screen.

My heart tightens.

For a long time…

Damn, he's got endurance, the horny devil!

I jump out of my chair and bang my fist against the wall.

"Really? It's two in the morning, damn it!"

They absolutely don't give a damn.

They pause for five minutes and are right back at it again.

All. Night. Long.

And I haven't written a single word.

***

The next day, my alarm goes off at nine AM. I skip the shower and don't bother to get dressed. Mind focused, I position myself by the entrance door, watching for any activity in the hallway. No way am I letting the newcomer disrupt my routine. I need to work in peace. But those fucking images are plaguing my brain and twisting my stomach. *You're going to see what I'm made of, Casanova!*

Around noon, he finally leaves his place. I don't miss the opportunity and rush into the hallway, more wound up than ever.

Then, all the air around becomes dry. I stop in front of a man who is busy locking his door. Squinting, I observe him. His build is imposing, giving off something naughty… very naughty… This is not the same *quite-good-looking* guy from yesterday. Oh, no, definitely not!

My heart starts pounding as he turns toward me, looking surprised. Without a word, he scrutinizes me from head to toe and stands his ground.

Damn, he's handsome. He could easily be a book hero with his broad jaw, three-day-old stubble, fathomless eyes framed by thick eyebrows, and his dark brown fade haircut. A walking cliché!

A walking cliché that takes my breath away. I grimace inwardly.

"That was you, last night?" I attack as a form of greeting.

His lips curl slightly as he nods.

To think that I'm in my fluffy pajamas.

I continue before letting my confusion show. "Are you planning to live here? Or are you squatting in your friend's new apartment? Because I'm warning you right now, there's no way you're going to disturb my nights with your sex life. I work nights, and I need *silence.* That's why I moved here. Tell your chick to keep it down when you're screwing her."

Now it's his turn to be dumbfounded. I didn't bother with politeness, that's for sure, so he knows right away who he's dealing with. With wide eyes, he remains just as unresponsive as before.

Annoyed, I continue, "I hope we understood each other. You can pass the word on to *Milo.* Which one of you lives there?"

He keeps staring at me, then points to himself with his finger.

Is he messing with me?

"The least you can do is answer me!"

I'm well aware that I'm coming off as the grumpy neighbor, but nothing beats the peace and quiet of my nights. Not even this almost unreal, charismatic individual.

The Apollo-like man answers with a shrug, then with the edge of his hand, he points to his throat.

No… don't tell me that he…

"Oh, for god's sake, all that noise when you're mute? Next time, ask your partners to keep it down, out of courtesy."

I leave him standing there, speechless, before slamming the door shut with a resounding *thud* and burying myself under the covers to catch up on my sleep.

I think I made myself clear. So… why is this lump in my stomach weighing me down? Why does the idea of a man like that living next door mess with my guts? Why does it tie knots of anxiety inside me?

I bury my face in my pillow, shivering with fear. Somehow, I manage to fall asleep, with the burning hope of erasing these last hours when I wake up.

CHAPTER 2

I knew it…

The next two nights, I was treated to a concerto of moans in various tones. Not to stray from the cliché, all the chicks were different. Of course.

Two possibilities. The first: he's not only mute but also as deaf as a post and didn't hear a word when I gave him a piece of my mind. The second: he's one of those bastards who think they can do anything because of their amazing looks. Or maybe his dick is out of control. In which case, he would have come to apologize the next day… Unless he finds me terrifying?

This morning, I sent Vampyr to Mr. STD's apartment through the terrace. His mission was to pee on his things. I hope the instructions were clear. When my cat is upset, he pees. He never fails!

He came back two hours later, using the same terrace, while I was reveling in the neighbor's misfortune. Whose name I still don't know, by the way. The only way to find out would be to come out of my foxhole. A rare activity, especially during the first gusts of autumn. I don't need to; my cocoon is far more calming and secure than the outside reality. The wooden floor gives my living room a cozy feel, and the filled bookshelves reassure me. My pen name on the colorful spines fills me with pride. A few plants decorate the large living space where a couch, coffee table, and a desk are arranged. I might feel cramped if a large bay window didn't fill my wall. I could suffocate if the view of the

Sacré-Coeur Basilica's domes wasn't splendid. If I didn't have a terrace where I could settle down to draw inspiration.

Today is definitely not my day. My phone hasn't stopped ringing, displaying calls from my mother that I've ignored. Without a doubt, she'll barge into my lair and try to pull me out of it. I have had enough with Gala's lectures; I don't have the strength to fight an additional enemy.

As a bonus, Delphine, my fantasy book editor, is not satisfied with my seventh manuscript. She sent it back to me with varying degrees of annoyance. Our exchanges are tense. I'm aware I'm only a money-maker for her. I can't stand her narrow-minded ideas about literature. But she works for the biggest publishing group in France, and therefore, she considers her opinion to be absolute truth, which gives me hives.

Fortunately, I still have Marshall. My confidant editor, and the one I let transform my thrillers from start to finish without hesitation. He never undermines me or ignores me. His advice is always wise and kind, even the suggestion to use a masculine pen name. A woman writing gory thrillers is less welcome by the readers, apparently, especially if she also writes romance. Marshall is the one who boosts me during tough times, the one who knows my weaknesses, and even though he gains nothing from it, he's saddened by my blank page syndrome when it comes to love.

It's after one of his calls that my internal engine starts to run. After my daily scrolls on social media to check the impact of my works, I throw myself at my keyboard. The chapters of *Bloody Stars* that I couldn't write last night sprawl across my screen. They tower over the groans that ate me up for hours. The salacious words that gnawed at me.

Suddenly, the doorbell rings. A glance at my watch tells me it's three in the afternoon. If my mother has shown up while I've been lying low, I'm moving to hell!

"Zee! Can you open up?"

Phew! It's Galati.

The obnoxious fairy is glowing in one of her sexiest dresses. She gives me an excited smile, framed by a blow-dry that she rarely does. Her pumps pound my floor as she greets me, then plops onto my sofa. Too much cheerfulness. She's up to something.

"Explain yourself?" I grumble.

"What do you mean?"

"Your presence. Your outfit. Your dopey smile. All these things that are getting on my nerves."

Restless, she rushes into my kitchen to pour us both a glass of soda. "Some things can't be explained. I think I'm going to write a book!"

I roll my eyes and take a sip of my Coke. "But since I always read your stories in advance, you're going to tell me what it's about. Because I was working, you know!"

She raises her eyebrows and crosses her pretty legs. "Has inspiration struck again?"

"For *Bloody Stars*."

Her disappointed pout annoys me. She'll see—the sales will exceed those of my romance novels. That's my goal, and I'll show her.

"Listen, I ran into Milo at the supermarket near my place. Turns out he doesn't live in the building at all! It's his buddy, Ervin, who just moved in. We exchanged our Insta accounts, and in a few comments, he invited me to spend the evening here."

"Here?" I frown.

"Well, next door. They're throwing a housewarming party, and we're cordially invited."

"No way."

Outright refusal.

And her puppy dog expression won't change a thing.

"Why not? It'll do you good to socialize, and it's perfect for you—you don't even have to go out."

A lump forms in my throat. *Ervin.* Of course, he couldn't have a name like Bob or Joe, right? Those kinds of men are sexy. He must be dumb as a rock, because he didn't understand me the other day. Concealing his lack of neurons at first sight… Fate is ironic.

"Forget it, Gala, go by yourself." I keep our first encounter to myself. She would use it as material for her novels, no doubt.

"Come on, doll, I don't know anyone," she protests.

Abruptly, I stand and head for the kitchen, but my friend follows me.

She won't let go of the subject and begs me to accompany her, planting disturbing images in my mind. Those of the mute Adonis on the doorstep, his piercing eyes scanning me from head to toe. Images prompted by those too-loud moans over the past two days. I focus on fabricated images of the crowd, the judgment.

The tension between us escalates, as it often does. The pretty blonde concedes, as she often does, and leaves without asking about my upset.

These quarrels that tear us apart suck my energy. They sadden me and tarnish our friendship more and more. I dread them because the lingering emotions they leave behind weigh on me for days.

Gala has my best interests in mind; I'm aware of that. She doesn't say anything, but she senses something has been wrong for years. I hide behind my workload, but she's known me long enough to understand it's not just that.

Angry at myself, I slump into the chair behind my desk and activate my idle screen. My fingers start typing again, pouring out my frustration. Hours pass without me realizing it. A few bursts of voices can be heard from the next-door apartment. The jerk didn't even tell me about his little party!

Tomorrow, first thing, I'll set things straight with him! His disability is far from holding me back. No, it's his gaze, really, that unsettles me. His gaze and whatever he seems to have in his pants, given the screams of the girls he's entertaining!

Did Gala really join them?

Would I dare admit that I envy her and her ability to overcome her shyness?

While my best friend is far from being extroverted, she refuses to be consumed by her inhibitions. And I know her persistence tonight wasn't just about changing my ideas. She was seeking my support. Which I bitterly refused, like the excellent best friend that I am.

I close my eyelids, take a deep breath that pushes away the lump.

Spanish music starts playing, now preventing me from writing. My phone vibrates.

[Gala: The vibe is cool; I'm sure you'll be comfortable. I'm bored without you...]

Despite our argument, she persists.

[Zee: You can just come back?]

[Gala: No, Milo is great, but his friends are keeping him busy.]

[Gala: By the way, your neighbor is hot! You really should come and have a look…]

Well, thank you very much, I've been hit in the face by his perfection! Going over to his place is trouble waiting to happen.

However, Gala keeps tugging at my heartstrings, adding to my guilt, especially when she rarely gets the chance to go out and meet people…

Lost in my turmoil, I'm startled by the doorbell. I freeze until the second ring, which gives me stomach cramps.

Shit…

I drag my feet as I walk toward the door like it was a march to purgatory.

Much to my surprise, I discover my best friend, beaming, accompanied by the infamous Milo flashing his Colgate smile at me.

"Hey, neighbor!"

Baffled, I frown, reminding myself that I'm in my pajamas. "What are you guys doing here?" I can't help blurting out.

"Don't worry," Gala reassures him. "She's grumpy, but she doesn't bite. It's just how she is." She turns back to me. "Milo was wondering why you weren't coming, and Ervin felt bad that he didn't invite you in person."

"That's the only thing he feels bad about? Really?"

They exchange a questioning glance before shrugging and insisting that I join them.

No matter how much I push them away, Milo—whose little beard intrigues me—is far more persistent than my friend. While I'm unsure what she might have told him about me, tears brim in my eyes. My chest tightens.

I absolutely *don't want* to go to this damn party. Yet, I can't seem to escape it.

I'm pissed off, but I head to my room. Avoiding my mirror, I search for an appropriate outfit that flatters my disproportionate body. The choice is quickly made. I opt for a black dress with cap sleeves that hugs my waist then flares loosely to just above my knees. I put on opaque tights and heeled boots, which are supposed to give me a slimmer figure.

As I think about the handsome guy next door, I hesitate over undoing my messy bun. No, I don't want to attract his attention or let him scrutinize me. I'm sure the comparison to the chicks he fucks would be excruciating. I outline my green eyes with kohl to conceal my tiredness and find a small box of chocolates hidden in my cupboard to use as a polite gesture. This is the chance to set him straight by choking him with chocolates.

Ready, I endure my friend's appreciative look, her new friend's unwavering smile, and leave my apartment with an immeasurable sense of anxiety.

Once we enter the living room next door, the smell of cigarettes hits my throat. Even though the smoke is being drawn toward the wide-open bay window, it has already tainted the air. I recognize the wooden floor, the cream-colored walls, and the high ceiling characteristic of the Haussmann-style building, but the layout is completely different from mine. Much more masculine, my neighbor has chosen dark leather armchairs and a basic coffee table. A few framed photos adorn the place—which is still without rugs—and a small bar separates the open kitchen.

In the center of the living room, a few couples are dancing a *bachata*, and I take stock of the other guests. There must be about fifteen. Following Milo's lead, I navigate through a sea of men, as well as two or three women that look like they stepped straight out of fashion magazines. I don't belong here.

"Make yourself comfortable and help yourself. The kitchen is open to all," Milo informs me.

Wasn't my neighbor supposed to regret not inviting me personally? He could have welcomed me if that were true. *Pff, it was just a trick to trap me! Gala is going to hear about this.* In the meantime, I look for a place to put my chocolates and head toward the aforementioned kitchen.

In the hall beside the minibar, I accidentally drop my chocolate box. It crashes to the ground with a dull sound, echoing the missed beat of my heart.

Fuck.

My perfectly virile neighbor is currently making out against the kitchen counter with a lost lamb.

I swallow hard, hypnotized by the obscene game of tongues, and superimpose this image on the one inspired by the melody of his lovemaking.

My skin tingles, even though I would like to warn this woman. The poor girl probably has no clue where that mouth has been after midnight. Otherwise, she wouldn't be so enthusiastic about cleaning his tonsils.

During their languorous dance, the serial kisser's gaze happens to meet mine. And the contact is intense. It electrifies my belly.

Frozen in embarrassment, I can't tear myself away from the spectacle. He, on the other hand, takes too long to stop. When his partner notices me, a soft laugh escapes her swollen lips before she returns to the living room with a bottle of vodka.

My neighbor stands there looking at me with a smug smile, his hands in the pockets of his torn jeans. Tonight, I detect a slightly disconcerting bad-boy vibe in him. His expression turns my embarrassment into irritation. I pick up my chocolates and put them on the countertop, right in front of him, masking the slight tremors that his fiery eyes provoke in me.

"Hey," I shout.

His smile widens.

His muteness isn't an excuse. His chin raised, he's looking down on me.

"It's very nice of you to invite me. I was bored at home, especially since I couldn't work due to the music. But I guess that's not something you care about, huh? Apparently, it doesn't stop you from breathing."

His expression remains unchanged as he crosses his arms—arrogant prick!

"Here are some chocolates, because I'm nice," I spit out, not looking nice at all. "If you could return the favor by giving your crotch some time off, that would be great. We can decide on the days, if you struggle with scheduling."

He raises an amused eyebrow. I can't stop myself; my heart is beating too fast.

"For instance, you could get laid on weekends and Mondays. It would allow me to focus without interruptions the rest of the week."

He uncrosses his arms and walks toward me with the look of a predator that has hooked his prey. If he starts yelling at me, I swear he'll suffer my wrath! Ah, but no, he can't talk. Thank god…

"Mondays aren't really convenient for me, actually."

But… he's speaking.

Dumbfounded, I remain freeze for a few seconds, wondering if I've hallucinated. A few inches away from me, he towers over me with his imposing muscles, his bewitching spicy scent sending all my senses toward my lower belly.

His dark eyes scan my face, travel down to my non-existent breasts, cascade over my too-wide hips, and end at my boots.

"I like to relax during the week," he whispers, bringing his face closer to mine.

My breathing becomes shallow. Damn, and on top of that, his voice is husky and devilishly sexy. I swallow, then, unable to retreat, I admonish him, "You're not mute at all!"

This time, he squints and steps back. "Not at all, no. I still don't understand why you jumped to that conclusion."

Is he kidding me? I mimic the gesture he made to me on the doorstep, furious.

"So, you figured that I don't speak from that?"

"What should I have thought?"

"To put it on mute. You were screaming so loud the whole building could hear. I wanted to spare you a reputation as an asshole."

Now, it's my turn to be speechless. His handsome face takes on a mischievous expression. He licks his lips, surveys the room behind me with a casual glance, and then locks his dark and slightly glazed eyes back on mine.

"Instead, your prudish reaction titillated my curiosity."

"The prude invites you and your curiosity to go—"

Without warning, his index finger crashes into my lips. I startle and instinctively move back, cornering myself against the minibar.

"Instead of giving me crap," he says, seriousness returning, "why don't you tell me your name?"

My mouth still burns from his touch, and the air around me feels dry, much like everything else around us. Only a soft salsa and my magnetically attractive neighbor, with his horrifying behavior, remain.

"What if I don't want to?" I breathe out.

"I'll find out sooner or later."

He tilts his head to one side, fully aware of the effect he's having on me. This stinks… He must be used to changing the women's minds; I'm just another victim.

No way. I'm not going to be fooled.

I blink, regaining my composure, and glare at him once more. "Alizee Roy. Your neighbor and biggest pain in the ass. You better watch yourself."

This time, he lets out a genuine laugh, and then extends his hand. "Pleasure to meet you, Alizee. Ervin Shiro. Your new neighbor, incapable of silencing his conquests, much to his own chagrin."

I roll my eyes but don't refuse his handshake, which is both firm and gentle. He takes a few seconds too long to let go. Seconds where his teeth bite into his lower lip and my belly contracts. Where I start to feel scared.

***

At midnight, only our host's intimate circle remains. Empty bottles litter the coffee table, and the scent of Alix and Lionel's weed overwhelms me. I focus on Gala's shy smile as she's devoured by Milo's sparkling eyes.

Undeniably, he's very charming. And very interested in my friend. But they both show the same restraint. Obviously, it's not his biological clock that's ticking. *Come on, man! Be brave and get closer to her!*

The evening was relaxed, as Galati had predicted. I ate, drank, reacted to a few jokes, refused two dances, criticized Ervin three times. Wiped away his unkind and terribly arrogant remarks. Stopped my stomach from tumbling with each of his fleeting glances.

Given his lustful gaze, he would have eaten Marlene, the chick he'd been making out with in the kitchen, if they were alone again.

What's it like to be kissed by a man like him?

The images resurface. Legs spread, overshadowed by his massive chest. His teeth sink into his lower lip. Into the flesh of his prey. Into delicate, perfect, female flesh. The complete opposite of mine…

Fuck! It's been too long since I've had sex. Just the sight of a handsome guy is making me go crazy, even if he's obnoxious.

I remember one from my college days. Jean-Michel, with a cock as disappointing as his name. The one-night stand ended with a… flavorless penetration. His loud orgasm after ten minutes confirmed my belief that selfish lovers existed, thinking their pleasure is the sole purpose of a romp in the hay.

I lost my virginity just before my high school graduation, with my boyfriend at the time. Giving in after three weeks hadn't been very wise. He took what he wanted and dumped me without further explanation. So, I wanted to get revenge during my last year of college. I didn't come out of it satisfied. Since then, I've been avoiding sex and content with writing about it. Give me gangbangs and seventh heaven; I'm the queen of debauchery!

"I'm a customer service manager, and Zee is a writer." I hear Gala chattering.

All eyes turn to me. Dual feelings rush over me: mistrust over their possibly hostile attention and pride over being able to share my resume with them.

The usual questions start pouring in:

"What do you write?"

"How many books have you published?"

"What do you do to make money on the side?"

"Can you make a living from it?"

If they only knew that bookstore shelves are dominated by my bestsellers… I've always declined TV invitations and face-to-face interviews. Since I refuse exposure, my various pen names protect me from the spotlight.

I explain that I studied literature and criminology, that I'm trained in those fields, and that it's my fucking job. The one that allows me to afford an apartment in the beautiful neighborhood of Montmartre.

Their admiring expressions boost my confidence. The mocking

look from Ervin, standing behind the couch, grates on my nerves.

"And what do you do with your time, apart from… you know what?" I ask.

He walks over and flops down on the sofa beside me, just a few unfortunate millimeters from my person. Paralyzed, I try to remain immune to the warmth of his thigh against mine, his piercing gaze, and his dominant posture.

"I'm a cameraman. I make sports documentaries."

My throat dries up. The presence of his arm stretched over the back of the chair, behind my neck, makes me tense.

"That's great!" Gala exclaims. "What kind of sports?"

"A lot of motocross," replies Alix, one of his buddies, running his hand over his blond curls.

"That's right. And I didn't need any diploma to learn everything, Miss Smart Girl," Ervin says.

I glare at him with my most disdainful look, my pride stung. "Good for you. My brain must not be developed enough to teach myself."

Milo and Gala exchange a worried glance, as if our disagreement is embarrassing them.

"Considering the amount of crap you're capable of throwing at me every minute, I have no doubt about your brain's capabilities," Ervin retorts.

I can't help but smile. "I've been rather inspired these days."

"Inspired, huh?" he murmurs, getting closer to my ear, like a wolf ready to attack.

All right. That's enough. I jump up, searching for oxygen despite the stifling atmosphere. "I'm going to bed; I've had enough!"

CHAPTER 3

The agreement has been set.

I have my weekends, Tuesdays, and Wednesdays to write in silence, at any hour of the night. The rest of the time, I suppress the concerto taking place in the next room through Boy Epic's delicate voice. It transports me, accentuating the unease that creeps over me when my imagination overflows and I try to put down on paper the words that come to me then. So painful. Like stabs in the heart.

It's been two weeks since I last saw him. I often hear him—in his living room, on the landing—but we've never crossed paths. I've made sure of that.

Of course, I checked his Twitter, Facebook, and Instagram accounts. I held my breath over his almost indecent photos, his chiseled torso, his suggestive poses, all commented on by a horde of appreciative, willing conquests. What was he looking for by exposing himself in that way? What were they all looking for, these well-built men, with their inciting images? Ervin doesn't need to lure women with that; he doesn't have any trouble flirting in real life. So why? Moreover, no woman ever appears by his side. At least not a girlfriend.

It's amazing how revealing social media can be. We barely talked, yet his photos reveal his love for travel, nature, and animals. He went on a motorcycle road trip in the United States, spent two years in Albania—his home country—and then a year in Indonesia, where he did some brilliant reporting before returning and working for one of the biggest sports channels in Europe. He also filmed the construction of a villa in Andalusia and posted the videos on Facebook.

I felt like a stalker, an intruder, but immediately remembered that his profiles are public. Consequently, he allowed me to spy on him, and even indirectly encouraged it.

Galati has been quite busy, but she was hoping to get closer to Milo. I'm the only one too bitter to be insensitive to the boy's kindness. He fits my friend's criteria perfectly, except that apart from a few casual messages—initiated by him—he hasn't texted her back.

After having lunch with leftover pizza, I gather the children's books I ordered online into a bag and put on my puffy jacket. My phone starts ringing. I glance at the screen.

Alan. Editorial Director at LoveRomance Publishing. I roll my eyes, activate the speakerphone, and begin putting on my shoes.

"Hello, Alizee, how are you?"

That honeyed tone doesn't work with me, and he knows it. "Great. To what do I owe the honor of your call?"

"The organizers of the upcoming romance festival contacted me. They really want you to host their conference."

"No."

"They're paying generously."

His insistence used to irritate me, now I don't care. "You'll tell them, as you do every year, that I prefer to remain anonymous. And besides, it's been two years since Jade Evans published anything."

"Yet, you're still on the shelves. I assure you, revealing your identity and promoting you could increase your book sales tenfold. Even two years later."

Ever the opportunist.

"Appearing under the name Jade Evans, huh? You forget I have several pen names. What if I decided to reveal myself under one of my other names? I've been invited on TV shows for my thrillers. You know that will never happen for my romance stories."

He mumbles, offended. Despite being the number one publisher of romantic literature, this genre is far too unpopular in France, unfortunately.

"As you wish, Alizee! Just remember that your favorite genre is romance, and if you delay bringing me a new book, readers will forget about you."

I grab my bags and open the door with my phone in my pocket. "I'm aware of that, Alan."

When I turn around after locking the door behind me, a confrontation with my neighbor freezes me in place. He also stops, on the last step of the staircase. Apparently, he's unwilling to risk the building's outdated elevator, too.

"Yet, you continue to write for others! Do you think I don't know that? The world is small; don't try to feed me lies."

This time, he manages to get under my skin. I grab my cell phone and bring it closer to my mouth. "Listen, Alan, it's not my fault if nothing inspires me! I just can't do it. Don't blame me for wanting to make a living differently. Maybe it's the pressure you keep putting on me that's preventing me from moving forward! Perhaps if I worked with Ludivine, who's known to be ten times less of a pain in the ass than you, it would be easier. On that note, Have a good day!"

This is a perfect example of Alizee Roy losing her nerve in front of her neighbor, the pheromone diffuser. She's most likely going to sabotage her great relationship with her amazing editor.

"Are you blackmailing your editor?" Ervin chuckles in front of me.

I exhale loudly and try to reorganize my thoughts. "He'll get over it. An occasional outburst won't finish him off."

Dressed in a leather jacket over a navy turtleneck and distressed jeans, Ervin is to die for. His slicked back hair clears his face, except for a rebellious strand falling over his brow. Probably dislodged by the helmet he is holding.

Just yesterday, he was giving pleasure for hours…

Fuck! Can't get it out of my head! Whenever I see him, my thoughts go straight to his sexuality.

For once, his smile seems kind. He walks toward me, taking advantage of my distraction to peek at the books I'm carrying.

"I never pictured you writing for children at all."

"I don't have enough heart for that," I grumble as a warning.

He squints, a pout distorting his full lips. "Do you plan to burn all these books, hoping to find your inspiration again?"

The rascal, not only did he listen to me, he remembered everything!

I don't have time for another verbal joust.

"I'm taking these books to an orphanage," I explain with a shrug. "If you'll excuse me, I need to hurry. After that, I have a masterpiece to finish, and since I couldn't write last night…"

He remains still, and I try to slip between his frame and the railing. He grabs my wrist. Taking advantage of my surprise, he snatches the bag from my hands, eliciting a cry of indignation from me.

"Let me take you."

I size him up, my heart racing. The burn from our contact still lingers. "No need. Give me back my bag."

He keeps it out of my reach, a mysterious smirk on his lips. "You have to hurry, right? Let me make amends for last night. I have half an hour before an appointment; I can do you this favor."

Silent, I don't manage to read his expression. His deep irises are covered by a frosty veil, despite his smile, despite his offer. He makes me uncomfortable as much as he attracts me. It's inexplicable. Impalpable.

"I… don't want to ride with you." I sigh.

"I have a second helmet. I insist."

***

He got the best of me.

I surrendered.

On the sidewalk, I try to put on my helmet, but my head refuses to fit into the damn thing. Already suited up, Ervin comes to my rescue. With his helmet, he gives off a nervous energy that commands attention. When he places mine in my hands and undoes my bun, his gaze through the glass visor finishes me off.

"It'll be easier like this," he says as he sweeps my hair down my back.

"Thank you."

For the first time in my life, I get on a motorcycle. And not just any motorcycle, a breathtaking classic—a beautiful black Harley Davidson. Scared, I spend a long time trying to figure out where to put my arms until he takes control and positions them around his chest. Fortunately, his leather jacket makes the drumming of my heart undetectable. We weave through the traffic jam of Paris, the bike swaying us from side to side, increasing the adrenaline that twists my stomach. Out of breath, I leave no doubt that this is my first motorcycle ride. Ervin doesn't make fun of me; he asks about my well-being with disconcerting consideration.

Today, I don't linger in the orphanage. Vadim and Maeva, my favorite kids—because they fear me—won't get my reading session or progress updates on my thriller. I'm quick, hoping to get back to my den soon, still reeling from my motorcycle ride and leaning against my hot neighbor's back. It's probably the most extraordinary thing I've done in… well, I don't know, to be honest.

Too damn long.

CHAPTER 4

Friday, after work, Galati shows up at my place, anxious as usual. She doesn't like the fact that I'm still in my fluffy pajamas at five o'clock, and once again, I tell her I don't like the idea of dirtying my clothes when I'm not going out. It would mean doing more laundry. An eco-friendly vegetarian like her should understand, damn it.

"Well, I think I'll give up on Milo. He's hard to figure out," she complains as she slumps behind my desk.

Vampyr, who was napping on my turned-off computer, startles, and then runs into my arms. Poor thing… That's what happens when they cut their nuts!

"I thought he liked you. What's his problem?"

She sighs, fiddling with my pens while I prepare us some coffee.

"I thought so, too. But although we spend a lot of time texting, he's never asked me out. When I bring it up, he says he's tired or he's with his family."

"Hmm, doesn't sound good…"

Did we cut Milo's nuts, too?

"Yet, he's the one who starts all our conversations. It's not like he doesn't like me. But I'm tired of overthinking things. I really want to see him; it's driving me crazy."

She seems to be pretty smitten, actually. With her parents retired in Greece, her siblings scattered all over France, our friends with their own lives, her job, and writing, her routine hasn't been so great these last months. The opportunities to meet a guy who also interests her are quite limited. So, giving up on Milo seems too fast.

I serve her a cup of coffee, then pick up my phone. "Look at this, Gala! I knew I had seen something about it this morning."

She approaches me as I scroll through Ervin's Facebook page.

"They're going out with friends at Bloodybar tonight."

The information makes its way into her mind. "I didn't know you were Facebook friends with Ervin," she says.

"You're kidding! I'm not."

She raises an eyebrow, glances at my phone screen, looks back to me with an annoying sparkle in her eyes. "So… If you knew about their outing, it's because you stalked his profile."

Mouth agape, I try to figure out how to defend myself, while she raves, hands on cheeks.

"Oh, my god! You like him! You like Ervin! You like *a man*!"

"Never in a million years!" I retort vehemently.

She gets up without warning, rushes into my bedroom, chirping in her high-pitched voice.

"Gala! Where are you going?" I rush after her.

"To find something for you to wear tonight! But it's great—*you like Ervin!*"

"Keep repeating that crap, and I'll kick you out!" I snap as she searches my closet. All I need is for her to get the wrong idea.

Even Vampyr meows in disagreement.

"Don't jump to conclusions," I insist, standing in front of the dress that she throws on my bed. "I can't stand him. He prevents me from writing, and he has a bad fucking temper!"

"I don't think so. And if that were the case, why did you, who only goes on Facebook for your books, end up on his profile, checking his schedule?"

Is this some kind of investigation? "To see if he'll bother me tonight!"

Her wary gaze assesses me for a few seconds before she sighs and sits on the edge of my bed.

Even though I hide my clenched fists behind my back, she's not fooled.

"He's hot. I'd understand, you know."

There's nothing to understand.

"He changes partners like shirts. It's just a deal-breaker!"

She shrugs, caressing the tight burgundy dress she selected. One I wore before, when I still imagined I could have some effect on men.

"Let's say you're not interested in Ervin. A part of me doesn't want to give up on Milo. But I need a little support, my dearest best friend… If you agree to come with me to the Bloody, I might have a chance to get answers to my questions."

And that's how Galati once again dragged me into an environment I loathe. Wearing down my resistance by taking me by my feelings is a tactic that works sometimes.

The advantage of these bars is the darkness that hides us. I should have remembered that before arguing with Gala about my wardrobe. She insisted that I put on *the* dress. The one that shattered me in the past, leaving an indelible mark on my soul. And big loser that I am, I gave in to her unbearable persistence. A donkey would lose its head in front of her determination.

She did my makeup, curled my hair for the occasion, and swiped one of my old outfits—a frilled black dress adorned with small, candy-pink hearts. With the patent pumps she always wears at work, she looks like a Lolita.

In my dark red outfit with a plunging neckline, hugging my curves down to my knees, adorned with pretty lace sleeves, I move through a crowded mass following my friend, drink in hand. We settle at the back of the room, scanning for familiar faces in the crowd.

"What if we're in the wrong place?" She starts to worry.

I roll my eyes, sip my Red Bull Vodka through a straw. A popular track blares through the speakers, igniting the drunken bodies on the dance floor. I need to relax. What if they changed their minds? Deep down, a small voice rages at that thought while my conscience desperately hopes for it.

"All right, come on, let's dance!" she impatiently insists.

She gets up, and despite me shaking my head, she drags me along roughly.

A few glances have already traveled across my face. They lingered too long on my non-existent cleavage, shamelessly roamed the rest of my anatomy.

I squeeze my eyes shut and try to ignore them. I don't know them, I'll never see them again. I don't care.

I start moving to the rhythm. I don't move away from Galati, preventing any unwelcome closeness. This place stinks... My only desire right now is to get out of here.

When I open my eyes, the first image that comes to me, behind Galati, is Ervin, his hands resting on a lovely, swaying butt.

Stunned, I realize he saw me long before. His playful gaze, the provocative smile that is specially addressed to me, leaves me feeling trapped. I can't get rid of it, can't warn my friend that they are there, that we're not in the wrong bar.

Suddenly, I'm too hot. While he gropes the stranger who turns her back to me, his eyes half-closed, probably questioning my presence here, shame consumes me. He knows. He knows I'm not here by chance, there's no doubt about it. Why would I set foot in a bar, me, his neighbor, the recluse?

"Oh, Milo's here!" Gala exclaims.

I swallow hard, cough up my lungs until the main person of interest pats me on the back.

"Hey, are you okay?" he worries. "Hi, ladies, what a surprise!"

The guy seems sincerely delighted. No awkwardness; meeting Galati doesn't seem to bother him. Excellent news. I'll be able to leave them.

Alix and Lionel, his two party companions, warmly greet me. Lionel is all dressed up, with his semi-long black hair cascading over his temples, his fitted shirt and tight jeans completely different from the sweatpants he wore at the housewarming party. As for Alix, he remains faithful to the image I had of him at the apartment. Some kind of hippie with golden hair, shamanic clothes, and an adorable smile that manages to smooth out the wrinkles on my forehead.

"I didn't know you guys hung out here," says Milo, who hasn't abandoned his baggy T-shirt, which falls over slim-fitting pants on his slender legs.

"Us neither, don't worry," I grumble, a grimace frozen on my lips, as Ervin joins us with his conquest.

It's Friday, his *relaxation* day. The physique of this mermaid leaves no doubt about her fate. Tanned skin, long ebony hair, a goddess's body, and sophisticated makeup… she'll scream through the walls, too.

I start to feel irritated. Frustrated, I let out a sigh, trying to catch my breath.

He doesn't even know her name; he just keeps touching her. My eyes shoot daggers at his hands on her hips and the way his muscles stretch his T-shirt and jeans.

Torn between jealousy and repulsion, I'm furious with myself for not being able to divert my attention.

The gentlemen offer us a drink, then they go hunting for women. Milo sticks to my friend like glue. Although he devours her with his eyes, he doesn't make any moves. What an idiot!

I slip away and return to our original seat. This place inspires me. I take out my tiny notebook and scribble on the paper.

Minutes pass, jokes flow. Then Ervin's unexpected remark to me makes me raise my chin.

"Did you get bored with the silence at home? I got you too used to moans; I guess I have to up my game."

Fuck! He gazes at me with that damned mocking smile. Holding two drinks, he sits next to me.

"What do you think, smartass? I was just keeping my friend company."

When he places the Red Bull Vodka near me, his eyes scan my cleavage and then travel to my lips. Damn, he's already a bit drunk.

"Where's the brunette?"

He scans the bar and shrugs. "She left, I think."

"It's a bad night for both of us!"

He pisses me off so much. He manages to poke at that thing deep inside me that makes me addicted to our exchanges.

"A horrible night. If only you hadn't shown up…"

I swallow hard. My heart rate quickens. "Don't tell me I screwed your hookup."

He chuckles, and his nose brushes against my neck as he leans closer to my ear, sending a thousand shivers down my spine.

"Just my mood. There are at least five chicks I could still go home with."

I stiffen, aware of every touch, every drunken breath on my skin. What do I have to do with his mood? "Five? Only that?"

He continues to breathe against my skin, erasing everything around us. The Wonder Woman in me seems incapable of any movement. My heartbeat is erratic, and my fingers tighten around my glass until he finally moves away. The surroundings take shape again, saving me from his intimidation.

"Five at a time, if I want."

Such arrogance, my god! His charm doesn't work anymore; he can go and ravage his dick if that's what he desires. I'm going back to my notes!

✳✳✳

"Are you sure you don't mind?" asks Milo.

"Yes, I do mind, but I don't really have a choice. We can't leave him in this state," I rant as I position Ervin's leg on my bed.

"He deserves it," says his friend, placing the pillow behind his head.

He helps me remove his drink-stained T-shirt, jeans, and shoes, leaving only a lifeless, exquisite body in my bedroom. I place a bucket next to the bed just in case and dismiss Milo as quickly as possible, eager to find some semblance of silence.

Once the door is closed, I lean against it and close my eyes for a few endless minutes. The room still sways a bit. I've had few drinks, too, but not enough to disconnect. I don't know what Gala's plans were, but my evening wasn't supposed to end like this.

At two o'clock in the morning, exhausted beyon belief, it will be impossible for me to close my eyes. My completely wasted neighbor lies on my sheets, because the slightest stain on my ultra-expensive couch would have pushed me to commit murder. And let's admit it, depriving the world of such a visual pleasure would only increase my punishment, no matter how obnoxious the guy is.

Five women, he said… He did get in more than five shots, that's for sure. If his friends hadn't stopped him, I don't know what kind of disaster he would have caused. And the moron lost his keys. Thank goodness, this sucker of a neighbor was here to take care of him.

His presence bothers me. To the point that I send a text to Marshall—my favorite editor—to explain to him that a hottie straight out of the romance novel I can't write anymore is sleeping in my bed, almost naked.

I switch on the kettle, then head for my bedroom, where I try to ignore his snoring. Even asleep, he remains a nuisance! I trade that ridiculous dress for my fluffy pajamas before settling on the empty side of my bed.

Only the lights from outside illuminate the room, piercing the pristine curtains. Ervin is sprawled out, massive and bulky. The Instagram photos hadn't lied; he looks just as sculpted in real life. *How much time does he have to spend at the gym? What kind of routine does he follow to create such a muscular body?* Without breathing, I approach him, lie down on my side, facing him, without noticing the interruption of his snoring.

I examine every inch of his skin: the bulge in his floral boxer shorts, his sparse body hair tracing a darker arrow toward his navel, only to wander even lower.

His eyes are still closed, but the corners of his lips lift. "You should go; I'd rather sleep alone," he mumbles.

I tense in surprise, waiting for any movement. Then, his words start to resonate.

"*I* should go away?" I repeat, dumbfounded.

No, but he's serious!

His head turns toward me, his expression crinkles, and he attempts to open his eyes, struggling.

Now sitting up, I glare at him, sternly trying to maintain my composure.

"The… neighbor? Shit. Damn it…"

He places his hand on his forehead, in the grip of an invisible pain, when suddenly his body is shaken by spasms. I rush to his side and place the basin nearby, but he draws in a deep breath and manages to hold everything in.

Uneasily, he lies back down while I vanish into the kitchen for some sort of remedy. When I return, he's watching me, looking unwell. I bring him an aspirin, a glass of water, and a strong coffee.

"You don't have to do this."

"Don't worry, witnessing your downfall is quite entertaining," I retort, sitting cross-legged next to him again. "Five chicks, you said?"

He chuckles, staring at the ceiling. "In the end, it's you who put me in your bed. Taking advantage of a drunk man is bad."

I raise my eyebrow, trying not to linger on his profile, made even more desirable by his vulnerability. "If it saves me from your sexcapades, I might as well get you drunk every night."

"What am I doing here?" he asks suddenly.

"You lost your keys."

After a weary and deep sigh, he sits up and drinks a few sips of the coffee.

Does he realize the effect his presence in my home has on me? He's probably used to hanging out in various bedrooms, but here, it's my sanctuary. Only a few close friends are invited in. So, a guy like him, in the bed of a girl like me... he can tease me all he wants, but I know for sure he doesn't see it that way at all. I'm the uptight neighbor who's helping him out, despite the fact we're at war with each other.

"I'm sure my fucking sessions turn you on," he says as naturally as possible.

His seriousness makes me burst out laughing. "Well, I didn't see that one coming! I've told you before, they distract me from work. They also make me wonder about your emotional stability. You never sleep with the same girl."

He chuckles, his slightly glazed but still piercing gaze drilling into my brain, even in the dim room. "How closely have you been studying my partners' voices?"

His comebacks are becoming exhausting. "How far are you willing to go to avoid my questions?"

He sighs, places his half-empty cup on the nightstand, and turns onto his side, facing me, his elbow folded under his head. "There's no need to evade. I just don't want to get into a serious relationship."

"Why not?"

"Because it's easier that way. In the morning, I get up, go to the gym, and then, depending on my contracts, I work. Sometimes, I'm abroad for a few days for work. In the evening, I like to relax with my friends, I like to go out, drink, and have sex. I don't need a woman in my life. I'm not interested."

His last sentence resonates with me. I'm not interested either. Maybe not for the same reasons.

"You see, I'm not a complicated guy."

"I'd even say you're quite primitive."

"What about you? You don't fuck; why don't you have a boyfriend?"

Offended, I stiffen. There's no way I'm opening up to this jerk. "First of all, who says I'm not having sex?"

His smile says it all.

Fuck! With clenched jaws, I glare at him with my most angry look. Then I remember that provocation is his fuel.

"There's more to life than sex," I argue. "I'm focused on my career; I don't think about love."

On those words, Vampyr, who our conversation woke up, climbs onto the bed and rubs himself against my folded legs.

"You stole his spot," I scold Ervin, whose attention destabilizes me.

I pet my cat and pull him onto my lap. I can't resist kissing his head.

"I see…"

"See what?" I reply, a bit aggressively.

Ervin moves his hand toward my baby, who growls a warning, showing his teeth.

"Have you had a lot of boyfriends?"

Why is he even concerned about this? "No," I can't help but admit. The atmosphere, fatigue, and the remaining alcohol in my veins prevent me from keeping quiet.

"How many?"

Shut up, Zee. Shut up, shut up, shut up, shut up. I hesitate about the number… Bury some memories. "One." Damn it!

"How long?"

"Three weeks."

"When?"

"My senior year of high school."

He remains stoic for a few seconds, during which his black eyes roam over my body.

Uncomfortable, I curl up behind Vampyr, feeling exposed. I hate his reaction, yet I stay there, eager for his responses. *What is he thinking? Does he understand no man has ever wanted me?*

"Did you sleep with him?"

I swallow. Nod silently.

"And then?"

For once, he remains serious. For once, I'd rather not confront him. "That's none of your business."

I chase my cat off me and prepare to leave, but he grabs my wrist.

"Wait. Answer me."

My breathing stops. I fear revealing myself in the next breath. I fear he'll be able to read me if I stay in this room any longer. "No. Torture yourself with your existential questions. I need to sleep." And to get out of this suffocating room.

"You can stay," he insists, still not letting go of me. "I won't jump on you in my state."

"Oh, I'm not worried about that. Even in your full capacity, I doubt you'd ever throw yourself at me." I yank my arm free and get off the bed.

"Why?"

I look at him for a few seconds, irritated to no end. What is he really looking for? To get me to talk about the fact that I'm below his standards? To get me talk about my extra pounds? About my stringy hair? My too-pale skin?

"Are you seriously asking me that question? Well, goodnight."

CHAPTER 5

When the first light of morning enters my living room, I regret not having left my drunken neighbor to his fate, alone in the hallway. It's seven in the morning, and I can't fall back asleep, no matter how comfortable my sofa is. The thought of returning to my sheets gnaws at me, but confronting the snoring madman will keep me from falling asleep. Not because of his snoring, no…

A creaking noise catches my attention. I focus on the approaching footsteps. I open one eye, but he has already made his way to the kitchen.

Okay, I can say goodbye to sleeping in. "Did you get lost?" I yawn as I join the clattering of dishes.

Ervin walks around in front of my countertop, cup in hand, still in his boxer briefs.

Fuck! Nothing but boxers.

I swallow hard as my eyes lock on his aroused cock that peeks out from the edge of his underwear. Well, *peeking out* is an understatement, considering all that's showing.

Oh. My. God.

"Sorry, I didn't mean to wake you. Where's the coffee?"

Still groggy, I point to the shelf without taking my eyes off his erection. Holy di— uh, shit! What's that thing doing in my apartment? In my kitchen? Am I still dreaming? Well, more like having a nightmare.

"I don't understand why you bother with boxers," I mutter, scandalized. "Can you put that thing away?"

He takes a few seconds to understand, and he immediately follows the path of my gaze. To my surprise, he shrugs and tucks it completely inside the elastic fabric. Goodness gracious, it practically stretches to his hips! Then, Ervin turns his back to me to make himself some coffee.

"Sorry, morning wood. Besides, you're the one who undressed me. I couldn't find my clothes."

Exactly like on his Instagram photos, *Do not fear death. Fear a life of mediocrity* is tattooed on his back, just above a beautiful Koi fish.

"They're in the bathroom," I answer mechanically, hypnotized by his ass.

I gulp.

Curse my hospitality.

"Okay. Well, at least the vision of the monster will have immunized you."

"What are you talking about?"

Without missing a beat, he continues casually, "I mean, you won't see two like this."

Seriously, is he boasting about the size of his— what a jerk!

He goes on, "Since you don't have any experience, this is something that could have stopped you. I've known plenty of hot girls who backed out as soon as they saw the beast."

I'm left dumbfounded by his audacity.

"Who says I don't have experience? I explained I've only had one boyfriend. That doesn't mean I've never seen a naked guy before!"

"You wouldn't have stared at it with such curiosity, then."

Shit…

"So, I guess I should thank you, right?"

"My soul is generous; I don't need gratitude. I do it willingly."

I'm hallucinating this.

He continues to whistle, as if he couldn't care less that I caught a glimpse of his manhood. It's as if being at my place doesn't bother him in the slightest. After getting completely blitzed last night, he's cheerful enough to make me puke. Too many questions are swirling in my head. How do I look in my oversized pajamas, with my messy hair and sleepy eyes? Not that I care what he might think of me… but… I saw… his dick!

Even if he's taking it lightly, isn't this some form of indecent exposure?

OK… Don't react like a prude… Stay calm…

"It's seven in the morning," I complain. "How can you be so perky?"

He moves around me, serves me a cup of black coffee, and leans against the wall in front of me, wearing his ever-present smirk and dimple, which act as a trigger for murderous impulses.

"Habit, I suppose. It's time I go to the gym. You know, to maintain all this," he boasts, pointing to his perfect physique.

Although his erection has disappeared, this resting bulge unsettles me.

Suddenly, my nasal radars pick up a very particular minty scent. I raise my face and glare at him reproachfully. "Did you brush your teeth?"

He raises an eyebrow, brings the cup to his lips, and answers in the affirmative.

"With… my toothbrush?" I growl in low voice, feeling the anger bubbling up in my veins.

He blinks twice, as if he didn't quite understand. "Obviously. How else would I have done it?"

My toothbrush. In his mouth.

"No, this can't be true!" I explode, rushing toward the front door. "Get out of here!"

He stares at me, incredulous and motionless. "What's the problem?"

"What's the *problem?* You used my toothbrush to clean your mouth full of alcohol and all kinds of bacteria? It's disgusting. Since when do you use your host's toothbrush?"

"Don't worry, clean freak, I cleaned it up. Don't get yourself worked up over it."

I. Can't. Believe. It. This lack of manners!

Okay… My wrath has no effect on him. I massage my temples, trying to regain my composure.

"Your clothes are in the bathroom; you can take them with you. I'm sure the locksmiths wouldn't mind if you greeted them on the doorstep nearly naked."

He looks up at the ceiling, continuing to drink. Then he eyes my bookcase, increasing the pace of my palpitations. Not reassured about what he might do next, I approach him, being careful that he doesn't spill anything on my books.

"You're kicking me out?" he finally retorts, absorbed in the book covers.

I don't say anything, irritated and involuntarily intimidated.

Good god, in the harsh light of day, so much exposed flesh makes me uncomfortable. Despite his obnoxious behavior, his presence makes my stomach tingle. I think back to the questions he asked me last night, on my bed. His interest in my love and sex life, his hands around my wrist...

"Which ones are yours?"

Caught off guard, I grow more irritable. "Guess."

"Jade Evans... I can't imagine you reading Jade Evans at all. So, it means that it's you."

My chest tightens. Is he planning to turn the pages? The entwined couple on the cover is quite explicit about the content.

"Anna's life takes a turn when she learns her parents have been lying to her all her life: she's adopted, abandoned by her biological mother at birth. Today, Mike Field shows up at her door, her biological mother's lover and messenger, who wants to meet her. Anna agrees, but she doesn't expect all this man stirs up in her. Between forgiveness, revenge, sex, and manipulation, will the young woman let herself be trapped by her own demons?" Ervin whistles, impressed, and then reads a few pages at random. He squints, deeply concentrating, before moistening his lips.

Shit...

"So, you write smut, huh?" he remarks.

I sigh, my irritability at its peak. "Fuck! You guys are all the same! At the same time, coming from a horn dog like you, what did I expect?" I retort.

He gazes at me, stunned. "Hey, take it easy, I just made an observation."

"An inaccurate observation!" I get angry. "I write romance. And guess what? In love stories, there's sex! It's like in real life, you see.

Of course, you can't understand these two concepts aren't mutually exclusive! But don't reduce my books to pornographic novels!"

"Reduce? I'm sure there are very porno novels out there. Just like there are very good horn dogs," he mocks while putting my book away.

I sigh dramatically, finish my coffee, and pray he leaves as soon as possible. What a jerk!

Unfortunately, he lingers, exploring the works on my bookshelf, aware I'm getting impatient. He's clearly trying to drive me crazy.

"Liliana Fork. Is that another of your pen names? Do you write fantasy? It's like Harry Potter, right?"

My teeth grind together, preventing me from saying a single word.

He gives me a questioning look. "I don't know anything about literature. You have to help me out here."

"It's like *The Lord of the Rings*. Does that ring a bell for you?"

"Yep," he says as he flips through a few pages.

"Have you ever read anything in your life?"

He shakes his head. "No, Miss Writer, it's not my thing."

"Yeah, it's more about motorcycles and abs for you, right?"

My sarcastic tone doesn't seem to affect him. He nods as he puts my book away. "Pretty much, yeah." I don't mention photos, travel, and animals; he'd realize I've been spying on his social media.

"So, why are you asking me all these questions then?"

"You intrigue me."

Stunned, I lose my words.

"We're neighbors, right? Besides, it's not fair. You know how often I fuck, you've checked out my almost naked body, you know the size of my cock. You've even seen me drunk as a skunk. All I know about you is that you're a top-notch pain in the ass and dresses look stunning on you."

My heart misses a beat. I didn't see that coming. He enjoys my dumbfounded reaction, the bastard! Thanking him would choke me.

"I could return the compliment, but unlike you, I don't thrive on hypocrisy."

He grabs another one of my romance novels without reading the synopsis, staring at me in surprise. "Hypocrisy? Me? Sorry, I don't know how to do that. Why do you think that?"

I swallow and immediately regret my remark. I should have said thank you and kept quiet. Instead, I run away and dive into my still-steaming cup.

"I still don't understand how I could have gone out wearing it. That dress makes my ass look fat," I mutter. That too I hate to admit it in front of him, but testing his reaction was far too tempting.

"Tell me about it!"

My chest is cracking. He laughs at my indignation. Am I dreaming? Did he just make fun of me?

"Jerk!"

"No hypocrisy, remember?" he replies, approaching the desk with a feline step and an enigmatic smile.

He goes around it, stops in front of me, puts down the book, leans on the palms of his hands, and leans in. With determination, he gazes at me as if trying to probe my mind. "It's crazy that you write sex scenes that you've never experienced."

I raise an eyebrow, still shaken by his previous comment. Does he realize how much he hurts me? No, of course not. Mr. Muscles must not have the slightest complex.

"Because you think you have to commit murder to be a thriller writer?" *Idiot*.

"Maybe more practice would serve the realism of your writing. The only sentences I came across seemed to me—"

"*What?*"

He moistens his lips, mischievously studying mine. Then he straightens, arms crossed. "I just think you have a lot to learn. I'll take your book with me; I'll make up my own opinion."

"You're not taking anything with you!"

"You'll be the first author I read. You should be flattered."

"There are plenty of other writers who can feed your pitiful intellect much better!" I spit as I stand, panicking at the thought of him keeping his word.

"Getting feisty, huh?" He scoffs, grabbing *All Night Long*.

I see red and rush him, trying in vain to snatch my book back. He raises his arm, observing me hopping around, laughing. Even Vampyr has climbed onto my desk and is looking at me with Olympian calm, the traitor!

"Give it back!" I shout, undeterred.

"Easy there, tigress!" He chuckles, backing away.

When I lean on his pectoral muscles to better leap, he grabs my waist to immobilize me. Through the thick fabric of my pajamas, I feel each one of his fingers digging into my flesh, into those love handles I hate. I pull away, feeling like I've been punched in the stomach.

Breathless, I curse him with all my might. The fact he continues to trample my already shattered self-esteem drives me crazy. That it's not enough to annihilate my attraction to him terrifies me. And the idea that he might dive into my soul through my romance novels makes me nauseous.

Some sounds rise outside—the world waking up while our eyes are locked on each other. In mine, he must read the violence of my bitterness, which makes him regain his seriousness.

"What were you doing at the Bloodybar last night, Alizee?"

His question catches me off guard. "I was just trying to take my mind off things, like almost all the customers of the bar."

He shakes his head slowly. "No hypocrisy, remember? You're not the kind of girl who'd enjoy that."

"What do you think I was doing there, then?"

He squints, seemingly searching my eyes. "It's weird, I had the feeling that you were looking for me."

His damn arrogance ignites my rage. I was accompanying Galati! Who wanted to run into Milo. So why on Earth do I feel like I've been caught red-handed?

"Absolutely not. Is that what got you in a bad mood?"

He nods, taking a deep breath, avoiding answering me.

"Alcohol clouded your judgment. Why would you expect me to follow you to a party, huh?"

"You tell me, Alizee."

It's right at this moment that the doorbell rings.

Paralyzed by panic, I can't make the slightest movement. Who could it be? At this early hour, there aren't many possibilities.

Ervin takes me by surprise, heading toward the entrance, my book in hand and still wearing his boxer shorts.

"Wait!"

Before I can reach him, he opens the door, allowing my worst nightmare to come true. *Mother.*

Wide-eyed, I dare not appear in the doorway. I let him welcome her as if he were at home, his smile devilish as ever.

What they say to each other is lost on me, I'm so dumbfounded.

My mother's puzzled face becomes apparent as she steps inside. He makes room for her and Charles, my half-brother.

Fuck! The last thing I needed was him. At eighteen, he scrutinizes us both, then turns his wide-eyed gaze to our mother. She shakes her head, stunned.

"Alizee? Can you explain the presence of this Greek statue in your home?"

I take a deep breath while glaring at my neighbor. The bastard is clearly restraining himself from laughing.

Charlene Chamoux. My mother. The woman with whom I have a complicated relationship moves away from the male sculpture, who is busy closing the door behind her. She's dressed in a long, leopard fur coat that matches her blond bob. As usual, her complexion is flawless, her make-up accentuated. Her classic wide-leg pants perfectly highlight her slender and elegant silhouette. I've always thought she resembled Cher, with a kind of controlled exuberance.

She represents everything I'm not.

The way she devours Ervin's anatomy with her eyes would have made me laugh, if I weren't so mortified... and if Charles's bored expression weren't adding fuel to the fire.

"It's not what you think, Mom. Let me introduce Ervin, my neighbor."

"Hi," my youngest brother says nonchalantly. "Charles, her brother."

"Hi."

"He was sick and lost his keys, so I let him stay the night," I explain as I help my mother take off her coat. "In fact, he was just about to leave."

"Would you really let me go out naked?"

Now he cares about that! I shrug. "I'm not stopping you from dressing. Your clothes are in the bathroom—like I said."

While my family is settling in, he comes closer to me. Way too close. He whispers in my ear, "I would prefer you take off yours."

A horrible wave of heat overcomes me. I swallow, trying to control my undoubtedly scarlet cheeks. I don't know how to respond in front of my mother, who is looking at me conspiratorially.

His mocking expression betrays his intentions. He's trying to disturb me, playing with my nerves without realizing the depth of the impact. Does my lack of sexual experience amuse him? Why is he picking on me like this?

"If you don't step away right now, your underwear might end up stained with your blood."

He moistens his lips before taking a step back, allowing me to join my unexpected guests, my mind in chaos.

"All right, mind if the washing machine finishes its job, kitten? I'll go home once my clothes are clean and dry. I don't want to catch a cold, and they reek of smoke, I'm sure"

Kitten? He dared to call me *kitten?* I glare at him with lightning in my eyes. My brother's muffled chuckle dimly registers.

"Call me that one more time, and I'll emasculate you for good! We're not that close." I let go, my mother's presence forgotten.

As Ervin disappears into my bedroom laughing, my mother clears her throat after conspicuously eyeing the tattoo on his back.

Crap!

"You guys obviously slept together," she comments in a reproachful tone.

"I slept on the couch."

Her disapproving look starts to weigh on me.

"How chivalrous of you."

I sigh and explain the situation to her, even though she doesn't believe me, before serving them a coffee.

"Is this boy the reason you've been avoiding me for weeks? Your hormones are tingling. I'm totally open to that idea. I don't know when the last time a man touched you was, but we live a few miles apart, and I have to show up by surprise just to run into you!"

Oh, boy, here we go again... How can I explain to her that remarks like that push me further away from her and her family?

Charles is aware of it; he looks at me with compassion and a hint of weariness. I imagine she used some kind of emotional blackmail to convince him to follow her and her utopian ideas about family bonds. Thankfully, she didn't bring Gui, her husband, with her. Faced with the near-nudity of the other idiot, I have no idea how he would have reacted. Charles looks so much like Gui, with his hair as black as his eyes, his stocky build, and his lovely dimples. Often, I can't bring myself to accept that we share the same blood. Especially since this feeling seems to be mutual; we've never been close. Probably my fault.

"You should get out more, Alizee. I mean, look at you. Your job is slowly killing you."

With the encounter with my naked neighbor managed, reality catches up with us. She, of course, can't help but comment on my appearance. My hair is messy despite the bun on my head, I've barely removed my makeup, probably have eyeliner all the way to my jaw, and my pajamas are the type she hates: not flattering at all.

For this cabaret owner, I'm an insult to femininity. And yet, she doesn't possess an ounce of feminism. For her, men are the key to everything. They open the doors to pleasure, plant their seed in us, become our pillar, even though in her own relationship she's the one who wears the pants. A woman full of contradiction, indeed.

Ervin's suggestive insinuations come back to me along with my embarrassment. Asshole!

"The fact that I don't go out has nothing to do with my job, Mom. I'm comfortable at home, don't I have the right? And I do grocery shopping. Often."

"The grocery store is at the end of the street. That's not what I call going out."

"I went out last night."

"To a bar? That's a good start, but, kid, you need to meet people. Beyond your doorstep, I mean. You don't plan on staying like this your whole life, do you?"

"Excuse me, Mom, for never being good enough for you!" For not being like you, for not accepting myself, for not opening up to others.

"Being good enough for me?" she replies, irritated. "It's always about you, Alizee! You would be perfect for me if you were happy. I don't care about the rest. But it's obvious you're not!"

I know what she thinks. As long as no man enriches my love life, she will convince herself that I am unhappy. Because that's how she works. It's also the reason why she quickly replaced my father after his death.

Now, I regret burying her suspicions. Maybe introducing Ervin as a potential boyfriend would have calmed her down. Deep down, I would have been proud to shut her up, to show her I don't need to be skinny, pretty, and sexy to catch a hottie. Well, that's not counting the childish behavior of the aforementioned hottie. I would have briefed him before opening the door: be handsome and shut up!

"I'm doing very well, Mom. Thanks for your concern."

Charles sighs, exasperated, as he does every time we have a confrontation. He heads toward my bookcase. His presence no longer bothers me; he also suffers Mom's supposedly benevolent reproaches.

"I bet your fridge is empty! You only eat frozen pizza, which prevents you from feeling good about yourself. It makes you bitter. Even more so in recent years. People can sense that kind of thing, and that's why they won't approach you."

"Men, you mean? You can say it frankly."

Her jaws tighten, the result of her frustration.

Mine tighten my throat.

"You can't rely on your damned cat when you're in trouble! And in life, we all face difficulties sometime or another. I don't understand why you reject the idea of love so much."

"I don't reject it. I just don't have time for it. Look, if this wasn't just a courtesy visit, you can go back home, Mom. I've had enough of this." I stand, hoping she'll follow suit.

Settled on my sofa, however, she seems determined to make me see reason. "I came because I miss you! Every time I see you, my heart sinks at your ever more obvious neglect."

With a heavy stomach, I rush to the kitchen and pour myself a glass of orange juice. My heart thumps painfully. I need to breathe. Vampyr wraps around my legs, purring to get my attention. I serve him some kibble, noting my half-brother sitting behind my desk. Farther away, the door to my room is open. Ervin is leaning against the doorframe, still in his boxer briefs, arms crossed.

Fuck! I had forgotten he was there.

His dark expression doesn't bode well. He remains still, shamelessly spying on us. Charles exchanges a sidelong glance with him.

When my mother joins me, a sorrowful expression on her face, my neighbor decides to intervene. He steps forward, positioning himself by my side, wrapping his muscular arm around my shoulders.

"No worries, ma'am. I won't give her a choice. With me, your little girl will get back on track quickly."

My brain starts to boil. It explodes in all directions, pulverizing my synaptic connections before I leap out of his grip, his touch still burning. About to unleash my frustration on him, I'm silenced by my mother's sparkling eyes. Apparently, my neighbor's Adonis-like appearance intrigues her. Sly satisfaction stirs inside me.

"Hands off!" I say to him. "You see, Mom, it seems that despite my seclusion, I can still attract men. And as you can see, they're quite clingy!"

Confused, she examines us before repeating that she only wants what's best for me, that she didn't mean any harm by her sermon. I don't give a damn. At the moment, I just want to avoid having my business exposed in public, even though Ervin seems to enjoy it.

Mom calms down, gives me the benefit of the doubt, then asks for news about me. I watch her go through my bookshelf while Ervin tries to approach me again. I stop him with a step back, responding to his frown with an aggressive look.

"Are you still working on your thrillers?" my mother asks.

I had explained to her that for a few months, it was the only genre that inspired me.

"I'm reaching the end of the next one, yes."

"You still can't write your porn books," Charles retorts insolently, lips cruelly curled.

"Charles!" Mom exclaims. "We say e-ro-tic! You're still too young to understand the subtlety."

A weary sigh escapes me. Little brat. After my previous altercation with Ervin, I didn't need this. It's distressing; I know what he thinks of my work.

"Still *haven't*. It has nothing to do with can or can't," I snap at him. "I'm just giving you time to read all the ones already published."

He replies with a casual chuckle. "Gross!"

"No, you really should read them." I add, "It would save you from writing the word *cock* without a 'k'."

He looks at me, perplexed, while Charlene shifts her attention back to me, her hand in front of her mouth and her eyes laughing.

"You should double-check when you send a dirty message to your girlfriend… I know *Alizee* and *Alice* are bit similar, but still…"

Victory! Oh, lord! His expression could make me squeal with delight, right now! It didn't take two seconds for his cheeks to turn red and his eyeballs to pop out of their sockets.

Wide-eyed, our mother pinches the bridge of her nose.

Indeed, the years haven't diminished our bickering. Although, in reality, it's an underlying settlement of scores…

Nevertheless, she adds fuel to the fire. "Maybe you should learn the whole thing from Alizee, even though she just writes about it."

"Damn it, Zee!" Charles swears. Confronted with my smug smile, my half-brother fumes and clenches his fists, ready to explode.

But Ervin stops him in his tracks. "Next time, buddy, send her a picture directly. No mistake guaranteed!"

Oh. My. God. Did he just say that in front of my mother?

My younger brother bursts into laughter. His embarrassment is now a thing of the past. I'm mortified.

Before things get out of hand, my mother decides she's heard enough from me. After cordial—but tinged with bitterness—goodbyes, they depart, leaving me alone in the jaws of a predator…

CHAPTER 6

Silence. All week long. Finally.

I don't know what town my neighbor ran away to, and I don't care, as long as his work keeps him out of my den. Unfortunately, my focus hasn't improved at all. I can't concentrate. While writing *Bloody Stars*, images of those damned tented boxer briefs distorted my mind. *His* deep voice echoed in my ear on a loop. *His* body on my couch while the laundry spun in the washer, after my mother's departure. *His* uncomfortable silence after my threat to kick him out if he spoke up again. My palpitations due to our prolonged proximity until the locksmith arrived to let him in his apartment.

After my message, Marshall arranged to meet me at the coffee shop in front of my house to discuss it. He's happy that my crazy adventure with my neighbor is unsettling me and encourages me to use it as inspiration for writing romance. According to him, Ervin could be a source of inspiration.

I tried. Thinking about the jerk, putting sentences together about what he evokes in me…

However, the experience was more painful than usual. Words came to me, but as soon as I put them on paper, they acted like sharpened blades, reducing my mind to pieces. So I put away my notebook.

Galati, on the other hand, is even more confused than me. Milo couldn't resist; he saw my friend again, kissed her properly after a dinner. Then declined her invitation to come upstairs and ran off. Since then, they have gone back to their virtual exchanges. And that's it.

It's Saturday, and I'm not writing. I've lowered my defenses, started a movie on Netflix, and filled my apartment with coconut incense, all while scrolling through Ervin's latest Insta and Facebook pictures. It's a bad habit I've developed. But they are so well done! Besides, this way, I know he was working on a documentary about CrossFit, the latest trendy workout.

Around midnight, my screen shows a message request on Messenger. Seeing my neighbor's photo freezes my courage. No! Could he know who's snooping on his profile? Why now? And on my Jade Evans account, no less!

[MersEv Prod: I can do better than Mike, I assure you.]

I gulp. Why is he talking to me about my book character? My heartbeat intensifies as I reply:

[Jade Evans: You think you can be a bigger jerk? Because with him, I really set the standard high.]

[MersEv Prod: You know what would be great?]

[Jade Evans: No, but as the generous soul you are, you're going to tell me.]

[MersEv Prod: Show you that a guy can be more original than that walking cliché.]

Boy, what an ass!

[Jade Evans: You're really in no position to talk about cliché!]

[MersEv Prod: Appearances cannot be trusted, Shakespeare.]

[Jade Evans: I'm guessing you're reading my book.]

[MersEv Prod: I'm trying to. Not easy; your TV is loud.]

In an inexplicable reflex, I sit up straight in my chair. He's there. Next door to me. Reading me. Reading my guts scattered on paper. I squeeze my eyes shut and take a deep breath.

[Jade Evans: You see, when I told you I don't need sex… The idea of you not being able to focus because of the noise is enough to make me orgasm.]

[MersEv Prod: Don't try to make me believe sex doesn't interest you. I've read three-quarters of your book. You managed to get me hard. This blowjob, damn…]

After a rush of pride and excitement, my stomach tightens. I squeeze the bridge of my nose. Embarrassment raises my internal temperature.

What will he think now? Guys are complete idiots. Undoubtedly, he'll create scenarios in his head. He'll mix my heroine with me.

[MersEv Prod: I couldn't help but picture you in her place…]

I would have broken my cell phone if I had the strength. My trembling fingers are hooked into it, my wide eyes are pinned to it. My heart pounds so hard against my ribs, in my lower abdomen…

This situation is trouble brewing. And the effect it has on me stings.

I bury my phone under the pillow and curl up on the couch in the dark, the room lit only by the light of the television. I remain motionless, as if moving even the slightest toenail could split me open and expose me to the pervert who imagines me blowing him. Or sucking Mike. No doubt, Ervin has taken the place of the hero in my story.

What do I do now? Ignore him?

And what do I do now that he's knocking on my door?

Fuck!

"I'm not here!" I shout, turning up the TV volume.

The knocks persist.

"I'm busy watching a movie. Come back later!"

Or never. Never is good!

No, he apparently doesn't take no for an answer. He hammers on the poor door so loudly that I worry about the neighbors on the lower floors. Darn it! If he brings up that damn blowjob, I'll make him suck his oversized dick himself!

Furious, I consider my outfit. A Minnie Mouse T-shirt that reaches below my butt, which molds it outrageously. Hm…

I rush to the entrance to yell at him that I need to get dressed, when I realize through the peephole that it's absolutely not Ervin.

Screw Minnie, I swing the door wide open, giving Charles my deadliest glare. "Damn it, what the hell are you doing here at this hour?"

Glassy-eyed, he leans against the doorframe, emanating a strong smell of liquor. Given his wrinkled shirt, jeans, and polished shoes, I deduce that he was out.

"I can't go home, Zee…"

This can be true. "Call a cab and go back home. My apartment isn't a hotel."

I won't let myself be fooled again. When he drinks too much, he runs here for refuge. Intoxication doesn't seem to make him forget our mother's reprimands. Another of her paradoxes: she loves to party. However, the idea that her son could get drunk horrifies her. So, the next day, she always barges in and blames me for his poor choices. So tonight, it's a no-go.

"Listen, my little Charlie, you're eighteen years old now. You're going to own up to your bullshit and leave me alone."

"Come on, Zee, let me crash here," he answers in a slurred voice. "I promise, I'll leave before she shows up."

"Are you confusing my apartment with a church? It doesn't say *Virgin Mary* on my forehead."

"Mary, no. But the rest, I'm not sure." He stupidly chuckles.

"Get out of here!" I grab him by the shoulders and try a 180-degree turn, but he abruptly frees himself, shoving me backward. Ignoring my shouts, he staggers toward my living room.

"Come back here!"

I rush after him, before he roars, "What is your problem with us? You know what? I don't give a damn if you can't stand us." He collapses on my sofa. "I'm not the only one who has to put up with Mom."

Furious, I shout at him to make him leave, but he seems determined to camp in my living room, lying on my couch.

"Is everything okay here?" A voice behind me surprises me.

With a hiccup of fright, I spin around, facing my concerned neighbor.

"I heard some yelling, and since the door was open…"

What an idiot I am!

"It's… it's nothing," I stammer, eyeing Ervin's sweatpants. He's wearing nothing else. Is he tempting me on purpose, or what?

In the darkness, his attention shifts to the rascal sprawled next to me. "Are you sure?" he asks, stepping forward, his fists as clenched as his eyebrows.

"It's my brother. He thought he was at a hotel and doesn't care about causing me problems."

Barely conscious, Charles mumbles something that finally pushes my patience to the edge. I gauge Ervin's mood. He's amused by the situation.

"Do you want to help me drag him to the elevator?"

His eyes widen, as if asking if I'm serious.

"Let him take responsibility for his adult choices. No one forced him to get drunk, and he lives just a few minutes from here. I'm tired of cleaning up after him."

Ervin approaches, right in front of me, towering over me with his imposing stature. Although his eyes are looking at my face, he seems lost in thought. Mine don't have time to blossom.

"He's not in a state to go home. You can put him at my place, if you want."

Stunned, I flutter my lashes, asking him to repeat.

"Assistance to a person in danger," he explains with a shrug. "If I do nothing, there will be a murder here tonight. I think even the neighbors downstairs heard you yelling."

I must be turning pink. Now he thinks of me as a screamer. After the prude and the slut, he finds me hysterical. Disheartened, I don't try to contradict him too much. "If you only knew what I'm trying to escape."

A faint smile appears on his lips.

Damn, couldn't he have put on a T-shirt? Was he planning to play half-naked gallant knight?

"And why would you escape, anyway?" he asks.

His silence lingers. Our exchanges before my brother's arrival come back to me. I open my mouth to decline his offer, but he beats me to speaking.

"To thank you for the last time."

I raise an eyebrow, hands on my hips. "For real?"

He walks toward Charles's lifeless form. "It's a solid reason."

I sigh, surrendering. Anyway, I don't want the kid here. When my mother shows up, I'll be blameless. I could even blame her for bothering me for nothing.

I join my hero and grab Charles's ankles. "I'll take the legs, and you handle the upper body."

Ervin chuckles and grabs my hips from behind, causing me a heart attack. He shifts me to the side.

"Are you kidding me?" he says as I still struggle to recover. He then points to his muscular chest. "Do you think all this is for show? Move aside and let me do it, Pulitzer."

With his strong arms—because let's admit it they're quite robust, even in the darkness—he effortlessly lifts the slumped teenager and hefts him over his shoulder.

My wide-eyed gaze follows Ervin to the door, and I immediately rush after him, making sure he completes his good deed.

It takes me a short moment to adjust to the lit lamps in the adjacent apartment. Meanwhile, Ervin takes Charles to his bedroom. I assist him in arranging my brother and take off Charles's shoes.

"He didn't deserve your bed, I promise you."

Charles's sudden snoring confirms my statement. I roll my eyes, before noticing the serious gaze of the man in front of me. A sudden return to the present makes me step back, and I realize I'm wearing nothing but a Minnie Mouse T-shirt that barely reaches my thighs. Below it are my bare thighs, dotted with cellulite, and my pompom slippers.

In fact, at this point, I think my dignity as a woman has disintegrated.

Ervin runs his tongue over his lower lip, takes a step back to grab a dark gray T-shirt, and puts it on. It's nice of him to come down to my level—well, to get close to it, because even so, we look like a high-tech missile and a plain matchstick side by side. However, the damage is done. He burned my retinas with that Adonis-like body exposed, a Greek god who reads my books and mocks the sexual experiences I describe in them.

"Thanks, dear neighbor. I'll go. As soon as he comes to his senses, kick him out. No mercy for the kid!"

He follows me into his living room but grabs my arm before I reach the front door. My heart misses a beat.

I turn halfway, worried.

"We haven't finished our conversation."

I swallow hard. Ah, he didn't forget… "Do… you mind if I go get dressed?" To never come back.

"No. I love your outfit."

He reduces the space between us, and his index finger glides down my forearm in an outrageous caress. All the signals in my head are on high alert. When he intertwines his fingers with mine and draws me to him, I almost faint.

I don't know what I was expecting, but he leads me to the couch and tells me to make myself comfortable. He sits right next to me, way too close.

Panic freezes me. In his last text, he'd said he imagined me in suggestive situations. Does he see me as an easy girl? The little fat girl from next door, desperate, easy to seduce, who would spread her legs for the first handsome guy interested in her?

"What's your problem with your brother? With your mother?"

His question surprises me. I blink, trying to decipher his neutral expression. With his voice devoid of arrogance, I bet on pure curiosity.

"I don't have a problem with—"

"I was there when they visited you last week. And tonight is the first time I've really heard you lose your temper."

With his chest turned toward me, arm stretched over the back of the couch, reaching behind my head, he has casually folded his leg. Yet, his posture tells me something else. Something more... calculated. His muscles are tense, and it has nothing to do with his recent effort. The movements of his chest are broader. It's subtle, but distinct. Despite my wariness, his dark eyes manage to get into my mind, making me lose the little control I had left.

"Is it... possible to have a blanket?"

Disconcerted, he hesitates for a moment, before asking, "Are you cold?"

I wrap my arms around my knees, nodding. In reality, I'm hot.

Hot because of his presence.

Hot because of my embarrassment.

I don't know how he guesses my lie. He grabs my wrists with his powerful yet gentle hands, separates them, and runs his gaze down my legs with severe frown. His jaws tense, as if he's about to say something, then he changes his mind. "No, I don't have a blanket," he finally decides in front of my accusing expression.

My chest tightens. The heat of our contact spreads, incinerating each of my cells. I feel like I'm suffocating, like I'm being exposed both physically and psychologically. I don't want him to scrutinize my body. And he notices it.

"Don't run away, answer my question."

I fill my lungs with oxygen, and with a hint of courage, I savor the warmth of his fingers still wrapped around my wrists.

"They're old stories. Uninteresting," I begin, head down.

"I've already told you, Alizee, you interest me."

The confidence and the velvety tone of his deep voice, along with our proximity, make me tremble inside. A lock of hair falls on his brow, over his furrowed eyebrow.

He'll think I'm ridiculous. "My father died when I was eleven. Cancer took a year to finish him off. I… suffered a lot, during that year." The memories of his condition are painful.

"I'm sorry."

Still avoiding eye contact with Ervin, I try to calm the emotion creeping up in me. I only let my anger explode in front of Charlene and her family. I don't want Ervin seeing it.

"My mother remarried three months later. Gave birth seven months after the funeral."

On my skin, the pressure of Ervin's fingers intensifies. When they subtly caress me, I lift my eyes to his. The compassion I read there feels like an electric shock. No man ever cared before.

"She… she insisted he was premature. She thought I was too young to realize she was lying."

He nods, as if he finally understands my feelings.

"I never accepted her husband. He wasn't bad, but he stole my father's place. I felt like… I *feel* like she was waiting for him to die," I grind out, holding back my tears.

My breathing becomes erratic, and the knots in my throat prevent me from continuing. My breath catches when Ervin caresses my cheek.

"Looking back, I think I went through a depression that lasted for years, but she didn't notice. She was too busy with her cabaret and social gatherings. I built a barrier between the rest of the world and me; that's how I started writing. It's also the reason why I've never been close to Charles. Even now, just seeing him is enough for her betrayal to blow up in my face. It's constant, indelible."

With his thumb, Ervin strokes my chin. The trail he leaves there captures my attention, somewhat dissolving the resentment behind my ribs.

"You've never talked to her about it?"

A scoff escapes me as I turn my face away and shake my head. "Talk to my mother? No. I talked to my dad. A lot. He knew how to reassure me, while with my mother, I felt even more…"

My voice trails off. I refuse to continue and try to stand.

Ervin tightens his grip on my arm. "Even more…?"

The lump in my chest becomes unbearable. It has been a long time since I put words to my unease. Over the years, I've tried to live with it by externalizing my bitterness on paper, continuously skimming the overflow in my heart.

Until a stranger comes to shoot in the anthill.

"Even more miserable," I admit.

He stares at me, his eyes shining. Strokes my temple, freeing a few strands that escaped my bun. He's actually paying attention to what I'm saying. Despite the possibility that he's looking for my vulnerabilities, my tongue loosens. My heart opens up. And it feels good. The details I'm about to share with him, not even Galati knows.

"I weighed three times more than the others when I was a child. You can imagine those nasty brats didn't spare me. But I didn't let them get away with it; my father instilled enough strength in me to shut them up. He considered me a princess, whereas in my mother's eyes, I always understood I wasn't *enough*. Not smart enough. Not as pretty as the girls who work for her. Not worthy."

Ervin's nose twitches like a nervous tic.

"After my father died, I became a real spitfire. I lost sixty pounds in a year. I lived only by my textbooks and managed to graduate with honors."

"And to prove that you're worthy, you got two degrees," Mr. Curious finishes.

The weight of his attention prevents me from looking him in the eyes. I feel it like a magnet. His magnetism clashes with my modesty. I say nothing.

Despite him uncovering my intentions, the reality is pathetically sad. I've lost the weight and achieved multiple degrees, but I'm still that insecure teenager chasing after her mother's approval. And I hate that fact more and more with each passing year.

My neighbor lifts my chin, runs his gaze over my lips, then my nose, and anchors my eyes with a sly smile. "If it's any consolation, I find you way sexier than her."

Stunned, I recoil, taking a few seconds to catch on. I burst into hearty laughter immediately. A liberating laugh. Amid my nervous bursts, I don't miss the chance to remind him, "Don't lie; you think I have a big butt!"

He squints, a mischievous pout on his face. "Indeed. But damn, I love big butts."

My spasms stop. Trapped in the corner of the couch, I inhale too deeply. When he notices, a shadow crosses his face. Dark and unsettling. Bewitching.

"Your large, almond-shaped eyes are fascinating. I've rarely seen such beautiful colors. Your little, often-wrinkled nose is adorable. And that mouth…" he finishes in a whisper.

My heart drums. My blood pulses to the tips of my limbs. Aware of each of his movements, each of his breaths, and suffocated by his lingering lavender scent, I forget his words.

He leans in closer, towering over me, then engulfs me. Speechless, I didn't expect him to take me in his arms. That he would nestle my head against his shoulder and envelop my head in his broad palm. With his other hand, he encircles my waist to hold me against him.

"Your flaw is being the queen pain in the ass," he whispers in my ear. "It's probably why you don't get laid, but I assure you, it has nothing to do with your looks."

Am I dreaming? "Did you just call me a pain in the ass?" I exclaim, struggling in vain.

His grip tightens. "Shh, easy now, kitten. Let the pain in the ass sleep a little longer, okay? We're in the middle of a serious discussion here."

"Let me go!"

No matter how hard I try to hit him, he just won't let go! Out of breath, I give up, collapsing against his steely muscles, on the verge of tears.

"Let yourself go," he tells me in an affectionate voice.

His words, though tender, are almost too much to bear. They stir up a mix of emotions—anger, frustration, along with an overwhelming sense of relief. I hug him in return, in silence, without trying to spare his T-shirt.

He undoes my bun, runs his fingers through in my hair, giving me delightful massages. Thus, he elicits satisfied moans from me.

"I lost my father, too. Even though he's not dead," he says against my temple. "And I also have a bunch of brothers who don't think I measure up. And you know what, Voltaire? I don't give a shit. Because I know my worth."

His revelation crushes my heart. What happened to his father?

I want to ask him the question, but he presses his lips on my cheek, sucking away my tears. Suddenly, I'm on the verge of imploding. His stubble scratches my cheek. He slides down, licking languidly. Fear scrambles my senses, chops my breath. His fingers tighten in my hair, holding me firmly in place. My brain misfires; it's a blackout. My chin starts to tremble as he kisses my jaw with infinite tenderness. I think my nails have pierced his T-shirt; I can't be sure. When his tongue glides over my lower lip, a dizziness disconnects me. As it traces the outline of my lips, my stomach contracts violently. When he begins to pull away, I throw myself on his mouth, overcome by my desire.

Ervin seems surprised. Quickly, he starts growling, takes control, and tips me backward. His grip in my hair is deliciously painful, and the weight of his body strangles me with pleasure. The ardor of his kisses drill into my lower abdomen, awakening a monster rarely summoned. Damn, it's exquisite! He's fierce yet sensual. He leads the dance with mastery, provokes me endlessly. In turn, I moan. A sound that drives him wild and guides him to my throat. He kisses it, nibbling it in an extremely sexy way, until the moment he grabs onto my love handles.

I freeze. Push him away with all my strength, alarmed, to extract myself from the couch. Dazed, I catch my breath while he stares at me, equally stunned.

"Alizee…"

In incomprehensible stammers, I readjust my T-shirt, pulling it down as if it could hide the damage to my underwear, then begin my retreat. Ervin barely has time to get up before I rush out his door and through mine, then lock it behind me. Leaning against the door, I struggle to calm down. I sink to the floor, disheveled, my mouth swollen.

With my face buried in my hands, I exhale slowly, still trembling from his touches. Ervin kissed me. His lips collided with mine. And his tongue… Oh, my god…

What on Earth just happened? He was extracting undisclosed secrets from me, and suddenly, the atmosphere changed. I recall every moment, trying to understand the turnaround. When had he made this decision?

When I was telling him about my torments? At the last moment, during our tearful embrace, or the moment when he contacted me on Messenger?

CHAPTER 7

For three days, I've been trying to put my sensations into words. Those of his kiss, I mean. Burning. Softness. Arousal. Violence. Tingling.

However, it's impossible to formulate a single sentence. The images cut me off. And the more I try to dissolve them, the more they persist. It's all Charles's fault! The little drunkard got away with it: our mother, of course, seized at the opportunity to bother me. Traumatized by my night, I rebuffed her, pretending to ignore what she was talking about and went back to rocking out, hiding in the darkness of my room.

I haven't heard any woman in Ervin's place since Sunday. What does that mean? Was that kiss a spur-of-the-moment thing, or had he planned it for a long time?

Every time I think about it, my cheeks turn pink, and my private parts shamefully throb. But what upsets me more than his kiss is the confessions he extracted from me. I would have opened my stomach, serving him my guts on a silver plate, and it would have been the same. I don't know what came over me at that moment. His gaze, his expression, his interest in me despite our altercations. His gesture with Charles.

I'm lost.

So, I carefully avoided him in the days that followed, giving my brain some time to piece itself back together. I wouldn't want him to think that the poor girl next door had a crush on him. We've slipped up, and now I'm avoiding him. That makes my position clear! Anyway, he hasn't tried to contact me either.

Over my tracksuit, I've put on a thick, long cardigan and am about to go out to run some errands—no more frozen pizza in my freezer—when the next-door lock clicks. My heart skips a beat. With my hand on my doorknob, I turn it slowly, unsure whether to open the door. However, the damn mechanism is poorly oiled and causes a monstrous creaking. I freeze, just like my neighbor on the landing. Then, the steps hasten, rushing down the stairs…

Stunned, I still wonder about what has just happened.

He heard me behind the door. And he fled! He *fled! Him!*

I'm dreaming! What does he think? That I would have clung to him like a leech? I can't let him believe that! He's going to hear about this!

***

Of course, tonight he doesn't come back to his place.

He's disappeared. Poof! The fugitive has vanished.

The next day, Gala invites herself over. She's eager to share her love problems with a girls' night out.

Although she hasn't changed her appearance, her good mood shines through. Fortunately, she's not one of those women who are hysterical when they meet the ideal man.

"Zee, I absolutely have to tell you *everything* from start to finish. This guy is driving me completely crazy!"

Ah. Maybe she is a bit hysterical…

We settle on the couch with a hot chocolate for her, a glass of wine—well, two or three—for me, and she explains her complicated relationship.

From what she reveals, Milo seems attracted but terrified by their connection. A fine specimen of tortured souls! Maybe I should take inspiration from them, after all. It'll dominate the digital sales charts with its promising title: *Balls Up, Milo!*

They met again at his place and kissed once more. Without him attempting anything else. Good boy. Too bad for my friend's libido. The number of her lovers is probably not high. And a vibrator isn't enough to satisfy her. What she keeps yearning for is flesh, warm blood, and a velvety voice to whisper dirty things in her ear.

I digress.

"You two are together, then?"

She sighs, flips her long golden mane to the side, and crosses her legs. "I… think so. I think he wants to take it slow. His life is busy, and his previous relationship was quite recent."

"Finally, a sensible man in this town," I mutter, my nose in my glass.

"You didn't go to the orphanage this week," she points out.

I usually keep her informed, just in case she might have something to fill my bags. Her neighbor is the mother of five *adorable* kids who only hold interest in their toys for a month at most. Then they get bored. They squirm and whine in the toy aisle, demanding new entertainment.

If their mother didn't pass their trinkets on to Gala, who always gives them to me, their behavior would irritate me. But well… Then people wonder why I don't step outside!

"Zee? Is there a problem?" She brings me back to reality.

"No, not at all."

Going out with all my bags and risking attracting the neighbor's attention scared me. But since he's avoiding me… Another sip. "Do you have any news about Ervin?"

"He's in the Cévennes, participating in unofficial motocross races, or something like that."

I squint, not sure if I understood. "For work?"

"No. He's on the other side of the camera. Milo is going there on Friday to attend the final race. He suggested we should join him. I thought you wouldn't be interested, but—"

"I'm coming!" I exclaim, raising my glass.

She gives me an amused pout.

"This time, this arrogant guy won't escape me. I'm going to tell him what I really think!"

"What happened this time?" She laughs.

"If you only knew," I grumble.

"What?" Her seriousness returns, and she leans toward me, her eyes round. "What *exactly* happened?" she insists.

Damn it. The desire to tell her about my Saturday night and the fear she would make a big deal out of it tear me apart. Whenever we discuss men and my view that they're trouble, it turns into an altercation.

"He… helped me out… and then… we *slipped*," I say, mimicking quotes, evasive.

"Oh! Did you get hurt? Nothing broken, I hope?"

Yes. My poor little fragile heart.

"Uh… I've smashed my dignity a few times, yes. But it's not exactly what you think."

"Speak, damn it!"

"It was an accident, okay?"

"Did you break his leg?"

"He kissed me."

She opens her mouth, ready to respond, before realizing what I'm saying. The blonde freezes, dumbfounded. The lightning that crosses her eyes warns of trouble. "What?"

"He kissed you?"

"Is that so… unlikely?" I retort, feeling offended.

"Um… Is he still alive?"

This time, I giggle. "No, but seriously. Let's just say that… he didn't exactly jump on me."

"It's you who jumped on him?" she articulates, horrified.

"Have you seen me? Never in a million years." Well, technically, after he licked my lips, it was me who took hold of his. But I'm not sure if he remembers that, so let's bury this thing in the abyss. "It just happened… by itself."

"I want details! Oh, my god, I can't believe it!"

I downplay my confession, give her the essential details and then explain that the brute is avoiding me.

My friend seems uneasy. I know her; she's hiding something.

"Your turn, spill it! What's with that constipated look? Before we went to the Bloodybar, my interest in him seemed to enchant you."

Her hand slides over her neck, a recognizable tic. She hesitates to deliver some bad news.

"Come on, free yourself from this burden. Is he married? Does he have mononucleosis? Am I going to sleep for six months?" I'd like that, actually.

She shakes her head, looking apologetic. "It's not that… Milo talked to me about it. Let's just say… he's not the kind of guy who would consider a long-term relationship."

"Because I would? And with him? Did you listen to me, Gala? I'm telling you that I'm trying to reach him to clear things up."

Outraged, I cross my arms and sit back down in the corner of the sofa. Does she also think his Adonis-like physique makes me lose my mind? She might be desperate to avoid ending up alone, but not me.

"I've been enduring his unwelcome lovemaking in audio since he moved in. Do you really think he fits my ideal man?"

She apologizes before I get more upset, admits to projecting her expectations onto mine. Then she fills in the Friday slot on my agenda.

✳✳✳

With my face buried in my hands, I realize my mistake. I should never have made this trip.

With Gala and Milo, we hit the road on Thursday afternoon toward Occitane, France. Judging by the Milo's surprised expression, I conclude my friend kept the reason for my presence a secret. In the back of the car, I felt like a third wheel, an intruder in this fresh intimacy they had created. The undeniable and dominant chemistry between them would make me nauseous if I weren't happy for my favorite blonde. It was only halfway through the trip that I realized that if she had followed her boyfriend, I had no reason to be there. Motorcycle races? Not really my thing! Moreover, consumed by my goal, I had forgotten what normally terrified me: Milo had warned us a real community attended these mini championships. They were all very friendly and would be delighted to socialize with new followers.

Socialize.

Initially, I just wanted Ervin to understand that I wasn't chasing him. And in reality, here I am, abandoning my cat for an entire weekend and traveling four hundred miles to confront him.

I felt even more foolish when we arrived at the inn, and participants informed us he had disappeared with a girl from the village. Despite logic, the idea pinches my heart. Thus, I find myself slouched over a table in the lobby, berating myself for my ridiculous decisions, drained of all energy.

The next day, Milo wakes us up at eight o'clock. The plan: head to the location of the first elimination races to support the participants after having breakfast.

I originally came for anything but to support Ervin. So, getting up at the crack of dawn… Good lord, I'm boiling. If he dares speak to me the wrong way this morning, I swear I'll eat him alive.

Fortunately for him, he's already getting ready. Therefore, I have my meal with some fans, consuming whatever the inn offers. They chatter about a lot of things that my lethargic state prevents me from focusing on. From what I understand, this isn't motocross but EnduroCross. To select the participants for the long course tomorrow, several rounds will take place today. Six hours of challenging track, after which only a few competitors will be able to claim victory. No more country rides; this is some real tough-guy sporting!

Ribbons delimit a path of overturned soil littered with obstacles like tires and logs. A small crowd is gathered, while a little farther on, in the camps, the bikers are getting ready. In the distance, I spot Milo joining my fugitive neighbor.

Our kiss is only a few days old, yet it feels like an eternity. And just the sexy image of him makes me melt like ice in the sun. In his red and white suit, he seems to be in a great mood, laughing with his friend. Enough to sabotage my good humor! Our eyes never meet; he goes back under the tent, and the race begins.

✳✳✳

I must admit, those bikers have balls. They're giving their all, climbing the mounds, trudging through the mud, getting knocked over and disqualified for the most part. Fierce, Ervin holds his ground on his bike. I'd have butterflies in my stomach if the thought of him discovering my presence didn't have me in knots.

He makes it through the second elimination race of the day, and I'm seriously getting into it, wanting him to beat the rest, hands down.

That was before the intermission.

It's four in the afternoon, and more supporters have gathered in the area. I never imagined the atmosphere at this kind of event would be so family oriented. Milo's friends suggest Gala and I join them at the local café. A beer and food refill before the last round of the day is in order.

We decide on a bistro, typical of the region and welcoming. Made of stone and wood, it's undoubtedly a symbol of the local culture. The atmosphere is cheerful, with about ten guys making us feel at home, inviting us to sit around a long table as if we were members of the group. I even forget the reason for my visit, laughing heartily with them, avoiding the pointed glances of a guy named Pat, whose kindness leaves me skeptical.

I'm *socializing*. Unbelievable!

Suddenly, the door swings open, triggering a chorus of cheers. The gang greets Ervin, who's accompanied by Milo. Some give him pats on the back while others tease him mercilessly. Way too much love for my bitter eyes. The atmosphere is festive until my attention focuses on the hottie joining the two best friends. She puts her hand on Ervin's shoulder to grant him a kiss on the lips.

Stunned, I feel like I've swallowed shards of glass. The pain in my throat is searing; the overwhelming sense of betrayal taking over. I knew it… I knew it. Yet a small voice inside me screams that he could have clarified things the day after our kiss, before landing on other mouths. Despite my effort to avoid him, he didn't even try. Against my will, I share a distressed look with Galati. She had warned me, too…

My attention falls again on the doll. Her large doe eyes, her delicate, sensual nose, and her chin framed by long jet-black strands harmonize perfectly. Her plunging neckline is highlighted by an elegant silhouette, and her ass is… small. Muscular. Well-rounded. Adorned by the huge hand of the one I currently hate with all my being. Who claimed to love big butts. Liar.

No wonder he hurried away when he thought he'd run into me in the hallway.

A second attractive redhead enters the café. She, too, rushes into the arms of the heartbreaker. Hanging on his neck, she gives him a deep kiss that leaves me dumbfounded.

This time, I exchange a scandalized look with my friend. She shakes her head, wide-eyed, then lifts her gaze to the ceiling.

So, if I understand correctly, he French kisses hello, and these bimbos have no issue with it. Of course not. I feel absurd for having come all this way. What an idiot I am!

And it's even worse when his dark eyes meet mine. They freeze in surprise. An indescribable mix of emotions animates them, leaving only a desert of frost.

A twitch makes him frown, but the redhead catches his attention back with her splendid smile.

Watching them feels like being stabbed. She's beautiful, sunny, and elicits a satisfied grin from him. While I…

"Forget it, Zee," Gala whispers in my ear.

She gets up and greets her guy while Ervin is pulled to our table by his friends.

He sits far away from me, engages with everyone, making himself comfortable like a king in the center of his subjects. Not once does he acknowledge me; he's carried away by their joy.

As he marvels, I soften. An intruder—that's me. An intruder in his environment, in his court. Next to me, Pat fills the empty space. I ignore him when he tries to get my attention. After the hand he placed on my backside during the races, I won't fall for that again.

"Alizee, would you like to go for a walk during the last run? I know a great place nearby… It might get your panties wet."

Is this a dream… Does he really believe I would, with his drunkard appearance?

"No, thanks, but very kind of you to offer," I reply, turning away from him.

"Come on, what have you got to lose?"

His remark annoys me. I admit I look out of place next to the two other bimbos, but that's no reason to think I'm desperate!

"Hey, Alizee, answer?"

It's better not to insist. Annoyed, I glare furiously into his eyes. "What do I have to lose? My self-esteem, damn it! I might have accepted if you didn't have that drunken face, who knows? Although, I'm not sure, actually…"

Now it's his turn to be offended. His expression suddenly sours. "Oh, now she's acting all high and mighty. Who do you think you are?"

"Watch out, I might decide to choke you. At least then your hand would leave my ass alone."

Caught off guard, he seeks support from his companions, whose attention is elsewhere, and then turns back to me. "But that's disgusting! Look at yourself and your—"

"Pat, could you let me sit down?" a voice says behind us.

Ervin slipped through the crowd and is standing behind my chair. He shoots Pat a stern look, unyielding to the brute's persistence. Pat complies and reluctantly gives up his spot, much to my dismay. I'm not prepared for this.

"Really? You insinuated you'd hurt him?" the Adonis jokes.

I scrutinize him for a few seconds, squinting my eyes, before shrugging. "He groped me earlier."

"Little jerk," he mumbles, his eyebrows furrowed.

Ervin glances at his friend, then he gives a subtle nod. He smiles at me. A faint, almost shy smile, contrasting with the airs he's been putting on since the beginning of the day. A smile that would make me blush. "Hi."

I clear my throat and manage to say, "Hi."

"You came a long way," he throws at me.

An anvil weighs on my chest. "I… Gala and Milo convinced me…"

Fuck! That wasn't the plan. *I came to shove your face in your mess and explain my point of view, idiot!* But, no, nothing like that escapes my pursed lips. He's so glowing, masculine, sexy, so… everything, that he silences me. Ugh, what about my resolutions as a strong woman? *Alizee, you're not better than a groupie.*

"Did you enjoy it?"

What is he talking about? The races? The kiss? My brain glitches.

"It was… impressive," I answer uncertainly.

His lips stretch even wider. His gaze lingers on mine. My heart skips a beat. The images of our last conversation come to me. Without controlling anything, I moisten my lips, grip the armrests.

"You're staying for the final round tomorrow?"

I nod, my temper carried away in the autumn breeze.

"When are you leaving?"

"Sunday."

"Hey, Ervin! You need to get ready, man!" calls a guy at the entrance to the bistro.

Ervin waves at him before turning his attention back to me. "I have to run the next race early in the morning. I hope to finish the course tomorrow. If I make it, I'll celebrate properly," he finishes with a wink.

This simple gesture triggers unpleasant shivers down my spine.

When Ervin leaves, I scold myself for remaining silent as a fish. Because of that idiot, I'm making one mistake after another. What does he think? That I'm like those two girls, unbothered by sharing my saliva with a Don Juan and the rest of his conquests? What a joke! I won't be part of his harem.

****

That evening, after his victory, I overhear the tall redhead from earlier complaining that Ervin collapsed in his room, exhausted. Satisfaction flares inside me, despite everything. His buddy Milo bragged how Ervin had promised the two hotties a threesome. Hah!

Near gloating, I return to my room and get ready for bed. But as I climb beneath the warm comforter, a subtle unease takes hold of me. He'd kissed me then promised to celebrate properly if he won. Had he really intended to fuck both girls at the same time? Had his wink meant… more? Did our kiss mean… so little?

I toss the unending questions around until god knows what time. Great. Even when I can't hear his lovemaking, the jerk pollutes my sleep.

***

The next day, we gather around the starting line. On his motorcycle, wearing his helmet and suit, Ervin exudes a combative aura. I find myself hoping he wins, even though my little inner devil has already impaled my voodoo doll of him.

When he revs up his engine, my throat goes dry. Once they all start, I learn we won't see him again until the end of the day unless he drops out before, as is the case for the majority of participants.

"Seriously? All these people to witness a two-minute start, and nothing else? We came all this way," I complain to Milo.

With his arm around Galati, he laughs heartily, despite his sleepy demeanor. "We're showing our support."

"I'm not supporting anyone. I just wanted to assess the difficulty of the route and revel in Ervin's give-up. That would have been satisfying!" I exclaim, arms crossed over my little quilted jacket.

"There's mad love between you two," he observes, amused.

I swallow hard, avert my gaze. "Your friend is very irritating."

He chuckles again. "Not sure Charlotte and Lyne would agree with you."

The two Barbies? "Of course, everything he arouses on them is between their legs. While he attacked an organ further north in my anatomy."

Milo raises an eyebrow.

"The brain!" I immediately correct his thoughts.

It's during the final straight line that a rocky ascent is right of Ervin. The sky has darkened by the time he joins us at the same bar as the day before, exhausted. In his worn-out jeans, snug military T-shirt, and with his shaggy hair still damp with sweat, he reeks of testosterone.

Everyone congratulates him for finishing twentieth out of five hundred. A good score, it seems. A result he wants to celebrate by stuffing himself, drinking, and, I assume, fucking.

He approaches me, slumps into the chair next to me. His sparkling eyes turned in my direction, he raises his eyebrows twice. "I want to eat you."

My heart skips a beat. "What?" I answer immediately.

"I want to eat stew, I'm starving. Hey, Greg," he asks the waiter, "serve me your special stew, will you?"

Shaken, I can't tell if it's him or my mind playing tricks on me. It must be the smell of his sweat. His confidence must be short-circuiting my brain and making me hear nonsense.

"I'm hungry, too," I mutter, slumping my shoulders.

"It's excellent here. Right, Pat?" he addresses the troublemaker of the previous day, his arm resting on the back of my seat.

The latter, sitting opposite a few chairs to the left, shoots him a furious look, filled with frustration.

"I don't doubt it. Infused with an extremely masculine scent, it must be amazing," I say.

Ervin doesn't seem to understand.

"You could have showered before joining us," I continue, leaning my body to the side. "Or sit a bit farther away—your choice."

He stares at me, bewildered, before putting on his cheeky expression. "Happy to inconvenience you. I've thought about it, and that's precisely why I avoided the shower."

"To annoy me?"

His smile widens. "To make your head spin."

I swallow, sensing the slippery path he's taking. In that, he hasn't changed! A thought of the two Barbie dolls, and I regain my composure.

"Ah, you've won the bet. You've even managed to suffocate me."

He approaches me, his armpit still exposed, sharing his scent full of... fucking pheromones! Is it possible to be so attracted to a smell?

"A pleasant way to suffocate you. I have other ideas that come to mind."

"Me, too," I retort, getting irritated. "Much more lethal ones."

He laughs and gives me a tender look before apologizing. "I didn't have time to stop by the inn. I'll eat, then I'm going back. I'm exhausted."

Images of a tongue running over his damp neck invade my mind. "Weren't you planning to celebrate your hard work on the course today?" I reply as casually as possible.

He squints as if wanting to strangle me, but in good spirits. "Yes,

I was. I changed my mind."

He sure changed his mind! His two groupies didn't escape my notice. They're busy chatting on the other side of the table, occasionally looking in his direction. The fact he hides his plans instead of bragging about them disgusts me. My discomfort intensifies. I need to put things straight to get rid of this burden.

"Ervin, I—"

One of his friends calls him, diverting his attention. A well-timed joke triggers general hilarity. It's impossible to get a word in, damn it! I give up and eat in silence.

Time passes. My best friend has left the restaurant with her prince charming. Kiko, a fifty-year-old member of the biker gang, has monopolized me for a long time. Now, it's just us. Delighted to meet someone with a higher level of cynicism than mine, I chat until the bar closes. Hooray, what a blast…

After he drops me off at the inn, I head toward my room with the urgent need to crash and make up for my night spent tormenting myself.

Of course, fate has other plans.

I open the door to a butt.

A back, legs, short-cut hair, sure… but what jumps out at me is a pair of butts moving.

Fuck!

Over his shoulder, Milo turns his head toward me. His body barely hides Galati, on all fours, receiving his blessing with euphoria, given her scarlet cheeks.

Oh. My. God. This is an angle I would have preferred never to discover. Wicked libertine!

Face hidden behind my hands, I whisper loudly, "What the hell? Did it not occur to you that I might come back to my room?"

"Sorry," says Milo, still not ready to surrender. "Take mine. My bed is free; the keys are in the pocket of my jeans."

Wide-eyed, I hesitate to ask if he's serious. His hands are still caressing my friend's hips. I have the answer to my question.

"Please, Zee," Gala begs, with Milo's cock still inside her.

"I can't believe it, damn it! Don't mind me, of course," I grumble, rushing toward the pile of clothes on the floor.

And these horny rabbits take me at my word! He resumes his back and forth gently, while she stifles a moan. Probably out of consideration for me. What a joke!

I grab his clothes and run away with them at full speed—too bad if he has to go back to his room naked! In front of his room, I fume while inserting the key in the lock. The darkness is only weakly lit by an outside lamp. The musky smell grabs my throat. Not surprising coming from that rutting animal. Damn, Gala chose the wrong day to satisfy her frustration.

Once the door is closed, I can see Milo's individual bed. Another one is arranged a foot from his, a dark mass curled up under the sheets.

Stunned, I can't believe he sent me to sleep with a stranger. Those lustful lovebirds will hear from me!

In a sigh, I evaluate the two options before me: run down the corridor separating me from my room in exhaustion, interrupt Gala's best night of the year, and convince Milo to leave, or lie down in these sheets, fall asleep next to an already sleeping person who probably won't wake up until tomorrow. A little bonus: the satisfaction of having confiscated absolutely all the clothes from my room thief.

I opt for immediate sleep. After tucking my sneakers at the foot of the bed, I dive under the blanket fully dressed, wrap myself in the warm softness, and close my eyelids. Then, it's oblivion.

CHAPTER 8

"Alizee?" A familiar voice says my name.

Numb, I mumble some protests. Now, it's my shoulders being pressed. I make a half-turn, trying to understand what's happening through the slit of my eyelids.

My neighbor's face stands out in the dim light, very close to mine. My breath catches. I blink, struggling to open my eyes wide.

"What are you doing here?" he asks, looking surprised.

I recoil, gradually regaining my senses. "What time is it?"

"Three o'clock in the morning."

I've only dozed off for two hours. In Milo's bed. Why on Earth didn't he mention that Ervin was in his room? Crap.

I sit up, increasing the distance between us. He remains kneeling, elbows resting on the edge of the mattress. The dim light reveals a strange expression on his face.

"I thought the room would be empty. Milo is sleeping in mine. Besides, it was either that or watch live porn."

Ervin remains impassive.

"And you… what are you doing here? Roommate issues?" I dare to ask since he keeps silent.

"Let's say it's something like that," he grumbles, sitting on the edge of his bed.

I rub my eyes, discovering his penetrating gaze is burning with intensity. Darn! He's shirtless, wearing only boxers that are presumably tented, and he's cleaned up!

"You… shared a room?" I ask.

"With two people, yes."

"Oh. I get it." Unable to stop it, my voice betrays my bitterness. "Milo told me about your plans for tonight. I guess your roommates are the two dolls you were hanging around with all weekend."

I hear him swallow, then reply with an accusatory tone, "Why are you here, Alizee?"

"Your buddy is busy screwing my friend," I snap. "Don't get any ideas!"

"Why did you come to the Cévennes?" he asks, visibly annoyed.

Speechless, I search for words, for a way to bounce back from the tone used before explaining myself. I can already see the path traced by his mind, his misguided deductions, and the resulting irritation.

"I'm warning you, Ervin, I have nothing in common with those two girls—"

"I confirm," he interrupts, vindictive.

Teeth clenched, I take his uppercut with dignity. Asshole! "I wasn't talking about the physical aspect, but—"

"Me neither," he continues, approaching. When he leans toward me, balancing on his fists on my mattress, my blood pulses.

I panic. "You should know I don't want to replace them!"

"But you're here for something, and it has nothing to do with the bikes."

So here we are. I take a deep breath and steel myself. "We kissed the other night."

In response, his eyes, filled with desire, shift to my mouth.

"I… just wanted to make sure it was a slip-up," I say, regretting my choice of words. *To inform you* would have been more accurate.

"You slipped onto my lips, yes," he murmurs, moving closer to my face.

With a raised palm, I stop him, annoyed. "*I* slipped?"

A sinister grimace distorts his features. His hand creeps toward my leg under the covers.

"You're the one who licked my lips, I remind you."

"Oh, did I? Your memories are accurate," he mocks.

The predator advances farther, making my breathing shallow.

Embarrassment might extinguish my arousal if this Adonis weren't shirtless.

"Ervin… Don't do this," I implore, pulling the blanket up to my chin.

He looks down at it, grabs my arm to lower it. His face is only inches from mine, and my heart races. I shake my head, alarmed, held hostage by my traitorous body.

"You came all this way to make sure we made a mistake, huh?"

I swallow.

Credibility, hello. Well, goodbye. Farewell, even!

"Exactly. You can do whatever you want with other girls."

An unfamiliar emotion crosses his dark eyes. The outside light dances on his harmonious features, making his fine beard sparkle. Tension tightens my throat. Why do I feel like he's not fooled?

Suddenly, he stands, takes a few nervous steps, runs his hand over his head, down his cheek.

What's happening to him? I don't understand his behavior. He should be happy. He probably isn't used to the chicks he hooks up with driving miles to justify their frivolity, especially those he kisses.

"What do you know about my desires?"

I part my lips, about to answer, but he interrupts me, "Why run away right after opening up to me?"

"It was… a moment of weakness. I shouldn't have opened up."

His eyebrows furrow. With fists on his hips, he shakes his head as if struggling to untangle the situation.

"You're used to it, right? You thought you'd make me scream like the bimbos you tend to jump, is that it? I told you, I'm not like them."

He comes back, and settles on the edge of my mattress, facing me. "Stop. Maybe you're not like them, but you'd like to be in their shoes."

"Where they bleat in your room?" I ask, wide-eyed, accusing another stab. "You overestimate yourself, I assure you. Nothing about you attracts me."

His smirking face horrifies me. Ready to counter his next missile, I inflate my lungs when, once again, he shakes his head.

"All right… I get it, the novelist. For you, it was nothing. You prefer nerds, is that it?"

Bewildered, I blink, trying to break through his disillusioned expression. Nerds? They're bastards, too…

"We hate each other. What's the point?" I say.

"I don't hate you. Do you hate me, Alizee?"

His smooth tone puts me back on my guard. It's impossible to retort.

So, I deflect.

"And those girls—why didn't you stay with them? You made them a promise. Aren't you a man of your word?"

Thrown off balance, he'd have preferred if I had answered his question, undoubtedly.

"I struggle with commitment. I've told you that already."

"Oh, and what a commitment!" I scoff.

Tension is at its peak. I'm close to storming out, failing to explode without waking up the inn's guests.

He leans forward, lowering his face to mine in order to hurt me with more precision. "A parasite prevented me from spending the night with them, if you want to know everything."

Stunned, I don't know how to respond. I should have never set foot in Cévennes. I was blinded by my pride, my decision was much too hasty.

"That would be the first time that the parasite prevents you from getting laid. I would have liked that, though."

The rascal bites his cheek! He restrains himself from laughing at my expense. Ready to add more, I lean toward him as well.

We're forehead to forehead when he confesses, "Listen, I didn't know why you came. It disturbed me. Now I know."

The unexpected sweetness of his voice seeps into my chest, crackling each of my organs. He's reassured by my intentions, and I'm devasted by his, against my will.

"You can go join them, then," I spit out, hiding my emotions as best as I can.

With a teasing smile, he answers, "I really don't feel like it."

That would be a first.

My belly quivers. My heart pounds under his piercing gaze…

"Do you know what I want, Alizee?" His gaze pierces with

lascivious undertones.

"I…" I swallow. "I'm not sure I want to know."

He licks his lips—a real habit for him—and closes the distance between us again. I move away when he catches me off guard by slipping under my blanket. On the verge of leaving, I'm held back by my arm.

"Don't be afraid, kitten. I won't fulfill your fantasies today. Just share some of your warmth with me."

Bewildered, I examine him for a while. The look on his face, though playful, seems devoid of sarcasm.

"Don't think you know my fantasies; your mind is too narrow for that. What do you really want? You're not a man who shares his warmth. You were ready to kick me out while you slept, after I hosted you."

"Come on, come here."

He pulls on my arm, making me fall backward onto his chest. Restless, I try to free myself, but his grip is firm.

"Let me go, for god's sake!"

He pins me on the mattress, sliding over my body while immobilizing my wrists on both sides of my face. Trapped by the big bad wolf, the idea of being devoured generates a panic in me. I struggle like a demon, but the man is strong. My screams are muffled by his palm, my attempts to scratch thwarted.

Is he really going to force me? Take what he desires as revenge?

Breathless, I pierce him with my most murderous glare.

He exhales dramatically, and rolls to the side, wrapping his arm around my waist. Upon my release, I inhale a large gulp of air, wide-eyed and focused on the ceiling.

He turns my head in his direction. Our face-to-face electrifies me.

"I'm not going to do anything you don't want me to, okay? I want to prove my good intentions, despite my raging hard-on."

His last words bounce in my mind, setting my cheeks on fire. Despite the compelling urge, I can't lower my eyes to verify his words. The touch of his fingers on my jaw clouds my thoughts. I don't understand why or how I ended up in this situation.

"I'm not supposed to get you hard," is the only stupidity my mouth utters.

He traps his lip between his teeth, runs his thumb over mine, and lets his eyes linger on my breasts. "You're the only one who was able to make me so, this weekend."

My heart beasts erratically.

"Liar."

He smiles, commands me to turn onto my side, and presses against my back. His cock hardens against my butt, and my body heat surges suddenly. Jaw clenched, I try to manage my reactions, thinking about the best thing to do.

Should I send him packing and forcefully get out of bed? Or should I surrender, perhaps providing him with some ammunition to fortify his confidence, arrogance, and everything that I detest about him? Everything that tortures me.

The friction of his beard against my neck seals my surrender.

In this darkened room, where the only sound is that of our heavy breathing, I despise myself. I hate myself for letting him disturb me, for allowing my lack of confidence to prove him right.

His thighs are steel against my butt, yet it's the less voluminous bimbos he desired. It's with their big breasts that he had made an appointment.

But I found him sleeping alone in this room. A reassuring thought. Just like his strong arms that envelop me. Like his breathing, which is getting heavier. His fingers caressing my belly. When they reach my bulges, my breath stops. Despite my will, my body crystallizes.

"Relax, Alizee. Is that what bothers you?" he inquires, pinching my fat flesh.

I want to cry in embarrassment. "Don't touch me like that."

I grab his hand, but he resists, massaging that detested part of my body without reservation. At the same time, he pulls me even closer to him, and that damn erection presses against me, then his lips sneak close to my ear.

"It's not how I touch you that bothers you; it's what I touch. Fuck, Alizee, feel the effect it has on me. Get those stupid ideas out of your head and enjoy the moment."

I squirm, shivering under the impact of his words. "You promised me..."

"Hush, we're not doing anything wrong."

The rhythm of my palpitations is frenzied. In addition to encroaching on my intimate space, he reads me like an open book.

His hands cling to my too-wide hips, tracing the curve of my waist. Torn between shivers and repulsion, I squeeze my eyes shut, reprimand myself, and see degrading moments of my life flash behind my eyelids.

"That's why you ran away the other day."

I shake my head vigorously.

"Your body drives me crazy," he says in an even huskier voice.

He lies. He lies. He lies. He can't mean it; it's impossible. "Stop mocking me," I growl, the touch of his fingers now painful.

His hip thrust translates his displeasure. It's so strong that it pushes me, shakes me, both outside and inside. My blood pulses between my legs, in my jugular, and my temples.

"Stop convincing yourself that you hate it."

I hate it. This exposure, more psychological than physical, I hate it deeply. It crushes me, delves into my depths to tear them up, piece by piece.

Yet, I remain motionless against his chest. Savor his scent. His attentions, his words, although I doubt their sincerity. Our reunions and their cutting exchanges.

"Stop acting like you understand me," I retort, pivoting toward him. I stare at him with my intoxicated eyes, diving into his, which are ignited.

He caresses my cheekbones, my hair, as if I were made of porcelain, ready to shatter at any moment. Once again, he sees right through me. Our breaths mingle. His hand travels up my side, and his thumb pauses beneath my breast. Thus, he guesses when I hold my breath.

Memories of our kiss return in flashes.

"Stop looking at me like that."

My eyebrows furrow. "Like what?"

"As if you want me to kiss you."

My attention shifts to his mouth.

"Stop…"

The air freezes, time stands still. The thread connecting us, thickens considerably. The atmosphere is so charged that my stomach aches. My reason clashes with my instincts, with my barriers. His thumb caresses my cheek, his black gaze plunging into my mind, transmitting all his desires. Those that remind me of his horizontal exploits and all that I could imagine on the other side of the wall.

But I can't give in to him. It would be insane. It would be terrifying.

Without asking me, he buries his face in the hollow of my neck, grabs my hair to hold my head in place. When his leg wraps around mine, I stop fighting. I close my eyelids while granting him all my trust. I give in. And it's during my surrender that I understand.

Every sentence Ervin said resonates within me. Yes, I'm ashamed that he discovered my excess weight when his hand was groping the curves of a hottie a few hours ago. Yes, I enjoy his touch despite my repulsion. Yes, I had a strong desire to repeat the experience the day after our kiss, without admitting it to myself. Until I ran into him with those two other women.

His free arm encircles me, presses me against his rigid shaft. Despite my panic, my begging when he nibbles on my throat, Ervin doesn't stop. However, his hands don't venture below my hips or above my stomach. When he licks my collarbone, I falter. A moan escapes me. I cling to his hair like it's an anchor, then dig claws into his massive muscles.

"I… don't know… what you're doing to me," he growls.

The acute awareness of his moist lips against my skin sends me into a frenzy. I can't suppress a damn moan. His muscles ripple against me; I'm hot, so hot… until he abruptly pulls away. He deserts my neck, creating a painful void.

Out of breath, I can read his expression of surprise with difficulty. Embarrassed, I don't know how to react. I'm probably turning crimson, even if he can't see it.

When he muffles a curse, loosens his grip on my hair, and releases me, worry takes over. Ervin pulls himself out of the sheets, hand on the bulge in his boxers, and explains that he needs a shower, leaving me stunned. I hear the door close, as he makes his way to the bathroom.

Alone in the dark, I feel my heartbeat go wild. What happened in that bed? It stinks… It really sucks… How long has it been since I felt such intense arousal? And this extreme frustration is killing me!

Questions swirl, consuming me, and Ervin doesn't come back. Not until dawn when, finally, I fall asleep.

CHAPTER 9

My fingers are itching. The urge to write is terrible, yet what comes out is very ugly. Suffering, morbid kisses, bloody abrasions. My calling: zombie romance! Gather the necrophiles; I have enough to satisfy them! Well, just a few paragraphs, borrowing emotions here and there from the memories of that night.

The journey home was painful. I got up before everyone else, dazed by my one hour of sleep, and sneaked off to catch the train. Ervin can go to hell with the bikers, and I didn't feel like facing Galati and her lover, even with their covered butts.

Once home, I fell asleep until Monday morning. I woke up starving and tormented. In front of my chocolate croissant, I scribble, anxious about the image I project to Ervin, the threesome enthusiast. I bet he replaced my nickname of "Desperate Chubby" with "Insecure Chubby." After all, it's fair play; his nickname changes every day. If he hadn't bolted after my moan, I might have given him the nickname "Big Dick," but that would be too much of an honor.

The hours pass, and now I can't progress on any of my manuscripts. Every micro-image of Ervin haunts me, every word he spoke, every sensation felt two nights ago. I don't know where he went after slipping into my bed. Was it just a game to him? Make me surrender only to take me down! What if he was so excited that he went back to his two bitches?

That's why romantic male-female relationships are not for me. I'm so annoyed by this inner turmoil. My relationship with Gala is not much better; I've rejected her countless calls, trying first to sort out the mess in my head. In vain.

That's the reason why she barges into my place during her lunch break. Undoubtedly, her night of erotic fun did her good; she looks stunning.

"You look bad!" she greets me.

"Hello, Gala, it's always a pleasure to see you."

"Can I know why you're ignoring me?" she scolds, making herself at home in my apartment.

"Do I need to draw you a picture? Or you can open one of those books there on the shelf; it'll be more explicit."

"Don't play the smarty," she retorts, blushing. "Listen, I'm sorry that you found us."

"Well, in my room, the risks were high, don't you think?"

She gives me a puppy dog look, almost enough to make me feel guilty. Almost.

"I didn't realize. We'd been drinking, and… in the heat of the moment… we didn't think."

"I hope you didn't think. I would have doubted your lustful delusions! I'll never forget the image of your boyfriend's butt! I'll visualize it every time I see him! Can you imagine?"

She doesn't know where to put herself. Well, that'll teach her not to *think* when she's getting laid! But how can I blame her? All I have to do is recall my state of mind on Saturday night to understand how much our hormones can make us lose control. At least one of us had a night of pure pleasure. The witch!

"Is that why you left on the sly?" she asks accusingly. "Since you took his clothes, Milo had to walk the halls butt-naked in the freezing cold!"

It's the freezing cold that bothers her?

"Too much skin for my eyes; I couldn't handle it. Consider it an acquittal for kicking me out."

I imagine my excuse isn't convincing enough. Her perplexity is obvious. She knows me, knows that under normal circumstances I would have taken great pleasure in roasting them.

"And in reality? It wouldn't have anything to do with Ervin, would it? He was nowhere to be found, too."

Oh really? Where had that deserter gone?

"Speaking of Ervin! Did you know he was occupying your boyfriend's room when you threw me in there?"

She stares at me with her pretty round eyes. "I thought he was in the company of the two models."

"So did I."

"And… did you guys talk?"

On a roll, I explain my night to her, leaving out no details. An outside opinion is welcome because honestly, I'm lost. Skeptical, she delves into the matter with me, equally wary of the alpha male who clouds my judgment.

A knock sounds on my door.

Without interrupting my conversation, I open the door.

Speaking of the devil… The runaway is standing in front of me, chin held up. Cap backward, wearing sweatpants, he looks like he just came out of the gym.

Frozen, I lose track of my words. Galati remains silent, much like the handsome guy who greets me.

The mere sight of him is enough to stir me up. He doesn't seem bothered at all; his confidence makes me sick. Faced with my inertia, he hands me his bag with a friendly smirk.

"I spent the morning at my brother's—brought you some children's books. My nephew wanted to get rid of them. Thought you could give them to the orphanage."

Bewildered, I nod and take his gift. We scrutinize each other in silence, and then I realize he's waiting for my invitation to come in. Heart pounding, I glance at Galati. The beautiful blonde stares at me, questioning, when suddenly, fingers press against the back of my neck. Before I can react, a mouth collides with mine, like a cyclone sweeping through the air.

The bag falls to the floor, and I cling to Ervin's shoulders as he makes me stagger, bewildered. On the verge of a heart attack, I vainly try to pull away. His lips stifle my protests, and he ushers us inside my home, slams the door with his heel. His kisses are incredibly sensual, clouding my questions, reigniting those damn shivers from my feet to the top of my head. Despite Galati's disapproval, I loop my arms behind his thick neck and let myself be carried away in his storm.

He slides his hands under my ass, carrying me to the desk, where he sets me down. "You won't escape me anymore," he whispers against my mouth.

Am I the one trying to flee?

"Ervin," I complain before a scraping sound is heard a few feet away from us.

My neighbor barely glances at Galati, who's trying to capture my attention.

"I'll leave you to it, then." My best friend leaves.

I think she grabbed her things and closed the door. I think so… I'm not sure anymore; his assault on my lips is causing my synapses to malfunction. I kiss him back, devouring him with all the anger he stirs in me. I could berate him, but evidently, it's with persistent frustration that we free ourselves. So, with the thrusts of my tongue, I inflict my sermons on him.

Bastard. Bastard. Bastard. Hopeless bastard!

I make his cap fly away, nearly pull out his hair when he undoes my bun. His fingers weave through my strands, gripping them.

"Leave your fucking hair down." His desire-roughened voice growls in my belly. "And these damn pajamas…"

Out of breath, I retaliate by digging my nails into his cheek. "My pajamas tell you to fuck off."

He bites my throat. "I might end up tearing them apart."

His thighs make their way between my legs, and he tilts me farther, eagerly caressing my face.

"Do that… and I'll emasculate you," I retort, panting.

His tongue crushes against the base of my neck, slowly goes up to my ear. The sensations he triggers are entirely unknown to me. It's indefinable, unqualifiable, surging between my legs, buzzing in my temples.

"You want me too much for that," he whispers, Machiavellian, before nibbling on my earlobe.

Fuck! His insolence never ceases to amaze me. But the worst part is that he's right. Again, he reads me like a book. And again, I hate him for it.

My arm acts as a barrier between us; he gently pushes it away. Feverish, Ervin scrutinizes me, a dreadful smile on his lips.

"Stop acting like you didn't run away on Saturday night," I scold.

His cupped hands around my face, he furrows his brow. The setting has nothing in common with the shadowy atmosphere of last time. Daylight abounds, and I distinguish every part of his skin, every sparkle in his obsidian eyes. And what does he see? My open window allows the gentle breeze to caress us. It makes a few strands of hair flutter over my temples, which he brushes away with an affectionate gesture.

"On the contrary, I'm acting accordingly," he answers.

Too many conflicting emotions traverse his eyes in this moment. A voracious fire allied with a complicated restraint, tenderness, assertive assurance…

"I was scared. I may not show it, but I can control myself. I wanted to prove it to you, gain your trust. Then I realized that if I stayed there, despite all my determination, I would devour you. I know you want it, Alizee, even if it scares you. And that certainty doesn't make it easy for me, believe me."

His words seem unbelievable to me. Unthinkable, despite the evidence that overwhelms me. His erection was real, and that tension between us, I didn't dream it…

"Where did you go?"

He places his forehead against mine. "To get some fresh air."

I settle for that answer. "What's happening now?"

Without answering, he seeks my lips, caressing them gently. With languor. He locks us in a cocoon away from the external noises, where nothing else exists but our kisses. He fills me up with emotion and joy for endless minutes. Again and again.

And again…

CHAPTER 10

I spent the day in a parallel dimension. Ervin and I kissed for a long time. Afterward, he offered to ride with me to the orphanage. I think I spent half an hour in front of my wardrobe before he came to pick me up. My mind was fuzzy, and I didn't know what look to go for. Get dolled up for him? When pigs fly! I had to stay casual without looking like a sack of potatoes. But no matter what I wore, I felt enormous. So, I opted for a black, bell-flared dress and opaque stockings.

Getting on his bike reminded me of his performance this weekend. Clinging to him after we had just kissed excited me. I hadn't realized it until now.

He was quite comfortable with kids, making his presence easier to handle when it otherwise made me lose my composure. Then he dropped me off at home before heading to his appointments.

And here I am behind my desk, staring blankly, nibbling on my pencil, trying to define the nature of my emotions.

***

A week of texting. Ervin is having a blast with *All Night Long*, telling me he has everything to teach me with a disconcerting nonchalance. With my regained confidence, I remain sharp and prevent him from intimidating me. He won't teach me success, at least; my romance was number one in sales for months.

I miss him.

His two kisses ignited a new thirst. His eagerness mixed with gentleness still turns me around, although I don't show it. I'd rather die! He hasn't mentioned it either. With his busy week, we haven't crossed paths on the doorstep again. And it's not for lack of watching! I sometimes spend half an hour with my ear glued to that damn door, hoping to catch him, but nothing! Mister turned into a ghost!

***

My mother knows perfectly well not to wake me up before eleven o'clock. This makes me even grumpier than usual; nonetheless, she persists. It didn't take me five minutes to kick her out of my apartment, a new record that fills me with pride. I'm about to slam the door when my neighbor appears on the stairs, leaving me breathless.

My mother, on the other hand, eyes his sports attire with surprise. "Well, well, you do get dressed sometimes?"

I roll my eyes, praying she leaves before I head back to my quarters.

Her attention shifts to the bulge between his legs.

"It happens when I'm not at your daughter's place," Ervin retorts, mischievous.

Is he not embarrassed to tell her something like that?

"Don't listen to him, Mom. See you later!"

She shakes her head, exasperated, then points her finger at him. "If you ever find her lifeless body, call me before the paramedics, so I can fill her fridge. I might get charged with malnutrition."

"I'm almost thirty, Mom!" I snap.

She gives me a compassionate look, as if I had some mental deficiency, then turns on her heel, tosses her scarf over her shoulder in grandiosity, and bids us a cordial farewell.

Eye to eye, Ervin and I stand still amid the echoes on the marbled steps. Their reverberation hangs in the air, like a gentle melody trapping us in its notes.

At this moment, I wish it never ends. I'm reluctant to return to reality. The reality where I have sleep in my eyes, where my hair is a mess, where I'm wearing those fluffy pajamas that he hates—thanks to the autumnal temperature—and I have bad breath.

"Are you hungry?" he asks with a surprisingly serious tone.

I blink, remembering my mother's last words. "No, but don't pay attention to what she says; I have enough reserves to last the entire winter." I gesture toward my plump body.

My retort makes him laugh. An adorable laugh enhanced by a three-day-old beard that's incredibly sexy.

"Come on, I'll feed you," he says, heading toward his apartment.

Go to his place? Just like that?

"No thanks, I'm good. I'm not in the mood."

"Not in the mood for what?"

I watch his key slide into the lock, my arms hanging limp. "For nothing. It's nine in the morning."

"I forgot, you're not a morning person," he mocks. "Come on, I'll put you in a good mood, you'll see."

My belly is tingling from the inside. "You overestimate your skills."

About to enter, he freezes, scrutinizing me from head to toe.

"I know what you're thinking, and I don't care if you've joined the anti-pajama squad. I'm not changing."

This time, he bursts into laughter.

I fall for him a little more.

"I didn't ask you to change. I'll be satisfied with your crappy face for now, kitten."

My mouth forms a big 'O'. The nerve!

"Yeah, you're right, I'm in a better mood now!" I exclaim in disbelief. "Besides, are you planning to kick me out after an hour?"

"My tolerance limit for your pajamas."

My raised middle finger responds aggressively before I retreat to my place and slam the door. Leaning against it, I hear him knocking, bursting out laughing, blending his apologies with insincerity. My lips stretch involuntarily. He'll get me eventually, that idiot.

"Go home and admit your defeat: you don't know how to handle girls, moron!"

"You're not making it easy for me! Open up!"

My smile widens. He continues pounding, emphasizing my satisfaction.

"If you beg me, maybe."

"Oh, damn! I was planning to make you pancakes like you've never had in your life."

Okay. I give up.

I open the door and, without freshening up, find myself at his place in no time. In the morning light, I discover his lair in a new light. I'm at the enemy's place. It's masculine, minimalist. He clearly hasn't taken the time to settle in. His environment makes me jittery. He leaves me standing in the middle of his living room and disappears into his bedroom.

"Are you going to make them from there?" I say to maintain my composure, while inspecting the absence of his personal effects.

In the corner of the room, what I believe to be his video equipment is piled in a heap. Some cameras lie on the floor, piquing my curiosity. I approach them, fondling the cameras while recalling his splendid Instagram photos.

"Are you a photographer in your spare time?" I ask.

Dressed in a gray T-shirt adorned with fake paint stains and distressed jeans, he appears in the doorframe and leans against it. "I've traveled a lot. It's when I want to immortalize my journey that I truly enjoy photography."

I'd like to learn more. During his housewarming party, I saw a few photos that adorned his walls. Were they his? Why have they disappeared?

"Would you show me your photos?"

His eyebrow goes up, along with the corner of his mouth. "Are you interested?"

"I thought you were a brainless piece of muscle. Knowing that behind this mountain there's something like passion, yes, that interests me."

He shakes his head, dumbfounded. "You never stop."

As he heads toward the kitchen, I wonder if he read between the lines. He's everything I'm not. He is that confidence I envy, the narcissism that annoys me, the self-sufficiency that pierces me, and the arrogance that knocks me down. Yet, his involvement in motocross, or EnduroCross, the love for his work, his enthusiasm for exploration, and his artistic sense intrigue me.

"Do you like cinnamon?"

I give him a challenging look. "I'm more into frozen pizza and canned macaroni. You're speaking a foreign language."

Disappointed, he shakes his head while equipping himself with bizarre utensils straight from his cupboards. "Why do you harm your body?"

I stand up, scowling. "No time or desire to cook."

"Do you have breakfast?"

"Barely."

More than his disapproving look itself, what he must be deducing irritates me.

With his permission, I slip into his bathroom to freshen up. Different from mine, it boasts a large walk-in shower, a toilet, and two wood-effect sinks adorned with various masculine products. Their number doesn't surprise me, given the man's profile.

When my reflection in the mirror hits me full on, I fall apart. Fuck! Screw pancakes! With my fingers, I tame my hair after letting it down, splash my face, and my eyes land on his toothpaste. Then his toothbrush…

Dare I…?

A few steps away, his "throne" stands, the toilet seat raised… An irrepressible smile blooms on my lips. I take great care of my dental hygiene before going back to my cooking neighbor, cheerful.

"What's put you in such a good mood all of a sudden?" he asks suspiciously.

"Your dedication to satisfying my taste buds."

And he falls for my answer, too! Full of enthusiasm, my personal cook invites me to his table, right in front of his bay window. The pancakes are buried under a mountain of fruit.

"It's a fruit salad turned upside down, *in fact*."

From his sigh, I deduce his disappointment.

"You're worse than a kid, actually," he says.

I glare at him, but caught in my own trap, I stumble upon the darkness of his fiery eyes. His seriousness is almost frightening, reminding me that our relationship has been different from this incessant teasing. A week of communicating without seeing each other. Seven days where our kisses played on a loop in my head, driving me crazy.

Ervin is in front of me, cooking for me after my mother's remarks, throwing back my nasty remarks, betraying no particular emotion. And here he is, plunging into the window of my soul with the same expression he wore back then. He leans in, picks a piece of strawberry from my plate, and directs it toward my stunned face. My wide eyes follow his fork without me opening my mouth. He doesn't force it, caresses my lips with the red fruit, moistening his own.

"You wouldn't refuse me that...?" he says in a husky voice.

I flutter my eyelashes and part my lips, creating a small opening he gently enters, his attention focused on the piece of fruit that I devour. Good lord, the aura he exudes eroticizes this simple bite. I swallow, my heart pounding.

"So?"

I take a deep breath, nodding my head. "It's... good." Divine.

With determination, he moves his chair back, stands, and comes right next to me. What on Earth does he want from me? Wasn't *good* flattering enough?

With his fingers, he takes a second strawberry from my plate and once again brings it to my mouth. Astonished, I voice no objection, letting him press his index finger against the curve of my lip. Fueled by an audacity that I don't recognize in myself, I lick the tip, my face turned up toward him.

His gaze is electric, unsettling my entire being.

Then, he kisses me.

Elicits a deep moan from me.

Sends a thousand tingles racing down my spine.

His kiss doesn't last. He pulls away, not taking his eyes off me.

"Hey, you," he greets, as if we're only now meeting again. His usual demeanor cracks, revealing the man who turned my world upside down a week ago.

I flutter my eyelashes, holding back a barrage of lingering questions.

"I couldn't help it," he justifies. His thumb presses against my lower lip, wanders over my chin, traces circles on my throat.

Holy crap! I'm already wearing fluffy pajamas; there's no need to raise my internal temperature!

"We… should eat, if I have to leave in an hour." That would cool us down and keep my thoughts clear.

When he steps away, regret immediately assails me. I want more. A whole day devoured by the wolf wouldn't be unwelcome. But he doesn't insist and empties his plate in silence. I do the same, unable to concentrate on the flavor on my plate.

I clear the table, start doing the dishes, despite his fierce objections. It's a matter of politeness; I might be grumpy, but I'm not uncivilized.

Soaked up to the wrists, I become aware of the hourglass that is ticking away. We have twenty minutes left…

Suddenly, his presence behind me takes me by surprise. He places his hands on my waist and slips them under the thick fabric. I shiver, instinctively sucking in my stomach. His nose nestles in the hollow of my neck to inhale me.

"Too much kindness from you. It turns me on, kitten."

The heat increases.

His fingers climb slowly.

"Relax," he murmurs, caressing my skin with soft kisses.

Emotions collide—fear, confusion, desire. The memory hits me that I'm not wearing a bra. If he goes any further…

"Ervin… Ervin, stop…" I whimper.

His nails bite into my ribs. His hips mold against my backside, expressing his desires. My heart beats like a drum.

"I'm—" I'm completely freaked out… "I think I should go," I say, putting a glass in the sink.

"Stay… Just ten more minutes before I head to work."

I cling to the edge of the kitchen counter, trembling. Millimeter by millimeter, his fingers approach my breasts… What will happen next?

You know the answer, Alizee.

No… I can't endure it again.

With a sudden movement, I step back and free myself from his grip.

"Wait, Alizee!" He grabs my wrist to hold me back.

Terrified, I avoid facing him.

"What are you afraid of? You want it, too. You know you turn me on. What more do you need?"

I close my eyes, trying to gather my thoughts. For a week, I haven't heard any of his conquests moan. Was it due to a lack of desire or time? I turn him on, and then what?

And then, *me*?

We are too different.

"I don't know how, Ervin…"

His fingers tighten. "What are you talking about?"

"I'm not like you."

He comes closer, pressing himself against my back, and holds me captive, encircling me with his free arm. "You don't need to know how. I'm good enough for two."

"You idiot! I'm not talking about that." Although that concerns me, too.

"What's wrong?"

"I don't know how to handle… all of this."

His breath hisses in my ear, and his hand releases my wrist to settle on my stomach. I close my eyes, hating this feeling of being trapped by my insecurities. My skin vibrates under our contact; if only I could fully enjoy it…

"Don't move. Let me show you something," he whispers in that fucking sexy voice.

Torn between my reason, my desires, and my fears, I remain frozen, only to be assaulted by new kisses on my neck. My breathing quickens, and shivers resume coursing through my entire body. I suppress my moans, not expecting his next move at all: Ervin caresses my lower abdomen, slowly infiltrating beneath the elastic of my pants.

Damn it! What is he doing?

"Ervin…"

"Shh," he murmurs, nibbling my skin.

I arch my back and collide with his erection while his fingers continue their seductive advance. My heart races. I want to escape, but the sensuality of his kisses makes me a captive. I feel like a stick of dynamite ready to explode. The fuse burns between my legs as he goes down farther.

When he slips beneath the elastic of my panties, I cling to his forearm, shaking my head. "No, no, no… Get your filthy paws off there," I squeak in an unrecognizable voice.

A small laugh escapes his throat. He tightens his grip on me, breathing heavily against my cheek. "I assure you, Alizee, you'll like it. Let go. Don't think about anything else but the way you feel. The rest is just pollution."

He doesn't understand…

His touches are more insistent. He freezes like me, holding his breath. Between my legs, my blood pulses relentlessly.

"Fuck…"

He takes the words right out of my mouth.

My thighs close, and I shiver in terror. His scorching body against mine suffocates me.

"Spread your legs," he urges in a low voice.

Staring at the minibar in the living room, I vigorously shake my head. "Don't give me orders."

His hand delves in, cupping all my flesh, shocking me.

"I'll cook pancakes for you every day. Spread your legs."

It's outrageous to lure me with sweets! "Don't bullshit me… it was a disguised fruit salad."

He sinks his teeth into my neck again, extracting a small whimper of pleasure from me.

"The next ones will be chocolate pancakes."

His promises include a daily exchange. Reassured by this prospect, a barrier within me shatters; my thighs are spread by eagerness.

He smiles against my skin.

His fingers brush the lips of my pussy, and his gentleness brings me to the edge of the precipice. If I jump, I'll drown in it.

"However, I have a few conditions…"

My eyes widen, witnesses to my astonishment. "You swindler!"

His hand on my shoulder slips down to my breast, gripping it, cutting off my breath. Fortunately, my thick fluffy pajamas serve as a barrier against my total downfall.

"You never come to my place dressed like this again."

Asshole.

His middle finger slips between my folds, sending a powerful shock before withdrawing, gliding over my clitoris.

"Fuck, you're soaking wet," he chokes, his cheek pressed against mine.

He can't do this to me. My legs tremble, silently begging for him to come back.

"Deal?"

I surrender, nodding, cursing him with all my soul for the too brief glimpse he gave me. My flesh contracts in spasms; I would accept anything to get him inside me again.

Ervin tortures me, caresses my folds for a long time before his index finger boldly slips between them. My moan betrays my distress. When he teases my clitoris, I curse him.

"Keep insulting me, and I'll stop everything," he articulates, biting my cheek. "Kiss me."

I turn my head away, despite my monstrous desire.

His finger plays with my focal point of my desire, and when he presses it more eagerly, I melt. My face ends up turning to the handsome man. I yield my lips, which he seizes with passion. His tongue doesn't wait. It dances with mine, just as he dances with my emotions. Between my legs, he proceeds gently, with an expertise that propels me into the throes of pleasure. His two fingers rotate slowly, tormenting me explicitly.

"And I want you to kiss me when you greet me," he mutters against my mouth.

Yes. Yes. Yes, fuck, as long as you keep going!

"Don't stop…"

He doesn't stop; his concentric movements increase in speed, making me faint. My legs give way. Ervin holds me with his body and his kisses.

The dizziness is intense, the urgency between my loins, heavy. His tongue invades my mouth more deeply. Ervin growls into it, pressing his hard cock against my butt. He holds my hips while he pleasures me.

I want so much more. It feels so good. My hands cling to his forearm, stabilizing me. Right now, he could do whatever he wants with me, as long as pleasure is the outcome. There is no more kitchen, no apartment. There is no more confrontation between us, just this inexplicable attraction that ignites us in an instant.

The mass grows, swells in my belly and under his fingers until it explodes throughout my entire body. Overwhelmed by delicious shocks, I abruptly close my thighs, even though he continues his caresses.

Oh, my god!

I try to free his hand from my panties, but it's stuck. I squirm under his torture, begging him to stop, but he's stronger. I suffocate in pleasure, my clitoris now too sensitive.

"If I could fuck you on the kitchen counter, damn…" Ervin laments without letting me go.

I imagine myself bent over the stove, receiving his famous thrusts that have haunted my nights.

"You can dream!" I retort when he finally grants me the hoped-for release.

I pant, devoid of energy, like a limp doll between his arms. He gives me a few seconds to recover, then turns me toward him, pinching my chin between his fingers. Exhausted, I feel like my eyes are empty, yet filled with too many emotions. My heart is pounding, and I wish I could snuggle into his powerful arms and let myself sink, preserving this moment in my memory before crashing into reality.

He brings his face close to mine, infiltrating me with his gaze, and a smile appears on his wet lips. "Now, kitten, are you going to jerk me off, or you heading home so I can take care of it? I can't work in this state."

With wide eyes, I step back, almost stumbling, my body still fragile.

"Don't look at me like that. It was good. Don't regret it," he adds.

His features have taken on that irritating mask, distorted by arrogance and damnable smugness. His beauty has been tainted with ugliness, but he's still as attractive as ever. After this bewildering orgasm, I need… something else.

I knew I should never have given in. I knew it!

Disappointed, betrayed by my own weaknesses, I flee through the living room, with Ervin on my heels.

"Alizee!"

"You wanted me to leave, right? Unless you've changed your mind? No more need to jerk off, Mr. Super-Fuck?"

With these words, I leave, my mind in disarray.

CHAPTER 11

"Reassure me, Vampyr—you're on my side, right?"

Without flinching, my cat stares at my moving lips.

"Ervin is a complete jerk."

No reaction. The buzzing of a fly catches his attention.

"I should never have let him put his vile mouth on mine!"

Face down on my bed, head planted on my crossed arms, I try to keep my friend focused.

"Don't be jealous; he kisses like a god. Your cat kisses are cute, but they don't provoke the same things in me."

My cat yawns in my face, spreading his foul feline breath.

"And he smells good. I swear, nothing else existed when that idiot touched me. I didn't even have awareness of my body, my weight. I loved his caresses. I loved that he wanted me so much."

Vampyr gets up and jumps off the bed. Ungrateful! And what about my heart problems? I already see him begging in front of his bowl. Let him go to hell!

*****

At noon, I have lunch in the old center of Paris with Marshall. He is flabbergasted by my morning experience, thinks I encountered a jerk by definition. He advises me to stay cautious—a man like Ervin is only looking for satisfaction without bothering to respect the other.

"He takes what he wants without considering your sensitivity. This kind of guy moves on once he gets what he wants, and you'll be condemned to live in the apartment next door."

The ambient clamor makes our discussion difficult. I eat my pizza with little appetite after Ervin's pancakes.

"I got played by a specimen of the worst kind. I wonder why he set his sights on me."

"Maybe for the challenge," Marshall suggests. "You're smart, pretty—no matter what you say—and you don't let yourself be pushed around. That must be a change from all the superficial girls he sees. Men like to challenge themselves when it comes to girls. Once they win…"

I finish my glass of wine.

Once won, they move on to something else. I know that.

That's the problem. What he did to me this morning… I liked it. A lot. Our verbal sparring was charged with sexual tension as well. It stinks…

I'd be pissed if he moved on. And again, that's an understatement. Moreover, his tactless asshole behavior is unbearable; he might grind me down slowly.

Him and his damn jerk-off!

"So?" Marshall calls out to me.

My attention returns to him. "Excuse me, you were saying, my cotton bud?"

Yes, I also give people nicknames. They are appropriate, given my editor's physique. With his slender figure, I'm sure he's close to six foot five. His thinness doesn't help. At thirty-six, his thin face is framed by a dark curly mass of hair that falls on his cheeks. I like the little vests he wears over his fitted shirts, as well as his loafers, which give him a truly typical Parisian style.

"I spoke with Ludivine on the phone last night. Did you sign with Alan again?"

What had my romance editor's competitor told him?

"I haven't signed anything at all. Why?"

Dubious, he looks at me with his beautiful blue eyes. "You're not hiding anything from me—reassure me?"

"Spit it out, Marshall!"

He dips the tip of his lips in his glass, takes a deep breath. "During the book fair last week, she ran into Alan. A film producer specializing in romance adaptation was also present. Ludi heard that Alan would have given her the film rights to your upcoming release with LoveRomance for next year. The dates are set. I thought you were planning something for him."

Stunned, it takes me a moment to realize the exact meaning of his words. He can't do that. Promise something that isn't even signed.

"But… that's illegal! I haven't committed to anything! He hasn't even talked to me about it!"

Marshall's expression wrinkles. "I don't understand how he could sign anything with that woman if you haven't put anything on paper. Haven't you mentioned your film rights?"

I quickly shake my head and rummage through my tote for my phone. Under Marshall's worried gaze, I dial that shark's number with a frenetic rage.

"Alan!"

"My dear Alizee! What a pleasure to receive your call!"

Oh, he probably imagines he's about to hear some good news from me.

"Pleasure not shared! What have you schemed during the last book fair?"

A few seconds of silence. *Come on, think about your spiel.*

"So many things. It's impossible to detail them all. You tell me, Alizee, why are you calling?"

This old man has a way of making my teeth grind! "I heard a rumor. My next book will be adapted into a movie; that's really classy, isn't it?"

He laughs in my ear, the cheeky bastard!

"I see gossip spreads fast."

"Can I maybe have a say in this? Or, you know what? No, I won't. Not in person, not in writing, nada! Just find another author to screw over!"

I hang up on him, furious. I don't answer when he calls back. Then he sends me a text.

[Alan: Nothing concrete, just promises. I had to cover my back before she went elsewhere].

I show the screen to Marshall, who sighs dramatically. "Wrong. He claimed the deal was signed."

"He's trying to put pressure on me," I rage.

Marshall grabs a cigarette and twirls it in his hands. A furrow creases his forehead as he ponders.

"Do you think I should send him my cat's poop as a thank you gift?"

At least I manage to lighten his mood. He chuckles.

"No. I think Ludivine would take much better care of you than that money-hungry guy."

I sink back into my seat. Yes, Alan thinks in euros, but he's my first publisher. He took me in when I was just starting, knowing nothing about publishing, and propelled me into the spotlight. His marketing is perfect, and he brings my books to the forefront.

"Ludivine is more compassionate and admires your writing," he tries to convince me, sensing my reluctance.

"You say that because she's your friend."

He smiles. "Those are precisely the reasons why she's my friend."

I let out a long exhale.

"Tell me you haven't signed an exclusivity clause?"

"I'm not crazy I was a novice, not unconscious."

Leaving for the competition… Maybe. But first, I need to manage to write this damn romance.

CHAPTER 12

I heard Ervin come home in the late afternoon. Since then, no message or the slightest sign of life. I'm simmering. I scroll through his Facebook and Twitter pages, scan his Instagram and Snapchat. A few links and sports videos feed them, but nothing tells me what he's up to or planning.

Remaining in this uncertainty, hormones still boiling, is unbearable. I need to clear things up with Neighbor Jerk-off!

After a glance in the mirror, I hesitate to give our deal the middle finger and present myself to him in my pajamas. On the other hand, maybe I want him to see me differently. Sending him away in a dress seems more appropriate, so I put on the dark one with red polka dots that falls over my black stockings. I tie my hair in a ponytail, accentuate my eyes with a hint of liner, and put on some polished Charleston shoes. I'm now ready for battle!

I take a deep breath and suppress the images from this morning. Those little sneaky thoughts haunted me all afternoon; because of them, I had to change my underwear twice!

Dreadful Apollo!

On the threshold of my den, I come face to face with an angel straight out of a reality TV show. Long jet-black mane, hourglass figure with everything in the right place, big doe eyes, and a mouth made for other things. Pressing my neighbor's doorbell, she scrutinizes me with an innocent look that could make her pass for an angel. Or something else, take your pick.

I swallow, gaze at her white, faux leather miniskirt, her deeply plunging pullover, her ankle boots with six-inch heels, and the down jacket she holds in the crook of her arm.

No way! He called a hooker!

I join her, standing in front of the door. "What are you doing here?" I almost attack.

Innocently, she blinks before pointing her finger at the entrance. "I came to see Ervin."

Well then!

"And who are you?"

"I'm Nabilla, and you?"

Fuck.

My jaw drops. I immediately suppress a burst of laughter. It would figure her name was identical to the most notorious French bimbo on reality TV.

"Really?" I ask with a traitorous giggle.

She questions me with her eyes. "Yes, why? What's so funny?"

Trying to regain my composure, I shake my head. "Absolutely nothing. What are you here for?"

At that moment, Ervin opens the door, then raises his eyebrows. "Ladies?"

I swallow. Barefoot and bare-chested, he's only wearing jeans, revealing his obliques to make me drool. *Does this nudist ever get cold?*

"Care to explain?" I assail him, pointing at the woman of ill repute.

She stares at me as if I'm missing a few screws, then quickly moves to escape my wrath.

"Explain what to you?" he asks.

Hands on hips, I accuse him with his disapproving gaze, feel my pride plummeting inside.

"You didn't have time to empty your balls this morning? Needed to call a hooker to fix that?"

Flabbergasted, he glances over his shoulder, takes a step toward me, almost closing the door behind him.

"What the hell are you talking about? She's not a hooker."

Of course! She works in shampoo sales, right? "Yeah, yeah, my ass. Have you seen how she's dressed? Don't feed me your nonsense."

"I'll make you swallow something else if you don't calm down right now," he threatens me, narrowing his eyes.

At his insinuation, my traitorous cheeks flush. I'm such a hopeless romantic. Damn it!

"I'm very calm given the situation, believe me. Don't you think you could have discussed this with me instead of calling another girl? Especially after you touched me this morning."

His jaws tighten, making his cheek twitch.

"I'm telling you she's not a— you know what? What if she were? Is that a problem? Do you want to replace her?"

My heart twists with the feeling of being played like a fool. His behavior confirms that he's no better than the most basic jerks.

Seeming to realize this, he runs his hand through his hair and tries to explain. "Nabilla works with me. We're collaborating on a women's sports project. I had some details to clarify; that's why she's here tonight."

Sports… in the bedroom?

My pulse quickens. The heat of embarrassment washes over me. I cross my arms, a protection against the awkwardness. "And… you were expecting her half-naked?"

He frowns. "I just got out of the shower. Want to check out the bathroom? You might find something else to scrub with my toothbrush while you're at it."

This time, I return a triumphant smile. Childish reaction, I know, but giving him a hard time brings me immeasurable satisfaction.

"Ervin?" calls *Nabilla*.

Crushed by my own stupidity, my dignity tells me to withdraw. To leave this bare-chested scene to the care of this perfectly redone nymph.

I'm seething despite myself!

Without answering, he scans every inch of my body. I take a step back. When his eyes lock on mine, their intensity shakes something within me. Dang it… He invites me to enter by opening the door. I refuse with a shake of my head.

"I'll let you discuss work with your colleague," I say emphasizing the term. "I have things to do, anyway."

"What did you want from me?"

I shrug, releasing a sigh. "Talk… about this morning."

He nods. "Wait for me here."

He enters the apartment without closing the door behind him, and I hear him reschedule his appointment with the pretty brunette. She appears in the doorway, annoyed.

"I did warn Cem, though."

"He'll understand," retorts Ervin. "I'm sorry, beautiful, come back tomorrow. I promise it'll be worth it."

Skeptical, I watch her pout before crushing her plump lips on my neighbor's cheek. He apologizes, contrite, while she says goodbye to me. I respond to her bitterness with the desire to crawl into a mouse hole. Well, unfortunately, my ass wouldn't fit, so let's forget that idea…

Once alone, Ervin and I scrutinize each other. Him, with frustration, me, like a child caught in the act. A sensation I hate.

"Go get a coat while I get dressed; were going out."

"We're going out?" I repeat, stunned.

"We're going to talk outside."

"I've already been out today. It's freezing!"

"Well, put on something warm," he says, slamming the door in my face.

What the hell! Twice in one day—it seems my life is becoming exciting.

***

The glowing lights of the cafes create a fascinating atmosphere in the night. I've rarely wandered through the streets of Montmartre after sunset; I had forgotten this magical ambiance. It's teeming with tourists, who increase as we approach the hill. Lost in the crowd, I struggle to accept that I'm walking with Ervin. In his down jacket, the idiot looks adorable. His gaze remains fixed ahead, and sometimes his protective arm wraps around my shoulders to shield me from the crowd.

"Let's cut this way," he informs me, taking my hand.

He leads me onto the cobblestones, into the shadow of a deserted alley. A breeze makes me shiver. We're alone, in the center of Paris. We're alone in the silence of the night. We're alone, facing each other.

"Why were you aggressive? Tell me what's on your mind."

His husky voice scratches me from within. I stop, letting him take a few steps ahead before he stops and turns around. He plunges his hands into the pockets of his jeans, seemingly waiting for me to speak.

I shrug, letting out a few curls of condensed air as I sweep the old facades with my eyes. "What are you thinking? Are you trying to get me into your bed? Is it a game to you?"

"Look at me when you talk to me," he commands.

I obey, a frown on my face. His seriousness baffles me.

"You can't just show up at my place and kick out my guest just because she's attractive. You're completely crazy to call her a whore!"

"Excuse my mistake. I'm in a bad mood today."

"Oh really?" he scoffs. "Does having an orgasm make you more annoying than usual? If so, I understand why you avoid them."

His tone isn't teasing; it oozes cruelty. Why is *he* putting himself in this state?

I shake my head, worn out by these offensive exchanges. "My editor is getting on my nerves."

The sound of a violin rises in the distance. A tourist musician, most likely. A concerned expression animates Ervin's face. His beautiful eyebrows furrow, his delicious mouth tightens.

"You're not answering my question," I throw back to him.

He never averts his gaze, unlike me. His ease intimidates me, and the context prevents me from taking him down, from having the upper hand on my flaws.

"Of course, I want to get you into bed. I've been clear about that."

"And then?"

"And then, what?"

"And then you move on to another girl, like you usually do."

He takes a step closer, lets out a sigh. "What difference does it make?"

Despite being prepared, it hurts. Can I applaud his honesty? At least, he's not trying to deceive me.

"It makes a difference because I don't like the idea of being treated like the bimbos you fool around with. I've already told you that, Ervin, so stop teasing me."

Surprised by my honesty, he smiles. "Is *mademoiselle*'s pride shaken?"

With my eyes locked on his, I try to stand firm and not let myself be crushed by his confidence. I've been through this situation too many times. There's no way I'm going to be fooled again. "I'm worth more than a tissue."

He takes another step in my direction. His index finger caresses my chin in a sensual gesture. "You have nothing in common with those girls. But I've been clear—I don't want to commit."

I remain silent, taking in his rejection.

"And neither do you," he adds.

I blush. "Indeed. Especially not with you."

His hand completely cups my cheek, forcing me to step back.

"What's the problem, then? We'd both be winners."

He's wrong. I'd lose much more than the satisfaction gained.

"Why promise me pancakes every day? Why ask me to kiss you when we meet? Are you trying to fool me?"

He shakes his head. "I don't understand your hang-ups, Alizee. I enjoy making you breakfast. I like kissing you. It doesn't mean anything more."

Frustration torpedoes me. Without saying a word, I imagine my mornings with him, savoring delicious chocolate pancakes. I imagine myself under the influence of his most sensual kisses. I imagine falling for him.

The sound of the violin sends shivers down my spine. I wrap my arms around myself to chase them away, much like the perilous scenes playing in my head. "I can't. I don't want to sleep with you."

My body screams with desire, my heart cries for help. My reason hurls the most colorful insults in my repertoire at him.

Ervin opens his arms, exasperated. "Whatever you want!"

"*Whatever I want?*" Is that it? Well, he really seems to be dying of desire for me, the Casanova.

We resume our walk in the streets of nighttime Paris. In front of the funicular, he takes my hand, intertwining our fingers to lead me in front of the ticket office. With two tickets paid, he invites me to step into the cabin where we find ourselves alone again.

Ervin is captivated by the scenery outside, presenting me a perfect profile. Without restraint, I scrutinize his features, letting my insides squirm.

To use me and toss me away. That's all he's interested in, that's all that would happen. I must repeat this mantra, or I might change my mind.

"I know I'm handsome, but you'll still have plenty of time to admire me. Instead, enjoy the view," he recommends with frightening nonchalance.

Too gloomy to react, I turn my face toward the window. I see nothing but my dull life, chained by too many wounds, stifled by too many fears.

I revealed a part of myself to Ervin before our first kiss. Opening up felt good at the time. The attitude he continued to adopt made me regret my confidences. Yet, today, I feel like an invisible thread connects us. A thread fueled by our nastiness, by our mutual animosity, but nonetheless special. This man had his hand in my panties just this morning. This guy knows my weaknesses, and despite his inappropriate language, he manages to lessen them in his presence. Does he really appreciate my curves, or is it just a ruse to gain my trust? He has never lied, even if it means provoking my wrath… But the chicks he hooks up have nothing in common with me.

Fuck! I'm lost!

"By the way, you look very pretty tonight, too."

My heart somersaults.

"I didn't give you any compliments," I say.

He points his phone camera at me. Before I have time to react, the photo is taken.

"Ever hear of asking permission?" I protest.

He smiles, takes a second snapshot. "Let me immortalize this moment. You look truly beautiful."

My cheeks warm up. Uncomfortable, I turn back to the window, trying to ignore his interest.

After the ascent, we both admire the view from the top of the hill. The lights of Paris sparkle, and many tourists' cameras flash, immortalizing this wonderful tableau that I rediscover alongside my neighbor.

An artist's neighbourhood, to which I belong. A favorite district for tourists, where I feel different. Outside my den, I would have appreciated him capturing my lips, despite our previous discussion. A parallel reality that I would have erased once the threshold of my apartment was crossed. To my disappointment, he does nothing of the sort. He simply sits on one of the numerous steps, pressed against my side, wrapping his arm around me to raise my internal temperature. A gentle moment, a truce in our volcanic relationship. I nestle against his chest and rest my head on him, receptive to his friendly gesture.

Minutes pass, faces change, yet we remain there, motionless and entwined, suspended in time. Until the magic shatters, and we return home, parting ways with a simple goodbye.

CHAPTER 13

Two days later, I'm awakened by a message from my neighbor.

[MersEv prod: Pancakes?]

[Jade Evans: It's eight AM…]

[MersEv prod: I just got back from the gym. I'm waiting for you.]

Wearing a woolen dress, I freshen up and drag my feet to the neighboring apartment, feeling groggy. He seems delighted by my effort to dress up, while I'm blinded by his morning enthusiasm. We chat about trivialities, exchange a few barbs in all friendliness.

We repeat the ritual the day after. And in the following days, every time he has breakfast at his home.

I gain two pounds. I panic. Yet, I'm incapable of giving up his pancakes. Unable to forgo visiting him. Deprived of his presence.

A week later, he invites himself to my place and fills my fridge with strange things called *vegetables*.

In my database, I create a folder named Ervin, and put the few pages I managed to write in it.

During November vacation, when students have two weeks off, I go to the orphanage with Gala. She seems worried about his interest in me.

"Be careful, Zee. After what Milo said, I don't trust him."

I hide the irritation she provokes in me. "It seems like he's committed to feeding me. I don't understand why he's doing it, but he hasn't tried anything more since our discussion."

With a dubious expression, she confides in me, "From the start, Milo keeps telling me that you shouldn't get close to his friend. When I ask him, he explains Ervin's a player, not serious, and not good for you. But I feel like he's hiding something from me. I'm worried. I don't want your first experience with a man, after years in the desert, to hurt you."

I roll my eyes. "Do you see me as that fragile?"

"I see you as bitter. I don't want him to make things worse. People are already scared enough of you."

Scared? No, way!

"Don't worry, he's given up the idea of putting anything into me. Anyway, I don't want to sleep with him."

I omit a detail that's more important than anything else: I'm so busy protecting my ass that I continually forget to barricade my heart.

On the same evening, Ervin prepares us a delicious dinner, paired with an excellent bottle of wine that we indulge in. As if to affirm my friend's concerns, he kisses me before heading back to his place, leaving me breathless on my couch.

I can't sleep when I try, besieged by too many conflicting emotions. Was it some sort of slip-up? A latent desire despite his easy acceptance that our relationship remains friendly? And damn it, it was so good!

The next morning—because yes, his succulent pancakes punctuate my sleep cycle—I find myself at standing in front his door. He must have just returned from the gym by now.

He opens it, a towel casually thrown back on his bare shoulder, exposing his chest. I eye his sweatpants, instinctively closing the flaps of my long, oversized cardigan.

Although he smiles, his usual insolence isn't there. He's still undeniably sexy, with his wet hair and the sparkle in the dark depths of his gaze. And that mouth... soft and inviting...

"Hey."

I regain my composure and smile back. "Hello. Can I come in?"

He steps aside, brushes the lower part of my back as I pass by him, then leans against the closed door, hands in his pockets. "I'm sorry for yesterday," he starts without hesitation.

He hasn't prepared anything yet, but the smell of pancakes

permeates his apartment.

After an about-turn, I cross my arms, captivated by his onyx eyes. His face, so familiar and beautiful it complicates my breathing.

"I didn't mean to push, we had been drinking and…"

I take a step toward him, my eyebrows furrowed.

"You looked sexy in your pretty dress," he continues in a deep voice, without averting his gaze.

I shake my head, just inches from him. The seducer tenses against the door, his chest heaving. I want to tell him that it's wrong, that things were clear, that it was too good to be repeated. But all I manage to do is press my index finger into his plexus. In a ridiculous attempt to annoy him, I press harder, bumping against his steely muscles. Resigned, I let my finger slide along his abs.

"Alizee…?"

That voice, damn it! How do I suppress the wave of heat spreading through me?

"Let's pretend nothing happened, okay?" he says.

Is he mocking me? As if I could!

I grab his neck, rise on my tiptoes, and take what I've craved since he left my apartment.

When my mouth meets his, he groans in surprise. His scent immediately gives me a sense of fullness, and his soft touch electrifies my nipples. Unable to control myself, I devour him, rummage through his wet hair. His passion awakens instantly. He grabs my waist, gropes me, bites my lips, eliciting moans of pleasure.

My heart beats too hard. I break our kiss to catch my breath.

Our eyes don't leave each other. In his, I discern surprise, turmoil, and lust. A fierce desire. Frightening. I dare not imagine where it would lead us; I prefer to calm our passion.

"That was the deal," I justify myself.

He doesn't seem to understand.

"You cook me chocolate pancakes every day, and I kiss you to greet you."

Finally, he catches on and frowns. "The deal is quite convenient, you little brat. Nothing more?"

"Nothing more. Take it or leave it."

CHAPTER 14

Scandalized, I freeze in front of my cell phone screen.

"Alizee?"

Ludivine Jumet regains my attention, under the disapproving look of Marshall. I blink, feeling the blood pulsating in my temples. The jerk dared to Insta me!

"Sorry, I—"

I just found out that my neighbor posted a picture of me on Instagram. A souvenir from our nighttime walk in Montmartre, designating me as his muse. He has no shame!

My text message notification lights up.

[Gala: Ervin is posting pictures of you now? Are you guys together yet?]

A week ago, I assured her that between him and me, there was nothing more than delicious chocolate pancakes. Apparently, there are also snapshots with *#sosexy.*

"Are you thinking about it, Alizee?" calls the Ludivine's voice.

"Yes, of course." I force myself to smile, eager to leave this gourmet restaurant.

Marshall places his hand on mine. "You don't seem yourself. I hope our meeting didn't make you uncomfortable. You don't have to do anything, you know that."

"No, you know me."

He nods, pointing to my manuscript in the envelope. "*Bloody Stars* will be a hit, believe me. We start the promotion in two weeks. We'll have time for corrections; it will be very well-received."

His words are reassuring, given my uncertainties. I didn't have any before. Since Ervin appeared in my life, I'm riddled with them.

"I'm glad I met you," Ludivine says, extending her hand. "I hope everything goes well with your editor, even though I don't appreciate his way of doing things. With me, you know what to expect."

I shake her firm and friendly grip. "Thanks for your interest. Anyway, I don't guarantee writing romance, for now. I'm blocked."

She nods, lips draw on her sixty-year-old face. "No pressure from me, that's not my goal."

When Gala harassed me on the phone, informing me that her own editor had mentioned the film adaptation of a book I hadn't even started, I saw red. Despite my reprimands, Alan had continued to spread false news in order to trap me. I contacted Marshall, accepted Ludivine's presence at our meeting in order to clarify some points…

I rushed back home, and am surprised to encounter Ervin on his motorcycle, entering the small courtyard of our building.

I chase after him, furious. "You!" I burst out as soon as he removes his helmet.

At first surprised to see me, he immediately smiles.

"Don't make that face!" I command, pointing my finger at him.

"Why?" he taunts before cupping my cheek in his gloved hand and kissing me.

Caught off guard, I'm unable to react. And, god, it feels good! His tongue massages mine, sensually, and his arm encircles my waist, bringing me closer to him.

When he pulls away, his hazy eyes locked with mine, I almost faint.

"You don't have the right to do that," I pout.

In response, he gently nibbles the curve of my lip. "I have the right to kiss you. You gave it to me yourself."

My heart races when he whispers like this. This week, he has not stopped bantering, delighted to have the upper hand in our strange relationship.

"Don't abuse it!"

His nose traces a path under my jaw, triggering waves of warmth. "I only have to fuck you…" he finishes in my ear.

A wave of anger overwhelms me. I give him a proper slap and free myself from his grip. "No, what an idiot!"

He laughs out loud, holding his cheek. Then, he gets off his bike. "Damn, bullshit is ingrained in you! Every little hope to discover some neuron in you, I get disappointed!"

He doesn't give a damn about what I say. Rubbing his cheek, he heads toward the entrance of the building.

"Like posting a picture of me on Instagram. Seriously? *#sosexy?* I remind you that I'm an incognito author!" I bark, trotting behind him.

At the foot of the grand staircase, he tilts his head toward me. "That's why I called you my muse. I didn't know you were following me on Instagram, kitten."

I'll shove his *kitten* down his throat!

"Because that's not the case!"

He raises an eyebrow.

"Gala reported this annoying fact to me. You could have told me about it," I argue, climbing the stairs alongside him.

"So you could stop me? That would have been a waste."

On our landing, my foot stumbles over a soft mass. Fuck! How did Vampyr end up out here?

While Ervin opens the door to his apartment, I take my ball of fur in my arms, check that my home is securely closed. Crap…

"Ervin…"

But he doesn't hear me. He continues to rant about my image rights as he disappears into his place.

Suddenly, Vampyr leaves my arms to follow my neighbor.

"Oh no!"

I rush after him, colliding with the other moron.

"Easy, kitten. You slap me, then crash into me—I really don't know what to think anymore."

No, but stop!

"You're annoying me. Think about my cat who sneaked into your place, who's going to be completely lost and pee all over your stuff."

A flash of panic crosses his eyes. He closes the door behind us, takes off his leather jacket. "How did he get in?"

"I don't know, the door to my apartment is locked!" I exclaim while searching his place.

He scratches his head, rushes to his video equipment. "If your cat pees on… Oh, fuck!"

I turn around in a leap, expecting the worst. I face an irritated look.

"It was him, with Otto!"

"Otto?"

His whole body tightens before he rushes to his bedroom. I collide with him in the entrance. He's stiff, his hands clinging to his hair. "Fuck, no!"

I follow his gaze until I see my cat on his bed, wriggling on some furry mass.

"What the hell is that—?"

Ervin jumps on him, greeted by Vampyr's threatening hiss. I've trained my cat well. Vampyr grabs the other furry thing by the mouth, settles in in the corner of the room, and continues his business.

"Your dirty beast is fucking Otto!" Ervin exclaims, furious.

"Who the hell is Otto?" I reply, alarmed.

"My damn stuffed animal!"

I freeze, eyes wide open. Indeed, my cat is busy on a blue teddy bear. The big guy camps in front of the lovebirds and stomps his foot.

"Shit, stop that, you dirty pervert! Shoo!"

Vampyr doesn't want to hear it; he keeps rubbing himself, his fangs sunk into the synthetic material.

When Ervin turns to me, bewildered, I can't hold it anymore. I burst into a guttural laugh, my face hidden behind my palms.

"Take back your Vampyr and get out of here!" he roars.

I close the gap between us and size him up, paying no attention to the little party happening at my feet. "First, you're going to lower your tone! I thought you were in solidarity as womanizers. What's the problem?"

"Otto smelled like piss the week I moved in."

My mouth twists into a guilty pout. Yes, indeed, I had sent Vampyr on a mission to get revenge for the nocturnal vocalizations of the other chicks.

"He's clearly not peeing on it!"

Ervin tries vainly to shoo him away with a hand movement. My cat is very focused.

"But isn't that damn beast spayed?"

He has a point. I don't know why he's so aroused, but the blue seems to please him.

"Do something, don't just stand there!"

I cross my arms and say, sardonically, "If you delete my photo from your Insta."

Ervin shakes his head, dismayed. "Fine! Go ahead!"

I coax Vampyr, who's not ready to give up his lover, then get the idea to grab a chair and drop it right next to him to scare him. He ejects himself and runs to hide under the bed.

The owner of the raped teddy bear grabs the victim and sniffs it deeply. "Now I have to wash it! Shit!"

No way, I can't believe it. This thing looks like a turtle.

After grabbing my cat, I scrutinize my neighbor with a mocking expression. He just came back from the bathroom, still red with anger.

When he notices me, his nostrils flare.

"What?"

"You have a teddy bear."

His eyelids form two deadly slits. "Is that forbidden?"

"It's ridiculous."

His strong jaws clench. Damn, I'm enjoying this!

"No more than living in seclusion with a pet!"

The grin on my face emphasizes my disagreement.

"I care about it, okay? I've had it since I was born."

"It's too cute!" I mock.

He bypasses me, heading to the living room. "Let's figure out how your cat ended up in the hallway."

"First, you delete the picture. Otherwise, I release Vampyr on… Otto. My cat hasn't copulated in a long time, and it saddens me to deprive him of it. He's has a crush, you know."

"Shut up and come here. The post is deleted."

I giggle as I comply. It feels so good to see him embarrassed, Mr. Big Arms.

At my place, there's nothing wrong except my open window. Ervin goes to the terrace, climbs on the railing to observe the roof. The contraction of his muscles under his sweater sends tingles through my lower abdomen. To distract myself, I fill my valiant, neutered cat's bowl.

"There's a skylight that opens onto the landing. He must have come in that way," concludes my teddy bear-loving neighbor.

"Well, at least I know there's no psychopath waiting for me under my bed."

Ervin's silhouette stands before me. His look is murderous. And I—I gaze at him with my chin held high.

"Thank you for checking. I hope Otto will recover."

My jubilation is palpable. His teeth nervously pierce his lip. He must be dying of frustration.

"Not a word about what just happened," he commands.

"Or what?"

His eyes roam from my mouth to my laughing eyes.

"Cat got your tongue? Too bad, he prefers Otto's!" I burst out again. My childishness will be the death of me.

Ervin grabs my bun and brutally crushes his lips onto mine.

My euphoria fades away.

His kiss is beastly, feverish. Vengeful. He silences me when he seizes my butt to carry me to my bedroom.

Once he throws me onto the bed, I berate him.

"What the hell are you doing?"

He climbs on top of me, trapping my wrists on the mattress. His nose is only a few millimeters from mine; I can feel his breath on my moist lips.

"Don't play with me," he growls. "Don't make me angry, don't mess with me. The consequences could be terrible."

"I'm not playing."

I'm not playing; I'm losing control. Every day a little more. I try to resist in every possible way, like just now, with the idea that he keeps a stuffed animal. But here he is, more animal than ever, threatening me, generating within me a heavy ball of magma, ready to disintegrate me.

"You provoked me with that photo," I blame him, toneless.

His eyes trace the outline of my face, while meowing invades the silence of the room.

"So what? It's just a snapshot. Why do you have such a hard time accepting your image, damn it?"

I swallow, craving his mouth.

Our breaths mingle, yet he remains focused on my response.

"Not everyone has your excessive narcissism. And then… it's more complicated than that. Someone made me an offer…"

He frowns. "What offer?"

The velvety tone of his deep voice runs over my skin. His hips make themselves comfortable between my legs, hitching up my skirt indecently. Breathless, I struggle to escape his grip. Each particle in him attracts me. His physique, his confidence, his weaknesses… Hypnotized, I spill everything.

"Promoting my next book on the set of *Restez éveillés.*" Surprise flashes in Ervin's eyes. He remains silent for a moment, before brushing against the tip of my nose. "That's great."

Kiss me…

My lips graze his when I tilt my chin.

"I don't know."

"You'll reveal your identity."

My tongue caresses his mouth as I moisten my own.

"I don't know."

A few kisses are placed on the corner of my mouth; then, they burn my jaw, electrifying the delicate skin of my throat. My wrists still captive, I arch my back and exhale slowly to keep from getting carried away.

"Talk, Alizee. Distract me, or I'll devour you."

Devour me…

"I handed my manuscript to Marshall. Thanks to Ludivine's contacts, it's highly likely that I'll be invited to the show. It would mean putting a female face on Elie Roy, my other pen name. I was against it, but the audience is huge."

He sinks his teeth near my jugular, then soothes the bite with his tongue. "Do it."

"My image will become public," I confess in a sigh of pleasure.

"And who is Ludivine?"

Unlike Marshall, I've never talked to him about her. I stretch my neck, then rub my cheek against his three-day-old beard and elicit a growl from him. I'm caving… Despite the deals, my insecurities, and his vanity, the attraction between us is unbearable. It nibbles away at us a little more every day, weakens my will.

"A romance editor and a friend of Marshall's. She's wanted me for a long time."

Suddenly, Ervin's breathing intensifies. His face still buried in the hollow of my neck, he questions me, "Are you changing publishers?"

He might be trying to distract me, but his solid member between my thighs makes that impossible. "I don't know."

"You don't know much."

"You're distracting me," I moan.

His heart pounds behind his ribs. "If you don't spill it right away, I'll let go of you and grab these breasts that are tempting me."

"We have a deal," I retort vehemently.

"I don't care. I want you too much."

At this passionate declaration, all the reasons why I absolutely must not give in explode in my face. So, I divert his attention. "I made sure that in case I offered my next manuscript to Ludivine, she could secure Alan's agreement for the film adaptation. Since it's not official, nothing commits me to it."

Ervin lifts his head, looks at me with surprise. "Would you double-cross your editor?"

A few seconds of silence accentuate my feeling of guilt.

"If you knew him, it wouldn't surprise you. He's a shark who deceived me first. He's been pressuring me for two years."

Ervin lets go of my wrists. However, he doesn't go after my chest or any part of my body. Instead, he rolls to the side, propping himself up on his hand, elbow bent. With relief, I turn on my side to face him.

He wraps my rebellious hair around his free fingers. "Are you planning to go back to love stories?"

A disenchanted laugh escapes me, and I shrug. "I have a few ideas, yes. It's still unclear, and I get stuck when I try to develop them, but after my thriller, I'm seriously considering trying again." I close my eyelids, savoring his caresses on my temples.

"Why are you stuck?"

Because… because my love and sex stories have played dirty tricks on me, because my writing painfully brings me back to them. Because the scars run deep.

Understanding that I won't talk about it, he adds, "Your porn books are fascinating. I'll help if you want."

Without opening my eyes, I can't help but smile. "My hero will have a teddy bear named Otto."

His hand wraps my throat, exerting a gentle pressure. "Your hero will be a sensitive man, nostalgic for his childhood when he didn't know certain things."

Suddenly, I lock my gaze on his obsidian eyes, my interest heightened. "What things?"

He bites his lips and tucks a strand of hair behind my ear, betraying his hesitation. "Adult things. A couple on the decline and its consequences."

I swallow. This little jerk manages to shake me up. He had already told me about his father's abandonment. Could it have affected him more than it seems? To the point of keeping a stuffed animal at thirty years old?

"He will become an erotomaniac."

"Ah, because the heroine won't screw him?"

"Of course not." I smile. "That would be the last thing."

He remains silent for a moment, then takes a deep breath. "You should say yes to appearing on TV. And you should go back to romance, Shakespeare. It suits you well."

He extracts himself from my bed in no time, stretching as if he was waking up from a deep sleep. "I'm going to go, Alizee, or I'll break my promise."

He crosses the living room, spouting colorful curses aimed at my cat, leaving me panting on my mattress.

CHAPTER 15

Eyes glued to the huge wall clock, I count…

One kiss. Two kisses. Three kisses…

I no longer enumerate them. Often, they are brief. Unstoppable, yet controlled, so as not to slip away.

Ervin hasn't tormented me with his innuendos anymore, our last intimate encounter having proven to be perilous. Our exchanges are less hostile, but still sting. I learn to get used to them, him, and his exasperating attitude. A complicity has been established between us, despite the short duration of our tête-à-tête. I enjoy his presence, feeling more and more at ease in his proximity.

He has never invited himself over again. The sexual tension between us is too obvious. Every one of his lingering looks fries my brain. It's obvious, and the rascal relishes in it, but he doesn't take advantage of it. It seems he has more decency than I imagined.

Forced to wake up early, my mind on pancakes, I've learned to go to bed early. Therefore, I have no idea what he does with his nights. A detail that kills me. Ervin is a ladies' man. Moreover, he's a sexual guy; so there's no way he's going to be satisfied with our kissing sessions. Considering our deal, I try not to think about it. I'd quickly risk torturing myself with painful comparisons, and then blame myself for no reason.

***

Christmas music resonates through the bass of the cabaret, complemented by some remixed samples suitable for the evening. Seated at the same table as my stepfather Gui and my half-brother, I'm bored out of my mind. Every time a dancer moves on stage, I pray for her to stumble, hit the floor, or even break a leg. Something interesting, in short. A perfect revenge for everything they indirectly inflicted on me, putting sparkle in the eyes of my mother, who never found me up to her standards.

I hate the holidays. Ridiculous Hallmark movies to make housewives' hearts melt, kids who max out their parents' credit cards just because an old, bearded guy handles the finances. I'm sure it's a conspiracy against adults. Kids know no one goes down their chimney to leave a present under the tree; they pretend to believe it to make their mom and dad pay up. The magic of Christmas—my big fat ass!

Today, like every year, it's lady Charlene, my mother, who hosts the evening. On stage in her flamboyant costume, she's in her element. She expresses herself with lyricism, performs grand gestures, still captivates her husband. This Mr. Average… The custom-tailored suit chosen by his wife fails to elevate his dullness. I've never understood what she sees in him, especially when she was always with my father. Despite being sick, my father was much more fun than the square Guillaume!

The venue is packed, and the customers seem delighted. After all, they are at *La Chaumière*, the most beautiful cabaret in Paris after the *Moulin Rouge*. The wooden walls are adorned with black stones and golden arabesques, glittery veils embellish the ceilings, a majestic Christmas tree sits at the back of the establishment, and the waiters are dressed in Santa Claus-themed suits, complete with beards and hats. The show is spectacular, yet I can't seem to get into the spirit. Charles fiddles with his phone, prompting me to take mine out of my bag. Another hour before they serve us the turkey—I'm not out of the woods yet! A whole night of my crazy mother, her ghost boyfriend, and Charles lays before me. Joy!

I would have asked Galati to come with me, but it's her chance to meet her important siblings who have gathered from the four corners of France. Not to mention that, for New Year's Eve, my blondie is flying to Malaga in Spain with Milo while I'll be freezing my butt off. Lucky her!

Those two are deeply in love. After just two months of dating, she's already thinking about moving in with him. He's very much in love; however, something seems to hold him back. Personally, I find him odd. A week ago, at Ervin's party, he watched me way too often, giving me dirty looks during my banter with his best friend. The icing on the cake was when he stumbled upon our stolen kiss in the kitchen. It was like he was jealous.

I was jealous then, too. The chicks Lionel and Alix brought hovered way too close to Ervin. They perched on his lap, leaned against his chest. Their lips wandered on his cheeks, into his neck. The little show-off was reveling in it, and I was well aware. I feigned indifference, even contempt, but deep down, it twisted my guts.

[Alizee: Entertain me, I'm bored.]

[Playboy: I miss you.]

Well, this is something! I sit up straight in my seat, feeling like I've been hit in the face. The music fades, and all I can hear is my pounding heart. What a pathetic mess I am. Why do these simple words provoke such a reaction, damn it?

[Alizee: A major first. Is your night as crappy as mine?]

[Playboy: I don't think so. I'm chilling with my nephew, watching a Christmas movie.]

[Alizee: A Christmas movie and a kid. I confirm, your night is even worse than mine. In my opinion, you would like to be in my place. The dancers are hot and work with their tits exposed.]

I receive a laughing emoji.

[Playboy: And do you dance?]

A smile plays on my lips.

[Charles: Who are you chatting with?]

I look up at the brat; he's radiating unmistakable distress.

[Alizee: Do I ask you questions?]

[Playboy: Often, yes. Do you want to go dance?]

Fuck! Wrong person!

I glare at my disturber.

[Charles: I'll do you a favor wherever and whenever you want if you help me sneak out, big sis.]

Oh, please! If he could sober up somewhere other than my neighbor's, it would be a big step forward.

[Alizee: I don't like dancing, but I'd prefer that to spending the evening here.]

[Playboy: On my way to pick you up.]

Stunned, I look at my cell phone, wondering if he's serious. He doesn't answer my numerous calls, just sends me a message fifteen minutes later, letting me know he's waiting for me at the entrance.

When I leave the table without warning, the disappointed face of my brother almost makes me cackle in glee. *In your face! You may be ten years younger, but I'm the one who's dodging the family gathering this year!*

I flutter to the door, where there's absolutely no one. The street is nearly deserted, swept by the magic of Christmas. I'm dumbfounded. Feel like a fucking idiot! And yet, it doesn't surprise me.

"Bastard!"

A homeless person a few feet away turns toward me, thinking I'm addressing him. "Have you looked at yourself, bitch!"

Oh, calm down, dude!

Disappointed, I give up, leaning against the wall, my heart empty. No way I'm going back inside—I won't give my brother that pleasure. Shit… It's freezing! In front of my wardrobe, I had to choose: stay warm or be elegant. Wanting to avoid my mother's reproaches, I opted to freeze.

At the end of the street, I see a man approaching. What an idea to go jogging on Christmas's Eve! Here's someone more desperate than me.

"Alizee!"

Oh! Surprise! It's the guy who stood me up. "I thought you were waiting for me in front?"

"The cops hassled me; I couldn't park my bike in front of the cabaret."

My heart palpitates. Even more when I see he has two helmets. It's awful how my skin starts to tingle whenever he's around. He looks adorable in his down jacket, with his pompom beanie and fitted jeans. His nose reddened by the cold makes me smile.

"Hi," he murmurs, leaning in to capture my lips.

All my irritation disappears with his touch. His mouth is cold, yet so soft. Despite the cold, he takes the time to be tender, does it damn well, and warms me up in seconds.

Then he hands me the second helmet. "Come on, let's get warm."

On his motorcycle, I feel like I'm eighteen again. We cross Pigalle Street, weave through small alleys dotted with snowy mounds. Nestled against his back, I realize no one has ever made me feel this way. My adrenaline is at its peak; his fervor, his nonchalance are refreshing. He's elusive. My heart races when he kisses me, my retinas are exhausted from watching him prepare pancakes—a man who cooks, even pancakes, is sexy! My body suffers every day from the memories he's left all over it. And my brain keeps tying itself in knots.

Ervin takes us… home.

"You're getting to know me. I thought you wanted to dance."

Opening the building's door, he turns his face toward me, looking mischievous. "Oh, but we're going to dance."

What's he talking about? I sense the vintage music and a slow dance in the middle of the living room. Not in my wildest dreams. Did he think he was in a Christmas movie or something?

In the stairwell, his phone suddenly starts to vibrate. When he picks up, I hear a familiar voice getting excited on the other end of the line.

"Wait, wait, calm down, Galati!"

What do you mean, *Galati?* Since when do these two talk to each other? With a dry mouth, I try to control the feeling of betrayal that takes hold of me.

Ervin stops his climb. I follow suit, a nasty feeling behind my ribs.

"All right, I'm coming," he says abruptly, looking puzzled. He hangs up, turns around without a glance at me. "Milo had an accident. I'm heading to the hospital."

A cruel sense of relief washes over me, quickly replaced by worry. "Is it bad?"

"I don't know; your friend is freaking out. I have to go. I'm sorry, Alizee."

"I'm coming with you."

We hurry to the hospital, traverse the emergency room corridors, and arrive at Milo's room. It's small and cold, with several empty beds separated by white curtains. Typical. Gala is sitting on a chair by his side, welcoming us with a furious look. Her boyfriend is sitting on the mattress, not looking so bad.

"What happened?" my neighbor asks, alarmed.

With a scratched face, Milo shrugs, eyes looking up. "Nothing serious, man."

"Are you kidding me?" The blonde startles me. "He had a motorcycle accident! He was fooling around somewhere in the forest, playing in the snow, slipped, and ended up in a ravine!"

"Is anything broken?" Ervin asks, unusually serious.

"Just some bruises. I need to get X-rays and a scan in case I have a concussion. In my opinion, it's unnecessary."

"Of course it's necessary, honey!" the blonde rants. "That bike will kill you, I'm telling you!"

Intimidated by her turmoil, I realize the extent of her feelings for Milo. She, usually so calm, almost scares me.

"Let's calm down," Milo retorts.

"What were you thinking? How did you end up face down in a ravine?" Ervin now teases him.

Gala turns red, stares at them in turn, before putting her hazel eyes on me. I freeze.

"You're not at *La Chaumière*?" she asks me.

I remember I'm wearing heavy makeup and glittery stockings under my coat. I glance at Ervin, who's relaxed, busy chatting with his friend, then turn back to Galati. "I couldn't take it anymore; he pulled me out of there. We were heading back to the apartment when you called."

She nods with a concerned expression. For reasons we both don't know, she distrusts him. Well, I have my own idea: who would trust a jerk who's obsessed with his image and anything that comes with a pair breasts and shapely legs?

The boys' laughter grabs her attention. "Well, I need to stretch my legs!" she exclaims, on edge. "Coming, Zee?"

I shake my head. Paris takes holidays seriously, and even hospitals operate on minimal staff. I have no desire to wander through the sinister, empty corridors on Christmas Eve.

"I'll be here all night," Milo complains. "There's only one doc; the others are with their families."

"It'll teach you to act like a jerk," Ervin says.

"What were you two doing together?"

"I saved her Christmas Eve; she was ready to shoot herself." Ervin laughs.

"Let's not exaggerate," I lie, unable to give him any ground.

"Weren't you at Cem's?"

Ervin nods.

"Who's Cem?" I ask, curious.

"My brother." His hand glides over the small of my back. "And *Nabilla*'s husband, you know, the hooker…"

Suddenly, I feel like an idiot. His colleague was actually his sister-in-law… and I insulted her. I'm ashamed!

"Oh yes, that's right. You were celebrating Christmas with your family. You abandoned them because of me."

No need to dwell on my little jealousy crisis.

The handsome dark-haired man covers me with a tender gaze under his pompom beanie. "In our family, we don't celebrate Christmas, kitten."

Is he crazy to call me that in public? Fuck! I'm blushing!

"And why is that, *Otto*?" I retort, mischievous.

He squints, looking like he wants to shoot me, then grabs me by the waist and pulls me close to his hip, his face just a few inches from mine. "Because it's not our tradition. And my mother can't… be there right now," he finishes with a grimace.

"Guys, spare me your nicknames, I can't!" exclaims Milo, nauseous.

"Oh, you don't know Otto?" I smirk.

Ervin gets my attention back by pressing on my love handle. "No, and he doesn't want to meet him, believe me."

I revel in it. "Good, Otto belongs only to Vampyr," I say.

My neighbor rolls his eyes, letting go of me abruptly.

To annoy him, I've often sent my cat into his apartment through the terrace. It never failed; he rushes to his cuddly toy, soaking it with his smelly fluids.

"You're lucky you look hot tonight. I feel compelled to forgive all your nastiness."

Damn, here we go again, I'm getting hot. He can't decently say something like that to me, and with such intensity in his eyes. I could have returned the compliment if Milo wasn't focused on us.

Ervin wraps a lock of my hair around his finger, admiring it. "Never tie your hair up."

"If you want it down so you can paw it all the time, no thank you" I reply with a shy smile.

He returns the shy smile. My heart stumbles.

"Well said," Milo interjects, exasperated. "Don't let him fool you, girl, you're worth more than that."

In unison, we turn toward him. He shakes his head, rolling his eyes, and I giggle softly.

"He's right," I concede to Ervin, who grins even more.

At this moment, I'd like to bite into his lips. Our kiss in front of *La Chaumière* was too brief. I dare not imagine how our evening would have unfolded if Gala hadn't called. The way he looks at me allows many indecent scenarios to bloom. The most terrifying ones.

"I'm sorry about your brother. I didn't mean to steal you from your family," I tell him quietly.

My friend reappears in the room, piercing me with her gaze.

"No problem, I was dying to see you."

I swallow, ignoring where these impulses of kindness come from.

"Besides, we gather regularly, don't worry. I'm close to my older brother; his son is fed up with Uncle Ervin."

Him talking about his family touches me. While we often discuss trivialities, he never opens that door to me, remains quite secretive about his private life. Yet, the affection he holds for them is obvious. I remember his confession during our first kiss. This feeling of inferiority that they try to impose on him... His confidence is his strength; it's remarkable. If only I had his temperament.

Gala's outbursts pull us out of our bubble.

"Milo doesn't want to cancel the trip to Spain," she complains to Ervin.

He pauses, exchanging a glance with his friend. "I imagine, yes…"

Wide-eyed, she seems to be on edge. "What do you mean, *you imagine?* I called you to talk some sense into him; I didn't think you were so reckless."

"Let's wait on the X-rays," my neighbor suggests.

"If anything is broken, you don't take him with you; you stop him from driving!"

"Milo's a big guy; there's no need to castrate him," says my biker, getting annoyed.

"Uh, my best friend is worried sick. Lower your tone, please," I interject.

He raises his hands and steps back in a sign of surrender.

"And then, what's this about riding in Spain?"

"If we go to Malaga, it's for the gentlemen to have a motocross race in the mountains."

"Are you going there, too?" I ask Ervin.

He nods.

"Me, Milo, Lio, and Alix."

And Gala…

No one told me about it. Not even my friend. After all, if her boyfriend invited her, there's no reason for anyone to ask me to come along. Especially since traveling with mere acquaintances isn't like me. Anyone who knows me knows I would have said no. So why does this feeling of being left out gnaw at me?

"By the way, would you like to come?" asks Ervin, as if the idea had just popped into his brain.

"Not even in my dreams!" I retort immediately.

"Come on. It's warm over there. We'll stay in a villa that was lent to me for four days. The race only lasts one day—we're going to have a blast."

I swallow hard. Four days living with Ervin, with no walls to separate us. "Nope."

"Leave her alone," Milo intervenes with a murderous look in his eyes. "It's not her thing; she'll be bored in Spain."

Mind your business, dude! What if I wanted to make myself desired? He should say it right away if it's him who's bothered.

Gala nods, still looking for my approval. I ignore her, answering my neighbor, "I already struggle with tolerating you when you live in the apartment next door; can you imagine four days in the same space?"

He chuckles. I should have kept my mouth shut! It's pointless; my smile betrays my agreement.

"I'm taking that for a yes," he boasts, ruffling my hair.

I push away his hand with a slap, my heart pounding. "I admit, Spaniards are handsome. It'll please my eyes."

"For the pleasure of your eyes, there's me."

Speechless, I clench my teeth as he laughs aloud. So many possibilities, but my eyelids roam over him, eager, before I retort, "Oh, really? Let me think about it because it doesn't jump out at me right now."

"Do so. In the meantime, you've a bit of drool on the corner of your mouth," he mocks, pressing his thumb to my lip."

I step back, destabilized by his gesture. "That's probably the only place you'll get me wet."

"I'm not so sure."

"You'll never know."

"Wanna bet?"

"Damn it, stop pretending like you want to fuck her," Milo mutters.

A dead silence surrounds us. Gala and I stare at the injured man, dumbfounded. Ervin glares at his buddy, weighing down the mood.

"Give me a break for two minutes, will you?" growls my neighbor.

With a dry throat, I feel like the ground is opening under my feet. My heart twists. Painfully. Shame makes my breathing uneven; my chest heaves like that fateful day when I collapsed.

The room becomes suffocating. They watch me with concern, shrinking in my field of vision, and without understanding how, I find myself outside, panting in front of the building. Galati quickly joins me, incredulous.

"What happened, Zee? Why did you run off?"

To escape. To avoid being hurt again. I shake my head, pull out my phone to call a cab.

"What the hell are you doing? Did Ervin do something to you?"

"He didn't do anything to me," I reply while giving my address for the cab.

"Is it because of what Milo said?"

It's because of me and my damn self! "Go back inside, Gala. I don't feel like talking right now."

Her cheek twitches. She's used to my confessions, but my exclusion surprises her.

Ervin rushes over as well. He stops in front of me when I don't have the courage to face him.

"You shouldn't leave your buddy alone," I mutter.

"He's in the X-ray room. Go on, Galati."

Once my friend disappears, Ervin grabs my shoulder, which I shake off abruptly. Accidentally, my eyes meet his, questioning.

"Don't listen to that jerk, he's always trying to provoke me. A bit like you, he tries to joke."

My breath condenses into thick swirls; the cold burns the tips of my fingers. I don't know if he's the reason I start to shake.

"What did he mean by that? That you're playing with me?"

All those kisses? And his hand in my panties? And this attraction between us? Is it a challenge driven by the sole desire to pin me to his trophy board?

"I'm always teasing you, Alizee!"

"No, but…" The words die in my throat. "Whatever's happening between us…"

A nurse bumps into us, in a hurry to go home for Christmas, no doubt.

"What's happening between us? Nothing serious, as far as I know," he says.

I feel like I've been hit with a sledgehammer. Yet, my intentions are the same. Our deal suits both of us; we have breakfast together after his workout sessions, share passionate kisses whenever we want. He makes my stomach flutter. I must surely entertain him… Our exchanges aren't much deeper. So why this feeling of rejection when he downplays what binds us?

Because I want more?

"Nothing serious," I assert.

A few weeks ago, he claimed to want me. Is that still the case, or is desire now operating in one direction? Milo's comment disturbs me. What if I've been right all along?

"Don't string me along, Ervin. I'm not another name to tick off your list of bitches."

"To my great misfortune."

Don't act like you want to fuck her.

Behind the tall dark-haired man, snow begins to fall. I take a deep breath, notice the taxi pulling into the driveway.

Disappointed, Ervin takes off his hat to cover my head. Then he puts his finger between my eyebrows.

"Can you give me the pleasure of cheering you up? Tonight, I'm getting you plane tickets. We're leaving in two days."

CHAPTER 16

The Malaga sun manages to warm the tip of my nose. The temperature is around seventeen degrees Celsius, a summer heat compared to Paris weather.

Once inside the modern-style villa where Ervin is hosting us, I inspect the surroundings. It belongs to his producer, and since she never visits, this ladies' man has free access. I won't ask about what she gets in return. In the yard, there's an infinity pool with water that's far too cold. The interior decoration is basic. The floor is covered with stone tiles, the white walls have some abstract paintings, but the living room is rather spacious, centered around a comforting fireplace. Three bedrooms are available, two with a large bed and the other with two twin beds. Gala and Milo act like love-struck lovers, setting up their stuff in one of them as if it were a honeymoon suite. *Adiós* female solidarity! There's no way I'm sharing my bed with anyone. Like planting a flag, I drop my bag on one of the small mattresses.

Alix, the bohemian, enters the room and does the same on the second bed.

"Shall we share the room?" he suggests, looking friendly.

"If you don't move, snore, talk in your sleep, sleepwalk, fiddle with your phone in the dark, breathe too loudly, get up too early in the morning, go to bed too late at night, or—"

"Get out, Alix," Ervin interrupts, entering the room.

"No way! You're not sleeping here under any circumstances!" I say.

They both stare at me, bewildered, a mocking grin on Alix's face.

My neighbor sighs dramatically, running his hand behind his head. "What did I do this time?"

His friend chuckles as he leaves us. "Good luck, man."

Is he going to sleep here to take advantage of me? He'll be able to defend himself by accusing me of consenting, and the worst part is that he'll be right! So no, I refuse to take any risks.

"I don't want to sleep next to you."

He unpacks his things and approaches with feline grace. Facing me, he pinches my chin, a sardonic smile on his lips. "Are you scared, kitten?"

Trembling at his touch, I burn with the desire to lash out, but the presence of our friends silences me. Good god! Of course I'm scared; the air crackles in the space we both occupy.

Instead, he steals a fleeting kiss that makes me shiver.

"I agreed to come. Don't ask too much of me," I murmur.

He caresses my cheek, his gaze appreciative. "Relax, we're here to have fun. I'll crash in the living room."

I nod, stepping back to escape of the grip of his sex appeal. This long weekend won't be easy.

***

After settling in, we head to the city's historic center. Very different from my Paris, the mix of architectural styles is quite beautiful. The terraces are full, the beach lively, and the tapas bars inviting. We join a group of Ervin's friends who live in the area and explore the city's lesser-known sights. Gala expresses her anxiety about the races. Milo has recovered from his accident, but she doesn't understand his determination to put himself in danger. Lost in thought, I realize Ervin's thirst for adrenaline attracts me more than it worries me.

"How are you doing with Ervin?"

As we follow the group into a typical alley, I slow my pace. "There's nothing between us."

"Except for massive sexual tension. Despite what Milo says, Ervin devours you with his eyes every time you walk into a room. The girls he sleeps with don't have that effect on him."

The girls he sleeps with.

The beautiful blonde senses my shock, quickly correcting herself, "Well, I don't know if he sleeps with them. They definitely flirt with him, though."

Could she be aware of things that I don't know? What is she witnessing exactly? I swallow, struggling with her explanation. I tell her about my aversion to him, explain that he already occupies far too much my thoughts to give him even more space. And this hopeless romantic can only come up with one explanation for my torment: "Zee… you're in love!"

I widen my eyes at her. "No, but would you like a megaphone, too? Don't talk nonsense!" I tell her, exchanging fleeting glances with Ervin in the middle of a conversation.

Did he hear her? Fuck! I feel like a teenager again! My pulse is racing, and all I want now is to book a ticket back to France and barricade myself in my cocoon.

"You think about him all the time, and he gets you in all your states. You're into him! Don't try to fight the truth. And kissing each other all the time will only reinforce your feelings."

I panic. No way—I can't feel that way about him. It's laughable, I'm headed for depression!

"You should channel all this energy into writing instead of playing with fire. Anyway, you're stubborn. Despite my advice, you'll do as you please. Seriously, doesn't it inspire you?" she teases, her tone mischievous.

She never misses a beat, that minx! I shake my head vigorously. Bring my palms to my cheeks, my mind upside down. *Love.* Now that she's put the word out there, it's chaos in my brain.

And lately, I do indeed have a sudden desire to talk about love and sex. I just have no idea for a plot. "I need to purge myself of this pollution…"

Galati gives me an amused look. "Since we've reunited, this is the first time it's happened to you."

If she only knew…

"Nothing good will come of it, I'm telling you, my friend!" I add.

***

I hate this. I hate this. I hate this.

That ungrateful best friend should never have explained to me how I felt about Mr. Heartthrob. It's consuming me. Last night, we spent the evening in a bar where there was a flamenco show. The dim lighting, the music, and the atmosphere highlighted his unbearable charisma. And that "Rosa," or "Clara," or whatever name ending in "a" she had! Fluttering her doe-like lashes in front of him like a horny deer. Caressing his biceps over his shirt. And, darn it, that idiot! With his stupid look, used to this kind of attention… "A friend", my foot. I'd bet my hand that he fucked her. Even my whole arm!

This morning, my best friend was worried sick about her darling. Too stressed, she preferred to take her mind off things with a shopping spree rather than accompany him to the race. Poor thing! She should have known that with yesterday's revelations, my mood would be awful.

In the late afternoon, the men return without victory but cheerful. We plan to spend the evening at the villa, stuffing ourselves with tapas while playing poker. After my crushing defeat, I decide to get some fresh air, muddled by Lionel and Milo's burnt cannabis. Wrapped in a plaid, I let the breeze of the Spanish winter ruffle my hair. I need to sort out my thoughts. Sitting on the lounge chair, I mentally sail off into the Mediterranean, where the lights of the city below disappear.

Ervin meets me at the edge of the pool. Without warning, he kneels in front of me and kisses me. Again. Like a hurricane, he knocks the butterflies in my belly down with his possessive way of grabbing my neck. I cling to his veined forearm as his tongue invades me, struggling to catch my breath, drowning in his depths. When our mouths part, and he plunges his beautiful obsidian eyes into mine, I detect a special glow. Something raw, sincere, and utterly devoted.

"I've been dying to do that since this morning."

That's why I'm falling in love, damn it! Because, during our truces, the intense expression he wears leaves no escape. His desire is urgent but genuine.

Milo's troubling words are pushed to the back of my mind, and I snatch a second kiss from the hot guy standing before me.

"Missing some affection?" he teases me.

His gentleness makes me smile. This Adonis will be my downfall.

"I just hope to return home and find my Vampyr."

"Two days—it's a long time."

"Indeed. Plus, that traitor swears only by Otto."

His annoyed grimace draws a giggle from me. *I better go back inside.*

My hand caresses his cheek, my thumb presses against his lip. The tip of his tongue teases it, exciting my hormones.

Stop it, Alizee...

He seizes my fingers, bestowing them with gentle kisses, before complimenting me, "The nail polish is nice. It's the first time I've seen you wear some."

Gala painted me a pretty pale pink during our girly afternoon. She drilled into my head that Ervin would like it, despite my protests. Who said I wanted to please Ervin, anyway?

He's going to hurt you. Very badly...

His face moves closer to mine, and with a devilish smirk, he suggests, "A midnight dip?"

I burst out laughing. "Can you see? I'm under a blanket!"

"Nothing that can't be fixed."

"My cryopreservation will be irreversible if I dip even a toe in that pool!"

He straightens, hands on hips, eyebrows wagging.

"Not in your dreams!" I shout, panicked as I stand.

"Don't try to run away!"

Is he trying to kill me? He's crazy, damn it! It's not even fifty degrees, and Mr. Muscles takes off his sweater! Besides, it's not like his hair is protecting him from the cold, he probably doesn't have more than three hairs around his nipples!

"I'm warning you, Ervin, if you make any contact between me and this pool, I'll gut you! I'm not joking!" I yell as I back away toward the villa.

Suddenly, a screeching sound echoes behind us. My attention is diverted by the arrival of a Jeep in the driveway.

My feet leave the ground, the scenery sways. Of course, the deceiver takes advantage! I squirm, roar in distress, see my blanket fall to the lawn.

"I can't swim! Put me down," I beg, pounding his back with all my might.

That old snake chuckles. Worse, he spanks me! "I won't let you drown."

Red with embarrassment, I try to kick him. Nothing works—the guy is solid. Imagining the water temperature fills me with fear.

"I'm fat, I'll sink! It's a homicide by pneumonia that you're committing! I swear you'll pay for this! I'll release my cat on your ridiculous stuffed animal! I'll tell him to pee on your equipment, and I'll shove the tripod legs up your ass! You'll die of a scrotum infection!"

This idiot continues to mock me.

At the water's edge, I try one last resort, "Your lips will never touch mine again in your life!"

My reply makes him burst in laughter. Traitor! He doesn't care about our kisses.

Suddenly, a nasal voice rings out behind him. In front of me.

"Er-vin!"

I turn imploring eyes on a pretty young thing who had spent most of yesterday fawning all over Ervin. I'd forgotten she and her friends were joining us tonight.

The chief groper rushes toward us with an ecstatic smile, singing things in Spanish. I reach out, about to beg for her help.

Ervin turns to greet her, begins to put me down. Her high heel catches a puddle, and she slips. She clutches at Ervin, desperate to stop herself from falling.

A scream tears through the starlit sky.

Splash!

I've never been so afraid and so cold in my entire life!

* * *

"I swear, I just wanted to scare you! I would never have thrown you in the water."

Screw Ervin's lamentation! He can dance on his head, I won't speak to him. Anyway, my mouth is frozen.

Wrapped in my blanket, I shiver by the fire amid the guests enjoying the evening. My neighbor fell in with me, but he doesn't give a damn. He'll see—karma is a beautiful bitch that will make his life hell. The clumsy brunette briefly apologized before laughing with him.

After filling the bathtub, he comes back to get me, drags me into the bathroom, and tries to downplay the situation. I won't give in. Even Gala attacked him, fiercely defending my health, which says a lot.

After he leaves, I sink into the warm water. Immersed, I hear the bimbo's chatter, envision their little game, and fume. I visualize her tight jeans and her little crop top that reveals her belly button and realize Ervin probably didn't notice the neckline of my brand-new dress tonight.

I hate him, I hate him, I hate him. And fuck me, I want him!

I want his eyes all over me instead of on her. I want his mouth on my lips, unhurried, like that famous day we spent kissing in my apartment. And I want his hands…

Memories are invading me. The ones of his gesture, my sensations.

My fingers follow the same path as his, stopping at the bottom of my belly.

The sound of his voice near my ear, spewing obscenities, turns me on. His way of spanking my ass a few moments ago infuriates me. And excites me.

In my unspoken desires, his palms linger on my behind, caressing it. Frustration slowly envelops. I close my eyes, withdraw from the present scene, and return to every situation where he made me thirsty. What did I desire then?

My hand grabs my breast, rolls my nipple. I imagine it's him. That he's devouring it. My thighs spread, I arch my back. My blood starts pulsing in my clitoris. With my heel, I pop the bathtub plug. The water level drops. Quickly. When the tub is empty, I imagine Ervin staring at me, I imagine slapping him to punish him. Completely absorbed in my fantasies, with the violent impression living them, I exhale a discreet moan, as if, with silent wingbeats, those famous butterflies in my stomach were flying out through my mouth. I think back to his fingers dancing against my clit, and a second moan makes me stop everything. I pant, embarrassed to have indulged in my fantasies so close to these people in the living room. I feel all funny.

I don't like this. Besides, I can't seem to touch the most sensitive parts of this troubling body. I prefer writing rather than feeling.

Wrapped in a bathrobe, my face flushed, I try to slip away into the bedroom, but in the doorway, I bump into a mass as hard as steel.

Of course, I had to run into the hulk at that precise moment! Enough with these so-romance situations already!

"You took your time. I need to shower, too. I'm freezing," he explains. "What were you doing?"

"What does it look like I was doing?" I wanted to sound aggressive. The joke's on me: I squeal like a kid caught red-handed.

His lack of response doesn't help. I dare a glance to gauge the situation, but when I see his suspicious look, mine shoots up.

Fuck! I feel like *insatiable little debauchee* is engraved on my forehead. Especially when his attention slides to the neckline of my bathrobe. Damn it! My sex is still pulsating; if he starts drooling, I'll have to move to Ouagadougou.

"I have no idea." The handsome dark-haired man smiles. "You tell me. You're all red, yet there's no steam in the bathroom."

He knows! Oh, my goodness, he can tell I'm aroused!

I square my shoulders, narrow my eyes, and retort, "I was trying to scrub off your big paws on me, Sherlock Holmes. Dirt's tough, you have to scrub for a long time."

As I walk around him, he retorts, amusedly, "If I had been there, I assure you, it wouldn't have taken so long. And everyone would have heard you."

With my brain overheating and my dignity in the gutter, I rush to my room, wide-eyed and head down.

CHAPTER 17

At first, I consider hiding in my room until tomorrow. Often, embarrassment dissolves after a good night's sleep. However, the groupie with her nasal laughter is getting on my nerves. Ervin this, Ervin that… I don't like it at all, so I dry my hair, put on my fluffy little dress, my fuzzy slippers, and return to the holidaymakers.

Ervin is fresh as a daisy. How annoying he is, with his tight jogging suit and his wet hair slicked back. The Spanish girl has left the space next to him to dance, allowing me to jump on the occasion. Nonchalantly, I drag my feet to the couch and slump down next to Ervin. Let the girl dare to claim her spot.

I didn't miss the sidelong glance from the handsome guy. He smells good, like men's soap. He seems to hold back a fiery comment, one that fuels me with rage and desire. Instead, he pours me a drink.

The music softens, the buzz of conversation becomes clearer. Ervin chats in Spanish with one of his friends I don't know. He spreads his legs, brushes against my knee. I sip my drink in silence. His hand covers his thigh, brushing against mine in the movement. With my eyes locked on it, I struggle to pay attention to Alix, who is trying to start a conversation. The tall blond man refills my glass.

I have no idea what's in this stuff, but it burns my throat. When the groupie comes back to sit on Ervin's lap, I down my second drink.

The dizziness is still manageable. My jealousy, not so much. Before she barged in, he was sticking his mouth on *mine!*

I've had enough. As I turn in their direction to give him a piece of my mind, Alix grabs me by the arm. "Come on, let's dance!"

I reclaim my limb. "I don't know how to dance, take her instead." I jam a thumb at the groupie. "She's bothering Ervin."

When he hears me, Ervin stares at me. "Who's bothering me?"

"Her." I point with my chin. "She's too intrusive," I say so only he can hear me.

From behind, the main culprit doesn't realize I'm putting her down, even though my neighbor seems surprised.

"What? Is that how you sit on people's laps? She's not five years old anymore!" *Okay, shut up, Alizee.*

Ervin's gaze intensifies, shifts to his friend, before enveloping me, hypnotic. Meanwhile, Alix chuckles and refills my glass.

"Actually, alcohol makes her funny. Here, forget the dancing—have another drink, sweetheart!"

Oh, really? I underestimated my humor quotient. Yet, that wasn't a joke; this *Españolita* is getting too comfortable.

"Do you want to take her place?" Ervin asks, watching me struggle with my drink.

"What is this stuff? It's super strong!" I cough. "Oh no, I would crush you, Mr. Muscles! Despite your strength, you wouldn't have a chance against my super booty!"

Both men burst into laughter under the groupie's questioning eyes. Ervin dismisses her—well, he kindly invites her to leave his lap—to tap on his knee.

"Come here, my child. Do you dare challenge me on this field?"

"What field?"

"His muscles," Alix answers, looking exasperated. "A minefield! It's like touching his dick!"

I chuckle, my glass empty again. "His *huge* dick!"

Now it's their turn to stare at me, dumbfounded. And the glass refills itself, as if by magic. For what reason? To drown me in alcohol, since I didn't take a dip in the pool? I refuse to put my lips on it this time; I feel tipsy enough for the evening.

I observe both of them, wondering why this silent exchange of looks.

"Hey, hey, can I be in the secret, too?"

The feeling that my voice is dragging…

"Are you guys…?" Alix points at us, looking puzzled.

"Nope," Ervin replies after sipping from the same amber liquid as me.

"Nope," I repeat, not understanding a word of what they're talking about.

"Come on, come see if my legs aren't strong enough to support you."

I glare at my overly sexy neighbor, grumble at the thought of the other bitch spending time on him, and accept his challenge just to bother her. Standing, I lean over and try to aim for his thigh, when he grabs my waist and pulls me toward him. I collapse, panic-stricken, but he holds me firmly against his chest.

"I feel dizzy, Ervin…"

He tightens his embrace for a second that feels like an eternity, a second when he whispers in my ear, "And I'm getting harder, kitten."

"Liar."

I untangle myself from him and savor this brief moment on his thighs, then stand up completely.

"I'm going to rub up against someone else before I end up soaking my panties again. Gala! Where are you?" I grab my half-full glass.

He grabs my arm. Annoyed, I click my tongue.

"What now? Your legs didn't break, wow, congratulations! Keep up with your workouts, it even makes you super hot."

"The girl next door's getting feisty." Alix giggles, trying to stir up the crowd.

"Shut up, Al," my sex symbol scolds. "You need to put the filter back between your brain and your mouth, kitten," he remarks, holding me back.

What filter? A philter of love like in D&D?

"Are you trying to cast a spell on me?"

Confusion crosses his eyes. "Huh?"

Well, I'm already in love, no need for that!

"You want to mess me up, handsome? Know that I won't let you do it!" I shout, fist in the air.

My best friend suddenly appears in my field of vision. She looks worried. I dive into her arms, whimpering, spilling a bit of alcohol on my dress in the process. "Gala! I don't feel good. And that idiot wants to make me drink a love potion!"

"I have absolutely no idea what she's talking about," said idiot protests.

"There's something about soaked panties in there," adds Alix.

I turn my head toward Ervin. If looks could kill, he'd already be rotting in the depths of the Milky Way. Since my panties bother them so much, fine...

"Hey, what are you doing, Zee?"

In front of Gala's wide eyes, I slide my underwear down to my ankles, pass it over my slippers, and brandish it in the air.

"*Voilà*! Who wants my paaanties?"

"Zee! Damn, she's wrecked..."

Well, actually... I feel pretty good!

All their attention is on me when the Spanish girl starts giggling. Oh, she'll get what's coming to her, that one! Fueled by a newfound cosmic force, I rush to the pretty woman and try to cover her face with my lingerie.

Arms hold me from behind, while my friend grabs the end of white cotton. Against Alix's chest, I smile foolishly. "Hey, you're all hot. Will you hold me a little longer?"

Stunned and amused, he nods, patting my head.

"What I'm supposed to do with this?" Gala asks, shaking my underwear.

Ervin snatches it from her and stuffs it into his pants pocket. I don't care; I snuggle into the blonde's arms. "Wanna dance?" I announce.

We end up on the improvised dance floor, swaying to a Latino rhythm. I'm clumsy, but I don't care. Focusing on my steps helps me to forget everything else. A silly grin surely betrays my euphoria as the scrunched-up face of Ervin comes into my view. Seated on a chair next to a flirtatious groupie, he downs drinks, his gaze locked on me. I can't dance, but I accentuate my hips movements, delighted to catch his gaze. Alix's hands electrify me when they land on my waist. I shouldn't enjoy it, yet my body emits no repulsion, charmed by the tempo of the music.

Besides, Ervin's attention invigorates me. As long as he's watching me, I keep going. My head spins, but I want to sway with him.

As he ends up right next to the hippie and orders him to let me go, I cling to his arm.

"Why do you care if she's having a bit of fun?" Alix asks.

"You can see she's not in her normal state."

"So what? We're just dancing," says Alix.

Ervin smells of alcohol, too. His eyes are bloodshot. "Fucking hell, go dance somewhere else, let her go."

"Ervin." I emerge from my cloud. "Can you please give me back my panties?"

His eyes widen, his cheeks blush. "Come and get them yourself," he whispers in my ear before walking away toward the kitchen.

"But…?" Feeling crushed by the injustice of this universe, I watch him leave with a puppy-dog pout. "Alix… Ervin is unbearable!"

The blond man confirms mumbling, not expecting me to leave him and follow his friend.

In the dim light, it's just sexy-neighbor and me. He watches me arrive, his eyes dark. Suddenly, I forget why I followed him, I forget what I wanted from him, and I just settle down around the kitchen island, facing him and his half-full glass.

Our silence speaks volumes, his eyes full of anger. I take a sip of his water, press my cheek against the delicious coolness of the countertop.

"What's wrong with you?" I struggle to articulate. "What are we doing here?"

I'm in love. Damn it.

"Drinking doesn't suit you."

"On the contrary, I feel lively. As long as I don't end up blacked out in your bed… Doesn't that ring a bell?"

His eyebrows remain furrowed. "Alcohol makes you annoying," he says.

"If you say so."

Where on Earth is his usual banter, his enthusiasm?

"You should go to bed before you depress everyone, trust me. Although, the other bitch doesn't seem to be bored with you."

The words escaped me. Mortified, I bring my hand to my mouth, searching the kitchen for a hiding place. The cupboard under the sink seems large enough…

"Are you jealous?" he sneers with unexpected arrogance.

"Not. At. All. I know you're going to end up spending the night with her. I don't care."

I can't control my stream of words, damn it! And besides, I do care! Why did I leave his lap? I felt good there, I would have breathed him in forever. I would have soaked up his scent, rubbed against his muscles and his hard stuff.

"Are you kidding me?" Through his glazed eyes, he looks at me with surprise, making me feel like I just said something absurd. Let him not pretend she's a cousin or yet another half-sister; their looks didn't lie.

"You two looked like you were about to eat each other. I thought you'd make her scream, *Oh, Ervin, fuck me harder!*" I adopt a bad Spanish accent without losing my seriousness.

He, however, bursts into laughter. "Flora is a friend, I assure you there's nothing between us."

Liar.

"But there was. You've already fucked her," I state.

After a brief moment, he lets out a sigh. "She's the one who screwed me. I was wasted, and she took advantage."

The booze is a convenient excuse. "Pooooor victim."

"Absolutely! I actually wanted to hook up with her sister at first. She ruined my move. It was in Costa Rica, five years ago. A lot has happened since then."

"Yeah, right."

He shrugs. "I know you think I'm an asshole. I know my principles are shaky, and I assured you that there's nothing serious between us, but—"

He's piquing my interest here. His natural charm enchants me; I hang on his every word.

"I'm not going to stick my tongue in your mouth just to drag it into her pussy right after."

Ervin and his legendary class.

"Oh, that's too kind of you. I didn't think you were that considerate." I pretend indifference as a wave of heat swells behind my ribs. "I thought you had no qualms about sleeping with two girls at once."

"It's not the same."

What's the difference today? Special considerations for me?

"I understand better why you're wiggling against Alix."

"Alix is single. Alix thinks I'm funny. And he's funny. And I wasn't wiggling, I was dancing. Well, trying to!"

"Without underwear?"

"Ah!" That's why I was following him. Holy crap, I danced with the shaman bare-assed! "Give me back my panties." As I slide off the high stool, I stumble and almost fall.

He laughs, then shakes his head. "No, I'll keep them."

Stunned and completely flushed, I lose my words. Holy crap, this would make a great scene for a cheesy romance! Bingo, I'm going to write a bestseller! I'll call it *My Little Wet Panties*.

"I need to write!" I exclaim suddenly. The panties, forgotten! My shame, tossed aside! I rush into my room with a stroke of genius, despite the protest of my muse.

He follows closely, leaning against the door frame, watching me pull my laptop out of my bag and settle onto my mattress. I forget his presence, obsessed by my goal. I don't even turn on the light to stay focused on my screen.

In my *Ervin* folder, I open a new page, my fingers on fire, but when I try to put words down, everything gets confused in my brain.

"Did you really think you could write in this state?"

The killjoy who isn't planning to fuck Flora approaches in the dark. He sits at the foot of the bed without taking his eyes off me. Up close, he's intimidating. He gives me the impression of a predator ready to jump on me.

"I had a stroke of genius, I swear!"

My lament makes him smile. "You could have explained it on every TV show; what a shame."

"No, that's impossible." I sigh, closing my laptop in defeat.

He takes it from me and puts it on the bedside table, then sits down cross-legged right in front of me. I cross my legs next to him, facing him with a hint of defiance.

I suddenly become aware of my nightgown, which reaches above my knees, and my bare legs. While I despise my buttocks and thighs, my calves don't bother me much. They're a little bit chubby, but shapely, tapered by slender ankles. In the darkness of the room, his eyes roam over them without him making any comment. Is he comparing them to the Spanish girl's stilts?

"Nooo, nooo, no. I declined the invitation to be on the TV show."

His eyes widen as his name echoes from the living room. His groupie calls him, her voice dragging. Ervin leaps out of bed to lock the door. He returns, stumbling to my side, annoyed.

"Ah! So, you're not a jerk with just me."

Flora's voice cuts through the noise from next door.

"She sounds determined; you should answer."

Ervin shakes his head, his eyes locked on mine. "I can't believe you turned it down," he suddenly blames me.

"Turned down what?"

"Promoting yourself on television. How can you pass up such an opportunity?"

Oh, that! I frown, hiding under my hood. "Not interested."

"Not interested in what? Being recognized for what you do?"

I exhale forcefully. "Not interested in showing myself off."

Now Milo's voice covers the music. "Ervin, where the hell are you?"

I giggle into my hands, like a kid playing hide and seek. "Do you think he'll find us?"

"Who cares? I'm pissed off! Is it because of your body insecurities?"

I freeze, biting my lips. An unpleasant sensation invades me. He's already seen my vulnerabilities. Why reopen them?

"If you already know, what's the point of asking me?"

"Because it's fucking ridiculous!"

What does he know? Surely, my mother will scrutinize the show, point out every flaw, every poorly worded sentence, every misplaced bulge. She'll share it with me because I'm her daughter, but there will still be others. Those who will discover the identity of Elie Roy, the famous author of bloody thrillers.

Just some woman.

A blonde with a big ass.

Those words hit me like a ton of bricks, so painful, so cruel. I hear the laughter, like shards of glass in my ears.

"My ridiculousness pisses you off," I grumble under my breath.

A sudden noise startles me. There's a knock at the door.

"Ervin, you there?" Milo calls out.

In the darkness, Ervin urges me to stay silent, his index finger pressed against his lips.

"Alizee? Are you asleep?"

On the verge of shouting my presence, I find myself gagged by Ervin's hand. It's so warm… Wouldn't he like to slip it back in my panties?

"Why don't you open?" I whisper.

"Our conversation is very, very, very important, and I don't want them to interrupt it."

Unlike me. I'd like to interrupt it with passionate kisses, but I say nothing.

"You're fucking beautiful—what are you afraid of? Your ass? Is that what bothers you?"

"For example…" I challenge him, my heart full of anger.

He lets out an exasperated breath. "Ugh, people don't give a damn about your looks. You're a writer, not a singer! I mean, there are chicks who insure their butts for thousands of dollars."

"Haha! That's a good one! You compare me to J. Lo or Kim Kardashian? And besides, whether I'm a writer, singer, politician, or philosopher, of course my image matters. I'm a woman, and all these jerks judge women, even when they shouldn't. Plus, my readership is mostly male. I don't need sex appeal; I just know what will be said in the industry if I lose credibility."

Once again, he shakes his head, showing strong disagreement. "Let's say people do comment on your image, since it will surprise many. I find you much prettier than those superficial dolls. Your charm would light up the screen. But if you prefer to let your complexes ruin your life…"

"You're kidding me." I burst out laughing. He's so funny, my nice neighbor.

"Damn, are you guys messing with us?" Milo yells, pounding on the door.

A quiet anger emanates from Ervin, who's still standing at the window of my soul. In the darkness of my room, he enchants me through the few moonbeams illuminating his face. He grabs my ankle, climbs my calf, sends shivers down my leg, then my spine, finally torpedoing my brain.

"Damn it, I'll prove you wrong!" On all fours, he approaches in a leap, stopping a few inches from my face. His Jack Daniels breath tickles my nostrils. Tension takes my breath hostage.

He's going to kiss me… He's going to kiss me… He's going to kiss me…

"If I spend my nights with bimbos, it's because it's easier."

Or not! Bastard! Can't even give me a damn kiss!

"Because they're easier."

When he lowers my hood, the cold seeps into my scalp, I shiver.

"They're duller…"

He licks the edge of my mouth with tangible restraint, opening all my chakras. His alcoholic breath intoxicates me. Then he grabs my shoulders. "Turn around."

Oh my god, what's he going to do behind me?

"I just wanted a kiss, damn it!"

He squints, torn between anger and vanity. "Lie on your stomach and trust me, kitten," he taunts.

"Don't give me orders." Terrified, I cling to my mattress.

The drums on the door resume, probably because of my audible protests. Ervin takes advantage of my distraction to turn me over on the bed, giggling in my ear. My head is spinning. The brute has flattened me on my stomach. In the darkness, his chest swells and deflates against my back, heavy and stifling. God, it's so exciting!

"Don't answer them. I want to stay with you. Just with you."

I swallow, subjected to the mutiny of my body. His voice captures my neurons, crumbles them. I want him so badly, yet fear seizes every one of my limbs. When he sits up to remove my slippers, one by one, to caress my heel, run up on the flesh of my calves, I let my dizziness lull me.

Anyway, I poured my guts out to him talking him about my fears, the rest doesn't matter anymore. And if it allows me to be groped by a hottie, well...

The flat of his hand travels up the silhouette of my legs, descending sensually. Then begins its ascent again.

"You hide behind your skirts. I don't think you realize the effect your legs have."

I bury my crimson face in my folded arms. "What effect?" I want to hear it, know in detail what I evoke in him.

His fingers now climb up my thighs. I press them shut, just like my eyelids. Don't they repel him?

"They haunt me constantly."

Ervin kneads my flesh without restraint, I feel his breath growing heavier, his movements intensifying. Though I initially feel repulsed, the intense sexual tension makes his endeavor pleasant.

"Relax, Alizee. Enjoy every caress, don't you like it?"

"It's not that I don't like it, it's that you're stirring up indecent thoughts," I explain.

He seizes the hem of my dress and suddenly slides it up to my lower back. My posterior exposed, I prop myself up on my elbows and sit up quickly, startled.

Ervin's voice breaks the silence, defying its own rules. "Wait, stay like that."

"But you can see my ass! You little sneak!"

As my head turns in his direction, he stops me. "Don't look at me. Not now."

"Why?" I freeze.

"Because otherwise, I won't be able to stop myself. Come on, lie back down."

The desire dripping from his plea puts an end to my hesitation. My buttocks are exposed, offered. What a pervert. What a delicious pervert...

My god… I'm screwed.

His palms cover them. I hold my breath as he caresses them.

"How can you hate such an amazing ass?" he blurts out, so low, as if he's talking to himself.

Teeth clenched, I blissfully endure his hands on my skin, his words on my heart. "Ervin…"

In concentric movements, he spreads my cheeks, stretches them languidly outwards, creating new sensations in the small of my back. Again, I moan his name. Damn, it feels shamefully good!

When suddenly, he bites my behind, I yelp in surprise.

"I'm going to eat you…" he growls before licking the wound.

"Oh, you licked my butt! And it feels so good!" I exclaim into the pillow.

He chuckles to himself, continues, kisses me all over my rear, eliciting pleasure-filled moans from me. With my head buried in the pillow, I feel like I'm running out of oxygen, as I gradually lose consciousness, engulfed by waves of lust. When everything turns black, it's too late, I know that from now on, there's no going back.

CHAPTER 18

Chimes ring out. A powerful hangover assaults me, and my heavy eyelids ache. To shield myself from the sudden brightness, my forearm comes to cover my face. When a shiver runs through my entire body, I realize my nudity. Alarmed, I abruptly open my eyes, staring at the ceiling for two long seconds before sitting up in a jolt.

I am indeed naked.

Panicked, I scan the room, consider the bed next to me—never unmade—and discover my bra, my slippers, and pajamas on the floor.

What the hell happened? I can't remember a thing.

My phone indicates it's already noon. I hurry, slipping on a sweater dress, and cautiously stick a toe out of the room. Lionel and Milo are busy picking up the empty bottles while Gala sweeps. It seems the local guests have left. When I greet them, Milo shoots me a disdainful look before grumbling through his teeth. His girlfriend clicks her tongue, then adopts a contrite expression. Whatever the case, their attitude is strange. I don't insist, backing away toward the bathroom to freshen up before heading to the kitchen.

Suddenly, a flood of sensations rushes through me. Fragments of a scene come back to me: Ervin behind me. His sex rubbing against my ass. My breasts grabbed, his chest against my back, his mouth near my ear murmuring that I'm too sexy. That my ass is a gift from heaven.

I blink, my cheeks on fire, interrupting my progress. No, impossible, it couldn't have happened. Yet, the memory of his warmth scorches my skin.

My pulse races.

Everything is hazy like a palpable dream, one of those that I've already confused with reality. The last thing I remember is being in the living room with Flora-butterfly-eyelashes. The music was blaring, and my head was spinning, glass after glass.

Another scene unfolds: our skin caressing each other in a face-to-face encounter as rough as it is languid. Sweaty, he pants. My voice echoed in my head: *Go on, my elephant, pierce me with your ultra-sexy trunk! Oh fuck, it's so good, you're going to make me come with your nonsense! I want you to scream my name! Right now! You like this ass? Spank it!*

Nooooo…

In distress, I cover my ears. I can't hear them anymore, it's impossible I screamed such things. I must have been dreaming.

With every step I take toward that kitchen where male voices echo, I repeat to myself like a mantra: *No way. No way. No way.*

When strange contractions tighten my vagina, I squeeze my eyelids shut, nearly bumping into a beam.

No way. No way. No way.

My arousal? Blame it on the fantasies! I should never have fantasized in the bath.

And because I'm a brave woman, I'm going to face my emotional tormentor in three… two… one second…

Here we go!

Alix and Ervin are chatting around the counter, devouring their sandwiches like ogres. They notice me, showing no particular reaction.

"Hi, Shakespeare! You look like a zombie," says Elephant Trunk with his mouth full.

I eye him suspiciously, and then settle down beside them. "Migraine. Have you guys been awake for long?"

"Not really, no. Here, take the rest of the baguette. There's some chocolate spread. It's not pancakes, but it's nothing nutritious, so it should do the trick."

I gaze at the food on the counter, observing him out of the corner of my eye. He seems like his usual self… Then my eyes land on the pacifist and his cheerful face.

"Have you found your panties yet?" asks Alix.

Huh? Why is this savage mentioning my underwear? We don't know each other that well, as far as I know.

"Leave her alone," my neighbor defends me, laughing under his breath.

Stiffly, I stare at them both in turn. "Can I know what you're talking about? What happened last night?"

Now that I think about it, my panties weren't next to my bed. Damn it, Gala must tell me what happened to me; these two idiots won't! It's been a long time since I got drunk; I forgot my weak ability to hold my liquor.

"Forget it." Alix laughs as he gets up.

As he cleans his plate in the sink, I eye Ervin. When he notices me and gives me a strange smile, I abruptly turn away. He knows! He knows, and he's taunting me, that odious hunter!

But as I dare to confront him with more confidence, he eats calmly, as if nothing unusual had happened, dispelling my fears about these surreal images in my head.

Lionel arrives, busying himself alongside his friend, stacking the empty glasses under the water jet. They bicker, adding to the ambient noise.

My handsome dark-haired man, on the other hand, hands me an aspirin. Despite my attempts to reassure myself, an uncomfortable feeling lodges firmly in the pit of my stomach. I move closer to Ervin, pretending casually, his lavender cologne soothing my headache.

With our voices muffled by the running water, I put on a nonchalant air and try, "Hey… we didn't sleep together last night, did we?"

"We did. You don't remember?"

Wide-eyed, I feel like the ceiling is crashing down on my head. No! He can't confirm it so casually! *No way. No way. No way.* He must be messing with me…

After swallowing the pill, I nod slowly.

"Thank goodness," he says, smacking his forehead.

Suspicious, I dig in, playing along with his stupid game. "Would it have been a problem for you if I didn't remember?"

"Hell yeah! I fucked you like a god; it would have pissed me off if you forgot."

Flabbergasted, I choke and cough, alarming the two big men who stop the drain and rush to me, fussing over me.

"Don't choke or you'll die, I don't know the ambulance number."

"Here, drink some water."

I gulp down my glass, dazed. Then I notice Ervin's obnoxious smirk.

His facade cracks. As for the fragments of images that come back to me, there's no doubt. I feel nauseous. I lower my eyes, unable to meet his.

Go ahead, my elephant, impale me with your sexy trunk!

Oh. My. God… At this point, it's not just embarrassment anymore.

Did I scream for the whole villa to hear? I bury my face in my hands, deciding never to lift it again. It's over for me. As a woman, I have no credibility left. Ha! Ha! I don't even deserve to write romance anymore. What a joke; I should burn all my books to ashes.

Under their intense scrutiny, I make the chair squeak and retreat into the bathroom, where I can lament as I wish. Behind the locked door, I let myself slip down, trying to focus on the events of last night. My heart feels like a bongo, pounding until it chokes me, as the images flood in, drop by drop.

Why didn't I stop him?

I wanted him so badly, knew sex would inevitably drive us apart. Fuck! Getting drunk in Ervin's presence was a terrible idea; I fancied myself a lovemaking goddess. What a joke!

Suddenly, knocks reverberate against the door. "Alizee? Alizee, open up."

Not in a million years! I need to be alone to swallow the bitter pill. Me, who didn't want to be just another conquest on his list—look at me now!

I'll come out later like a warrior and confront him with a smile, ready to face his mocking. And the sensations he reminds me of.

"Zee? What's wrong? Are you feeling okay?"

Now Gala joins in, too. Rolling my eyes, I plug my ears with toilet paper. I brush my teeth, splash my face in complete denial, and suddenly, the volume increases. Intrigued, I remove my makeshift earplugs and recognize Milo's voice, further in the living room.

"You couldn't help yourself, huh? You're a fucking bastard!"

Stunned, I press against the door. Then I hear Ervin rebuking him even harsher. "Mind your own damn business, man! Keep your eyes on your girlfriend and leave Alizee alone!"

The coolness of the wood chills my cheek, just as this altercation sends a frosty current through my skull. Was it really my name that was just mentioned?

Gala intervenes, but by the time I open the door, the three of them have already vanished into the couple's room. Lionel and Alix look at me, as stunned as I am.

"What's going on?"

The tall blond shrugs. "Milo's losing it. You should go check it out."

I don't need to be told twice. Behind the door, the enraged man stuffs his things into his bag, frantic. Gala is on the verge of tears, and Ervin is furious.

"You're an idiot, man! I don't see why you're leaving!"

"Screw you!" Milo replies.

"Milo, tell me what's wrong, please!" Gala pleads, but he ignores her completely.

Instead, he locks eyes with me like a loaded gun ready to fire and noisily zips up his travel bag.

What's his problem anyway? I've barely spoken to him. There's no way he's going to make me his punching bag.

He slings the strap over his shoulder, pushes past Ervin—who despite his anger looks bewildered—and brushes past me with too much confidence. His expression as he passes me sends a chill down my spine.

"Pff, I thought you, at least, were better than that."

And he's gone, leaving me stoically in the doorway as Gala rushes after him.

Better than what? Who does he think he is, talking to me like that? I turn around, but Ervin stops me.

"Let it go, it's not worth it," he says.

I look at him for a moment. "But… Is he leaving, just like that?" I ask.

He nods.

"Why? What did he mean by *better than that*? Is he referring to last night?"

The tall dark-haired man sighs, runs his hand through his hair. His features remain tense, but he still doesn't let go of me, doesn't run after the revving engine. We hear Milo's motorcycle thundering down the driveway in leaden silence, and Gala calling at the entrance.

Thousands of questions swirl in my head. Ervin knows something I don't.

"Is there something between you and Milo?" Gala blurts out, having returned to us. She stands in front of me, her eyes glistening with tears that she keeps to herself, locked in her usual modesty.

Between Milo and me? Stunned, I don't know what to say. I seek solace from my neighbor. "Nothing at all, I swear. I don't understand his attitude. We've never really spoken."

"Alizee has nothing to do with your boyfriend losing it," Ervin defends me, wrapping his arm around me.

I'm lost. The blonde gives him a fierce look. "His mood changes as soon as he sees you two together! What happened last night?"

Frozen, I dare not confess to her, convinced she already knows. "I… had a blackout. I only have a few flashes," I confess.

Ervin tightens his grip around me slightly.

She squints, assessing my sincerity. Though I often decline to tell her about my troubles for my own peace of mind, I now feel a heavy discomfort. It's not just about me anymore. Her relationship seems at stake. As well as our friendship.

"You were there, don't you remember?" I dare to say in a small voice.

"You were dancing with Alix. You took off your panties, and then followed Ervin into the kitchen. Then I think I drank too much because I fell asleep on the couch. Milo carried me to my bed. This morning he was upset without wanting to give me a reason."

If I screamed during all of it, she must not have heard it. Thank god. As for her boyfriend, he had already shown me his animosity when

I visited the emergency room. I haven't forgotten his inappropriate comment. Why is he so opposed to Ervin and me getting together?

I don't dare imagine the answer.

"Ervin, you know your buddy," the blonde says, her precarious calm evident. "Tell me if he's interested in Alizee."

My chest tightens, I shake my head. "It's just unthinkable, Gala."

Her gaze narrows on him. "Did he go for me in an attempt to get her?"

Next to me, Ervin doesn't deny it.

I step away and accuse him, "Say something! He's your friend, isn't he?"

He pinches the bridge of his nose, exhales emphatically. A veil of regret immediately crosses his face. "I don't know. Maybe…"

What?

No! It feels like a punch to the gut.

My friend hesitates for a moment. Then, a fierce frown is her answer to Ervin. "You liar!" she accuses.

Simultaneously, Lionel calls her from the living room. "Come on, Gala, let's catch up with him."

She obeys without delay, after casting us a look full of anguish. Anguish that I've caused her.

Nothing makes sense. The situation is slipping away from me. Irritation and distress wash over me.

"All of this because of that shitty night!" I curse, fist clenched.

Ervin doesn't seem to agree. My remark offends him. His resentment hits me like a ton of bricks as he turns away and leaves the room.

Okay, I think tonight's New Year's Eve celebration together is off the table.

∗

After a soothing shower, I leave Alix sprawled on the couch of the living room, busy scrolling on his cell phone screen, wrap myself in a shawl, and join Ervin in the garden, feeling dejected.

Dressed in his parka and facing the sky, the sea, and the expanse of the city, he captures the scenery in his smartphone. When he hears me approaching, he surprises me with a sudden turn, aiming his camera at me.

"Stop!" I laugh, hands covering my face.

Finally, he brightens up with a smile. "One day, you'll pose for me, I swear," he says.

The tightness in my chest loosens. This hypothetical future both terrifies me and comforts me. I stand next to him, my eyes focused on the horizon. We're far from Paris and its buildings, from the grayness in the sky, on the walls, and the pavement. Here, the wind soars in a melodious song. The coolness is invigorating, and the sun, ever-present, regardless of the temperature.

Here, I need to cherish these last moments with Ervin before he disappears into our urban daily life.

"How did we end up like this?" I sigh, weary.

He swallows, then responds, "Who knows. Milo's starting to get on my nerves." There's no more bitterness in his voice, just a hint of distress.

"Do you really think it's because of last night?" I can't imagine that Milo feels any attraction toward me. Despite reviewing all our encounters, nothing stands out to me.

"Milo's a complicated man." Ervin justifies. "He has his own ideas, and—"

Nothing more, except for a sudden stiffness. What is he hiding from me?

I have the impression that the surface of this issue is covering something deeper. But Ervin won't tell me about it, that's for sure.

"We shouldn't have let things escalate," I confess, arms crossed to shield myself from the cold.

My neighbor reacts to my remark. He scrutinizes me, eyebrows furrowed. His presence is imposing to my left, enveloping me, emanating a masculine fragrance that no longer intoxicates me, since I'm so burdened.

"I was drunk, too," he admits.

I breathe in. Breathe out. Dread blooms, although I expected it.

"Listening to you belittle yourself, I lost my grip," he says.

"You wanted to prove to me that I'm not disgusting. I guess you really put your heart into it," I joke, trying to lighten the mood.

He laughs, tucking his phone into his pocket. I don't want him to realize how much it means to me. Thank goodness alcohol is a good excuse!

"I can't believe it. You had to be trashed to do it, too. You're an asshole even when you fuck…"

He laughs into his fist, unfazed.

"Oh, come on, give it some thought, I didn't even have time to come!"

"Poor you… Neither did I, believe me!"

"How would you know?" he challenges.

"I would remember it!" Unfortunately, my only memories are regrettable.

"Do you remember everything you felt?"

"I don't." I sighed, dramatically. "No, actually, I just have a few inglorious flashes."

He playfully nudges me with his shoulder.

"You wouldn't have told me if I hadn't asked," I reproach him.

However, I would have preferred… It's an episode I could have done without. At least, in these circumstances.

"I would have… I wouldn't have had the choice," he says, scratching his chin.

His nervous tone catches my attention. Uncertain, he stares at me, moistens his lips.

"Why?"

"I forgot the condom," he admits.

What the hell! Anger wells up inside me. "No, that's not true! No, it can't be true!" Panic seizes me. I pace back and forth in the garden, hands on my head, feeling like I've been infected.

"Alizee, I—"

"Shut up!" I interrupt, pointing a finger at him. "No, do you realize? With all the girls you sleep with, I'm probably going to end up with some disease!"

"Stop—"

"No, you stop! How can you be so reckless?"

The feeling of turning into a zombie haunts me. Then I imagine myself pregnant. The horror! "I don't want your diseases or your babies!"

Suddenly, he steps in front of me, holding my shoulders, caught up in my panic. "Hey, calm down, don't freak out. I'm careful, with the life I lead, okay? I get tested often. The last test was three months ago, and since then, I've always used protection."

"Oh, I feel so reassured! I have a one percent less chance of being infected!" I retort bitterly.

"I'll take you for every test imaginable, and we'll get a morning-after pill this afternoon. I'm sorry, Alizee, I swear I'm clean."

My heart rate barely slows down, countless scenarios clash in my head. I don't want to die yet! Or lose my vagina. I haven't explored it enough to give it up.

"I'm so mad at you!"

He brings my hands to his lips and kisses them gently. "I know. I'm sorry. But believe me, you're safe."

Despite the fear, I try to calm myself with a long exhale. He continues to kiss my fingers with rare devotion as my thoughts return to normal. If he's telling the truth, it's impossible to catch anything. I trust him…

"Okay, okay. Anyway, you're not the only one who forgot," I admit, taking back my hands.

We sit side by side on the lawn, facing the landscape. He puts his arm around my shoulders and I snuggle in, staring at my shoes.

"Ugh. All this fuss over some absurd joke. We were ridiculous."

He tightens his embrace and grimaces against my temple.

"I remember finding you very hot. I got off, before blacking out."

We exchange a knowing glance accompanied by a tender smile. Kind or sincere? In both cases, he manages to ease my embarrassment. His lips on my cheek soften me, and his nonchalance takes hold of my stomach. I'm comfortable here, against his side. It could continue until we get back to France or fade away tonight, but I'm living in the moment. Screw my pessimism.

The calm is short-lived. When Galati and Lionel return, the storm erupts.

On the way, they lost track of Milo, who refused to answer his phone. They only got a simple *I'm going back to France alone*, not even personalized for his girlfriend.

Lionel is distraught, while Gala seethes in her room. The guilt I see in her eyes when I join her weighs heavy on me. She's not one for melodramatic scenes, yet her suffering oozes out. I swallow, sympathizing. She ignores me, wanting me to leave her alone.

When Ervin steps in, she lashes out at him bitterly. "Don't you dare talk to me! Everything that's happening is your fault!" she says.

The tall dark-haired man takes her accusation with a step back. Jaw clenched, he seeks my gaze, then immediately avoids it, seething with rage. "How do you know?"

"For weeks, Milo has disapproved of your closeness! If he has feelings for Zee and you're hiding it from me, you're the worst bastard I know!"

He's about to reply, hesitates, then finally turns back. "You know what? I'm out of here, too," he says.

"Ervin," I call out, alarmed.

"Come on, let's go, Alizee." His voice comes from the living room.

Panicked, I run to catch up with him, passing by the boys with bewildered expressions. Next to his motorcycle, he hands me a helmet, looking determined.

"I'm leaving. With or without you."

I stare at him, speechless, reluctant to leave my best friend.

But he persists. "She's mad at you for all the wrong reasons. You better give her some space; there's no point in sticking around."

He's not wrong. Gala will resent me more if I linger. After we retrieve all our stuff, I agree to wear his helmet and let him take me into the unknown.

A terrifying unknown.

A refreshing unknown.

Against his soothing back.

CHAPTER 19

Unlike Galati, I understand Ervin's passion for motorcycles. The wind's lacerations, the speed peaks, the engine's roar, and the sensation of fulfillment are invigorating. I'm not sure which of these reasons makes my pulse race. Maybe it's my proximity to him that causes these palpitations. Despite his sporty driving, I feel safe against him.

During our stop at the pharmacy, he made sure I didn't panic and humbly apologized again for his forgetfulness last night. I found him touching.

It's five o'clock in the afternoon, and we arrive at a beautiful hotel. With determination, he heads to the reception and gets a room for us. I'd bet my leg he's stayed here before.

When I discover the lodging, a strange feeling takes holds of me. Vermilion walls. A huge four-poster bed surrounded by wrought-iron arabesques. Some beautifully crafted oriental sconces. A small window behind a satin curtain. A cozy atmosphere. A plant for an exotic touch, and a mini wicker lounge. Holy moly!

I explore the place, questioning my neighbor with my eyes. He looks bored.

"Is this where you bring your local conquests?" I ask him.

He gets rid of his things and settles into one of the small armchairs. "Not just that," he replies. His eyes scan me from head to toe, clouded by latent anger.

Curious, I approach, a little confused. "Why did you bring me here, Ervin?"

"I needed to get out. But I didn't want to leave you behind."

"Why?"

He ruffles his hair, letting a few stray strands fall over his temple. I expect a snide remark, ready to volley back, but he surprises me by admitting, "I didn't want to be alone. And you're the only one I can stand being around."

"Really?" I smile, taking a seat beside him. "I would have bet the opposite."

He smiles, too. Yet, his somber expression lingers, and his fingers hooked tightly at the end of the armrest remain tense.

"Chin up, you're not going to ruin the last day of the year. Plus, do you know how long it's been since I've set foot outside the country? So, grab life by the horns and order us a pizza! And make it snappy! Time is money!"

I hadn't signed up for a depression party. With the other bipolar guy and my friend mad at me for the first time, I need a pick-me-up.

"Pizza, huh?"

My comment elicits a laugh… of the disdainful variety.

"Sorry if I'm not the most exciting company. Tomorrow night, we'll go back to our own places, so you can console yourself with that, smartass."

He takes hold of my hand, his beautiful eyes locking onto mine. "Last night, I found you exceptionally lively."

Here comes the barrage of questions again! He's not going to start with his nebulous insinuations!

"Oh, come on! I was wasted, and I don't remember a thing, how unfortunate!"

My heart races as he leans in. Dazed, I recoil just inches from his lips.

He furrows his brows, searching for answers that twist my insides. When he cups my cheek with his palm, I don't move an inch.

"I can't kiss you anymore, kitten?"

That awful nickname now sends shivers of excitement through me. "Do… you want to?" I ask.

He assesses me, looking troubled. "Why not?" he replies.

I swallow. "Because of last night…"

More and more intrigued, he closes the gap between us and grants me a tender, sensual kiss. "What about yesterday? We talked about it. I don't understand your reaction."

Of course… How could he?

"What do you want, Ervin? Your signals are conflicting. I can't figure you out," I say.

A second kiss. More chaste.

"I don't want anything in particular, but your body calls out to me. I can't get enough of kissing you, touching you. You drive me crazy. Your face," he whispers, tracing my profile with his index finger. "Your curves obsess me."

My breathing quickens. More erratic, it becomes difficult to control. "But… you got me," I argue, a hint of resentment in my voice. He got me, like all those girls who saturate him so easily. Like those I swore not to resemble.

"And I still want more," he insists.

I'm not buying it. "Do you need a fully conscious prey to check off the *fucked* box?"

He pauses, looking angry, then abruptly backs away. "I thought we were better than that." He stands, hands in pockets, and heads toward for the window, tense from head to toe.

I shield myself from the guilt caused by his reaction. I won't fall for it again. I've suffered too much, I've only known that.

Fool me once, shame on you.

Fool me twice, shame on you.

Fool me three times, shame on me.

To be hurt a fourth time would be my stupidity on display.

Even if it's Ervin. Especially if it's Ervin.

"You think too much, Alizee. It's exhausting. Why does it bother you so much? Why do you feel like nothing but prey?"

"Because that's what I've always been!" I explode.

He stares at me, eyes wide.

Fuck, it slipped out… It opened the floodgates of my most painful emotions, of my suppressed memories.

"You've had, what, one or two bad experiences with assholes, and you lump us all together?" he continues.

I shake my head, pushing back the cruel words of that damn Laurent.

"Go on, talk, tell me what's holding you back so much. What makes you hate men and makes you so bitter? What prevents you from having relationships or becoming a couple? It's not just a lack of confidence in yourself, it goes deeper. Because I can't fucking convince you anymore that your looks are driving me crazy!"

I feel trapped.

Between my desires, his, those I felt for Laurent and what followed…

Ervin comes back, crouches in front of me to cup my face. "Shit, don't cry, Alizee. I'm not forcing you into anything, get that into your head. I'm just trying to understand you."

Tears won't fall. They're piled up at the edge of my eyelashes, at the brink of my wide-open eyes.

***

I've only had three relationships… very short ones. After my first time in high school, the guy dumped me as soon as he had me in his bed. It hurt me at the time, and it took me a few years to accept the fact that he was just a jerk. I wanted to relive the experience at the end of my university years, and although my partner was as skilled as a rabbit, it was he who then distanced himself.

No longer too excited by sex, I secretly dreamed of arms to cuddle into when I ran out of inspiration. Encouragement from a man who would understand me, who would share my daily life and appreciate who I was on the inside, since the outside repulsed me. I envied all those couples around me. I wanted to feel loved…

I met a man outside the orphanage—Laurent. Employed in a library, he was sent by his boss to offer some books to the kids. He flirted with me, was witty, quite simple, and rather kind. I didn't tell anyone about it. I started this relationship on cloud nine, jumped for joy when

I discovered his passion for literature. Excited, I revealed my literary identity to him. Even more surprising, he had read and loved me. I easily entered his circle of friends—a bit nerdy, very nice, too.

Then came the evening when I invited him to my place. He was so handsome, well-built, and so charming that when his kisses and touches became bolder, I felt those famous butterflies in my stomach. After sleeping with him, I fell in love with him. He had been gentle and caring and had also reached orgasm quickly as he seemed to have enjoyed it. I hadn't climaxed, but my heart had completely melted.

The next day, Laurent was more distant. A week later was his birthday. I was bedridden with the flu. I wasn't supposed to go to his party, but I forced myself. I put on a tight-fitting burgundy dress, thinking he would like it, and went to the restaurant where the festivities were taking place. At the end of a long table of twenty people, Laurent was bragging. They didn't see me approaching, all absorbed in a discussion that seemed to fascinate them. Close enough, I finally heard his friend Robert say to him, "So, did you hook up with the other writer?"

I froze, stared at this man whom I thought was pleasant. Others who I once found friendly also supported his question, almost mocking. But the worst came just after, when Laurent answered them, "Don't even mention it! She's a shitty lay. Then again, when you look at her…"

At that moment, a white light engulfed the scene. My asthenia stunned me, my heart was trampled with force, as if it were just an insect to be eradicated at all costs. I didn't understand. Why was Laurent reacting like this? It was he who had taken the lead. If he wasn't satisfied, why talk to them like that?

"What does she look like?" one of the guests asked.

"Some blonde with a big ass," echoed an unidentified voice.

They all burst into cruel laughter.

The same cruelty was painted on Laurent's face, the man I had fallen in love with. This man was laughing at my expense, in front of a gathering of human waste.

The treachery tasted sour.

I didn't have the guts to face them, me, the blonde with the big ass, shitty in bed. *I turned on my heel and disappeared from his life for good.*

I believe that day will remain etched in my memory. I'd never felt such shame, not even when I was a kid and teased relentlessly.

He never reached out to me again. Never sent a text, made a call. He had relegated me to oblivion. And my heart was shattered.

Before his birthday, I thought about telling Galati, Marshall, and my mother. In the end, no one ever heard about this relationship. It lasted a month, and it destroyed me for years...

***

And here I am, in a hotel room, facing this man who always manages to extract the darkest part of me, to put words to this pathetic story.

Tears flow, like the first time I confided in Ervin. And like that time, he wipes them away with his thumbs. In his onyx eyes, I see frustration, anger.

"What a son of a bitch!"

"I've never told anyone. If you spill, I'll emasculate you," I threaten, sniffling.

Once again, he kisses the back of my fingers. "I'll never do that. Ignore that bastard's words, why did you let them eat at you for so long?"

"Because I have some pride! And then, it all makes sense! If my relationships have ended in failure, it's because sex with me is a deal-breaker. This episode is proof of that. I'm just a blonde with a big ass, incapable of giving pleasure to a guy. Seeing me naked must have definitely turned them off them."

"Don't talk bullshit, damn it! The first one was just a stupid kid, the second was a one-night stand. Of course he didn't call you back— what did you expect? Do you think I call back the hotties who throw themselves into my bed? And this Laurent is—a weakling without balls who probably doesn't know how to take care of a woman! If you give me his address, I swear, I'll beat the shit out of that asshole."

"You'd do that for me?" I squeak, amused.

"A hundred times. Is it his fault you can't write anymore?"

I sniffle, lower my eyes, my heart as wrung out by these memories as it is swollen by Ervin's concern. "It's possible, yes. The dates match up."

"It's his fault that you're afraid to spend a dreamy night with me."

The bastard manages to coax a laugh out of me, even in these circumstances. "With anyone. You and I are neighbors. If you try to avoid me after a big disappointment, it'll be even more awkward."

The handsome man's jaw tightens. His hands rest on my thighs, their contact hindered by the nylon of my stockings. "We were drunk last night, but I remember everything. Yet I'm still here. And I'm not going anywhere," he finishes with a kiss on my knee.

I melt. I melt and it horrifies me…

He'll run away.

"I've been clear—I refuse to commit to any kind of relationship. But, damn it, Alizee… I really want to show you how much I like you."

I swallow, still bruised by my confession.

His hand gently wanders between my legs, slipping under my skirt, while his gaze becomes pleading. "I want to make you wet," he murmurs. "Again and again. I want you to feel me so hard that, no matter what happens next, you'll have no doubt about how I feel for you, at this very moment."

I feel like the noose is tightening. I'm scared, yet I want to give it a try. I'm tired of this constant protection, of this persistent aversion. What if he's right? Should I trust him because I've shared my most intimate secrets with him?

"What will happen? And what do you feel about me?" I articulate, feverish.

His fingers stumble upon my sex, triggering an avalanche of shivers throughout my body. I exhale deeply, slowly, internally shaken, my hands clenched on the armrests. When he increases his pressure, a moan escapes me. Blocked by the seat, it's impossible for me to spread my thighs farther. Unperturbed, he persists, pinches, ardently caresses. His breathing grows heavier, the devouring sensations he provokes disconnect me off from reality.

"Ervin…" The streaks on my cheeks are now nothing but a distant memory, my sole desire is for him to continue, again and harder.

Without warning, he interrupts to lift me up, as if I were as light as a soap bubble. When he lays me down on the bed, his face betrays his eagerness. The fact that he wants me so much excites me terribly. When he almost rips off my tights, I receive a shock right in my lower abdomen.

I want him to draw the curtains. Instinctively, I'd like to hide my body. He'll refuse. The way he eyes me leaves no doubt about it. And now he's pulling off my panties.

Taking me by surprise, he makes me roll onto my side, presses against my back, and lifts my skirt to reveal my butt. My heart is racing. He inhales at the back of my neck, then whispers, with a voice altered by lust, "I feel a fucking strong desire for you. Not just for body. It's your entire being that makes me hard, my little pussycat."

He accompanies his declaration with eager caresses on my backside. Ravenous caresses, playing at the edge of my wet pussy.

"Unfortunately, you might make some unpleasant discoveries. There are things about me you won't like at all," he mumbles before nibbling my throat.

"What could possibly turn me off about you?" I blurt in a nervous laugh, my mind consumed by desire. "I already hate you."

He smiles against my skin and slips a finger between my wet folds, stealing a surprised squeak from me. "I hope you never find out," he says.

With these words, he traverses my sensitive flesh, pressing on my clitoris at each of his strokes. Triggering tremors with every breath.

I'm so, so hot.

He descends, bites, licks, devours my two alabaster breasts, plunging me into the throes of embarrassment, of pleasure. It's so, so good.

"You're so hot, Alizee."

I bite my lip, aware of every millimeter traced by the tip of his tongue. When it touches between my legs, I startle, sending Ervin back to his previous place of play. He nibbles, caresses me as if in worship.

Suddenly, he straightens, his expression grave, cheeks flushed, and pants stretched. I watch him like a frightened cat, facing his blazing gaze. His sweater goes over his head in an excruciatingly sexy way, revealing a set of abs worthy of a magazine cover. When his thumbs slip under the waistband of his pants, he wets his lips, covering me with a fierce gaze.

"Take off your clothes."

Despite the softness of his tone, his voice acts as a command. Nevertheless, I can't do it. The thought of him possibly gazing at me in full light petrifies me.

That doesn't stop him. He dives between my legs, spreading them forcefully, and kisses my flesh. Wide-eyed, I watch him, propped on my elbows, trembling with anticipation. Fascinated by his misty eyes, I'm overwhelmed with bliss as his tongue delves itself between my folds.

"Oh, my god!"

When it brushes against my clitoris, I nearly faint. Despite the hardness of his features, he's so gentle, so attentive, playing with me with expertise.

Has anyone ever lavished pleasure on me with such devotion? My elbows give way, I collapse onto the mattress, feeling waves of ecstasy coursing through me, concentrating in my lower belly.

He sucks me in so suddenly that dizziness propels me far from reality. My limbs tingle, my back arches. Each of his laps tears a silent cry from me. Clutching the sheets, I surrender completely, forget all my nagging reservations as a violent orgasm overcomes me.

Breathless, I don't have time to gather my thoughts before Ervin looms over me, trying to gauge my impressions. My chest heaves in an uneven rhythm. He licks his lips, which glisten with my wetness.

"You're delicious, kitten," he smirks.

Thump-thump… thump-thump…

"Did you like it?"

I flutter my eyelashes, nodding, dazed. "Damn… You're good."

Before he can boast, I grab his hair, pulling him toward me to exchange the most languorous kiss of my existence. I'm not sure if it's gratitude, excitement, or relief, but I devour him eagerly, while he moves on top of me, slipping his hands up under my dress to caress my waist.

"Damn, let me undress you, Alizee. I need to see you."

The heat is dizzying, I lose control. "Okay, Okay." I surrender, swept away by his passion.

The wool of my outfit disappears, my bra, too, quickly replaced by Ervin's kisses. He kneads and licks in such an erotic way that I'm unable to look away. When his eyes lift to meet mine, something indescribable happens, a connection so deep that it freezes both of us. Damn…

My heart pounds close to him; his thuds against my stomach. Skin against skin, the temperature rises. He caresses me for a long time, lets me kiss him more until I can't anymore. Until he decides to lower his pants, without letting go of me.

Panic sets in when his hard cock presses against my thigh. He feels it, runs his tongue over my throat before whispering, "Take it in your hand."

Heaven help me, how could I have slept with him just last night with such confidence? I feel like I'm experiencing my first time, it's so distressing! I'll never drink with a guy again!

But I comply, swallowing hard in the face of the beast. "This thing was inside me last night…"

His grins against my cheek. "Fuck, yes. And my *thing* will be inside you in no time, rest assured. Jerk me off, Alizee."

It's soft, warm, and throbbing between my fingers. As I begin my strokes, he anchors himself in my eyes, inhaling and exhaling forcefully, jaws clenched.

Bewitched, I revel in providing him such pleasure. He takes my hand, licks my palm to moisten it, and lets me increase the pace of my movements.

"Stop, stop… I won't last," he stutters.

Mischievous, I refuse to obey, delighted by this new sense of power. "Come for me, baby," I murmur in a husky voice, unable to help myself. I could bring him to climax just for the joke.

But he grabs my wrist and immobilizes it, not receptive to my admittedly unwelcome humor.

In a suspended moment, he dives into his pocket, pulls out a packet that he tears open with his teeth. He puts on his condom with a disconcerting dexterity, then guides his cock toward my opening. When his edges inside me, I whimper.

"Relax. Open up," he whispers in my ear.

As he penetrates me, I wrap my arms around his neck. Ervin's cock enters slowly, sliding effortlessly inside.

Uncomfortable, I feel besieged, so small under his immense and sculpted body. He takes possession of my hands, immobilizes them on either side of my head, our fingers intertwined, to start languorous thrusts.

It takes me a moment to adjust to his enormity, but then, it feels so good…

His eyes move from my mouth to my breast. He's attentive to my reactions, kisses me affectionately. With each of his invasions, I feel on the verge of exploding. Physical sensations entwine with my emotions. His face sweats with effort, with desire.

"You're killing me, damn," he growls against my neck before positioning my legs on his shoulders. His grip becomes bestial, his thrusts more lascivious, giving me different, more exalting sensations.

"Roll on top of me, Alizee," he implores against my lips.

Me? On top of him?

Paralyzed, I make it clear to him that this request does not please me at all. He insists, peppering my neck with a myriad of soft, wet kisses to convince me.

And this Adonis prevails.

I straddle him, feeling insecure. He must realize this is a first for me. Aware I'm not at my best, I dread the look he casts on my body.

I read in it only animal desire. My body flush against his, I dare a few rubs, making him swear under his breath.

"Come," he orders, gripping my hips with one hand, lifting his shaft in his fist.

I let myself slide, leaning on his titanium abdomen. It feels so good… Obviously, he shares my opinion, his teeth sinking into his lower lip, torment evident on his face. He guides me, envelops my breasts, his mouth full of curses.

"Fuck, you're so beautiful…"

Transported by pleasure, I forget my insecurities, undulating on his pelvis, focusing on his moans, on this debauchery he emanates. I engulf him faster, harder, thirsty for these electrifying sensations. His cock swells inside me as he rises on his elbows and grabs my neck to pull me closer. He bites my lips while growling, imperious, planting his fingers on my ass to thrust me harder. Shaken by his storm, I cling to his shoulders, drown my moans in his half-open mouth, moaning his name when he tightens me against his chest.

And he becomes merciless, ravaging me at that pace until orgasm…

CHAPTER 20

"Hmm hmm… And so, what did you feel?"

I stare at Dr. Duriau wearily. Couldn't we switch the roles for once? She's forcing me to dig, put into words what I don't even know myself!

"A bunch of things. I'm sad because my best friend has distanced herself from me; destabilized because since we got back, Ervin has been acting as if nothing happened between us, even though he assured me he had a great time—well, at least he's not avoiding me—and I can't seem to shake off my euphoric state since our sexual experience."

Not to mention the lingering soreness in my thighs from lack of exercise.

"It's only been two days. Do you think that's a bad thing?"

The old lady scribbles on her notepad with her stern demeanor that I hate, although she's the reason I'm loyal to her clinic. A tough cookie, just like me. And besides, she agreed to see me on short notice, which is a big plus for her!

"I don't know. I feel guilty about Galati. We used to spend New Year's Eve together, but this year, it was ruined by a fight."

"You're not to blame, unlike her lover. Has your sexual relationship caused any changes in you?"

I close my eyelids, seated comfortably in front of this money drain. While I escape to Andalusia, in this Oriental-style bedroom, Ervin's piercing gaze electrifies me. Though hesitant at first, I ended up feeling beautiful through his eyes, under his tongue that caressed my hips, pressed between his tender fingers. It was the best evening of the past few years for me. And then, he hadn't lied—that bastard fucks like a god.

"Someone's… into me… I'm sure of it. His gaze didn't deceive. After my previous misadventures, that means a lot to me."

A ringtone interrupts us. The woman with the wrinkled face runs her hand through her graying bob, adjusts her glasses on her nose, and leans over her phone. "Our session is coming to an end."

Already?

"Do you have any availability tomorrow?" I want to heal from these stars exploding in my brain, and quickly.

She gives me a knowing smile. "Just go with the flow, Miss Roy, it won't hurt you. I've got nothing until next Monday."

Of course it's going to be painful. I'm in love, damn it! Head over heels. Fallen into the one-sided love pot. I knew it, yet I charged ahead blindly. In front of the elephant trunk, I didn't think. He had the words, got me hooked… And I regret nothing. I just want to get rid of these useless and cumbersome feelings. Press the *Delete* button then go back to my regular life with a wonderful memory and maybe a tad more self-esteem. It'll give me some extra ammunition when my mother scolds me about my lifestyle. I'll stick it to her that the hottie next door banged me!

Meanwhile, Maeva and Vadim, my two favorite kids from the orphanage, complimented me on my radiant look. Damn, sex is even better than a vitamin cure! Books don't lie.

Friday evening, as I return from shopping, the famous Nabilla is on the doorstep. She's still as beautiful. Still as sexy. And, I hope, still as married… I glance at her sideways, key in the lock, slowing down my movements until Ervin opens the door.

First time we've met since Monday.

He stops, his eyes on me, freezing me on the threshold of my door. He's drop-dead gorgeous, too, in his dark shirt and jeans. He greets his sister-in-law and asks her to wait two minutes. My presence draws a displeased sigh from her. She doesn't hold me in her heart, Miss Shampoo.

When Ervin gives me two hearty kisses, I smile, blissful. He smells like lavender, a scent that takes me back a week and hundreds of miles down on the map. His hair is tousled, not yet styled. His eyes, sparkle while mine roam over his torso, which is compressed in superfluous fabric. Geez, his bare skin was perfect.

I think about it. And I'm wet. Fuck!

"I… I have to go," I apologize like a schoolgirl before he even says a word.

Before I can even open the door, he grabs my wrist. He takes a step into my lair and turns me toward him. His mischievous look sends a loop through my ribs. Those dimples, for god's sake… I shiver, frozen.

His face is just inches from mine. He gazes at me with desire, letting me see all the things he's done to me that have tormented my mind ever since.

I swallow. He swoops in on my mouth.

My chest about to explode, I cling to his shoulders and drop my bags at the entrance to my apartment.

A female voice grumbles, "Ervin? What are you doing? Are you coming?"

Panting, he steps back, anchors his eyes on mine before murmuring against my lips, "I'll ring your doorbell at ten tonight."

Then he disappears. He leaves me with a mess in my head and in my heart, completely dazed.

✳✳✳

I ate. Not too much, to avoid feeling bloated, not too little, to avoid stomach rumblings. I've pondered over my wardrobe. For a long time. I've opted for this burgundy dress that reminds me of the worst day of my life when Laurent and his friend trash-talked me. That day, however, has been erased by Ervin's lustful gaze in the bar where I wore it recently. In front of the mirror, I touch up my eyeliner and dab on my lipstick, the burn of his kiss still burning. I give some volume to my cascading hair over my shoulders, feel ridiculous in my stilettos heels. But the handsome devil likes that.

What was he thinking? Did he realize that by kissing me he blew my mind? I thought that when we got back, the affair would be over, that his kindness would dictate maintaining a cordial understanding between neighbors, but that he was done with his little obsession with me. And now he's doing it again like a hurricane, both in my thoughts and in my emotions.

When, right on time, Ervin rings the doorbell, I get stomach cramps like it's our first date. I open the door to him and a bottle of wine. Damn, he's even hotter than before!

Without greeting him, I invite him in, hypnotized by his delicious mouth. He surely notices it, because suddenly, his gaze darkens.

He says nothing, places his gift on the table, allowing me to ogle his perfectly curved backside. Then he pivots, leans back on his arms, scanning me up and down unabashedly. There's a predatory aura about him, as if he's having fun with his prey.

"Thanks for the bottle," I say.

"I tried to get you out of my head," he replies bluntly.

"Excuse me?"

"Come here," he commands, reaching out his hand.

When I take it, he pulls me toward him, between his spread legs, and plunges into my eyes with his arsenal of sex appeal.

"I can't forget our night in Malaga. I want to do it again."

Images of last weekend come back to me, accompanied by a serious heatwave. "*I want, I want,* anyway, everything you desire, you take it."

"Exactly." He smiles at me, our noses touching.

After our pre-sex conversation last week, Mr. Great Lay knows perfectly what I think about his advances.

"You look super hot tonight. How do you expect me to resist?"

His compliment sends shivers down my spine. His hand wanders over my lower back, settles on my buttocks, sensitizing every inch of my skin. The air around us grows heavier, just like my breasts, whose hardened nipples long for caresses.

He still wants me? Well, that's perfect, because I still want him. *You're going to fall, Alizee.*

I'm aware it's a very bad idea, but damn it… *Carpe diem!*

Unable to contain myself, I devour his lips, eliciting a surprised moan of excitement from him. Today, all I can think about is giving back to him everything he gave me during our last embrace. Everything he made me realize about myself, my feelings, my body.

He fucks me even harder, more beastly, releasing all the pressure of his week of abstinence. Our gazes are locked, struggling to part, despite the transcendent pleasure. The connection is more powerful than our first time. I let myself be manipulated as if I belonged to him, taking the initiative without embarrassment. He's sexier, more beautiful, more exciting than anything I could have imagined, and already, I see myself losing control and surrendering.

Naked and breathless, I lie across my bed. My eyes are fixed on the ceiling, my head resting on his shoulder. His fingers caress the fine hair at my temples tenderly. In his chest, too, it's chaos, I can hear it from where I am. His breath is deep, setting the pace for mine.

When Vampyr jumps on the mattress to rub against my side, Ervin jerks upright.

At that moment, the look he gives me feels like a slap.

A dark look.

A violent look, devoid of kindness.

What's happening?

Chilled, I instinctively cover myself with my sheet as Ervin turns his back on me, sitting on the edge of the bed, my cat cuddling his lower back.

Do not fear death.

Facing his koi tattoo, a strange premonition creeps over me. I lean against the headboard, curling my legs up as a form of protection. What's wrong with him?

When he pinches his forehead, impatience takes over.

"Ervin?"

"Hm?"

"Are you okay?"

No response, just the tightening of his impressive back muscles.

That ungrateful Vampyr purrs, happy to find the scent of his lover on his owner. Now the beast starts to meow, no doubt asking for his Otto.

Ervin gets up. A weight in my stomach, I sense his agitation as he checks that he hasn't left any clothes in my room. No luck for him, we tore off our clothes in the living room before tumbling into the bed.

"Why are you so nervous? You don't work tomorrow. Don't you want to have a glass of the wine you brought instead of fidgeting like that?"

I wanted to play it cool. My reproachful tone betrays me.

He freezes, tall, muscular, and naked, his cock still a little stiff. Gorgeous with his locks falling in front of his eyes, his heavily veined arms, and his penetrating onyx eyes.

"Fuck, this wasn't planned…" he scolds himself without worrying about my presence.

I forget to breathe for a few seconds, shocked. "Excuse me?"

He ruffles his hair, looking concerned. "What happened in Malaga was supposed to stay in Malaga. But, sex with you is…"

Stunned, I blink between indignation and… something else indistinct. "It's… you who wanted to see me tonight. It seemed pretty planned to me."

"I know, I know," he admits, settling back beside me, thus displacing my cat's glue.

His hand cups my cheek, his expression softening, although behind the window of his eyes, I see a plenty of doubts and as many regrets.

With a tight chest, I dread his reaction. I know it's just sex. I know there probably won't be a next time. Still, I'd have preferred an unspoken agreement, no strings attached. No need to hurt with words, to explain to me how and why exactly this heartbreaker will break mine.

His fingers slide over my throat, caress my collarbone before descending to the base of my breasts. He removes the sheet and stares at them reverently. Shivers run through me, mingling with my bitterness.

"It haunted me all week. I don't know what you're doing to me."

I also don't understand the reason for the wrinkles furrowing his forehead.

When he closes the gap between us, placing a wet kiss on my nipple, a sigh escapes me. After he raises his face, blaming me for his woes. "I won't be able to do without you."

Neither will I. Especially if he keeps giving me that look.

I ponder. Mouth slightly open, I'm unable to answer, melting against his lips as they crush into the hollow of my neck.

"It's problematic," he whispers.

This man is devilishly sensual, my awareness of him burning me up. When I thread my fingers through his hair, his breathing intensifies.

"I'm not sure you can handle me."

"I'm not sure either," I reply, eyelids closed.

"You'll hate me," he murmurs.

"Doesn't matter."

No matter what he does, deep down, I'll hate him.

Tenderly, he kisses the back of my ear, slipping his hand between my legs to grasp the inside of my thigh. "At your own risk. I have a monstrous appetite, and yet, I'm incapable of consistency."

"It's just for sex, I get it."

His nails dig into my flesh, painful like the thorn he's decided to plant there. Then he pulls away, looking serious. Confused. "We've talked about this."

I swallow, the aftermath of our lovemaking bleeding through.

You don't care, Alizee. You've known him for, what, two months? Even if he turns my world upside down with his Adonis-like physique, with his arrogant yet incredibly charming smiles, with his charisma infused with passion, fervor, and a desire to seize life by the horns, he's still just my womanizer neighbor. Despite him cherishing every part of me that I despise, soothing my bitterness, it's just a matter of hormones.

My arms wrapped around his neck, I pull him close and steal a passionate kiss to silence my inner voices. *Carpe diem.*

Here we go again.

Damn, this guy is a sex machine!

I'm ashamed I've screamed again. Like *them…* Well, hopefully, something less ridiculous. Still, he could build a solid case!

This time, we lie sprawled on our stomachs, shining with sweat. Him on the mattress, me on top, heart pounding.

I've just had sex with that sexy thing right underneath me. Me, *the blonde with the big ass*. Take that, life!

"The advantage of having sex at home is that you don't have to get dressed when it's time to kick the other out," he mumbles into the pillow.

"Seriously? I'll be happy to avenge all the women you've thrown out at improbable hours."

The bastard grabs my waist, a mischievous grin lighting up his face, then hugs me. His warm, moist embrace feels like a balm, his spicy scent still intoxicating me. His hands on my back, strong and manly, are reassuring.

"I won't move my ass from this room, no matter what you say. If you're not happy, take the keys to my place. My bed is all yours."

He's incorrigible! And all proud, he kisses me, that little jerk!

Finally, fifteen minutes later, he's at his place. And me, I realize that I'm living the most intense moments of my life and the most dangerous for my heart.

CHAPTER 21

Naked, I stand still in front of Ervin's bed, as stiff as a board.

Through the white curtains, daylight floods the room, exposing even the most unsightly corners of my body. I don't like it; I'm just obeying the orders of my tormentor, lazily lying on his side, his eyes heavy with desire.

He examines me bit by bit with disconcerting seriousness. I feel as if he's dissecting me. Like he finds me ugly through my own eyes.

Everything is exposed. My ridiculous breasts, my stomach, my love handles, my sex, my too-wide hips, my thighs full of cellulite. Everything I hate.

Even though we've just had a thunderous orgasm, I struggle to give my body credit for it.

He urges me to come closer. Asks me to relax.

I step forward until I bump into the edge of the mattress. Finally, he sits up, settles on the edge, equally undressed, legs spread around me. As he envelops my curves with his palms, a sense of vulnerability twists my insides.

Despite being in his birthday suit, his stature gives him a robust, almost warrior-like appearance. His model-like face doesn't change a thing.

His nose nuzzles against my sternum. He inhales me, places sweet kisses that multiply until they reach my nipple, eliciting a sigh from me.

He tells me he loves my breasts.

His hands roam my curves, lower and lower, more languidly.

His teeth sink into my love handle. He tells me I'm appetizing.

I don't believe him.

He gets angry.

He grabs my buttocks, kneads them while scolding me with his gaze. According to him, it's one of the most enjoyable sensations he knows. He claims to love my anatomy.

When I point out my stretch marks, his tongue comes to smooth them away. His index finger traces every groove of my cellulite, getting lost on the inside of my thigh. He assures me I have a woman's body. That every imperfection is a mark left by my life, that together they make me who I am. He explains a crooked tooth can be cute, a tilted nose can exude charm. Nothing different from my curves, according to him.

He repeats that he loves them, adores them, that I should be as proud of them as those models who make them their trademark.

Without warning, he grabs his phone and takes some pictures. Furious, I try to snatch the device from his hands, but against him I'm powerless.

Collapsed on him, on all fours on the mattress, admitting defeat is the only option.

No matter how much I rage, he remains unmoved, then shows me the pictures.

I hate them.

He repeats that he loves my silhouette, that it drives him crazy. That he would like to see my love for my body match his.

Each of his sentences chips away my dark thoughts.

He says I'm the most beautiful woman he's ever fucked. To which I reply that he's lying, offended.

As retaliation, he crushes his lips against mine. With intensity, with brutality. He forbids me to question the words that come straight from his gut.

The power of his kiss could almost convince me, and the fire in his eyes incinerates my fears.

Incinerates my whole being.

I vanish in smoke.

CHAPTER 22

I'm living in a delicious hell.

It's been three weeks since our pact was sealed.

Our pancake breakfasts have become less frequent. Now, they're accompanied by a torrid sex session that depresses me as soon as Ervin heads out to appointments.

We sometimes go three days without seeing each other, then hook up multiple times in the same night. In the living room, in the kitchen, on the floor, in the shower, on any available surface. He never stays after sex, and when it happens at his place, he makes it clear me that I need to leave.

His absence accentuates his presence in my cave. His scent is everywhere, the memory of our lovemaking imprinted on every room, every piece of furniture. The memory of his smile haunts my nights and my writing sessions. His absence is wearing me down. Our only outing together: the appointment made at the testing center. He insisted on it as much as I did; our longest and deepest conversations now only happen through texts. During our time together, all that remains is the chemistry between us exploding, leaving our bodies to speak for themselves.

I'm living in a parallel reality.

I'd like to talk to Galati about it, but she shuts down as soon as I mention my neighbor. She notices my changes—tough—points out the joviality that has replaced my perpetual bitterness. Still, she warns me about the old habits of the man I used to call Mr. STD. What does he do when he's not at my place? Is he content with our lovemaking, or does he flinch as soon as some other girl bats her eyes at him? The thought kills me, so I force myself to push it aside.

As for Milo, he and my friend have seen each other again, but he's different. More tormented, more distantWhen he assures her that I have nothing to do with his outburst, no one is fooled. I tried to dig around for info, but nothing has worked.

No matter how much I grill Ervin, he won't spill anything, either, except that his best friend needs to *think things through*. The situation worries me, but Mr. Walking Aphrodisiac always manages to distract my thoughts.

On this late Sunday afternoon, Ervin isn't working. After five days of radio silence, he shows up with a feverish look and his muscles extremely tense. Feverish myself, I let him into my cave without a word. He moves forward, unbuttons the first button of my shirt even before closing the door with his heel.

I no longer wear fluffy pajamas during the day, afraid of falling into one of his ambushes.

His eyes don't leave mine until I find myself naked before him. There's no more embarrassment. He undoes the button on his jeans. Seeing his arousal at the sight of my body intoxicates me. With my back straight, I help him undress, pull him onto the sofa, and slide onto his hard cock.

Once deep inside me, he whispers, "I missed you, kitten."

Amid passionate kisses, lingering caresses, and slow hip movements, the tension builds, intense, promising a devastating orgasm.

Suddenly, the doorbell rings.

We freeze, eyes locked, tongues intertwined.

He continues, opposing anyone who would try to separate us. But my unexpected guest persists.

"Crap," I mumble against his mouth.

His fingers dig into the flesh of my ass, causing me pain. "Don't go open it," he urges, guiding me on his shaft.

My phone starts vibrating on the kitchen counter.

"It might be important."

He sighs, resigned and frustrated to the extreme. He grabs the back of my neck to kiss me one last time before I put on a robe.

After another round of doorbell rings, I crack the door open, my jaw dropping at the sight of Charlene Chamoux. My mother. Accompanied by her husband. And my brother.

Stunned, I watch them in silence.

Then it all comes back to me.

Despite my protests, she'd invited herself over for a family dinner tonight, since I never go to her place. Obsessed with Ervin's occasional absences, I had erased the appointment from my memory. And here they are, all dressed up, bags in hand, waiting for me to invite them in.

"Well, what took you so long? We agreed to six o'clock," my mother reproaches, her stern eye scrutinizing my attire.

She must think I just got out of the shower, with my cheeks flushed. But when it comes to Ervin… I catch my hookup putting on his boxers as she forces her way in with her entourage.

"Go get dressed while I take care of the kitchen?" she commands, authoritative.

No, no, no, no!

And there they all freeze in front of Ervin, who's wearing his Hawaiian-print underwear.

He stares back at them, not the least bit embarrassed, rather annoyed in fact. His swollen lips and tousled hair leave no doubt about what they've interrupted. Fuck!

"You!" exclaims my mother.

"I couldn't have said it better myself."

Gui breaks down, horrified, while Charles visibly struggles not to burst out laughing.

"We should leave," the insipid man says to his wife.

She vigorously shakes her head, taking off her fur coat and then placing it on a chair. "Since you're here, join us for dinner. I'll cook something other than my daughter's frozen pizzas," she boasts, winking at me.

I scowl, praying for them to leave immediately, but she seems determined.

"Thanks, but I'll leave you guys alone," Ervin refuses, grabbing his jeans.

"They're all the same," my mother comments under her breath, placing her groceries on the counter.

Mister Super-Ass freezes, sending electricity into the air. A palpable tension that shakes us all.

"I beg your pardon?" Ervin says.

She eyes him, busy with her ingredients. "No, nothing, go ahead, leave. You're only here to bed my daughter, after all."

"Mom!" I protest, utterly embarrassed. "Go, Ervin, I'll call you later."

He doesn't even look at me, his eyes locked on the blonde who pretends to ignore him.

"What's the matter? Perhaps he's too ashamed to share a simple meal with your family. It's outside your scope, isn't it?"

If she keeps it up, I'll leave my apartment in a robe! Good grief, is she trying to scare him away for good? Is she trying to sabotage me?

Embarrassed, I grasp Ervin's elbow, urging him to leave, when he retorts, "Not at all. If you insist, I'll stay."

She makes a noise of proud satisfaction, while Gui stares at me like an idiot.

"Make yourself comfortable," I whisper, my stomach twisted.

Ervin and my parents together—a very bad idea.

What a surprise to see that he has no intention of getting dressed further. My mother is scandalized; Charles has stars in his eyes.

"Since I'm staying, once dinner is over, your daughter and I will continue what we were doing. So why bother getting dressed again?" Ervin says.

Is he kidding me? On the threshold of my bedroom, I shoot him a furious look. "Come on, get dressed, don't be foolish."

"If I walk into this room with you, parents or not, I won't let you leave." He chuckles, his comment aimed at my mother.

She, who usually has a sharp tongue, seems stunned by his insolence. And I don't even dare to gauge the reaction of the other two jokers. As mortified as I am angry, I fiercely draw Ervin inside with me and lock us in the room.

His devilish smile infuriates me. As much as his hands grabbing my waist from under my robe.

"What the hell are you doing? Is it not enough to embarrass me like this? You calm down or get the hell out!"

The mischief on his features fades into a harder expression. "You don't have to be embarrassed. She's looking for trouble, so she found me."

"Great, so I'm just collateral damage."

Desire dominates his gaze. He presses me against his hard-on, his hands on my ass. "I'm sorry, it's you who drives me crazy."

I feel hot all over, even in my heart. Stupid schoolgirl!

"I'm going to get dressed. If you stay, behave yourself please."

***

Seated at the table, we begin the meal my mother prepared. She pours out her knowledge about literature, delighting in watching us enjoy her dishes. Ervin, with a T-shirt on, discreetly touches me. I see her tapping the table with her nails, as crimson as her long-lasting lipstick, eyeing on my neighbor furtively. Does she suspect our little game?

"So, tell us a little about yourself. You're an adult, surely working, and enjoying a good time with my daughter. Yet she's never mentioned you, even though we've already met. I deduce it's all about sex. So, what's stopping you from committing to her?"

We all freeze.

Did I hear correctly?

Yes, Ervin's hand has frozen on my thigh. When he removes it, my heart drops.

"Mom, who says it's him who—"

"It's obvious," she answers.

Hurt, I dare not ask her to elaborate. Surely her answer would hurt me. Ervin's reaction, too.

"Yet, she doesn't want anything more serious than me," Ervin replies, his voice serious.

Charlene shakes her head, rolling her eyes.

"Honey, stop," Gui intervenes. For once, he's useful.

"Why, Gui? I'd like to know more about the man who might hurt my little girl."

At the moment, she's the one doing it. My mouth dry, and likely white as a sheet, I set down my fork. "I'm almost thirty, Mom. I think I can handle a booty call without getting emotionally involved."

I can't believe we're discussing my sex life with my family, and with my lover, no less!

My mother, turning into a witch in an instant, sneers disdainfully at her husband's distressed expression and her son's stunned one. *Yes, Charles, never bring your girlfriend home.*

"My poor child, stop fooling yourself. We're all the same. This kind of story always ends badly, and I have no doubt which one of you two will be hurt, my darlings."

"Your daughter is different," Ervin tries to convince himself, his fist clenched around his fork.

"Very well, let's move on to dessert so you can kindly take your leave, Mother." I rise abruptly, although not everyone has finished their plates.

"Please, Alizee," she protests.

She can scold me as much as she wants. Anger buzzes in my ears. "I should kick you out right now. I don't even understand what he's doing here." I point at her husband with my chin. "You don't have to spill my private life in front of everyone!"

"Alizee!" she retorts, imitating me. "Guillaume isn't just anyone. He's been your stepfather for eighteen years!"

Her words grate my ears, and I reject them with all my being. Hands clenched on my plate, I decide to flee to the kitchen, despite my mother's reprimands. The tap running full blast, I don't hear her coming up behind me.

"I forbid you to address him in that tone, he's never done anything to you."

I hear two chairs squeak. The pale replacement for my father announces that he's leaving, accompanied by the teenager.

Eyes closed, I pray for Ervin to make the same decision, but he doesn't. He remains seated, witness to the ugliest aspect of my life. I've talked to him about them, but subjecting him to them tramples on my dignity. Yet, with him, it's just one more time.

Charlene tells Guillaume she'll join him, standing by my side, furious.

"Are you proud of yourself? For heaven's sake, grow up! Your father died a long time ago! Why do you resent Gui so much?"

Fists on the stove, I seethe. Did she have to wait for an audience to open Pandora's box? "Stop pretending like I don't understand. Do you think I'm incapable of figuring it out? Charles was never premature. He's the product of affair, of betrayal."

With force, she slaps me across the face. The pain is striking, forcing me to hold my cheek, stunned.

Around me, everything turns red. All that remains is her expression, marred by anger.

She hit me.

For the first time in my life.

"Mom—"

"I forbid you to say that! Charles is your brother," she snaps, her eyes rimmed with garish makeup, shining with emotion.

A lump forms in my throat. She never lets this stern, albeit capricious, facade crack. Why today? She knew inviting Guillaume over carried risks.

"Charles is still my *half*-brother. I don't forget the circumstances of his conception. Dad was dying!"

"Your father was cheating on me!" she explodes, gripping my shoulders.

Uppercut.

Instant denial.

"Bullshit," I say.

She grabs the hand on my face, forces it down, and immediately replaces it with hers, warm and so unfamiliar. A tear rolls down her cheek. My insides twist with pain.

"Henri was a wonderful father. He protected you, and you were the apple of his eye. He succeeded where I failed. He expressed his love for you like I never could. I'll be forever grateful to him. He was a wonderful man, with many qualities. He was handsome, intelligent, charming, and funny. But he was always a ladies' man. He always had been. I knew it, I accepted it, convinced I was special, that he would change for me. Then, life showed me there was no point in trying to change his nature.”

“Stop!” No. No. No. I don’t want to hear this!

“He never stopped cheating on me.”

“You were never there! Always obsessed with your cabaret!”

“To forget! To think about something other than what your father was doing behind my back! I was too in love with him to leave him, but his infidelities were unbearable. And then, he loved you so much more than me, it made me jealous!”

The tears well up at the edge of my lashes now. This woman lies, corrupts the memories of my father out of pure vengeance.

“My darling, don’t for think for a moment that my love for you isn’t strong enough,” she continues, raising my face, locking her eyes with mine. “You were the product of our union, Henri and me, and I assure you, I was crazy about him. But when Guillaume came into my life, when he gained my trust, I fell for him. It wasn’t hard; I was tired and resigned to your father’s imminent death.”

No, that doesn’t excuse anything!

“You should have waited! Grieved, cried over his grave!”

“I cried the whole time I was with him, can’t you understand?” she bursts out, tears streaming down her cheeks. Mine are flooded, too. A heap of memories crackles in my mind; some ambiguous, taking on new meaning after these revelations.

I squeeze my eyelids shut in a poor attempt to escape this dreadful reality.

“Look at me, sweety! Please, stop blaming me.”

“Why are you telling me this today? You had eighteen years to do it,” I murmur, my voice choked.

“Because I see clearly. Because you worshipped your father and now idealize him, while I recognize men like him. I’d rather spare you from walking the same path as me. Because I love you,” she finishes, wrapping her arms around me unexpectedly.

Shaken, I open my eyes to see Ervin staring at us, impassive, slumped in his seat. His witnessing such an intimate discussion unsettles me. His hearing these abominations about my father disheartens me. His being the subject of such a comparison fills me with sorrow.

It shouldn't. He's just a fling, he sleeps with whomever he wants.

And my father wasn't a womanizer, I refuse to accept it.

I refuse.

I refuse.

I refuse.

His love for my mother was as strong as the love he had for me. So much so that sometimes, it pained him. I remember.

I push her away, ask her to leave. Without screaming. Without animosity. I just need space. I need her to go away. Sort through my memories, erase her lies.

When she disappears, I remain motionless against the kitchen counter for a long moment, distraught.

Finally, Ervin stands and approaches, his steps slow and hesitant. I lower my head, avoiding his gaze lest he notice my distress too closely. When his feet appear in my field of vision, my muscles tense. When, unexpectedly, he takes me in his arms, I stagger.

My mother's words still echo in my ears.

His masculine scent envelops me, his solid body is reassuring. Alarming. I want to bury my face in his chest, melt into him to pour out my sorrow. My fears grow as my need for him increases.

"Do you want me to leave?" he whispers against my head.

No!

"You should go…"

He doesn't move. "Do you want to be alone?"

I shake my head. "I want to go back and erase these last few minutes." My tears have given way to bitterness.

His mouth crushes against my temple. "You're right, I should go."

I hold him back, craving kisses. His kisses. Those that, so intense, obliterate any feeling. When his tongue finds mine, everything evaporates. Emotions explode like fireworks, and his hand at the small of my back sends me reeling. It's a different Ervin kissing me. His way of touching me, of moaning into me, like a cry of despair, plunges me into a dark abyss. His confidence wavers, his facade cracks.

Then he deserts my lips. He lets go of me. He apologizes and runs away, looking almost as devastated as I feel. He leaves me to an evening alone, a night of solitude in bitter distress, with only my keyboard and screen for comfort, into which I pour myself.

214   —   THE ROMANCE OF MY LIFE... NO WAY!

alone, a night of solitude in bitter distress, with only my keyboard and screen for comfort, into which I pour myself.

CHAPTER 23

Crimson lips. Extended eyeliner. Amber eyeshadow. Peach blush.

Galati finishes styling my blond locks, praising my appearance endlessly.

Yes, I dare. I've been invited to a fancy restaurant with Marshall, and I plan to dazzle Marshall.

"Congratulations on your success," says my friend. "I'll recommend *Bloody Stars* to Milo, even though reading isn't his thing."

"Shouldn't you start by reading it first?" I tease, pursing my overly bold lips.

"Well, maybe. I promise to read your thriller when you finish writing your romance."

"Wow, what a great bargaining chip. Wait… inspiration strike me, right here, right now!"

She gives me an amused smile, spraying something weird on my face. "It's a makeup setting spray," she explains.

Ah… cool, I'll be able to rub my face all over the tablecloth and nothing will smudge.

I sigh, checking my appearance in the mirror. My satin wrap dress hugs my figure perfectly. Its deep green brings out the color of my eyes, and for once, I'm not ashamed of my curves, even though it falls mid-thigh. Thank you, Ervin.

Speaking of whom—I wish he could see it. That jerk has been missing all week, claiming to be swamped with work. We promised there would be no awkwardness between us, yet I'm convinced he's lying. That he's keeping his distance since that disastrous dinner with my parents. Since that open-hearted kiss.

I would understand. His absence just hurt when I thought back to my mother's revelations about my father. He abandoned me. I needed to forget, and writing couldn't clear my head.

And I don't care about suffering from my feelings for him. I don't care about imagining him banging other chicks and feeling sick to my stomach. I want to see him. His posts on social media aren't enough for me, especially when he's posing next to some gorgeous TV reporter.

Fortunately, the great start of *Bloody Stars* has taken my mind off things.

Like a gallant knight, my favorite editor comes to pick me up. Since he's early, I invite him to wait in my living room. When he sees me, his jaw drops. The way his eyes focus on my cleavage amuses me.

"Well, I bet that took you by surprise!"

He pulls himself together, sheepish at being caught off guard, then takes in the rest of my outfit. "I'm not used to this. You look stunning. And that red on your lips suits you perfectly."

I slip on my heels, smiling broadly, letting him stroke my ego as I return the compliment. My Parisian is quite dapper!

All set, Marshall and I step through the door of my apartment when, oh divine coincidence, I run into Ervin, who's just returning home.

On the landing, he freezes. Then, facing my friend and me, he puts on a placid face.

"Hey," I venture, after clearing my throat.

He approaches without relaxing.

I inhale deeply. It's good to see him. And never-wracking at the same time.

When his eyes shift from Marshall to my outfit under my still-open coat, I remember my appearance. And revel in it.

"Hey," he returns, stopping about a yard away from me. Then, he abruptly extends his hand to the tall man, not particularly welcoming. "Ervin, her neighbor."

My editor eyes him with disdain, having a poor opinion of the ladies' man. Nonetheless, he shakes his hand. "Marshall, her friend."

Their handshake is firm. A bit too firm. It lingers. A bit too long. Men.

"Well," I interject, taking my colleague by the arm, "not that I'm not delighted to see you, but we're running late."

Cheerful, I pull Marshall toward me, forcing Ervin to let go of him. Ervin's jaw tightens, much to my delight. Since his eyes are locked on my scarlet lips, I smile for Marshall's benefit. "I think we have a reservation for eight-thirty?"

He nods, just as cheerful.

I sweep back my wavy hair, just to provoke Ervin, whose gaze is now diving into my cleavage. Then I press myself against the tall, dark-haired friend, emphasizing our intimacy.

"Come on, let's hurry, I'm starving!" I chirp, fluttering my eyelashes. "See you later, Ervin!"

"Wait."

Breathless, I stop on the first step and turn around, pretending nonchalance. "Yes?"

He seems like he wants to say something, but his mouth is sealed. His fists, clenched. His gaze, piercingly intense, drying up my throat.

"Alizee?" Marshall calls out to me.

I exhale.

I turn my back on my neighbor without a word and leave the building, triumphant and anxious at the same time.

✳✳✳

My small breasts have never been so successful.

Thank you, push-up bra! I notice a few men in the restaurant eyeing me, and strangely, I don't feel uncomfortable. I think about what might have crossed Ervin's mind when he scrutinized me.

Even Ludivine compliments me when she arrives. Once served, we discuss the purpose of our meeting.

"Where are you with your manuscript?"

"I just need… a dramatic element impactful enough to flesh out my story. That's all that's blocking me now." As for the emotions and the romance itself, phew! I'm really inspired! "I should finish it within the year."

"Very well." She sets down her fork, pulls a cardboard folder out of her bag. "Here's the publishing contract. Keep it, analyze it at your leisure, and if you feel ready to join Pink Feathers Publishing, give me a call."

Hesitant, I accept and tuck the document away. My heart beats slightly faster.

There it is, it's real. One signature, and I betray Alan. Full of doubts, I'm not sure if I'll take the plunge. Perhaps a final clarification with him would be necessary before I make up my mind.

"I find it such a shame you didn't present *Bloody Stars* openly. You know, readers are becoming more and more open-minded. It wouldn't have harmed your sales; the book is excellent."

I smile politely, moistening my lips with red wine. I'm not ready. I'm just starting to wear bold lipstick, so exposing myself to all of France… let's not go overboard!

"I also understand why Marshall didn't insist further. He wants to keep his little protegee all to himself," she adds, giving him a wink.

Intrigued, I watch my friend squint, prepare to argue, then reconsider, and finally sigh. "I don't want to rush her," he answers.

"Hm," comments Ludivine, taking a sip of wine.

"Alan is pushing me, and that's one of the reasons why I'm reluctant to work with him." Let's be clear: she's not going to impose anything on me. If I have to do it, it'll be at my own pace.

"I understand." She nods before changing the subject.

Once the meal is finished, Marshall drives me back home in his sports coupe, traversing the surprisingly uncongested roads at this late hour.

"I had a great evening. Ludivine is actually funny."

I wait for him to say goodbye to me before opening the car door.

He gives me a satisfied half-smile. "She's not my friend for nothing. I really enjoyed seeing you today, but we didn't get the chance to talk about anything other than work. How about extending it over a cup of coffee?"

A glance at my watch—almost midnight. "Sure, why not. I'm not sleepy anyway, and I've a lot to tell you."

His presence will mainly help push my neighbor out of my mind.

As we reach our way to the fourth-floor landing, I see Ervin leaning against the wall, arms crossed over his chest, and a scowl on his face.

"What are you doing here?" I ask him by way of greeting.

Marshall's hand slides over my back, under the scrutiny of the handsome guy.

"I was waiting for you," he says.

And I wasn't expecting that. "You could have let me know with a text."

He shakes his head, eyeing me up and down with irritation. "I didn't expect you to bring your… friend," Ervin says.

I swallow, torn between satisfaction and annoyance. "Well, why not? We're going to have one last coffee. Feel free to join us if you want," I retort sarcastically.

Surprised at first, he chuckles under his breath, looking sour. "I need to talk to you alone," he insists, directing his words at Marshall.

Behind my back, Marshall's hand tightens as he concedes. "I'll leave you two alone. Seems like he's in distress," he mocks.

As if I needed this. I should hold Marshall back and tell my neighbor to leave me alone, but my lips remain sealed.

Quickly, Marshall gives me two overly enthusiastic cheek kisses and a hug before retreating. As he descends the stairs, Ervin and I stare at each other in silence, caught in a tense atmosphere. He doesn't hesitate to scan me up and down again, wearing a tight-fitting T-shirt that accentuates his muscle, his favorite sweatpants, and his running shoes.

As soon as we hear the building door close, he demands, "Who's that?"

Stunned, it takes me a few seconds before I reply, "He introduced himself. I've mentioned him before, but you seem so uninterested in what I say that you didn't make the connection." I refrain from telling him that he's only interested in my rear end. It would be inappropriate. And yet so true.

"I would have remembered something like that. What's going on between you two?"

Really? Is Mister Booty Call jealous now? Unbelievable! After a week of radio silence, during which I don't even know who he's been fucking!

"You're playing the possessive card, huh? I don't think it's any of your business."

"I've got a right to know, don't you think?" he barks, unfolding his arms.

I seethe, stepping back and bumping into the safety rail. Typical guys, all the same.

"Not at the expense of my evening. Is that why you brushed him off? Pff, I should've expected it, it's so cliché! You could've been original and let me have a good time with my friend. And even if I wanted to get laid, huh? We didn't sign an exclusivity clause, did we? I don't ask you questions about the bitches you fuck, do I? Although I really want to, but I know how to control myself," I retort, the words tumbling out in a rush.

"Coming from the one who called my sister-in-law a whore out of jealousy," he cuts in, closing the distance between us.

As the timer on the stairwell light clicks off, darkness envelops us. He seems more imposing, more intimidating. Yet, I find my confidence rising. Under his intense gaze, I feel more desirable.

"The situation was different back then. Now, you disappeared for a week while I was at rock bottom, and then you reappear out of nowhere, claiming some right over me?" I counter.

He frames me with his arms, gripping the railing on either side of my body, his face too close to mine. "If you have any questions, go ahead. Ask me anything, I'll answer honestly."

He doesn't acknowledge my distress, probably avoiding it on purpose. He smells good. I want him to kiss me, damn it. I missed him— why did we have to meet like this? And my heart is beating way too fast, way too hard.

"Why did you wait for me?" I ask, not the question he was expecting.

He still answers me, "Because your brother showed up an hour ago. He was making a huge racket banging on your door, so I had to let him into my place. He's wasted, and it's not even midnight. The kid has a problem."

He catches me off guard. I feel foolish with my theories about his jealousy. Damn it, when is this teenager going to grow up?

"His only problem is not knowing when to stop. Because his mother made the decision for him too many times," I reply, relaxing and taking a deep breath. "I'm sorry. You should have turned him away," I say.

"He could barely stand on his feet," he retorts, his hazy gaze stumbling over my lips. "I'll talk to him tomorrow morning."

Silence falls over our motionless bodies, torturing my mind about my earlier outburst. He doesn't respond, doesn't add another word, doesn't even compliment me on my appearance. Yet I had imagined him seeing me while I was getting ready. I crafted reactions for him, fashioned an expression full of desire. A hungry smile. A predatory look.

None of that. All I got was disapproving glances.

Ervin abruptly steps back, just when I was dying for him to take me in his arms, then he heads back to his apartment door. I barely hear his good night as he closes the door behind him.

What a jerk! He could have said something, anything, instead of mentioning his sister-in-law.

In turn, I go back home. I drop my coat on the floor, immediately kick off my shoes before sitting down on the floor and leaning against the armrest of my couch. I hate what I'm feeling. It's bitter. It feels like disappointment, even more painful.

Suddenly, a beep sounds from my purse. I pull out my phone and read Ervin's message.

[Man Whore: You look stunning tonight].

Is it possible to feel so much joy? To the point of tears.

Thump-thump, thump-thump.

I'm not *fine* or *hot*. He said *stunning*.

I don't want to reply. I prefer to savor this moment, a silly smile plastered on my lips.

New beep.

[Man Whore: I'm not fucking anyone else but you].

New heartbeat.

With closed eyelids, I process the emotions triggered by his messages. Once again, it's through text that he really talks to me. What happened to our bond? It's real, though.

It's in these moments that, for a few seconds, I miss the time when we hadn't yet given in. We were searching for each other, teasing each other, but man, I was thinking so much less. Everything was more natural, more instinctive.

That's not to mention all the positive changes he has brought about in me, as well as the phenomenal sex we share. Although it makes my stomach ache, I know I'm ready to give him whatever he wants, to accept the kind of relationship that suits him, as long as he keeps making my heart beat this hard.

[Alizee: OK…]

CHAPTER 24

ERVIN

Accompanied by a grumpy Milo, I stand outside my brother's place. Cem has called us in for the day, my friend and me. He needs extra hands for his house renovations.

He invites us in, senses the heavy tension between us, and silently questions me with a raised eyebrow. I ignore him, not wanting to come up with some bullshit excuses.

After a coffee, we get to work, boards in hand. Milo is killing the mood with his gloomy face. I better loosen him up soon if I want to avoid the older one's questions. I take advantage of a moment alone with him to say, between two hammer blows, "Relax, man. This isn't the time nor the place to sulk."

He sighs, continues working, and ignores me even more.

Then it's my older brother's turn to show up and take me aside, even though Milo knows everything about our lives.

"Any news of…?"

I shake my head, sheepishly. "I'm doing everything I can, believe me. But so far, no luck."

Suddenly, the front door slams shut. Nabilla and Ryan, my nephew, make their presence known from the hallway. She greets us warmly, and the kid jumps into my arms, thrilled to see me. He wants to help, too, he says. A real little man, that one.

As I return to work, my sister-in-law checks in on Milo, leaning against the doorframe with her arms crossed over her snug little sweater. She's always had a thing for my best friend; in fact, she met my brother through him. Since she didn't match his Italian type, it's a good thing that Cem showed up and stole her heart. Nabilla is the perfect match for him.

"How's your neighbor?" she suddenly asks me.

With hammer in hand, I freeze. Then I turn to her, avoiding my pal's inquisitive gaze. "Fine, I suppose. Why do you ask?"

That's when my brother joins us, hands full with a toolbox.

"Something going on between you two, huh?" she teases me, sensing my discomfort. "Seeing the same girl twice—it's more than just a fling. I know you."

"Between who?" Cem interjects, intrigues by our chatter.

"Ervin and his neighbor. The first time, she would have gutted me if he hadn't stepped in. She even called me a whore, that little bitch. Well, it was just pure jealousy… I've assaulted chicks who hung around you for less than that. The second time I saw her, Ervin jumped on her to kiss her. No, don't deny it—I'm not stupid! For once, a girl doesn't leave you indifferent."

Hell, I'd like to shut her up. Women are impossible! She hadn't said anything to me at the time. That sneaky one waited until she was in front of my brother to spill the beans. My brother is laughing, amused by my bachelor lifestyle.

"Jeez, you should introduce her to us," says my brother.

"Yeah, in your dreams. Nothing's going on, damn it. Leave me alone."

"Watch your language in front of the kid," my older brother scolds. "It's the first time you've been interested in a woman. It must be something."

If he only knew…

"It's definitely something," grumbles Milo, focused on his work.

"Milo," I warn him.

He shrugs and turns his back to us, a sign he won't say another word. My brother and Nabilla chuckle to themselves, heading into the kitchen with their kid to prepare a snack for us, determined to leave me in peace.

"You went too far," my friend says, his tone sharp.

"Another time, Milo."

"You weren't supposed to fuck her."

I swallow, feel my muscles tense up. "Don't tell me what I'm supposed to do or not."

He puts down the plank he was holding and turns to me, his accusatory gaze laden with frustration. "How am I supposed to face Galati knowing what you're doing to her best friend? When Alizee finds out the truth, this shit is going to blow up in my face! And damn it, I like this girl. It's serious, not like your inability to control your dick!"

When Alizee finds out the truth. Shit, it hurts deep down. She must not find out. If she does, I lose her, and that thought tortures me more than I could have imagined.

"Sorry, Milo."

"Instead of apologizing, do things right! Stop your bullshit, tell her you can't be together. Just do what you have to do and get the hell out of this building. And don't touch her! There are plenty of other girls hanging on your balls in this town, so don't destroy her!"

Don't destroy her.

***

I'm a piece of shit.

Unable to control myself, I gave in.

Fired up by the sight of those eager lips around my dick, I feel frustration creeping in.

She teases, tracing my veins with the tip of her tongue, knees on the ground, and a mischievous look in her eyes. As I lean against the front door, the floor doesn't seem to bother her. With each hesitant lick, I shiver, a fiery mass forming in my core. This creature is stunning, so submissive yet dominating my pleasure. Teeth sunk into my lower lip, I slide my hand into her silky hair and grip her locks. She lets out a faint moan.

How the fuck am I supposed to resist?

As a warning, she goes for my balls, first massaging them with extreme gentleness, then nibbling on them, enjoying my uncontrollable groans. This chick is driving me crazy.

"Do you like that?"

In response, my grip tightens on her hair.

Her lime-green eyes, wide, innocent, and filled with doubt, are locked onto mine.

"Don't be afraid, you can go for it."

If she only knew how much I'm holding back from shoving my dick down her throat and setting my own pace… But watching her take the initiative is even more arousing. *Don't destroy her.*

How do I avoid that?

For the past few days, I've been anxious at the thought of seeing her, trying to compartmentalize my life to keep her from invading my thoughts. How can I resist when she's teasing me with that pajama tee that barely covers her ass, her wheat-colored hair cascading over her shoulders, her coconut perfume, and those doe eyes? Shit, I'm only human! And a horny one at that. Abstinence has never been my thing.

As she swallows me whole, her name escapes me. It earns her a smirk, that naughty girl. Her back-and-forth movements, accompanied by her wet hands, send fucking shivers throughout my body. I've never felt anything like it. She moans, captures my pearl of arousal with the tip of her tongue in a captivatingly erotic way, circles around my tip, and eagerly licks my balls while never breaking her eyes contact.

Spasms shake my cock, and my breath quickens even more. If this novice keeps going, she's going to make me come. And I want it. Emptying myself into her throat becomes a necessity. "Suck me, Alizee," I beg.

She toys with me, putting me through agony with her tongue without obeying, a mocking look on her face. "You know, blow jobs are great," she relishes against my cock. "I love torturing you with pleasure."

This minx never stops! Too bad, she asked for it. I grab my dick and push it into her mouth to silence her. Her slender jaw widens. Trapped by my grip, she has no choice but to suck. Her eyebrows furrow as she realizes I'm proudly watching her.

"Yeah, I love it, too, kitten."

First thrust, extremely slow to avoid hurting her. It's so warm, so wet, rolling on her tongue propels me to cloud nine. Alizee clings to my thighs, her eyes wide open. God, she turns me on.

At the second thrust, I curse.

At the third, I whisper a compliment, echoing her languid moans. She's so beautiful.

She's the only one with whom I take certain liberties without pretense, without playing a role. I just have to strip down, in every sense of the word, to have a wild time.

There she goes, setting pace on my cock, shattering all my confidence with her feline eyes. And she keeps going. Assaulting me with sensations more intense than the last, digging her nails into my quadriceps, scraping her teeth along my cock, as if seeking revenge.

It's divine.

I don't let her go, keeping her at my mercy with this feeling of domination.

But I'm not dominating anything anymore.

Head thrown back, eyelids closed, I'm nothing more than a slave to her mouth, subjected to her desire. Because by bending before me, she was experiencing more than just submission. Knowing that she enjoys sucking me intensifies my pleasure, propelling me through the levels of heaven at dizzying speed.

I suddenly open my eyes, focusing them on her as she sucks me in, cheeks hollowed, returning a smile. A smile as devilish as her gaze.

Damn!

"I'm coming," I warn her.

Without letting go of me, her lips abandon the dance, to my great disappointment.

"Take it in your mouth, please, Alizee…" I know I sound terrible. But I want to come in her mouth; for once that damn condom doesn't hinder us.

When she closes her mouth around me fully, my sex swells suddenly, and it only takes a few movements for the explosion to occur in my gut. In several jets, I ejaculate my burning pleasure into her throat.

She swallows.

Everything.

Goes as far as to clean my hypersensitive cock, causing a few spasms.

Seventh heaven reached. Euphoric, I exhale ostentatiously. My heartbeat erratic, I feel her rising behind my closed eyelids.

"I can't believe it…" she murmurs.

"I know, it's huge," I retort, finally setting my gaze on her.

She widens her eyes, seemingly offended, in her sexy T-shirt. "No, but you're hopeless! I was talking about me!" she yells, hands on her hips.

My attention is all on her still-glistening lips. I want to melt into them, taste myself on her… "Yeah, I have to admit, you're not bad either." My voice is hoarse, shattered by her performance.

"I can't believe I gave you a blowjob in the hallway."

A half-smile stretches my lips.

Disheveled, she tries to regain her composure, readjusting the T-shirt that I'm dying to take off her to admire her adorable little tits. She acts shocked when it was she who intercepted me on the landing, just as I was coming back from my brother's place.

When she opened the door with her annoyed look, memories of the previous night flooded back to me. Her carmine lips, her tantalizing cleavage, her so-feminine heels… they scrambled my brain as they always do whenever she occupies my thoughts.

Pierced by guilt and determined to put some distance between us, I stopped without saying hello. While I don't know how she interpreted this long moment of eye contact, I didn't resist when she pulled me into her apartment.

Without kissing me, she pushed me against the door, knelt, and unbuttoned my jeans.

It was the first time she'd dared to venture into this territory. Panic initially engulfed me, but I quickly yielded to my instincts. I made sure she was convinced, not for too long, fearing she might change her mind. A blowjob by Alizee, damn, the ultimate pleasure.

Touched by her pouting expression, I pull her close, hugging her tightly, savoring her body against mine, sated. "Thanks, kitten. You suck even better than in your books."

Surprised, she giggles at my remark.

Tenderly, I add, "It was intense. I'm sorry I was so rough. Next time, handcuff me."

"Next time, I'll rip it off with my teeth. You seem to like that."

This woman is something else. I chuckle softly, slipping my hand under her T-shirt to caress her ass. I take pleasure in fondling her cheeks, venture under her panties to feel them better. Thinking about the insecurities they cause in her deeply annoys me. It hurts me. I could spend hours kissing them. Well, that's a lie. I can't resist the urge to spank them for too long.

Slowly, she pulls back into her apartment, closes the door, and draws me onto the couch. Despite her blowjob, our intertwined fingers ignite me. She looks like an angel, with her tousled blond halo all around her doll-like face. A diabolical angel.

Remorse consumes me, yet I smile at her, blissful, floating on cloud nine before slumping into the cushions. I'll have to take care of her; I can't let her sin go unpunished.

Never mind if she gets more attached.

Never mind if I get more attached.

I abruptly lay her down on the seat, eliciting a gasp of surprise from her, then seize her ankle to place a few kisses on it.

"Mm, Ervin… are you trying to return the favor?"

I nibble, insatiable, giving her a half-enigmatic smile under my piercing gaze.

She giggles falsely, hand in front of her mouth with her precious little air. "I don't think you can top my performance. You should have seen your face."

I close my eyelids, cursing myself for rubbing off on her. Poor lost bunny that I've contaminated.

"Wanna bet?" I growl, attacking her calves.

A shiver runs through her; the warnings in my head screaming louder and louder.

Her languid body enchants me. I could stare at her for hours, listen to her talk, with her wit and her ability to make me laugh. I learn all about her life and quench my thirst for her passion, to explain mine to her.

I could.

I don't.

I can't.

So I fuck her.

Our arrangement is clear, the boundary must not to be crossed.

I remain terrified by her eyes, which are laden with emotion, as they mirror the way of touching her, making love to her, my constant need for our contact.

My mouth against the inside of her thighs, I slide my hand under her T-shirt to grab her breast. No bra. My cock twitches, on the verge of waking up.

"It feels so good—why do you have to be such an asshole sometimes."

I pause, not entirely sure I heard her correctly.

She shakes her head as if to chastise herself.

"What did you say?" Am I dreaming or did she seriously just call me an asshole with her breast in my palm?

When she looks at me again, I feel trapped.

"Never mind, keep going."

"What do you mean by that?"

"That you run away at the worst moments, when being there for me doesn't commit you to anything."

It's a heart-wrenching blow. Like a dagger so sharp I didn't even feel it penetrate me. Indeed, I could have sent her a message, if I couldn't see her. Check up on her, support her like a friend would. I bolted, scared by the kiss we exchanged. Seeing her break down during of the revelations about her father knocked me out; I didn't realize I was so easy to reach. I've never felt such empathy for any woman before. It's so surprising that I wonder if it's just that.

This woman—she's something else, and I'm not talking about her looks. I don't think I've ever met anyone like her. This attraction drives me crazy. What she emanates beneath that already fragmented shell of insecurities touches me deep in my heart.

In an inexplicable way.

I should confirm her doubts and hook up with other chicks to restore the balance between my brain and my cock, but I can't. For an inexplicable reason. It sucks royally!

"I'm sorry, Alizee," I say, leaning against the inside of her thigh. "I told you I was swamped."

She sits up on her elbows, pushes me out from between her legs, and directs her raw resentment toward me.

And in that moment, ridden by my fears, I act like an asshole…

"It's not my role to heal your wounds," I say. "Unless our physical contact serves as a bandage, I'm not obligated to support you in the bad times."

CHAPTER 25

I stare at him, shocked by his words.

Unable to hear to any more of this nonsense, I jump up, straighten my clothes.

Upset by his behavior this week, I had undertaken to lead him into ecstasy to loosen his tongue. Well, I'll be damned! He's babbling cliché bullshit.

"It's not your role? Then never dare to meddle with my affairs again! What happened yesterday must not happen again! Under any circumstances!" I storm, pointing my finger in his direction.

Startled like a deer caught in the headlights of a truck, Ervin seems cornered. His cheek twitches, his fingers tense like claws ready to strike. Oh, I can already see him fleeing! But not before I've had my say!

"If it was just attraction, who I bring back to my apartment wouldn't have bothered you. You wouldn't have distanced yourself like you did either! Our relationship wouldn't have changed. I would have remained the annoying neighbor you occasionally fuck. One among many. We would have kept on pissing each other off, and you wouldn't have had these bursts of tenderness, those fiery looks. Who do you think you're fooling?"

He rises to his feet as well, imperious, dominates me with an angry expression and articulates so slowly and confidently, "I. Have. Always. Told. You. There. Would. Be. Nothing. More. Between. Us. Those fantasies you create, put them down on paper instead of spitting them in my face."

I know cruelty used as a shield when I see it. If he thinks he'll get to me this way, he's kidding himself! "I don't know what you're after with me, Ervin, but just sex isn't enough for you! I'm not stupid!"

He closes the distance between us even farther, fists clenched.

I've just gone all-in. Either he admits what I'm saying, or he confesses the real reason for his behavior to refute my allegations.

"You're pretty presumptuous for someone full of insecurities. Why would you interest me so much?"

Cruelty as a shield, huh… Fuck! There are limits to this! With tears in my eyes, I cross my arms. "Insecurities? I have such an effect on you that I don't have many insecurities left, you see!"

His breathing intensifies. I sense a real battle raging in the depths of his eyes. Trembling, I fear the outcome. Cruelty might prevail and crush me. Let it come. I'll cry, but I'll get my revenge!

"You asked for it…"

His reaction catches me off guard. His frustration still palpable, he takes a step back and shakes his head slowly to—once again—flee from what's happening between us.

***

I've had enough with this guy! On the phone, Galati urges me to let go. Well, she hasn't thought much of him for a long time, but she's right. As she recommends in her books, I should clean my mind, redecorate in Feng Shui mode, and eat soybeans to eradicate the Ervinian parasites from my system. I think I understand the mechanism: inflict this suffering to forget the one in the heart.

Well, I guess pizza works just as well, actually…

I work hard on my computer, pour out my hatred in the form of pretty, caustic, and scathing sentences, defining love as a great source of trouble.

Around one in the morning, Vampyr decides it's enough. My cat climbs onto my lap and emits sounds worthy of a Stephen King novel.

"Hey, you. You better not shit on my thighs," I warn him. "Diarrhea's good once, not twice. Otherwise, no pizza for you!"

He turns his back on me, tail held high with a perfect view of his animal anatomy. I lower his tail, irritated, prompting a growl and a proper claw planting in the fat through my pajamas.

"Ouch! Come on, shoo! You dirty cat!"

I get up as my cat rushes toward the wall separating the two apartments on the landing and starts scratching the baseboard.

"Missing Otto?" I grumble as I drag my feet in his direction.

Just as I bend down to grab him, voices faintly echo. I stop everything and concentrate, alert for any additional sound in front of Vampyr's curious snout.

Ervin is busy chatting… with a woman!

Wide-eyed, I feel like my heart is trying to dismantle my ribcage. Nausea creeps over me as I straighten up, beside myself. With clenched teeth, I think back to his last words. *You asked for it.*

Damn it.

I hadn't dreamed it; cruelty had indeed won out.

I don't know what he's trying to make me understand, but he's going way too far. He can't claim to not see others while pretending it means nothing, then throw it in my face.

I see red! My guts twist with pain. Unable to follow my best friend's advice, I rush onto the landing and repeatedly ring his doorbell.

He pushes the vice to the limit: it's his stunning evening partner who opens the door, all smiles.

I stare at her, speechless, her perfect appearance hitting me square in the face. A magnificent blond mane cascades down to her hips, which must reach my waist because she's so tall. Her porcelain skin betrays no flaw, her face is to die for, and her figure, under a burgundy satin nightie, would arouse even a gay man.

I must look ridiculous in my fluffy pajamas and hair barely reaching my shoulders.

"Good evening. Are we disturbing you? Are we making too much noise?"

The nerve! The lady has a charming Eastern accent.

I boil inside. He's probably standing behind the door. I'm a writer, for god's sake. He shouldn't take me for an idiot!

"Fine… you can tell Ervin that he knocked me out. I give up, he can sleep with you if he wants, but he won't lay a finger on me!"

As she doesn't seem to be getting it, I hope my voice carries inside. With my guts in a knot, I turn and head back to my cave, tears welling in my eyes.

Curled up on my bed, I close my eyes, imagine what he's doing in the next room, and let myself go, tears streaming down my cheeks. My mother was right—this kind of man doesn't change. His first weapon of war: women. What did she feel when my father cheated on her?

Vampyr notices my spasms. He snuggles up against me, licks my face, but it's no use. I can't stop my sobs.

I knew it—this relationship would destroy me. From the beginning, I knew I was diving into a pit strewn with sharp spikes.

I crash into it. Feel the blood slowly draining from my body. And it hurts so much.

I had hoped—because I'm convinced actions, attitudes don't lie. He feels something more unique for me. Something he apparently doesn't control. I had so much trouble considering it at first that now, having realized it, I won't give up on it.

And that bastard has no qualms about fucking another right in front of me just to push me away. To hurt me. To gut me.

CHAPTER 26

Three days of brooding, feeling bruised from within.

Three days of trying to put things into perspective.

Three days without success.

I'm boiling with anger, to the point where Vampyr has run off. Oh, he'll come back; he's used to it with my periods.

Tonight is Alix's birthday, and I'm cordially invited. Wisdom has told me to ignore Ervin, but I can't. If I were the virtuous type, I'd know it. I want to confront us—Mister Big-Asshole and me.

I know it's pointless and childish, but I can't help it. So, I put on my high heels, a little black dress recently bought for a very specific purpose, and paint my lips red. Hair down, of course, I line my eyes with deep kohl, ready for battle.

While I had planned to encounter Ervin at the restaurant, I didn't expect to run into him at the entrance. When he sees me in my chic coat, his eyebrows furrow immediately.

"What are you doing here?" he reprimands me, planting his furious gaze into my eyes.

"I got the invitation on Facebook," I reply, shrugging casually. "Were we supposed to avoid each other?"

He glances at the doorway, revealing his masculine and tense profile. His three-day-old beard eats into his cheeks, his hair neatly slicked back, and he's particularly well dressed, with his dark jeans, parka open over a navy-blue shirt.

He sighs, rolling his eyes, then pushes the door open, inviting me to go ahead. "You're right. After you."

Fuming with rage, I return a sweet smile that he probably doesn't understand much and walk into the restaurant, head held high.

Alix, Lionel, Milo, Gala, and about ten other friends are already there. The remaining seats for Ervin and me are on the opposite side of the table. He has a fantastic view of my plunging neckline.

Well, yes, I noticed that despite my tiny breasts, he appreciated anything plunging. So, naturally, I went all out. For Alix's pleasure, since he couldn't stop eyeing me under the murderous eye of my asshole fuck buddy.

When it is time to move on to a more festive place, I announce I have other plans. At the entrance, as everyone decides on the best mode of transportation, I walk away toward the corner of the street.

He looks at me.

Without seeing him, I feel him. So strongly that his eyes could bore holes in my back.

Once Marshall's sports coupe appears on the perpendicular street, I rejoice. As he steps out of his car to open the door for me, I place my hand on his arm, stare at him with a determined look, and murmur, "Do you mind helping me make him jealous?"

He understands immediately. A playful gleam crosses his eyes. He notices the crowd behind me as a half-smile stretches his lips. "Anything you want," he replies, already caressing my shoulder.

I moisten my lips, urging him to kiss me in a sultry whisper.

Naturally, he freaks out. Well, he didn't expect that the little woman with insecurities could be so direct. But now she's wearing bright red lipstick and talking about herself in the third person. So a kiss, huh…

His fingers weave their way into my hair, cradles my head before pressing his mouth to mine. My heart undergoes a shock, I close my eyelids, try to imagine Ervin's face as Marshall's tongue enters between my teeth. Startled, I widen my eyes, emit a moan that makes him pull back.

Quickly, he winks at me, crosses in front of the bumper, and settles behind the wheel. I get into the car, slam the door, and turn around. As soon as we drive away, Ervin rushes toward us, his face flushed with rage, barely held back by his alarmed friends.

It's once we turn into a small alley that my heart dances. He was furious!

It's impossible to suppress the smile on my face. A bitter smile, for sure, but I needed to externalize my pain. Gratuitous cruelty can't go unpunished.

Vengeance accomplished!

CHAPTER 27

I was afraid I had gone too far. Asking my friend and editor to kiss me was not the greatest revenge plan. I realized that after receiving a billion messages from Galati. I didn't know I could be so vindictive, to be honest. Fortunately, Marshall didn't mind. I think that after the other jerk's behavior in the hallway, he enjoyed making him mad. A guy thing, I guess…

At two in the morning, I head home. Alone this time—and slightly tipsy—despite Marshall's insistence on walking me home. Of course, tonight had to be the night the stairwell light went out! With blisters all over my feet, I fumble my way up four floors, reluctant to remove my shoes, given the suspicious stains on the marble. And, *naturally*, I stumble on the last step, landing flat on the ground in front of Ervin, who's sitting against my door.

"Fuck! What the hell are you doing here? You scared the shit out of me!" I grumble on all fours, my knees throbbing. I barely lift my head, feeling oppressed by the darkness in his gaze.

Oh no! There's no way he's doing this to me again! I straighten, stand before him, and glare back, scrutinized by his glassy eyes. He reeks of hatred and alcohol.

"You can't react like this," I scold, fists on hips.

He runs his hand through his hair, clenches and unclenches his jaw before spitting out, "I didn't sleep with her."

Well, isn't that a surprise!

"Move aside," I retort, trying to step over him to get back home.

His icy fingers suddenly close around my ankle, making my heart leap behind my ribs. "Wait."

"Don't mess with me, Ervin, I don't need this."

His grip is so tight it becomes painful. "I'm sorry, Alizee. I was a jerk." *No kidding!* "But in my head—it's a mess."

"To subject me to your fits of jealousy and then fuck another chick, I can believe that, yes. Get out of my way, please."

In his state of nerves, I feel like he won't obey. Annoyed, I take the keys out of my bag, surprised to find my hands trembling.

"I freaked out, okay? You're imprinted in my head. You're right, it's more than just a hookup. But it can't happen! I tried to break this connection by sleeping with another girl, yet I couldn't even get a hard-on."

"Am I supposed to believe you?"

"Why would I lie to you? If I had fucked her, I wouldn't have been so messed up. I would have bragged about it like the biggest jerk."

"But you kissed her," I say coldly.

"And you kissed the other fucker. We're even."

"Go back home."

"I can't get you out of my head. I don't want to leave you in anyone else's hands."

A shiver runs through me. His fingers slowly trace up my calf, electrifying me completely. *Stay strong, Alizee! Don't let yourself be charmed by this seducer!*

My shoulders slump in a sigh. "What's your problem with commitment?"

I drop that bombshell, obliterating the part where I don't want a real relationship. Which, in essence, raises a serious question.

He finally lifts his face toward me. Tries to maintain eye contact. Quickly flees to the crimson of my still intact lips. "Let me in."

Stunned, I let out a nervous laugh that echoes in the darkness of the stairwell.

"I'll explain."

Well... Explanations are like our pancakes deal. Since they're key, I surrender.

We enter my home and I offer him nothing. Invite him to sit on the couch without even undressing, and stand facing him, straight as an arrow.

"Aren't you going to sit down? I feel like I'm being judged," he says, tapping the seat next to him.

"No, I'll stay in a position of strength."

He raises an eyebrow, a weary smile on lips that have fucking drooled over the Eastern European model's mouth. I feel nauseous.

"At least take off your coat, this will take a while."

I shake my head, arms crossed.

He inhales deeply, holds for a few seconds, exhales slowly before starting. "I'm married."

My jaw drops on its own.

"And I have a child."

My eyes almost pop out of their sockets.

"Well, it's more complicated than that… I was married."

The blood rushes through my veins like burning magma, a bunch of movies playing in my brain, making me dizzy.

I stagger to the sofa and finally sit down.

"*Are* you or *were* you married, Ervin?" I demand, my voice growling.

His brow furrow. With his elbows on his thighs and his hands intertwined, he seems hesitant to continue. "I was. I spent two years in Albania with my wife."

I remember seeing the Albanian pictures on his Instagram account. I never saw a wife there. After all, Ervin posts a lot of photos related to himself or his passion, but I know very little about his life. He never mentioned his family, although I discovered he has strong ties with them. He barely talks about it to me, either.

"Go on," I squeak, frightened by the hypothetical continuation of the story.

He pinches the bridge of his nose then stands up so abruptly that he stumbles. "I can't do this, damn it!"

As he heads toward the front door, I leap up and grab his arm, on edge. "No! You're not backing out! I want to know everything!"

He gives me a look burning with profond distress.

"What are you afraid of, Ervin?" What a good joke. I'm not sure which of us is more scared.

"Of hurting you," he mutters through clenched teeth.

"It's a bit late for that, don't you think?"

Heavy seconds weigh down on us with their silence.

He lowers his eyelids, clenches his fists, and, without sitting back down, spills out his story in one go, his voice chillingly flat. "I got her into my passion. I introduced her to motorcycling, and when our kid was just a few months old, she wanted to get back on the bike. Then… no… an accident… She had an accident," he states, frowning. "Fatal."

Oh, god.

When I reach out to his forearm for support, he recoils in a gesture of repulsion.

"She was the only daughter among five brothers, all crazier than the next. As soon as they found out my wife wouldn't wake up from the coma she was in, they made my life hell. Then they kicked me out of their country, threating me with a knife to my throat."

"Good lord, I'm so sorry… my deepest condolences for your loss. And your child?" I exclaim, horrified.

"They won't let me see him. One of them swore he'd shoot me if he found me. I first fled to Indonesia, then came back to France, to be with my family."

Shocked, I reel from his revelation, hand covering my mouth. It was an accident; how could someone be so cruel to a father?

"Is it… out of love for her that you won't commit? Do you still love her? Are you planning to go back and get your child?"

He squeezes his eyelids shut and shakes his head vigorously. "It's… a real mess in my head. I've mourned, but the guilt eats me up. So does the fear. If those lunatics find out I've moved on, there's a good chance they'll take it out on my partner."

Dumbfounded, I can't stop the tingling on my skin. Suddenly, Ervin takes on a very different identity in my eyes. A father… This first-rate womanizer is a dad, and he's been deprived of his child. There's a heavy tragedy hidden behind this nonchalance, and I was completely oblivious.

Damn, what possessed him to fall for a woman from a family of butchers? She must have been really nice…

"I don't want anything to happen to you. That's why it's better if we keep our distance," he finishes, already rushing toward the door.

"Ervin, wait!"

Hand on the doorknob, he turns in my direction, a grimace twisting his face. "I'm sorry, Alizee. This whole story is frying my brain, it's making me stupid. I don't know where I stand anymore."

The sensation that my ribs are being crushed. I want to insist that he stay. To press him for more details.

But paralyzed by my fear, I let him cross the threshold of the entrance. Leaving me to this whirlwind of bewildering information. Disrupted by this newfound truth.

CHAPTER 28

Ervin has a child.

Ervin's wife died.

His in-laws want to kill him.

All of this, thousands of miles away.

That's the reason why he's pushing me away.

Un-believable.

"You think he's telling the truth?"

On the phone, Gala takes a few seconds before giving me an honest answer. "It's true that it's big… At the same time, Milo's behavior might make sense now."

"I don't know. Why would this matter so much to him?"

"Because he has no secrets from me, and this one is a big deal. And you're my best friend."

Indeed… Goodness, if that's the case, I hope at least now her boyfriend will be less distant. But this story… sounds crazy to me. That said, it's Ervin we're talking about, the adrenaline junkie, passionate about travel and discovery, who has no fear. The tattoo on his back speaks to that.

"What are you going to do?" she interrupts my thoughts.

In front of the mirror in my bathroom, I hesitate. My eyeliner is thicker than usual, my cheeks tinged with a light peach, and my lips glossy.

"I don't know. This story has been weighing on me for two days.

I've been turning it over in my mind, looking for a solution, but I have too little information. I'd like to help him, one way or another. If it's true, the poor guy can't even contact his kid."

The kid will become an orphan even though he has a father—it's inconceivable! How can they behave like this?

"Aren't you scared? You only have his side of the story. Who knows, maybe he did something worse."

"His wife died. What could be worse?"

Behind the first-class arrogance he likes to show off, there's someone deeply human hiding, I'm convinced of it. His reactions to his weaknesses are childish, and they hurt, but deep down, Ervin is kind. I don't believe he's done anything so reprehensible that they should take away his child. And I understand their anger, as long as it only lasts for a while.

"I'll dig around. Milo must know the truth. They've been childhood friends."

"Pff… It's been two days, and I miss him so much… And no, assuming it's true, it doesn't scare me. On the contrary, it inspires me."

"Oh!" she exclaims, intrigued.

I step back and examine my new jeans—embarrassingly tight. The fact I could actually buy a pair like this is credit to my neighbor. He would love it.

Did I do the right thing?

"Why don't you use it for your manuscript?" the blonde interjects. "It's exactly the story you've been missing!"

"I couldn't help it, and in my despair, my fingers flew to the keyboard. I had to let it out or I was going crazy. But I'm hesitating to delete everything… It doesn't feel right."

"Of course it does! We all draw inspiration for our surroundings. Your hero is inspired by Ervin. Just take a few elements, transform them, and who knows? Maybe it'll help you sort things out in your head about this story."

That's worth considering. After all, this drama effectively nourishes and enriches my romance.

"I need to let things settle."

Nothing settles at all; my need to see him swarms through

my entire being. My desire to feel him against me, to hear his voice whispering near to my ear, kills me. The longing for our passionate lovemaking ignites my insides.

A glance at the clock forces me to interrupt our discussion. Feverish and angry, I pull my hair up into a loose bun, adjust my sweater, and send a message to Marshall:

[Alizee: I'm on my way out. See you in thirty minutes at our spot.]

I put on my coat without closing it, wrap myself in my scarf, and slip into my boots before grabbing my keys.

On the landing, I stop dead in my tracks. I can't help but glance toward Ervin's door. Since he deserted my apartment, I haven't heard anyone compliment his elephant trunk. A few noises from inside kept me on alert, so I know he's at home this late afternoon.

I lean over the railing, hands gripping the rail. The spiral staircase across the four floors forms a dizzying geometric spiral. Do I want to go downstairs? I can't stop thinking about what's going on upstairs.

A tumultuous battle rages in my mind, my skin constantly tingling. An impulse drives me to pound on *his* apartment door.

"Ervin, open up! I know you're in there! I won't leave."

After ten endless minutes, the door cracks open.

The least we can say is that he doesn't look very good. His hair is uncombed, his beard has grown out again, and above his bare feet, he's dressed only in his sweatpants and an oversized old top. The sad look he gives me tightens my throat. Poor guy really looks like shit.

"I don't care," I start.

He frowns imperceptibly, a sign that he doesn't understand. I push the door, trying to make him step back, but his body continues to resist.

"I don't care, Ervin."

My hands cling to his T-shirt, to the massive chest I've missed so much.

"I'm ready to take all the risks for the relationship we have. I don't care if it doesn't lead anywhere. If you stop yourself from living because of fear over some hypothetical danger, you'll never do anything again."

He shakes his head, even more shriveled than when he opened up to me.

"I remember, you warned me in Malaga. You were afraid I'd find out something about you, thinking I'd hate you. Whether it's this unbelievable story or something else, I don't care. I don't hate you."

He takes hold of my hands to detach them from his T-shirt. "It's because I hid it from you that you should hate me. I deceived you."

I don't care. I don't care. I don't care. I just want to hold him in my arms. "I know. I know you weren't honest. It's okay, I understand the reason. It's not the kind of confession you can drop on someone the first time you meet."

"Aren't you scared, damn it?" he exclaims, sounding irritated.

I shake my head vigorously. Of course, I'm not completely at ease, but my fear is less than that of losing him completely. "No, I'm not."

"I might disappear without warning. I might have to go back or even run far away from here. And you can't be part of the equation. I have things to take care of; I can't leave things as they are, and what I feel for you won't change that."

I gulp down those dreadful thoughts. Of course. He has a kid to retrieve. And there's nothing I can do about it.

"And what do you feel for me?" I ask.

With his jaws clenched, he stares at me with slightly widened eyes, in disturbing silence.

Come on, big boy, spill the beans! I know you're not madly in love, but tell me you feel something, anything!

He grabs the door handle, about to close it on me, when I push him back abruptly. He barely stumbles, far too strong for my feeble hands.

"Be stronger than this, damn it!"

This time, he slams the door behind me, shaking the walls around us. Then, without restraint, he roars at me, "It's not about strength! You can't imagine what it all entails. You don't want to be around the man I am, I assure you! I don't want you to suffer!"

"I don't care about suffering!" I shout back, as determined as him.

A deep anguish now fills his dark eyes. I pound on his chest with my palms, emphasizing my discontent.

Then, I grab his collar and pull him toward my mouth.

He crashes into it without resistance, plunging his large and warm hands between the folds of my coat to pull me close. Our kiss takes only a few seconds to ignite. Like an explosion, it takes possession of our two beings, spreading this wave of sensations without warning. I feel dizzy, accepting his curse without flinching.

My coat falls to the ground. Ervin's fingers are on my face, my waist, my butt. "I swear, you're making a big mistake," he says before devouring my lips.

"I don't care. Take me. Now."

His limbs tense. Before he can pull away, I remove his ugly T-shirt and kiss his burning skin. He sighs, slowly giving in.

"Shit, shit, shit, shit… It's when you do this to me that I lack strength," he exhales in a groan. "I should push you away."

Suddenly, my phone rings in the back pocket of my jeans. No way I'm letting Mister Freak Out escape. I seize his mouth again, but it seems someone is determined to reach me.

When I grab my phone, Ervin recoils with a repulsion that alarms me.

"Shit, it's Marshall," I mutter as I see the caller ID.

Staring at my screen, I remain motionless, unable to pick up. Giving up my fight to make the man of my desire surrender is inconceivable. On the other hand, my friend has probably arrived at our meeting place. Standing him up wouldn't be right.

Ervin's shadow envelops me. His face above mine, he reads the name on my cell phone.

"We had an appointment. Initially, I was going out to see him, but I'm really late now," I mumble, resigned.

Suddenly, he snatches my phone out of my hand, throws it on my coat on the floor, and steals a violent kiss from me. His newfound fervor surprises me, especially when he leads me into his bedroom. He lays me on the bed, carefully, devouring every part of my anatomy.

He resents me.

He desires me.

He's angry with me.

He forgot the condom.

In our trance, I neglect to remind him. The urgency prevents me from doing so.

When he releases himself inside me and collapses against my exhilarated body, I realize that today, he didn't just fuck me. He made love to me with devastating passion.

CHAPTER 29

In early February, my spirits are soaring. As predicted, sales of my book are skyrocketing. Elie Roy is being hailed as a revelation in the thriller genre. Marshall is over the moon, and Ervin keeps sending me photos of my book on the bestseller shelves in bookstores.

Thanks to my neighbor, I'm living on cloud nine. Sure, he refuses to put a label on our relationship, and we both we know it could fall apart any day, but between us, it's volcanic. It's intense. It's tender. This man drives me crazy. And unlike previous weeks, we're communicating.

Tonight, Milo, Gala, Lionel, and Alix are invited to his apartment. I've done some shopping, prepared some zakouski—chips in bowls and mini frozen pizzas; that's my specialty—and welcomed the guests.

Once again, Monsieur Great Lay's best friend gives me a sideways glance. He' better stop that!

As we lounge on the couches, watching a replay of motorcycle races, the jokes are flowing. I'm nestled against Ervin's chest, happily sipping on my beer when he snatches it from my hand.

"Easy there, kitten, I've lost count of how many bottles you've already emptied."

Oh, he's so thoughtful! I love it! I can't help myself; I lean in and give him a sloppy kiss on the cheek.

"Please!" Alix pretends to gag.

"But he's just too nice!" I defend myself loudly.

The man I'm secretly in love with muffles me with his large hand, the one that knows so well how to give me pleasure.

"Okay, we get it," he says.

I feel the urge to lick his fingers.

Suddenly, I'm feeling incredibly aroused. Despite the need for a break among friends after indulging in a thousand delights, I can't seem to control my hormones.

Ervin gets up to get me a glass of water. This absent-minded guy has left his cell phone on the couch. Well… this is my chance.

I grab it, entering the code I spied over his shoulder, and start snooping through his texts.

A whistle to my right catches my attention. Galati gives me a stern look. I squint, unsure if I understand. Then I notice Ervin's friends staring at me with either surprise or disapproval.

Oops! I forgot they were there.

Very, very slowly, as if it masks my crime, I place the phone back where it was. I feel ashamed, overcome by a slight dizziness.

Of course, they can't know the doubts that are eating away at me. My lover is always glued to his phone. And it's not about posting his photos on Instagram; he seems to anxiously await certain calls. Whenever I mention the story about his child and his crazy in-law family in Albania, Ervin becomes irritable. I can forget about getting answers from him. And forget about assessing its truthfulness, too. That's why I snoop around whenever and wherever I can, in search of the truth.

It's ugly, I know. But it's not just curiosity; anxiety is my main driving force. He could leave from one day to the next, and I refuse to be caught off guard.

As he returns to place his sublime ass by my side, Milo is staring at us oddly.

"What's wrong with him?" I ask Ervin too loudly.

Him has certainly heard me, but without getting upset, Milo continues, "So, Ervin, when are you moving?"

What?

Silence fills the room, accompanied by the annoying hum of the TV.

"You're moving?" Lionel inquires.

I stare at Ervin, my hands starting to tremble. He frowns, glaring at the Italian. Gala's boyfriend remains unperturbed, confident in his demeanor.

The arm around my shoulders tightens. My stomach churns. No one ever mentioned any moving!

"I have no idea, Milo. It's not in my plans, right now," Ervin responds.

Can he feel my heart racing? Can they see my face go pale? Second after second, the shock sobers me up.

His body shifts slightly, and from his expression, I sense his simmering anger. Holy crap! I should be the one who's most upset. Especially since he doesn't even glance at me once.

"Are you planning to fly abroad, or are you staying in Paris?" Alix adds, just as disappointed as I am, but accustomed to his friend's travels.

Uncomfortable, Ervin holds me tighter against him. I need some air.

"I'm not planning on going anywhere, I'm telling you!"

Apparently, they're not aware of his story like Milo is. So, it's true… Would he move constantly to cover his tracks? Or is it part of his plan to find his child?

"I guess you like the apartment." Alix chuckles, referring to our proximity.

"Indeed, I do," Ervin retorts. "I've grown attached to it," he adds, planting a kiss to my temple.

Milo sighs, shaking his head. Does he think it's not reasonable? Am I a danger to his friend?

Between guilt and reassurance, I snuggle against my lover's side. Yet, I'm still trembling.

I tremble as they change the subject. As they laugh, my Adonis remains tense. As they get drunk, no one notices my turmoil, except Galati.

Past midnight.

I busy myself cleaning up the remnants of this strange evening. The silence is charged. Ervin seems to be avoiding me. For him, too, Milo's casual mention wasn't insignificant.

When the apartment is tidy, I notice that practically nothing has changed since the beginning. The decor and furnishings are minimalist. No personal effects lay around. Some of his belongings are still in boxes.

Four months he's been living here. Four months, and he's never really moved in.

My heart tightens. He gives me the impression of a frightened animal, ready to bolt at the slightest anomaly.

Leaning against the doorframe of his room, I tell him my theory about his not planting roots while he puts on a casual outfit.

"Did I hit it right?" I ask coldly, indicating I won't move until he tells me the truth.

With his dark eyes, he nods, irritation evident. "I warned you."

"I know you did."

I haven't forgotten. Our relationship has evolved so much, only I imagined he'd have less trouble talking to me about it.

"One day, I'll have to leave. Regardless of the reason, I won't be here anymore. You need to prepare yourself for that," he says in a hoarse whisper, standing before me, chin held high, covering me with an incandescent gaze.

Feeling tiny against his massive frame, I'm overcome with a sense of injustice. Though he might seek to intimidate me into silence, my distress prevails.

"Don't make that face. Who cares, let's live in the moment! You think I won't survive the absence of your amazing cock? At worst, my suffering will fuel my inspiration. I'll dedicate my future bestseller to you, and my pockets will be full."

My declaration manages to soften his features. A faint smile plays on his delicious mouth, while a wave of tenderness extinguishes the bitterness in his eyes.

I raise my eyebrows twice, proud of my comeback, even though deep down, I know his moving would shatter me.

CHAPTER 30

"I love those jeans. They make your ass look great."

In front of the mirror, I accept Ervin's compliment with a joy that's hard to contain. Nothing adorns me but a slim, high-waisted pair of pants. Underneath my usual messy bun, my breasts are exposed, fully displayed.

Behind me, Ervin gazes at me in the mirror, lying on my bed in perfect nudity. The afternoon light casting on the puzzle of his body makes him devilishly appetizing. I'd give up my frozen pizzas for that!

"You shouldn't wear a bra; your tits hold up on their own."

Sometimes, the relevance of his remarks bewilders me. "Thanks, I guess. It's what you call having small boobs," I retort, sarcastically.

"It would turn me on to see your little nipples pointing through your sweaters."

"Points for me, baby," I tease in a husky voice.

He laughs as I place my hands on my nipples, massaging my breasts languidly, igniting a new flame in the deep darkness of his eyes.

"You're perfect."

Seeing my skeptical expression, he adds, "You have a Kim Kardashian silhouette with boobs that defy gravity."

"Yeah, right. I'm more of a blond woman who stuffs herself with pizzas." I chuckle, my cheeks turning pink.

"If you say so… You're my very special blonde, though," he replies with a wink.

I wish this moment would never end. I want to keep reading that desire in his eyes indefinitely, linger in this room, and make love until we're both satiated.

Suddenly, my phone starts ringing. I hastily slip on a purple, fine-knit top and pick it up. Fuck, it's my editor.

"Hey, Alan," I answer, grimacing at my lover, whose cock lazily peeks out from under the sheets.

Can't he get enough? We've just had sex like rabbits, and I'm tired of this relentless arousal. Damn it! Damn libido!

"I'm in a great mood, so watch out," I warn Alan, smiling, as I sit on the edge of the bed.

Ervin wraps his muscular arm around my waist, radiating warmth against my back.

"No, I still haven't made any progress on my manuscript," I snap back in response to his aggressive tone.

The fingers of the best fuck in the universe—I can attest to that, despite my limited comparison—wander against my neck, soothing my budding tensions.

I'm lying to Alan. My conviction that Ludivine will take better care of my story has significantly strengthened in recent weeks. My novel is ready, printed on my desk, and I fully intend to hand over the rights to her.

After a heated and sadly familiar conversation, I hang up with a tired sigh.

"Seem tense between you two," comments the handsome dark-haired man, peppering my neck with wet kisses.

I flutter my eyelids, savoring the sensations for a brief moment. "I can't stand him anymore. Everything about him screams profit. Maybe that mattered to me once. I'm not like that now and I want… more than a fat check."

Ervin's hot palm on my stomach comforts me. How could I have lived all these years with the certainty of giving up on relationships? How can I do without his touches, his caresses, his kisses now? They're a bandage to each of my frustrations, erasing them with ruthless efficiency.

"You must be almost done now. Send him your novel and agree to the bare minimum. He wants you at all costs, no need to kiss his ass for him to take care of your text."

I don't kiss anyone's ass. It's not my philosophy. And I still haven't confessed to Ervin that I've finished my manuscript. Drawing inspiration from his problems, the ones he's so reluctant to mention, is a serious block.

Hey, you know what? I plagiarized your life. You can find it in The Misfortune of Ervin, *the walking sex toy, his wife six feet under, and their kid held hostage by a crazy family. A wild comedy sprinkled with steamy sex scenes!*

My shoulders slump.

"Alizee?"

"There's… something I have to tell you…"

How do you announce something like this? It's like with breakups, there's no right way. Maybe I could send him a text, yeah! That's it, a text. Except if he decides to bail on a whim, I won't be able to stop him. Goddamn it, he'll hate me!

"Are you too sore to go another round right away? I get it, you know, I fucked you so hard, kitten."

Eyes rolling to the ceiling, I shake my head, take a deep breath before pulling the pin on my grenade, and once again, my cell phone jumps on the sheets.

Our attention simultaneously turns to the screen displaying the name of my thriller editor. Anticipating Ervin's reaction, I'm faster, grabbing the device and leaping out of bed to answer.

My sex machine glares back at me. If I can't stand Alan, he can't stand Marshall.

While I chat cheerfully with the man who restores my good mood, Ervin gets up and demands I hang up. I jump up to escape him, refusing to submit to his little jealousy fit. I explained to him perfectly well that our kiss was staged, meant to make him jealous. Marshall and I never crossed the boundaries of friendship. But he's so stubborn. He storms off to another room to show his disagreement, with a face darkened and his dick hanging out.

I ignore it and continue my conversation, agreeing to a decisive dinner with Ludivine and him, later tonight. Today, I'll be giving her my manuscript along with my publishing contract. Signed.

Since the moment of truth is imminent, I'll have to remember to call the other crook to let him know I'm bailing. Tense moment... very tense. Did I mention my love of ostriches and their politics?

Once the call is over, I join my fuck buddy in the living room. Bewildered, I freeze as soon as I see him standing behind my desk, pouring over my papers, his face drawn.

"Hey, you're not ashamed to snoop through my stuff?" I stamp my foot, a ball of anxiety forming in the pit of my stomach.

In response, he gives me a murderous stare.

I swallow hard. Almost stagger when I realize he's found out. And he's not happy about it at all.

"Care to explain?" he growls, waving a few pages of my manuscript in the air.

Damn it, Ervin's unexpected visit prevented me from hiding it away. Meaning anywhere other than prominently displayed on my desk.

"I... I..." I stutter like an idiot.

Fuck! Where do I start?

"*The Romance of My Life*? You finished it."

His reproachful tone makes me shrink into myself. Naked as he is, his angry face nullifies any comedic dimension of the scene.

"I... I was planning to tell you, I swear... but..."

The silence stretches, increasing my embarrassment. *But* what? *You didn't have the courage, you little timid thing!*

"I was afraid you'd be angry! The situation is complicated enough as it is, and I didn't want to give you another reason to push me away. For what it's worth, I changed a bunch of details, the names are different. No one will suspect I based it on your life."

His jaw clenched, he doesn't break his gaze from mine. Behind his placidity, I sense a terrible frustration. His cheek twitches, his fingers crumple the pages.

"When you told me about it, I was overcome with wild inspiration. I couldn't not put this story on paper. It was visceral. What happened to you touched me, and it's so unbelievable that it makes for a completely crazy story!"

"Unbelievable, huh," he interjects, his voice flat.

I nod, fearing I've said too much.

Still impassive, he remains silent for too long. Then he exhales deeply, as if in need to control himself. It's another document he's shaking next.

"You're sending it to Pink Feathers Publishing?"

Wide-eyed, I nod. "Yes… I… would understand if you don't want me to publish it. But please, think about the success it could have. I'll call Ludivine and ask her to postpone our dinner. You'll have time to read and approve it, if you want."

He shakes his head, thoroughly annoyed, folding my contract in his fist. "Without consulting me, you were planning to send your novel, which is inspired by me, to some shitty little publishing house?"

Shocked by his words, I don't know what to say. A vein pulses on his temple, his cheeks turn scarlet in the face of my total incomprehension.

"Ervin… it's not just some small publishing house…"

"It's the one owned by your asshole editor friend, isn't it?"

Jealousy again? This time, there's no way I'm going to indulge his whim.

I rush at him, trying to get the signed document out of his hands. Without success. He's too tall and determined to fight.

"Give it back to me! You have no right to decide where I publish my books!"

He steps back, walking around my desk to put more distance between us. Fuck! I'd love to kick his flaccid balls right now!

Furious, I go after him, when horror freezes me.

He tears my publishing contract into several pieces, turning it into multiple paper balls while glaring at me with spite.

"Fucking hell, Ervin!" I shout, appalled.

"No way you're sending your manuscript to this Ludivine!"

Is he out of his mind? What does it matter to him?

"I do what I want! Who the hell do you think you are? You barge into my life, mess it up, turn my emotions upside down by warning me that you could disappear without notice, and on top of that, you want to force me to make decisions I don't agree with! What difference will it make when you're gone? You'll forget about us, me, and my books, so keep your distance from my professional life!"

My heart pounds in my chest. One might think that pouring out like this would make me feel better. Not at all! In front of Ervin's steaming expression, I tremble, disintegrate inside. No matter how hard I try to stand my ground, his fury terrifies me.

He tosses the paper balls and storms into my bedroom. As soon as I hear the rustling of his jeans, I rush after him.

"Ervin!"

Without calming down, he nervously buttons up his pants. I don't understand; his reaction is completely disproportionate.

"Ervin, talk to me!"

"I have nothing to say to you," he grumbles without looking at me.

Helpless, I feel tears welling up. "What's the matter with you? You can't react like this!"

His koi tattoo mocks me as he searches for his T-shirt in the mess of our things. I don't know what else to say to make him stay, fearing at this moment that he might never come back.

Exasperated, he decides to leave without getting dressed further. He pushes past me, eliciting from me an indignant cry.

"Don't run away again!" I shout before he loudly shuts the door behind him.

Stupefied, I remain motionless for a long moment, unable to put words to what just happened. I hear him return his place, slamming several doors as he rushes out again and then down the stairs of the building. I feel sick. I felt this way before he discovered my manuscript, but at least then, I knew the reason.

Now it's emptiness. All I have left is my dinner tonight and my questions.

I can't let Ervin's moods guide my decisions... Yet, I cancel the restaurant, claiming an unforeseen event.

My choice is final. I will publish *The Romance of My Life* with Pink Feathers, but I need time.

I need to understand.

To be able to explain why this solitary tear is rolling down my cheek.

And to suppress that voice screaming in my head that…
Damn it, I love *him*.

CHAPTER 31

Hands on the handlebars, I feel the adrenalin fizzing inside me. On the winding Spanish roads, I clear my mind. It's been ten days since I deserted my apartment in Paris. Ten days of incessant rumination without finding a solution.

Alizee bombarded me with texts, a fine bouquet of excuses that don't mean a thing to me. While the sensation of betrayal is strong, it's my own that oppresses me whenever I think about it.

I had thought to recharge my batteries at my producer's villa in Malaga. The same villa where I slept with Alizee for the first time. The result: the feeling of being the biggest piece of shit in the world clings to me. Milo was right, I should never have gone that far with her. And all for nothing. My stomach churns at the thought of her learning the truth. As if she hasn't suffered enough, damn it…

I speed up, slaloming between cars and trucks.

I don't want to destroy her. Her helpless expression when I lost it has haunted me for days. Her pain would finish me off.

Who am I kidding?

I was well aware of everything she had already endured in her life, but it didn't stop me from fucking her. And it didn't stop me from continuing even when I knew she was in love. But damn, not seeing her, not touching her, not hearing her sweet and sexy voice when she lets her guard down… it's killing me!

In a parallel existence, I would have done everything differently. I would have shielded her from all the crap in life, I would have boosted her confidence. She would have loved herself as much as I—

Surprised by a jolt, I realize that my motorcycle has run over a dead and flattened fox.

Focus, Ervin!

Cem's words are also swirling in my mind. I wasn't supposed to return to France so soon, but family duty calls.

Despite arriving at midnight, I waste no time and head to my brother's place, nervous as hell. I park on the sidewalk across the street, examining the house. Of course, all the lights are on. However, I didn't expect it to be my brother Joni who opens the door for me.

He and I size each other up for a moment, our faces impassive. Now, small wrinkles adorn the corner of his clear eyes—a legacy from our father—his temples are graying, and his tall frame has slumped even more.

These past five years without seeing each other have left some serious marks…

"Hi."

I answer with a nod, shaking the cold hand that he extends to me. His grip is firm, his gaze piercing. I have no idea what he must be thinking right now. As for me, I'm only concerned about Cem's call.

He invites me into our elder brother's home as if he owns the place. The light is warm, warming my body from the cold caused by the long journey I've been on since yesterday, by my inner emptiness, and by the worries that have been gnawing at me for several years.

In the living room, Fati, the third of our siblings, is sitting next to Cem and Nabilla, looking downcast. It seems that the Shiro family is gathered—what a surprise! They, who have never lifted a finger until now…

I quickly greet my last relative, with whom relations are as frosty as the North Pole, before addressing our eldest brother.

"Where is she?"

"She's asleep," my sister-in-law intervenes.

My desperate gaze must touch her, because she immediately sits up to hug me.

"Where is she?" I repeat, annoyed.

She affectionately pats my shoulders, then points to my nephew's room.

"She was hysterical, it took us ages to calm her down," Joni warns me.

A violent nausea overcomes me, as quickly as my steps guide me into the famous room.

She's lying down, curled up as if all the pain in the world inhabits her dreams. I can't repress the infinite sadness that washes over me. My grip on the doorknob tightens, and my jaw clenches as I watch the last images of the person dearest to my heart, who turns her back on me.

On the other hand, seeing my mom again, and knowing she's safe with my brother, removes that constant anxiety rooted in me.

After a heavy exhale, I return to the living room. Everyone is watching me, anticipating my reaction. I'm no more angry than Fati but certainly the most affected by the situation.

"How did she end up there?" I finally ask, slumping into one of the armchairs.

"Remember when one of our cousins found her with another cousin in Albania?" Cem begins.

I nod, also remembering that she had taken refuge in the mountains with those ugly bastards and dislodging her from there was mission impossible.

"I called our father," Fati continues dryly, delivering a powerful uppercut.

Stunned, I stare at him, my jaw clenched to the extreme.

"Don't look at me like that. He was the only one who could do something."

"Don't mess with me," I growl, overcome by a surge of pure hatred. "What could Dad possibly do when he abandoned her when she needed him most?"

That's why things don't click between my brother and me. Besides our opposing temperaments, he always sided with our father, even when he left my mother to rot with *them*.

He plunges his piercing black eyes into me, as if he's ready for a fight, as always. I raise my chin, daring him to open his mouth.

After my father left, when I was a kid, my mother became very lonely and got close to a cousin with dubious morals. My brothers had already left home, leaving only me and my sadness over her loneliness. At first, I initially found their friendship comforting. Living my life, I left her to that branch of the family, which, I thought, filled the void left by my father. Over time, they took her over, whisked her away to Albania away from her children. When, between two trips, I visited there a few years ago, she seemed completely lobotomized. With the help of Cem, the only one who truly cared, we brought her back to France. Unfortunately, she presented worrying symptoms of decreased mobility. Having a family doctor is always helpful, and thanks to him and many expensive exams, spinal muscular atrophy was diagnosed. An incurable genetic disease gradually paralyzes the muscles, up to the respiratory organs. We immediately imposed physiotherapy sessions on her, although no medication exists for it yet.

I roamed around for a long time, for work and for myself, opening myself to the greatness of the world and its benefits, with peace of mind knowing she was in the hands of my eldest sibling. That's how I discovered an experimental treatment was available across the Atlantic. When I came back to announce it to my siblings, my mother was gone.

Vanished. Almost kidnapped with consent by some sort of middle-aged cult. Those bastards had lobotomized her again: her illness was the work of God, no medication opposing His divine decision was tolerable.

We tried our best to reason with her, in vain. So, knowing she's back, thanks to our father, gives me a wave of unpleasant shivers.

"Where is he now?" I ask Cem.

"He bolted as soon as she crossed the threshold," he informs me, with the same bitterness that fills me.

"In the meantime, he's managed to bring her back," Fati intervenes. "He even managed, through some connections, to make life hell for those who indoctrinated her."

I ignore him, massaging my temples, plagued by additional worries.

"We'll be able to get her treated," Joni decides before the situation gets out of hand.

Speaking of which…

With closed eyelids, I don't know how to tell them. Disappointment chokes me. Theirs will destroy me, and the reality of my revelation crushes my spirits.

"About that…" They all stare at me, brows furrowed. "I have something to tell you…"

I hear them stir. Nabilla comes and sits beside me, placing her hand on my shoulder. Like my brothers, she does know nothing good will come out of me.

"I think her treatment is… off the table."

***

Drained, I head back home. It's nearly six in the morning, and the night at my brother's was difficult. Undoubtedly, our parents' divorce has fractured the Shiro siblings.

The only reason our bond, though worn, still holds is because of our mother's recovery. Today, we face a wall that only I can break down. To save our mother depends on a deal I made to win over Alizee. However, the consequences seem insurmountable to me. Now, she matters. Alizee matters. More than I ever thought she might

At the top of the stairs, I take a deep breath and stare at the neighboring door. I wish I could shout her name, spit out all this frustration that fills me, but my lips remain sealed.

Suddenly, a clicking sound freezes me. The handle moves, the hinges creak, and the door swings opens slowly.

My veins feel like lead when Alizee's small head appears in the doorway. Her immense eyes scrutinize me with such intensity that I instinctively recoil. She looks so broken that my heart squeezes.

"Ervin…" she whispers in a hoarse voice.

Fuck…

My fists clench, suppressing my sudden urges. I want to rush to her, kiss her, apologize a thousand times for my asshole behavior, but shame petrifies me. What have I done? For god's sake, what have I done?

Just as she opens the door wider, ready to join me on the landing, I rush into my apartment. She takes advantage of the fact that I'm turning the key to grab my leather jacket.

"Ervln, look at me," she commands more firmly.

With my door unlocked, I grasp the handle, feel my pulse in every limb. My trapezius muscle tenses as she slips her small hand onto my elbow.

"Don't come any closer…" *Or I'll fall apart.*

"We need to talk! I didn't know you were so stubborn, and I had no idea you would react like this!"

Me neither.

"And… I have something to tell you…"

Terrified, I open the door, dart into this temporary apartment, and slam it in her face.

Her screams change nothing.

Nor the ringing of the doorbell.

Her insults, even less.

✳✳✳

Under the shower, I curse myself for being unable to tame my fucking dick, I curse myself for succumbing to her cat-like eyes, to her defiant smiles.

Naked and wet, I sprawl face down on my mattress. Knocked out by fatigue, I grab Otto and bring him close to my face, desperately seeking some kind of solace. With closed eyelids, I try to ignore the incessant vibrations of my phone, longing more than anything to sink into oblivion and forget these last stressful hours.

How am I going to manage to cure my mother? I can't leave her in this state… My stomach tightens, my heart skips a beat.

I should have found another way… or manned up and gone through with my plan.

If my cell phone makes another sound, I'll throw it out the window!

SHIT!

I leap out of bed and grab it.

But the name displayed on the screen freezes me.

I swallow, quickly open the message.

He's furious. And *he*'s asking me to meet him at the Puck Café in an hour.

CHAPTER 32

After countless sleepless nights, my head feels like it could explode at any moment, which is why I've encased it in a beanie. Well, actually, it's to track Ervin that I've wrapped myself up in a puffy coat he's never seen, under a big scarf and an ugly hat I hate. Maybe I went overboard with the sunglasses, but this way, there's no way he'll recognize me.

A ten-day period without a single sign, not even a post on social media. I thought I was going crazy! To the point of losing six pounds. The highlight of my life!

If the depression that followed my ordeal with Laurent traumatized me, this is a whole different experience. His absence added to my indignation and guilt. A crushing absence, digging a gaping hole within me that's impossible to fill. Luckily, Galati shook me off, chanting that I had done absolutely nothing to deserve such a reaction. She's right, however, if I hurt Ervin, we need to talk about it. If only he wasn't so stubborn!

Hidden behind a beam at the back of the Puck Café, I sip my hot chocolate while spying on the profile of my tormentor. Sitting by the window, he's staring into space, his posture tense and his expression anxious.

What's happening to him? Who is he meeting so early in the morning? Could it have something to do with his child or his crazy in-laws?

My curiosity at its peak, I can't help but lose myself in watching him, falling deeper into the abyss of love. I don't care if he has obligations, if he has to leave any day now to be with his family. I need to spend the time he has left in France glued to him, like a little koala.

When he looks up, his features instantly tighten. Intrigued, I glance toward the entrance, my stomach knotting, and discover the trigger for his state.

I spit out my hot chocolate. Fuck! It's everywhere!

Dabbing the table with a napkin, I focus my attention on the LoveRomance publisher. He joins my neighbor, their greetings indicating some familiarity.

As they exchange words, as they sit face to face, a weight settles in my stomach. What does this mean? What's Alan doing here, and how do they know each other? This smells fishy.

The old shark doesn't take long to get animated. He makes grand gestures, sporting a furious expression in front of a sheepish Ervin.

Damn, I have a very bad feeling about this. A rush of memories overwhelms me, bringing me to the brink of explosion. I recall the immense anger of the tall dark-haired man when he discovered my publishing contract with Pink Feathers, and immediately feel my blood boiling.

Beside myself, I stand up abruptly, almost knocking over the chair, and rush toward their table.

As soon as Ervin's eyes meet mine, he pales. Alan, on the other hand, is at first stunned, but anger quickly takes over.

"What does this mean?" I lash out at Ervin, his bewildered expression only fueling my rage.

Yeah, you scam artist! I caught you red-handed! You're going to have to explain to me why you're colluding with the devil.

The traitor pinches the bridge of his nose. Just what we need.

"Don't play the victim, Ervin! What are you plotting behind my back? Do you two know each other?"

Alan's contemptuous laughter catches my attention. He casually leans his arm on the table, trying to appear relaxed despite his tense demeanor.

"One wonders who the real victim is here… you ungrateful little brat!"

I glare at him, outraged.

"I called you, I explained to you why I was entrusting my book to another publishing house!" With a few well-chosen insults, granted, but still, I did the right thing. "I was upfront. And I have the feeling that's far from being your case!"

Alan remains silent, with a smug smile. Ervin slowly shakes his head, looking overwhelmed.

"Alizee," Ervin says, "let's talk about this at the apartment—"

"Not a chance!" I object, categorically. "You're going to explain this to me right here and now."

"Alizee, please," he pleads.

"I've known Ervin since he was a teenager," Alan interjects.

Those words alone send a wave of dizziness through me. I almost stagger but quickly regain my composure. "What?"

"Alan!" the other fucking imposter scolds.

My breathing quickens. I look at the man who transformed me in just a few months with a pleading gaze. No… No… No… He didn't really deceive me about that, did he?

"Why, Ervin?" I grind out, my chest and fists clenched. I feel like throwing up.

He remains silent, his eyes shining with despair.

"Damn it, speak up!"

"Alizee, you're drawing attention from the whole place," Alan calmly scolds me.

How can this filthy bastard keep his cool? My heart is racing at a thousand beats per a minute as I watch my lover's increasingly devastated expression.

"I don't give a damn about it!"

"When I think that Ludivine will reap all that we've sown," the editor spits at the other man so vehemently it becomes ominous.

All that we've sown…?

My breathing becomes labored. Ervin closes his eyes, a furrow forming on his forehead. I shake my head, feeling a chasm opening inside me, a violent earthquake shattering me to pieces.

"Look at me!" I shout, slamming my fist on the table.

He's seized, as much as our audience, of whom I care little about. In the midst of this increasingly crowded café, his eyes pierce me, betraying a myriad of emotions. Once again, his recent anger explodes in my face.

"What are you doing in *my* building, Ervin?" I must control myself… or I'll explode as soon as he opens his mouth.

It's the moment Alan chooses to sneer. "He was hitting on you. He inspired you, poor thing."

The shock immobilizes me. I can't breathe. This time, I'm really staggering. Ervin stands up to catch me, but I scream at him not to touch me.

At that moment, a waitress rushes to my aid, asking me if everything is okay. Dazed, I'm unable to say a word. Alan reassures her, placing an order at the same time, oblivious to the fact that I'm about to vomit.

"All this family drama abroad, the story about your wife, your kid—was it all lies?" I realize once the waiter leaves, annoyed by my commotion.

His slow nod confirms the horror of what I've fallen into. I stare, unable to find any response at all. Just pain. Unending pain.

My neighbor remains silent for a moment before finally whispering an apology.

Alan adds something, then explains that I needed a dramatic source of inspiration, while enjoying himself. I don't hear anything. His voice is drowned out by my internal turmoil, blending with the ambient noise of the place. Only the drums of my heart resound. My entire field of vision fades into the background except for Ervin's tortured face.

"You should thank me, actually. I knew the apartment next to yours was empty, so I sent him there with the conviction that he would cure your writer's block. Given his success, I was sure a man like him would not leave you indifferent. His mission was to seduce you and give you material to write. I was right, but the traitor you are ran to Ludivine."

Me? The traitor? I see red. Unable to control myself, I grab the water pitcher on the table and throw its contents in that bastard's face. He lets out a surprised cry and shoves his chair back, furious.

As he wipes himself off, calling me crazy, flashes assault me, images flickering in my memory. *You're perfect. Let me capture this moment, you're really beautiful. Your insecurities are ridiculous, you've got a great ass. Sex with you is—*

Bullshit…

Tears threaten to spill. The sensation of Ervin inside me torpedoes me. My confessions about my biggest flaws that preceded our first kiss, those concerning the most painful episodes of my life before we slept together, in Malaga…

His family secrets that are a web of lies.

I'm suffocating.

"You liar!" My hand moves on its own. It lands in a powerful slap across Ervin's face.

In an instant, I find myself running on the sidewalk, cheeks streaming with tears. How could I have been so deceived?

With my skin whipped by the winter chill, I don't hear Ervin following me. He grabs my arm, abruptly stopping me in my tracks.

Facing him, shaken by an overflow of anger, I pound his chest, unable to hold back. I hate him! I hate him so much!

"All this for a fucking book?! What about my feelings, damn it?"

The worst insults from my repertoire come pouring out. "I was stupid enough to love you. God, what a fool I am!" I'm broken. Shattered.

He tries to hold me still by the shoulders, but I struggle with all my might. He talks and talks, drowned out by a violent internal buzzing that prevents me from hearing him. The cry of my distress.

It's so painful…

Betrayal always tastes sour. In reality, Laurent was just a small player. This time, I've been manipulated by a master.

In one final burst of fury, I manage to break free from his grasp and flee at a sprint.

CHAPTER 33

The smell of chlorine saturates my nostrils. The dimly lit atmosphere of the indoor pool is relaxing, gradually managing to calm my internal turmoil.

But not enough.

At the end of my next lap, I cling to the edge, resting my sore muscles.

"Come on! Keep swimming!" Marshall's voice scolds me.

Oh boy, if I had known, I would never have agreed to this aquatic torture session. He reaches the wall just next to me, glaring at me behind his swimming goggles.

"I've never done any sport in my life! You can't do this to me!"

My whining doesn't seem to soften him. He shakes his head, his little blue circular goggles bobbing on his skull. "Stop it. You're doing pretty well for a woman who's never set foot in a gym. Your cardio is remarkable."

Thank you, endless sessions of sex with Ervin.

"Hey, what's with the teary eyes? Don't cry. I won't force you if you really don't want to."

A solitary tear rolls down my cheek. With a lump in my throat, I swim away, but am quickly caught by my coach. In the water, he grabs my arm and pulls me to the end of the lane, at the foot of the ladder. He climbs up first, grabs a towel, and spreads it out as an invitation to leave the pool. Hesitant, I adjust the shorts of my swimsuit before complying.

Once wrapped up, I let my friend rub my shoulders, then lift my chin toward him.

"Hey…"

I lower my eyelids, scolding myself for not being able to control my emotions. The poor guy invited me to spend a few days at his second home in Ajaccio to take my mind off things. He urged me to swim breaststroke to clear my head. Apparently, it didn't have the desired effect.

I apologize profusely as we both settle onto a sun lounger.

"Don't worry, it's normal. The wound's still fresh," he reassures me as he hugs me close.

Physically, we've never been so close. His warmth seeps into my body, instantly calming me. However, he's unaware of everything Ervin and I have shared, underestimating the depth of my pain.

"Everything was fake," I mumble against his damp chest. "Everything! And that bastard Alan—"

"Tell yourself he was caught in his own game. In the end, he went through all that trouble for nothing, and Ludivine seems to be thrilled about your manuscript."

I sniffle back my tears and rub my irritated eyes.

"I don't care about that… I'd have preferred to not write anything and not get fooled by that fucking seducer!"

Marshall's hands run through my wet hair.

"The way he looked at you, I doubt he was ever sincere. If he was, he wouldn't have bombarded you with calls a week afterward."

A shiver runs down my spine. Disgust, that's what his calls inspire within me, if it's just to hear him say he's sorry when every word was orchestrated from the start.

"Alan probably didn't choose him for nothing. He's an excellent actor. And with women, he's used to playing. He knows what's he's doing. I was such easy prey. Like the biggest idiot, I gave myself to him right away. I should have listened to my instincts and been wary. You and Galati warned me, too. For a guy like him to suddenly take an interest in me… He gave me confidence, convinced me I wasn't just a worthless, stranded whale!"

My editor recoils, taking my face in his hand and locking his hazel eyes with mine. The furrow between his eyebrows doesn't bode well.

"Stop with that! He's just a jerk who's used to hanging out with bimbos, you explained it yourself. You're so beautiful, inside and out— it's a good thing he made you feel uninhibited. You couldn't have left him indifferent, trust me. A man recognizes these things."

He doesn't realize his words are crushing me. I'm convinced of the opposite, but if he were right, that truth would be even more unbearable. If Ervin really hadn't played it all, what am I supposed to feel?

Before Marshall came to my rescue, Vampyr and I had taken refuge at Galati's. Well, under Galati's covers, where I hid the entire time was there. I flooded her sheets with all the saltwater my body contained. If I'd cried lipids, I'd be so skinny that I could have modeled for a prestigious brand, I'm sure of it. But nature is a bitch. When you're unlucky, it's all the way!

My friend was as devastated as I was to learn of the deception. Once she found out, the first action she took was to give her boyfriend hell over the phone.

Yes, he knew.

Yes, that was why he was against my getting closer to Ervin.

Everything made sense; he felt guilty about lying to his girlfriend and couldn't betray his *best friend*, as he called him. He didn't expect our relationship to go so far. He didn't expect me to sleep with him for the first time or to get so attached. He didn't expect me to be so stupid!

Galati took a day off to support me, and we both cursed them with the worst names during the whole period I crashed at her apartment. In the end, I urged her to forgive her man, but she didn't seem convinced. Before I left, she just promised to think about it.

✳✳✳

Tonight, Marshall invited me to dinner. On a heated terrace overlooking the mountains, we dine by candlelight. He loves it. The floor is wooden, giving the place a romantic rustic charm. He looks very elegant in his well-made sweater, next to my ridiculous puffer jacket. Well, it's not like I've had the heart to dress up lately. Wonder why!

While he orders for us, I receive a curious call.

"Hey sis, what's up?"

Perplexed, I immediately question Charles about what he wants.

"According to Mom, you've gone off to recharge in Corsica, or something like that?"

My mother barged into my place one morning only to find me gone, then alerted the whole building to my disappearance. I got wind of it, explained to her that I was taking an improvised vacation. Since it's not like me to step a toe out of my lair, she quickly suspected something was wrong. She also quickly guessed it had something to do with Ervin. Being as silent as the grave, I gave her no affirmation. She can keep her snide remarks to herself.

"Say, could I crash at your place until you get back?" the odious little brat dares to ask.

I'm flabbergasted! Here I'm crying my eyes out, and all that scavenger can think about are the keys to my apartment.

"You're dreaming. If you want your own place, figure it out and stop leeching off others."

"Please, Al! Just for a few days, Alicia's parents didn't go away this year, and she refuses to let us stay at a hotel."

"Oh, so you plan to dirty my sheets on top of it? You really don't know how to sell yourself, poor thing! That's a double no!"

Marshall grins in surprise, to which I respond by rolling my swollen eyes.

"I thought you were more open-minded," Charles spits out with a hint of disappointment in his voice.

… *given what you write*, I hear without him actually saying it. Ugh, idiot!

If he tries to sweet-talk me, he won't set foot in my den!

"Why don't you ask your great buddy Ervin? It's at his place you end up wasted. I'm sure he'll be more than happy to host you."

Take that, liar!

"You're a pain!"

"I'm well aware, yes. Bye!" I hang up on him before he can insist, then shake my head, dismayed.

The waitress serves us a basket of bread, which I dive into to vent my frustration.

"I tell you I hate my family," I grumble to Marshall.

He chuckles softly, with a glimmer of tenderness that raises my suspicion.

"I don't see what's so funny about that. Charles would be ecstatic if he knew how unhappy I am."

There's nothing classy about the way I speak while stuffing my mouth. I can't help it; my irritation makes me uncontrollable.

My editor leans toward me, elbows on the table, and squints under his beautiful brown curls. "After all the rejections he faces, don't you think your brother's persistence is to preserve your bond?"

His words hit me like an uppercut. In shock, I pause for a moment. Indeed, Charles never gives up. I thought that after the way I treated him, if he persisted, it was because he was just a stubborn brat. But if…

Yet, my grudge toward his father is obvious. He indirectly suffered from it, so why would he want to get closer to me?

Marshall must sense my turmoil; he takes my hand in his, warm and so gentle, and caresses my skin with his thumb. "Don't worry about that, consider the bright side of things," he says.

Despite his words, I'm unsure about Charles's supposed intentions, but they intrigue me nonetheless.

The phone rings again.

"Seriously! Can't I enjoy this moment in peace?" I pull my hand away to check my phone screen. "The whole family is getting involved, it's crazy!"

"Don't worry about me," teases Marshall.

If he had forbidden it, I'd have been grateful. Since I don't want to come off as a heartless witch, I answer the phone.

"Alizee! Why on Earth did you allow Charles to stay at your apartment? I'm still his mother, I decide where he sleeps!"

Stunned, I'm momentarily speechless before stammering, "But… I… never… agreed! I told him to buzz off!"

"That's not what he told me!" my mother exclaims.

"Well, he's got nerve! Put him on a leash and don't open your door to him! I can't believe it."

"Sometimes, that boy drives me crazy," she blurts like an irresponsible parent.

"Me, too! Don't let him conspire against us!"

She sighs audibly, mutters something before changing the subject. "How are you, young lady?"

Young lady—that's the first time she hasn't reminded me of the struggles of my biological clock.

"Fine, thanks."

Silence.

"I'm at a restaurant, Mom." Will she understand that she's bothering me?

"Oh, that's a good thing. Have fun and come back refreshed. I miss you."

I swallow hard. On edge, I'm not prepared for such a declaration. "I'll take as much time as I need."

"Yes. Go out, have fun, and above all, don't let disappointment get you down. You're strong; you don't need anyone."

My chest tightens, and I can't resist responding, "Oh really? I thought according to you, I should cling on as soon as I find a man. Because without a man, I'm just a poor old spinster with cat."

My sarcastic tone surprises Marshall, whose eyes scrutinize every feature of my face carefully.

"I was trying to motivate you, you see? I think men should be the least of your worries. I'm not stupid, sweetheart, I know when you're not well. And I know your pain. Cheer yourself up; you'll have plenty of time to go hunting again."

The warmth in her usually cold voice spreads through me. That she senses my heartbreak is one thing, but I imagined she'd be lecturing me with an *I told you so,* as it's her specialty.

Once again, my eyes well with water. Alarmed, Marshall leans his leg against mine for support. I clear my throat to dispel my embarrassment.

"Thank you… Mom."

She then launches into an endless tirade about her problems at the cabaret. Thus, my frustration takes precedence over my desire to cry.

A few minutes later, our meal is finally served. The other tables on the terrace are almost empty. The sun has set, creating a cozy atmosphere. With a sweet voice, Marshall talks about the manuscripts he plans to work on. Although the subject fascinates me, watching this distinguished man sitting across from me, so charming and so kind, troubles me.

As we mostly discuss work, I know little about his personal life, while he is aware of my main adventures.

"Can I ask you a question?" I venture.

He takes one last bite of spaghetti before nodding…

"How come you never tell me about your love life?"

…and nearly chokes.

After gulping down his entire glass of water while desperately clinging to life, Marshall wipes his pretty mouth and takes a deep breath. "You caught me off guard."

"I can believe that." I laugh at his expense. "So, what's the deal? You're pretty cute, and you've got it all, even a house in Ajaccio," I joke. "You must have had girlfriends."

With blushing cheeks, he gives me a half-smile, fluttering his eyelashes. "I was convinced it didn't interest you all that much, unlike my editorial adventures."

I wet my lips in my glass of wine, wondering why I've never asked him about his love life. "I was trying to hide that side of my daily life, maybe I didn't want to talk about it at all." I suppose.

He eyes my mouth, which is probably stained by the burgundy liquid. I run my tongue over it and push him further.

"I've had a few girlfriends, yes. It never lasts very long."

"Why is that?"

"I'm rather picky," he boasts, crossing his arms.

I roll my eyes.

"The truth is, they eventually get tired."

"Of you?" Good heavens! What idiots they are. A guy like Marshall, you do anything to keep him. Well, I think…

"Of my devotion to work."

"Oh…"

I understand better now. And I sympathize. Reproaches from a man who wouldn't approve of my love for my job would quickly get to me. For that, Ervin was…

No! Pull yourself together, Alizee! Enough of your heart-clenching and throat-knotting! Ervin is a lying scumbag who deserved to rot on his motorcycle!

I quickly add, shoulders tense. "What's your type of girl?"

His broad smile crinkles the corners of his eyes endearingly. "Who could you picture me with?"

Good question. I consider him for a few seconds, then finally rest my elbow on the table, my chin in my palm, and give him a mischievous pout. "Let's see… Which ears does Marshall like to poke…?"

A hearty laugh escapes his throat. "What a flattering metaphor!"

"I have much saltier ones." I chuckle in turn.

His eyes take on different shades. Something inside me shifts. The atmosphere suddenly changes…

"I could see you with a girl who's wise, but strong and independent. Pretty, but natural. Elegant, but simple."

"That's a lot of opposites," he teases.

"Maybe. But I'm sure I'm right."

His arrogant little grimace amuses me. He picks at his pasta, then settles back in his chair and responds to me, his arm stretched out on the table. "Not quite. I like them impulsive, with a hint of vulnerability. Pretty, of course, with flashes of madness from time to time. Not necessarily elegant, but sensual. I like feisty women. The problem is, they're rather rare."

The silence spreads as I swallow my bite of pizza.

"You like pain in the asses, basically…"

CHAPTER 34

In front of my building's door, I feel sick. Fortunately, Marshall is by my side. Unwavering support.

The fourth floor seems so high and yet so close. I've lived here for years, and it feels like coming back to his place. Everything reminds me of his presence; I half expect him to suddenly appear and shake me to the core.

"Look at this," says my friend.

He points to a *For Rent* sign on the front, and I glance at it, eyes wide. My blood rushes, and I hurry closer, immediately searching for the relevant floor. But there are too few details.

Dizzy, I rush inside the building and sprint up the stairs. Breathless, I stop abruptly in front of my neighbor's door, observing the majestic, motionless wooden door, my heart racing.

My editor soon joins me, my backpack slung over his shoulder.

"He's gone…" I whisper.

Marshall's hand envelops my neck. "It's for the best."

Yes, it's for the best. The apartment next door is empty, I can feel it. Like before he appeared. After all, he only lived there to seduce me.

After a week in Corsica, I had come to terms with being manipulated but emerging victorious, as neither Ervin nor Alan had achieved what they coveted.

So why did I feel so stripped, so hurt by his move?

My breathing quickens further; I need to be alone. "It's okay, Marshall," I exhale. "Thanks for everything. I... I'm going to the neighbor's to get Vampyr."

He examines me for a moment with that serious look I know so well, gripping my arms. "Are you sure you'll be okay, Alizee? Don't you want me to stay with you for a bit?"

"No," I reply instantly. "Really, I'll be fine."

I prefer to be alone, Marshall.

Especially after that week in Ajaccio. I needed him, and the signal he was giving off seemed ambiguous to me. Yes, we're attached to each other. Yes, I'm a woman and he's a man. However, some of his looks said a lot. I preferred to play it down; anyway, I wasn't in the mood, and he never brought anything up. Maybe I was overthinking it; I don't know, and I don't want to know. We're friends, period.

Concerned, he complies and leaves me in my apartment.

Sitting on the sofa in this quiet and empty room, I feel lost. Back to reality. My cheeks burn.

Unable to resist, I grab my phone and scroll through social media in search of Ervin.

Nothing but old images of his work freshly posted. As he has already pointed out, he sells himself but doesn't share anything intimate.

I scroll and come across old photos of him, his charming smile, and his sparkling eyes.

My tears splash onto the screen of my cell phone. Damn them!

The next day, Galati forces me to step outside. According to her, my good deed at the orphanage should not suffer from my broken heart. Amid many comforting words, I learn that neither Milo nor the Shiro family know where Ervin has disappeared to this time.

In my sadness, I'm relieved that my best friend has forgiven her boyfriend. While my resentment still lingers, I'm well aware that he's not the decision-maker in this matter. In fact, I distanced myself in the following days to no longer interfere in their relationship. I like to think that our friendship won't suffer. My beautiful blond friend worries about my mood, but she hasn't counted on Marshall.

He's the living being I exchange the most with. A huge support, he's the shoulder I don't cry on—because I try to be strong.

Yet my suffering is very real, reflected in the number of coffees I agree to have with my mother and my readiness to deal with my drunken little brother. I almost look forward to him on weekend evenings!

However, I no longer write. Instead, I find *myself* reading to the monsters at the Vanille-Chocolat establishment. Twice a week! And they love it, those kids! It's just goes to show how low I've fallen.

Marshall claims it's no big deal, that I should take my time, that there's no point in forcing it, especially after what I've just endured. But if I don't write anymore… well, then I'm no longer me.

And it's eating me up.

***

Exactly one month ago, I discovered that my boyfriend was prostituting himself to turn my life into a bullshit romance. He was far from perfect; he was even a prime specimen of a tortured soul (guilt, no doubt), but if there's one thing that didn't collapse along with my hopes and love, it's that tiny flame of confidence that my friends managed to maintain after the drama.

I paint my lips with a dark red. In all humility, I think I find myself beautiful tonight.

I've been thinking a lot these past few days. Ervin was right: Laurent is a deep black spot that I need to extract. It's because of him that I was so easy to deceive by the other gigolo. He shattered me and ruined two years of my life; I gave way too much credit to this fucking pseudo-literary scumbag! Today, I'm taking my revenge.

In my burgundy dress, I stand tall as a board in front of the bar I'm about to enter.

The excellent student that I am has done research: tonight, Laurent has reunited here with his usual gang of friends. Some familiar faces, probably some new assholes, too, no doubt, and a date with whom he's still in the seduction phase.

Come on, Wonder Woman, show some nerve!

I push the door open and step inside.

The place is warm and trendy, the music not too loud, the decor stylish, without altering the rusticity of the place. As expected, on a Friday, in the center of Paris, it's packed.

I wander around looking for my target, my stomach tied in knots. When I spot him, my breath starts to fail. Is this really this man I've let haunt me? Gosh, he's so ordinary! Maybe I had my eyes in the wrong place.

Laurent is seated at a table of six, wearing a lumberjack plaid shirt, his blond hair brushed back, and sporting a pair of glasses that don't suit him at all. No three-day-old beard, no mischievous smile; he has always been drearily serious.

No, don't compare, Alizee! They're both bastards!

Beside him sits what I presume is his girlfriend. She's pretty. Plain, but not bad at all. Much better than me. *Stop it, Alizee!* She's not wearing lipstick.

Okay. I take a deep breath. One. Two. Three. Let's do this.

Like a gladiator, I close the gap between us and stand right in front of my nemesis, on the other side of the table, hands on hips and chin held high.

He squints at first, not quite sure if he recognizes me, before widening his eyes in astonishment. My heart rate spikes. In the face of my impassive demeanor, his cheekbones stretch to the max. Embarrassment creeps onto his features, much to my delight.

"What a surprise! Um…"

"Alizee."

This jerk doesn't even remember my name.

"Yes, Alizee! It's been a while."

Some of his friends turn around, seem to recognize me, judging by the looks on their faces.

"Yes, it's been a while," I repeat, acerbically. "I'm sorry for keeping my distance. Well, I guess you didn't move heaven and Earth to see me again."

The man's face freezes into a visibly annoyed expression. His girlfriend whispers something to him, probably asking for my identity.

"I'm just a forgettable fling," I explain to her. "You know, the kind men go out of their way to seduce. The kind they even introduce to their friends just to laugh about later. The kind they end up sleeping with, then ignore the next day. To tell their buddies that I don't measure up, that I'm just a *dumb blonde with a big ass*." The awkwardness that falls over the table is delightful. "Does any of this ring a bell, asshole?"

Other customers have turned their heads toward me; I relish in my ex's pale expression.

"I don't… know what you're talking about," he stammers, turning a pleading gaze to his girlfriend.

From the high of my heels, I feel the blissful sensation of being able to crush him. "I remember it very well! A mediocre fuck that you couldn't own up. Apparently, it was my fault. You were afraid I'd tell everyone that you had a small dick? That that was the reason why that night sucked? It's not my style, but since you didn't react to the mention of my big ass, I don't see why I should keep quiet. Because, I know for sure today, I wasn't the problem!"

The woman with him can't help but giggle. Oh, sweet revenge!

Red-faced, he turns to her, then back to me, and gets up from the table.

Well, I guess there's no point in lingering. As powerful as I feel right now, it wouldn't take much for everything to fall apart and for me to become pathetic. Let's seize the best moment to make our exit.

"On that note, I hope the lady next to you doesn't have too many expectations! Good riddance, geek." I spin around, and as I head back to the entrance, a group of girls to my right applauds. I feel like I'm in a feminist ad, an irrepressible smile on my face. I sway as I walk, until I find myself outside the restaurant after a dramatic exit.

Finally, reality catches up with me. It slaps me in the face with surprising gentleness. The taste of vengeance. I did it! There's a tingling in my stomach, it's even better than an orgasm! With my fists in the air, I can't help but stomp my feet and let out a little victory cry. I hope I ruined his plan, that coward! That'll teach him to act like a jerk!

Feeling uplifted, I hit the road while calling an Uber. It only takes two steps for me to hear a too-familiar voice getting lost in a conversation. I lift my eyes from my screen, paralyzed.

I come face to face with Ervin.

Everything around me freezes. So does my heart.

He, too, is at a loss for words, much to the dismay of the two women with him.

But he doesn't stop.

In his sleek leather jacket, with his carefully styled hair and his neatly trimmed beard framing his cheeks, he looks more impressive than in my recent memory.

It's only after he passes me that my lungs sound the alarm, demanding their oxygen. My legs tremble. My hands find refuge in the pockets of my coat, and my eyelids refuse to blink.

Of all the rotten luck, this bastard had to cross my path right on the evening when I'm giving Laurent a taste of his own medicine. Does fate send him my way just when I'm feeling up and my vindictiveness is at its peak?

Don't look back, Alizee... don't look back.

I don't look back.

I continue on my path like a robot, my shoulders slumped, my confidence shattered.

I thought I had overcome my feelings, but seeing him again feels like a stab in the ribs. All the memories come flooding back, his warmth, his voice, his kisses…

Who are these two women? A double booty call? Will he forget himself in their sheets tonight? Will he make them pant, too?

Suddenly, a hand grabs my shoulder, causing me to lose balance and forcing me to pivot. When I realize it's Ervin, it's too late to scream; he's already pulled me into his arms, holding me tightly against him.

I breathe.

Then I suffocate.

CHAPTER 35

"Let go of me!"

"Alizee, stop, please!" he shouts, ignoring me.

Despite my struggle, his grip is firm. My fists are powerless, but when I drive my heel into his shoe, he roars in pain and lets me go. I run away, fueled by fury.

It doesn't take him long to catch up to me. I try to attract the attention of the worried onlookers. With luck, they'll come to my rescue. But Ervin is cleverer; he leads me into a narrow passage, presses me against a stone wall, silencing me with his hand. His forehead against mine, he plunges his penetrating onyx eyes into me, overwhelming me with all the distress of his soul.

"Alizee, don't turn your back on me now."

In every word, every syllable, his pain seeps through, echoing against mine, amplifying it. I blame myself for still feeling it. I should have moved on, learned from my mistakes, and not repeated them. But Ervin sticks to me like glue.

A tear rolls slowly down my cheek, moistening his hand, which eventually lets me go.

"Let me forget you," I plead. "What are you doing here, Ervin?"

He shakes his head, still pressed against mine, then immediately enfolds me in his arms. "I was going to the bar. Forgive me. Please, forgive me," his voice fades away.

Everything comes rushing back. The sensation of being held in his powerful arms, the sense of protection he inspired, the cocoon he represented. I hate myself so much for feeling so good, so snugly nestled. I despise myself for desperately needing it. I want him to set me free, yet I hope he never lets go of me.

All these contradictions.

And the tears.

He appears out of nowhere, two girls hanging on him, and tears open my heart at the moment when I was claiming a small victory in my life.

"You should go," I whimper against his shirt. "Your girlfriends are waiting for you."

"They're not girlfriends. It's my boss and a colleague. And I don't care, I'm not letting you go. I won't let you go again, Alizee," he declares against my neck.

"You're lying! Liar… Liar. Liar! Liar! Liar! Liar! Liar!"

I try in vain to escape our embrace, but his kisses on my throat render me powerless. I shiver to the tips of my hair, endure the burn of his hand on the curve of my lower back. God, it feels good.

"I never lied to you about how I felt," he continues, intensifying his caresses.

No matter how much I push him away, he traps me between his bulk and the wall behind me, wedges his thigh between mine. It's terrible how the magnetism between us fucks up the reality of our relationship.

"Remember, Alizee, I warned you when you joined me in the Cévennes. I knew… I knew you'd end up hating me. I didn't want to hurt you," he murmurs, inches from my lips as he undoes the buttons on my coat. "I also assured you that no matter what you found out about me, what I felt for you at that moment was real."

I remember. And I crumble a little more, my face streaming with tears. He warned me, and I think he did so repeatedly. I just didn't want to listen.

I hate him.

I hate myself.

When his mouth meets mine, I moan in pain. My fingers involuntarily grip his head as he grabs my waist through my dress.

"I knew you would hate me," he growls between my lips. "I left because I had resigned myself. But damn it, I can't move on."

His teeth nibble at me; his tongue wanders over my lips as I absorb in his confession with infinite sorrow.

"You're engraved in my mind."

I feel like I'm breaking into a thousand pieces. His fingers slip under my skirt, setting my skin on fire. So powerful that a cry rises to the sky, my nails digging into his sublimely masculine face, slowly lacerating it as deeply as he tore my heart apart.

With his free hand, he grabs my breast, squeezes it passionately, reducing me to a fleshly envelope craving his touch. He fills all the voids of this past month, pulverizes me with an ultimate declaration, vile and selfish. "I love you, Alizee."

With a thrust, he asserts his words.

I'm no longer in control of my body. Like a rag doll, I let him use it as he pleases, let him do all the good that it's been requesting since our breakup. He has demolished my defenses.

"Why?" I ask, enduring his insistent caresses, while he repeats that he misses me, that he dreams only of my skin, of my coconut scent, that he longs to hear my voice, hoping to meet me at every street corner, knowing full well that I never leave my home.

He adds that he fell in love with my flaws, with my strong character, with the kindness it hides, with my naturalness without pretense.

Intoxicated by these words, I no longer know what to think or how to react. I rely on my instincts, kiss him intensely, thrust my tongue into his mouth, battling with his.

I feel so hot in the gentle winter chill.

My anger multiplies my sensations, as does the pleasure instilled by his hands on my ass. He kneads it eagerly, mirroring his desire.

In the dark alley, I hear the sound of a zipper.

"You drive me crazy," his husky voice vibrates.

"I hate you."

Suddenly, my panties are pulled aside, and his cock presses against my barely damp entrance.

"Fuck, Alizee," he moans against my mouth.

Ervin forces his way in, eliciting a groan from me. I cling to his shoulders to endure it, as he thrusts deep inside me with one sharp movement.

Torn between irritation, sadness, and voracity, I tighten my vaginal walls. He emits a guttural sound, grabs my thigh to wrap it more tightly around his waist, lifts me slightly to slide back and come back to thrust.

It hurts. I feel disgusting, yet I'd die if he decided to stop.

On his third invasion, pleasure overtakes me, finally lubricating me.

"Please, forgive me, Alizee. I can't do it without you."

Sobs shake me in rhythm with his thrusts. I pull his hair, hoping he suffers at least a little.

"Why?" I cry into the hollow of his neck.

His free arm wraps tightly around me, as if he desires to merge our bodies.

"If you cared for me, why did you go all the way?"

His back and forth becomes brutal.

"Why… did you also lie… about your wife and kid?"

He speeds up, as if to silence me. "Alizee…"

His voice is hoarse, his breath, shallow. His cock inside me is divine and conquering. Pleasure intensifies my sobs, spasms shaking me against his chest.

"Why… did you lose control… when you discovered the contract… if you… loved me…?"

He grabs my hair, tilts my face to kiss me passionately. Tears glisten in his eyes. His thrusts amplify, eliciting small pleasure cries from me.

"For the money," he confesses shamefully before silencing me with his kiss.

For the money. I endure his final thrusts with clenched eyelids, cursing him with all my might.

"I'm sorry, I'm sorry. I'm sorry," he repeats like a litany.

Is it possible to inflict so much pain on yourself while enjoying so much pleasure?

He licks away my tears, implores me not to cry anymore, repeats that he loves me.

I hear nothing anymore, only receptive to the sensations he continues to give me, no longer able to savor them.

When I feel him swell inside me, my mind lights up.

"Ervin! No more pills!" I exclaim, frightened.

Wide-eyed, he withdraws just in time, ejaculating into his hand immediately, his forehead pressed against mine.

For the money.

It wasn't a favor he was doing for an old acquaintance… When I said he was prostituting himself, I didn't imagine being so close to the truth.

He used me to fill his pocket. And to empty others, incidentally.

His labored breathing becomes unbearable. The feeling of betrayal strengthens me. My sex is as bruised as my soul, as soiled as my dignity.

The urban clamor resurrects all around us, emphasizing my abrupt return to reality. I try to break free when this rat clutches me again.

"Don't leave."

A tear rolls down his cheek. Stunned, I remain there for a moment, then I remember my own fractures.

"I never want to see you again."

It takes him a few seconds to absorb it. As soon as his grip loosens, I break free and run away as fast as I can.

CHAPTER 36

TEN MONTHS LATER

I finally arrive at this fucking destination! Frozen in my very first car, I briefly regret the days when I lived in the heart of Paris. Since I bought my house in the suburbs, every journey I make is an odyssey.

The parking lot is full. I curse as I drop my keys and blame myself for not wearing a down jacket. Time flies so fast when you're overwhelmed with work and moving; I forgot it was December. This treacherous sun doesn't help. It shines for nothing, hanging in the sky without warming the ambient cold by even a degree.

My boots pound the pavement toward the hospital while a strange sensation gnaws at me from within, a mix of terror and joy.

In front of the indicated door, I take a deep breath and enter Galati's private room. Everything is quiet. The natural light floods the clean and impersonal space. There's no one here yet. Just my friend, who looks like she's at the end of her life. Her pale complexion betrays obvious fatigue, her tangled hair screams for comb, and the dark circles under her eyes provoke a little laugh from me.

"You could have made yourself pretty for me," I tell her as I hug her.

She pouts, then gives into a satisfied smile.

A smile hiding immeasurable happiness, despite the rough moments she's just endured.

"So, what does she look like?" I ask as I head for the pediatric bed. "I endured an hour-long freezing drive because the heat went out in my car, all just to see her, so she better be worth it... If she looks like Gollum."

I lean my head over the newborn and... under the soft pink blanket indeed lies a little Gollum. I sigh in disappointment, while my friend bursts into laugher.

"Stop it, she's cute!"

I raise my face to her, lifting an eyebrow.

"It's because you put a little bow hat on her... You're already cheating at this age. My god, what will it be like later?"

I return to my contemplation. Well, this little squished and sleeping thing isn't so ugly after all... "Well... she's Gollum's hot chick."

The blonde with neglected roots since her pregnancy complication can't help but giggle. I smile, relieved that she's doing better.

"How was the delivery?" I ask as I settle against the windowsill. She sits up against the pillow, rolls her eyes again.

"Don't ever do it. Remember, it wasn't planned. It just happened to me, and now, I have a wrecked vagina."

As a good friend, she tries to speak my language. However, I know that having a child was one of her dearest dreams. The way it happened though, wasn't ideal. She discovered her pregnancy after five months, thinking the extra pounds resulted from countless candlelit dinners with Milo. Consequently, they had to find a home for three and barely had time to move in before her water broke. The baby must have been excited to move in, but she'll spend her first night in their cozy nest after she leaves the maternity ward.

We exchange a few jokes about the joys of future parenting life, then suddenly, male voices echo behind the door. My attention is riveted on the door that slowly swings open.

Milo enters the room, freezes for a few seconds upon seeing me before greeting me, all smiles. Following him, Ervin enters, then freezes as soon as our eyes meet.

My blood runs cold.

"Hi, Alizee," the new father exclaims as he kisses me on my cheeks. "I didn't expect you so soon."

Shocked, I can only emit a polite clearing of my throat.

My ex… adventure colonizes the entire space of the room. Nothing else exists, not the baby nor its parents. Just this impressive build, this face to be damned, these powerful hands closing into two clenched fists.

Looking as surprised as me, he takes a step toward me, then just gives me a placid nod when he notices my hunched shoulders.

Immediately, he shifts his attention back to the mother and the newborn. I glance at Galati, silently pleading with her not to blame me if I leave right away. Her puppy-dog eyes beg me not to abandon her now. Not before her family arrives, she silently articulates.

Fuck…

I've managed to avoid him for ten months. With my move, I naturally distanced myself from the center of Paris. While I managed to see my best friend as often as possible, gatherings with Milos buddies happened without me. Ervin was indeed a taboo subject; Gala was obliged never to mention him to me. It was inconceivable that I'd cross paths with the man I'd fallen madly in love with. This impostor who had deceived me in a horrible way. This man who had been nothing but a joke from the start.

"Hello, little Laura," Ervin's voice rings out.

My stomach clenches as he takes the baby in his arms.

"She's so beautiful," he exclaims.

"You see!" Galati exclaims victoriously. "Zee claims she looks like Gollum!"

Dumbfounded, he turns his head toward me, but then quickly averts his gaze, as if meeting my eyes embarrasses him.

"No, but seriously, you can't say things like that," Milo protests.

"Come on, she's just a baby. She'll be pretty when she grows up. For now, just keep hiding her under a hat."

Ervin chuckles under his breath, though he doesn't lift his eyes.

Predictions about Laura's hypothetical appearance are flying around. Meanwhile, I'm completely mesmerized by those muscular arms cradling the tiny thing with an Olympian calm.

Like flashes, grim images of our last encounter flood back to me. The dark alley, our mutual despair, him fucking me against a wall as he explained that he betrayed me for money. The intense emotions I felt and the decisions that followed.

It's impossible to engage further with the new parents; a lump forms in my throat.

After that encounter, I had no choice but to move. I felt like I was suffocating in that apartment, despite it being so dear to my heart. But he was everywhere. Every square inch of the place bore his mark, carried his scent. The smell of deceit. It stabbed me like a knife every time I woke up in in that bed where we had made love so many times.

I did everything I could to never cross paths with him again. I changed my number, blocked him on social media. I forbade myself from stalking him, though I longed to. Sure, I often failed at first, but finding nothing about his private life killed me even more. I was suffering enough; if I hoped to move on, I had to be radical.

Ervin sneaks glances at me from time to time, thinking I don't see him. The awkwardness becomes too palpable. We're both stiff as boards.

"You can talk to each other, you know," Milo interjects, scratching his chin. "What happened between you is ancient history; a lot of water has passed under the bridge."

My *ancient history* freezes. Still not looking at me, he nods. Okay, if I object, I'll come off as the killjoy… So, I weakly nod.

I knew he had a certain love for children, but this focus today serves only to save face. It's obvious. I stand there, almost assassin-like, devouring him with my eyes as I replay our moments like a movie. It feels like it was yesterday.

My resentment isn't as violent anymore, but the bitterness remains stubborn.

Since our breakup, I haven't been able to write a single word on paper, in any genre. Ludivine's corrections—don't mention them! *The Romance of My Life* has been a torture to work on, a perpetual reminder of my failure. A constant rekindling of my pain. So, yes, thanks to this smooth talker, I've gained confidence and men approach me much more. Often, I even find myself quite pretty and… sexy, but I can't let any man get close to me. In reality, it would suit me fine to be lesbian, too bad that phalluses have such an effect on me.

It's incredible how *he* hasn't changed. The sleeves of his sweater rolled up, he still reeks of sex. And, boy, he's handsome. From the awe in his eyes as he looks at the wrinkled little being, I can tell that this jerk would make a fantastic father.

Rage once again gnaws at me from the inside.

I sigh, recalling the first time I met him, on the landing, thinking he was unable to speak.

Was that calculated, too?

My shoulders slump.

There's a knock on the door. The worried head of Agatha, Galati's mother, appears in the crack. Her features relax when she sees her daughter. She enters, followed by half a dozen members of their family. Her husband and their other children, I imagine.

After a warm greeting, Agatha sizes up the son-in-law she's meeting for the first time. Antonio, the grandfather, wastes no time and snatches the baby from Ervin's arms. Ervin, embarrassed, steps back to give them space. Of course, he settles on the windowsill right next to me! As if the situation weren't trying enough!

I find myself unable to move a finger. Like a statue of salt, I freeze, trembling from head to toe.

The Stravis family speaks loudly, bursting with joy to welcome a new member in their tribe. Milo seems intimidated, huddling in a corner of the room, covered by his girlfriend's benevolent gaze. I would have felt sorry for him if he hadn't brought his best friend, a heartbreaker, a prostitute, and a pathological liar here.

I keep my eyes fixed straight ahead on one of Gala's brothers to avoid the horrible tension between Ervin and me. Just as a laugh erupts, he leans in close to my ear and whispers, "I went back to your place after we saw each other last time. You weren't there anymore. Milo told me you'd moved."

His breath trails across my skin, disappearing at the base of my neck.

"My apartment reeked of lies," I retort, acerbic.

He sighs. Utters my name in a hoarse voice, tinged with resignation. Presses a little closer to me.

Our contact electrifies me, despite the thickness of his sweater and my coat.

I close my eyes. I hate him for the attraction he still exerts over me. It's powerful, capable of devastating me if I'm not careful. As if these past ten months had never existed.

If I had managed to ease the pain that his memory inflicted on me, he is now brutally rekindling it.

He knows it, understands it, because he keeps repeating that he's sorry.

"Sorry for being Alan's whore?" I can't help but blurt out, guided by a surge of bitterness.

He tenses against my arm, while Gala glares at me, surely having heard me lose my temper.

Feeling cornered, I swallow, take a deep breath, then step toward my friend. Faced with her big questioning eyes, I lean in to apologize.

"I'm going to go. Congratulations on the little bug. I hope she doesn't end up as an escort or a ballerina."

Galati takes a deep breath before giving me her most sympathetic smile. Hey! I don't need her pity! It's really time for me to hit the road. I say goodbye to everyone and rush down the hallway, feeling the fire at my back.

"You can't just leave like that!" Ervin's voice stops me in my tracks.

I pause for long seconds before turning around. My heart is pounding too hard in this space that's too confined to contain both of us.

He strides toward me, not giving me the choice.

"We should never have seen each other again," I retort, panicked.

Standing in front of me, he towers over me, crushing me with his imperious demeanor, his pleading gaze.

"We don't have a choice. Our friends are moving in together. We can't avoid each other forever."

I want to kiss him.

Fuck! No, Alizee! This man has humiliated you enough for a lifetime.

He shakes his head, crosses his arms behind his neck, runs his hands over his head, then down his face, stretching downward. "Fuck, Alizee…"

I take a step back at his tormented expression.

"This is completely insane. After everything that happened between us, the only thing that has been obsessing me since I saw you again is your mouth."

I exhale emphatically, trying to expel all the pain that his confession injects into me. The emotion twists my gut. "I have a hard time with paid relationships, especially when I'm funding them without my knowledge."

With wide eyes, he vigorously shakes his head. "Damn it, Alizee, we weren't supposed to sleep together. It wasn't part of the deal. It was completely out of control! Everything that happened between us was!"

"Don't say that! You lied all the way through, even when I was more than just a booty call! What was your need to invent such a crazy family drama? A wife dead because of you? You have no idea how I felt when you told me you had a kid! How they were out to get you, that—"

His wide-eyed stare reflects back my stupidity.

"I was stupid. I should have trusted my first impression and not believed in that completely insane story. Why did you have to go that far? Couldn't you just have inspired me by playing Don Juan?"

Ervin pinches his forehead, before explaining to me what I already knew deep down. "I didn't have a choice. I needed you to finish that book, and it required a drama."

"So, you gave me drama."

He nods, moistening his lips. "A drama that would fuel your inspiration and keep you at a distance. I thought you'd freak out, that you would distance yourself from me and my problems. But you didn't want to hear it, you didn't leave me despite the danger... It drove me even crazier about you... Listen, I'll never have enough words to express my regrets. I needed it, my mind was still clear enough to distinguish between right and wrong. It was wrong."

He takes a step toward me. "Terribly wrong."

My pulse quickens as his figure envelops me.

"Like everything I want to do to you today." he says.

I can't anticipate the passionate kiss he steals from me.

With fluttering eyelashes, I push him away, furious, struck by his fiery lips. "You take what you want, huh? That hasn't changed either."

His eyes fill with the same poison as mine.

"Indeed. I'm persistent, always have been. For once, I tried to let it go, but over the months, I became more and more insane, consumed by regret. I prayed to run into you again. I begged Gala to allow me to see you. I searched for your new address like a madman. I don't know what kind of fucking spell you cast on me—it's been almost a year, and yet I can't get forget you. Even though you disappeared, even though you rejected me, I'm convinced we're meant to be together, Alizee."

I'm short of breath. For him, too, these ten months have just vanished into thin air. Disturbed, I feel my heart crumbling.

"With such feelings, you were capable of lying to me about your intentions while making love to me… I don't know if that makes you even more horrible or a complete hypocrite."

With that conclusion, I turn on my heel and, under the curious gaze of the nurses, desert the wretched hospital.

CHAPTER 37

"Take that, you jerk!" I exclaim, flipping my middle finger at the driver who cuts me off.

Paris and its automotive delights.

Another idiot to my right winks at me, revealing all his teeth. Yet another creep excited by hysterical chicks in cars. Well, he's a creep, but not that ugly.

At the next red light, he rolls down his window, signaling me to do the same. After a quick check in my rearview mirror, I decide that my messy bun doesn't make me look like I just rolled out of bed without doing my hair, and that my bright red lipstick isn't smudged on my teeth. Unfortunately, the light turns green. *Too bad, handsome guy, you won't have the privilege of being shot down by my sweet, chirpy voice.* Smiling, I speed off, leaving the handsome man to his failed flirtation attempt.

It didn't take a week for Galati to be on the verge of new-mom burnout. This morning, she called me in a panic, begging me to meet her in a coffee shop, taking advantage of grandma's babysitting offer to leave Laura with her for a while.

Thank goodness Agatha is there, otherwise, I would have had to deal with bottles and diapers to give her some relief, all because of my big heart.

Wrapped up in my shawl and huge scarf, I enter the meeting place. A forty-something man sitting near the door immediately ogles me. I ignore him, though I'm pleased that it doesn't bother me. Even though

I'm wearing skinny jeans that show off my curves, the other people's opinions no longer intimidate me.

I scan the room but can't find my friend anywhere. Instead, a brunette mane catches my attention. Her silhouette is familiar, and I quickly recognize her angelic face.

Oh, no! What's she doing here? I try to make a discreet exit, but her gaze falls on me. Fuck!

At first frozen, I'm surprised by her delighted expression. Isn't Nabilla overdoing it a bit? Does she remember that I called her a whore when we first met?

The bombshell gets up and rushes toward me, making me feel like a slippery bar of soap ready to slip through her fingers.

"Alizee!" she exclaims, enveloping me in her arms.

And she remembers my name, too. My goodness, these specimens have an elephant's memory!

"Um… hi?"

She takes my hands, her eyes sparkling. "I'm so glad to see you. I was afraid I'd miss you!"

With that, she creates a bad feeling inside me. "What do you mean?"

The beautiful brunette takes a deep breath, her lips pressed together. "Galati won't be coming."

All right, I get it. No victim of baby blues…

"Great, thanks for the set-up," I snap, extracting myself. "Bye now."

My heels pound the ground as I head for the exit, but I hadn't counted on Nabilla's persistence. She follows me outside, urging me to listen to her.

My blood pressure spikes. I don't want to; I can't let her go on. When I reach my car, she blocks my way by leaning against my car's door, her expression imploring. "I beg you, let me talk."

I sigh, clenching my keys in my fist as I turn my head. "I don't want to hear about Ervin," I warn, firm.

"Then I won't say anything. I just ask you to follow me."

"Because I need to go somewhere else now? You have no idea how much I struggled to find a parking spot."

With her botoxed puppy-dog pout, she finally convinces me. She even wedges herself into my car to prevent me from fleeing. I can only bow to her determination.

As she directs me on the road, my stomach sinks. I wish I could turn back, even though she swore Ervin wasn't waiting for me at the end of the road. I wish I could be back in my suburban home, with my Vampyr and his purrs, reading a good book and escaping from my reality where, for the past week, depressing thoughts have been plaguing me.

We reach our destination, and I stop in a residential area in front of a charming little house, complete with fence, garden, and all the bells and whistles. With my eyes fixed on the facade, I wait for her to open the door, fearing what she has in store for me, if not an arranged meeting with her brother-in-law.

The inside seems deserted. The decor is basic but nice, and the place is tidy and welcoming. Family photos adorn a table. Indeed, Nabilla is the wife of Ervin's brother. The picture of her husband leaves no doubt about their genetic link. A little boy accompanies them; I assume he's Ryan, the nephew Ervin told me so much about. Nearby is the most beautiful of the wolves, alongside his older brother and an older woman. Their mother, no doubt.

It's a strange sensation to step into his family's privacy a year after we met, months after we broke up. He never allowed me in there.

His sister-in-law invites me to follow her into the living room, where I find an older woman sitting on the couch knitting. I tense, noting the wheelchair next to her.

"Come," Nabilla whispers, gesturing for me to follow her.

I follow her hesitantly as she approaches the gray-haired woman.

"Mom, let me introduce you to Alizee."

The woman releases her tools as if it were a liberation. Her concentration was so intense that she hadn't noticed me. When she looks up at me, her eyebrows knit together.

"She's Ervin's and my husband's mother," the brunette informs me, in case my keen observation skills weren't up to par.

However, I realize that she must be much younger than her appearance suggests.

"Hello, really nice to meet you," I greet, feeling uneasy.

What a brilliant idea to introduce me to the mother of the jerk who betrayed me! It's her fault he hurt me; she's the one who brought him into this world! Of course, I don't let any of this show, hiding my thoughts behind a more or less pleasant grimace.

"It's because of her that my son's in such a mess?" Mrs. Ervin interrogates with a touch of aggressiveness.

What? Seriously, is this happening?

Nabilla kneels, placing her hand on the other woman's thigh in an attempt to calm her. "It's not her fault. He wasn't right either."

Am I dreaming? Did she invite me here to be lynched? That's all I needed!

I'm about to bolt when Nabilla stands and faces me. "She's a bit straightforward, but she doesn't know the whole story."

"And do you know it?" I retort bitterly.

She nods, then casts a sorry expression at her mother-in-law. "You don't know everything either."

"Are we playing *Clue* here? What I know is enough for me, I assure you."

Nabilla's eyebrows furrow as she points to the wheelchair. "His mother has spinal muscular atrophy."

Dubious, I remain silent, not eager to hear more.

She explains, nonetheless, the ins and outs of the disease, manages to touch me, despite the shriveled appearance of the main person concerned. Her life won't be in danger if she continues to attend her physiotherapy sessions, however, the disability is already serious.

"Before, my boy would charm every girl he met! He was a great seducer, spoiled for choice. Now that he's met you, he's broken. He no longer wants to fool around. How do you think he'll start to make me a family, huh? Children are made by two! If he's not looking for his soulmate, he won't give me grandchildren! And my son loves kids! Plus, he lives alone! Who will take care of him when he wants to rest? Good god, all because of one woman."

Stunned, I don't know what to say. All the compassion she inspired in me vanished in a few sentences. *Calm down, Alizee, she's older than you, don't lash out at her. If she has a heart attack, it'll come back on you...*

"Jeez, I see where Ervin gets it from," I mutter to Nabilla.

She scolds her mother-in-law before continuing her spiel. "In the US, there's an experimental treatment for this disease. But it's very expensive."

There it is.

The missing piece sets my synapses on fire.

When Nabilla explains that Ervin has taken on the responsibility to collect the sum with five zeros, I don't hear her anymore. Only anger throbs in my temples.

"Ervin never mentioned this to me," I growl through clenched teeth. My frustration is overwhelming. So that's why he never told me. Why he never stopped the lies despite his feelings…

His mother.

My heart is close to exploding; it's pounding in my skull so much that I need to isolate myself. But I remain paralyzed. The pain is overwhelming, making me feel like I've been trapped by the fucking story of my life!

"Where is he?" I ask.

My voice jars, surprising the two other women in the room.

"Where is he? I'm going to give to that prick a piece of my mind!"

"She's talking about my son?" the older woman is outraged.

Nabilla clasps her hands in front of her mouth, looking apologetic. "He's not here; he's in Argentina."

"What's he doing in Argentina?"

"He's… gone to see kangaroos."

"Kangaroos? In Argentina? You mean Australia."

"No, he said he was going to Argentina!"

Okay, let's calm down, we're not going to contradict the young lady. There must be *one* kangaroo in Latin America… And Ervin went especially to meet it.

"So, he's supposed to prostitute himself to pay for his mother's treatment, but he has enough money to go on his little world tour?"

She shakes her head vigorously, glancing at her relative, who seems to have no clue about what I'm talking about.

"He went there to shoot a documentary. He's trying to do something quite spectacular to make money."

Fuck! Why did he choose such a time to exile himself to the middle of nowhere?

Pissed off, I pull my phone out of my bag and go to his Instagram profile. A sigh escapes me. Indeed, stunning pictures testify to his journey. No kangaroos, just his smile, people with warm faces amid breathtaking scenery.

I grip my cell phone tightly, cursing him before collapsing inwardly.

CHAPTER 38

ERVIN

The Hill of Seven Colors, better than a Van Gogh, a true work of art by nature. The majestic waterfalls, the crimson lakes, and countless breathtaking landscapes make this journey to Argentina the most beautiful trip of my life. As for the documentary, I'm pinning my hopes on it. This time, it's not about sports, but I'll whisper in the right ear. The unique angle from which I approached these lands has never been explored; it will surely pique the interest of a producer.

After two months of dreaming, the dreary winter of Paris welcomes me back. However, it doesn't dampen my good mood. I've seen too many wonders to let it get me down. After dropping off my belongings at my apartment, Cem invites me to his place, where the whole family is gathered. He knows this gathering would typically make me run away, but I must admit, I'm starving.

After a refreshing shower, I eagerly join the Shiro family, drooling and praying that Nabilla hasn't burned her dish this time. Upon arriving at my eldest brother's place, I realize it's only half family gathering, as neither the wives nor the children of my brothers are present. My mother is the last person I greet, planting a kiss on her forehead. She seems to be filled with renewed energy, her face appearing serene, much to my delight. I settle down beside her.

She immediately bombards me with reproaches. "You're too tan, son! Do you want to get skin cancer?"

I roll my eyes, offering her a wide smile.

"Don't worry, it's going to take more than a little tan to bring down a guy like him," Cem teases.

"It'll help me charm the ladies, Mom," I boast, in turn.

She loves it when I say that. The thought of having a son who is attractive fills her with pride, although she would love to see me settle down and give her a bunch of grandchildren. Cem and I are her closest sons. We've always been devoted to our mother, while the others tend to prioritize their own families. My travels have never stopped me from showing her all my love. She's the apple of my eye, and it only takes a glance for her to understand that.

"You don't need to get sunburned to be attractive. You're naturally the most handsome man in France."

Fati—pretty good-looking himself—shakes his head, dismayed. It's obvious he would have preferred to receive those compliments. A childish sense of satisfaction washes over me as our mother nestles into my arms.

"Thanks, Mom. I was in the sun; I didn't have much of a choice."

"I know, I know, it's for work, but I missed you, Ervin."

For work, yes. And to forget, to put some distance…

Nabilla adorns the table with traditional cookies and serves the coffee. She then settles into the armchair in a solemn manner that piques my curiosity.

It's Cem's turn to silence the room and speak up. "I have something to tell you all," he declares, barely containing a smile. "Mom knows, but I wanted to announce it to the whole family at once. She'll soon be able to start a more effective treatment for her illness. We've finally managed to raise the necessary funds."

Stunned, I remain motionless for a few seconds before letting adrenaline rush in. Damn, my mother might actually get better!

My brothers burst with joy, hugging our mother, while I rush over to Cem to ask him how this miracle is possible.

He pats me on the back, nodding toward his ecstatic wife. "It's thanks to her. I have an amazing wife."

The tenderness in his eyes moves me even more. "What did she do this time?"

She joins us, exchanging a glance with my mother, who smiles at her, and intervenes, "She's our guardian angel. The one who writes books. There's finally hope, Ervin."

Huh?

Nabilla giggles, nodding her head.

"What's she talking about?" Joni exclaims.

My chest tightens. What's this all about? "Who's writing books?" I interrogate my sister-in-law.

That pest keeps grinning. "I don't think we know many writers, do we?"

I swallow, gripped by horror. "What… have you done?"

Nabilla approaches, abruptly grabbing my shoulder and locking her dark eyes with mine. "We just told her the truth. The rest, she decided on her own. A check arrived a few days later, and we didn't ask her for anything."

Confounded, I feel my brain frying. My heart exploding. My legs carry me outside in a sprint, and I hop onto my motorcycle amid my brothers' calls.

***

Arriving at my destination, I curse Gala for her stubbornness. I had to explain the situation for her to finally cooperate.

In front of the building, I take a deep breath. My excitement is at its peak, feeling like my cells are fizzing throughout my body. If I'd taken drugs, it would've been the same.

I stride up the pathway and hammer the doorbell without second thought, ecstatic. After the incredible experience in Latin America, this news comes as the cherry on top.

Contrary to my erratic pulse, the door creaks open slowly and ominously. The face of the woman who has haunted me for months appears in the crack, faithful to my memories. Better. Her messy bun, her piercing cat-like eyes, her angelic beauty contrasting with her surly demeanor—I've missed them so much.

She doesn't have time to be surprised. I force the door open, and with authority, I dive onto her lips.

It's so fucking good. A dizzy sensation overwhelms me; the taste of her mouth is divine. Yet, as soon as I take a step inside, she violently pushes me away.

"What the hell are you doing, Ervin?" she screams, furious.

Dumbfounded, I blink, not understanding. "Alizee, I—"

The hell in her eyes destabilizes me. Could I have been mistaken? No… impossible. Nabilla would never have told me such nonsense, even to reconcile us.

"Alizee… what got into you?"

"I'll ask you the same question!" she retorts, looking distraught, her fingers on her lips.

For a few seconds, I'm petrified, my chest heaving with rapid, deep breaths, lost in a million questions. "What you did… it's beyond generosity. That check—it's the reason why I betrayed you. I don't deserve it." I struggle to articulate, more moved than I can express.

"Indeed," she asserts, acrimoniously. "You don't deserve it, but your mother does."

We size each other up, her wrapped in her long woolen cardigan, defensively positioned against the doorframe, me with my elbow on the jamb, unsure what to do.

"How can I thank you?"

"By disappearing permanently from my life."

There it is, an uppercut perfectly returned. I struggle to swallow, my muscles tense to the extreme. Her voice is hoarse, laden with sorrow.

"You can't ask me that after what you've done. If my mother recovers, it will be thanks to you. You don't realize, it's completely insane! You're…" *Amazing, beautiful, inside and out.* "The woman of my life," I finish, as if in revelation.

Alizee is made for me, there's no doubt about it. I've never had these damn feelings for any other woman. She's exceptional, different, a whole of her own, and I'm sure I can make her happy… after healing her wounds.

My confession leaves her speechless. "Stop," she implores, her voice trembling.

I bend my knee, placing it on the ground, and encircle her waist without warning, blocking her attempt to step back. I need her. "I feel so guilty. Being the source of your suffering disgusts me. If I could absorb it, I swear, I'd live it in your place without hesitation."

"You idiot!" she cracks, pounding her fists on my shoulders. "You could have talked to me directly instead of relying on Alan and lying to me like you did!"

I'm stunned by her words, by the tremors in her voice that tear me apart. I have fucking tears in my eyes! Her fingers grip my hair, tilting my head so that I look at her. So that I face her. So that I take responsibility for my mess.

My throat tightens with pain. "How could I have known? I was desperate. How could I have imagined that you would lend me that much? We never talked about money."

A grimace twists her features. "Of course, you never told me about your family! The only glimpse I had was some bimbo with a G-string sticking out of her pants and eight-inch heels."

"I know," I murmur against her stomach. "I was afraid it might become serious."

"It already was. My feelings were serious! And you, you idiot, that money, I didn't lend it to you. I gave it! Now, I want nothing more to do with you!"

With that sentence, she breaks free of my embrace and rushes inside, trying to slam the door. I quickly block it with my foot, wasting no time in following Alizee into her new home. I would have liked to admire her interior, but my urgent desire to get my hands on her overrides that.

She disappears into her living room at a run.

"Don't reject me!" I thunder, this time as a command.

Quickly, I circle around her large sofa and grab her arm. She turns to me, her resentment intensified, shooting daggers from her eyes.

"Don't reject me like this! I can't accept your check without giving something in return!"

Without warning, she slaps me with all her might. Despite the pain, I kiss her. With all my might.

She recoils and shouts, "Rot in hell, with my charity!"

Once more, I kiss her fiercely. Even more fiercely this time.

Despite her effort to push me away, the passion I ignite between us is consuming. In no time, it overwhelms us, guiding Alizee's claws to my neck, her breasts against my chest. It makes her surrender to me, overwhelmed by her own desires.

When my leg stumbles over the couch's armrest, I stagger backward and slump onto the seat. I imagine myself getting up, chasing this fury through her house. But it's not happening: she lunges on me, straddling me, looking menacing.

I break out in a cold sweat.

With narrowed eyes, she shakes her head, then grabs my neck. "I hate you!" she snarls before sinking her teeth into my lower lip.

From the movement of her hips on my cock, I deduce that my groan of pain excites her. So, without any further hesitation, I grab her waist, swiftly rising. But my eagerness betrays me; my forehead collides with her nose.

"Ouch! That hurts!"

Before I can apologize, she retaliates by slapping me again. "I hate you!"

"I love you," I say.

Dumbfounded, she stares at me, eyes wide.

I seize her lips, shedding my jacket and even my sweater, despite the cold.

Her tongue inside my mouth is exhilarating. Rediscovering her warmth, her scent, her little moans is liberating. My erection is already painful.

"Fuck, I missed you, I need you," I growl between our animalistic kisses.

She takes the opportunity to claw at my back. The irritation sends delightful shivers through me, making me even more bestial. "I love you," I can't help but blurt out, all my barriers down.

"I got it, yes!" she replies.

Her cardigan flies off, snagging a lock of her hair, unraveling her bun, and eliciting another cry of pain from her.

"Shit, let me help you."

She swats my hand away, managing on her own, visibly agitated, then pulls her little sweater over her head. She looks stunning in her lace bra, but she's still overdressed for me.

"Get rid of that," I urge. My fingers trace her back to unclasp the bra, as they usually do, but nervousness robs me of all dexterity. "Your clasp sucks. Is it welded or something?" I grumble into her neck.

"It's just that you don't know how to do it," she chuckles.

"Are you kidding? I'm a pro," I retort, offended. "I've done it before with just the power of my gaze."

She shakes her head, mocking me as she jumps up to take care of it herself. One step backward, and she bangs her calf on the sharp corner of the coffee table, then tumbles to the floor, on all fours and tits exposed.

"Damn it, are you trying to kill me or what?" she roars in pain.

I feel sorry for her, but my excitement takes over. I seize her pants at her ankles, swiftly removing them.

"Not exactly," I say, grabbing her butt.

She clings to my shoulders as I lift her, sighing as soon as our bare chests touch. The velvet of her skin is intoxicating, her warmth penetrating deep into my heart.

Noticing the dining table not far from the living room, I rush us there, oblivious to a fucking chair in front of it that almost hits me in the balls.

It hurts! A curse bursts in my throat as I lay Alizee down on the table.

Everything is chaotic, as if the universe conspired against the fervor of our desire. Damn, I want her so badly. So much so that my heart might explode at any moment.

My angelic demon busies herself with the button on my jeans. In vain. And it annoys her as much as it amuses me.

"Let the pros handle it." I brush off her hand.

She curses at me, breathless with impatience. She wants it as much as I do.

With my pants on the ground, I grab her hips and pull her toward me. Our sexes bump against each other behind the fabric of our underwear, triggering a first surge in my body.

Her breasts harden, as I palm them. My eyes scrutinize every inch of her body as she undulates against my cock. She feels so good.

"I want to be inside you," I feverishly confess. "I want to possess you."

Her eyes light up.

"Your body, your head, your heart. Then, you won't be able to escape me. You drive me crazy, Alizee."

At first her jaw is clenched, but she eventually furrows her brow, a barrier against her emotion, and retorts, "Shut up and fuck me."

I'm not sure whether to laugh or frown. So, I let my impulses guide me, push aside her panties, and dive between her legs.

Without delicacy, my tongue crashes against her folds. I inhale her scent, reveling in the familiarity.

Surprised, Alizee continues to swear, arching on the table.

I tease her clitoris, tracing hundreds of patterns around it, sucking and lucking, relishing in the wetness of her arousal. I could spend the whole day pleasuring her like this, hearing her moan, watching her squirm under my tongue. Her happiness is mine; I wish it were as easy to absolve myself of my sins and mistakes.

"I love you," I whisper between her legs.

"Shut up, you liar," she groans, gripping my hair.

"The liar is going to make you come so hard the neighbors will call the cops," I grumble before teasing her entrance.

"There aren't any neighbors for miles, idiot," she retorts before emitting a squeak.

"I know, that's the point."

I straighten, annoyed, lower my boxer shorts, and without warning, penetrate her with a sharp thrust.

She widens her eyes, locked onto my fiery gaze. Deep inside her hot and wet channel, I freeze. The sensations are exquisite, could make me come in five seconds. My cock pulses inside her, eliciting guttural pleading sounds.

"My elephant trunk is going to send you to nirvana, darling," I boast, a half-smile on my lips.

"Oh, my god, what a jerk! Shut up," she complains, rolling her eyes. "Oh, yes!"

She won't be so smug for long. As soon as I slide into her, her walls contract around me. It's fucking good, fucking liberating. The way her face flushes with pleasure hypnotizes me. Her little mouth uttering encouragement, admitting that I'm sexy, that I please her, that she missed it, sends me into a trance. Her gaze locked on my chest, on my abs tensing with each of my movements, blows my mind. The desire in her eyes kills me, galvanizes the narcissism that has been lacking in me these past months. Between her thighs, I feel like a beast.

I keep my promise, make her scream for the whole neighborhood, and join her when the end is near. I'd love to continue for hours, to pleasure her indefinitely, but finding her again stirs up my emotions. When she has her orgasm, I let myself go, bringing her to the floor to pierce her with my profound despair. The one that has consumed me this past year. Her body is shaking. My knees and elbows take the blows, however, the waves of pleasure override the irritation.

We both end up naked, lying on the floor, breathing shallowly.

Sweating, I stare at the ceiling's imperfections until I regain my senses. It's freezing in this house. Wouldn't she want to cuddle up against me like before? We could warm each other without having to get up. I don't dare ask her.

Shit, Ervin, when did you become such a pussy?

The silence stretches. Her breath slows down, taking mine with it. Frozen, I decide to break the silence. "Now, what do we do?"

No answer. Is she still so angry with me? Is she going to kick me out?

"Alizee?"

I tilt my head in her direction. Her eyelids are closed, the movements of her chest are regular.

Despite all the turmoil, she managed to fall asleep. I must have exhausted her. It's because I'm too good!

Proud of myself, I immerse myself in the contemplation of her beauty, then decide to take advantage of her warmth. Saturated with endorphins, I cuddle up against her, gently spooning with her, and take the opportunity to absorb her scent before she kicks me out of her life again.

***

"Get up! Get up! Seriously. What a pain in the ass!"

The violence in her tone startles me awake. Dazed, I sit up, assaulted by the brightness. Where am I? Was that Alizee's voice just now? If it doesn't match the one moaning in my dreams; it stings like my least pleasant memories.

A glance at the large table next to me reminds me of recent events. A torrid fuck with the woman standing behind the chair, dressed and fresh as a daisy, setting two plates on the surface.

"You must be hungry. I heated up some pizza," she informs me, her brows furrowed in a grumpy expression.

Pizza. So that's what that delicious smell is! Indeed, I wouldn't mind. Not bothered in the slightest by my nudity, I struggle to get up and flop into the chair.

The sight of the woman who's anchored herself in my gut upon waking puts me in a good mood; I can't help but let a smile slip through.

Alizee freezes, eyes wide. "Uh… Are you planning to eat naked?"

My head is still pounding. I'm glad to be here, but if she could spare me her grumbles, I'd appreciate it. "Is that a problem?"

"Eating without washing up is disgusting. You stink," she retorts, darting into the kitchen.

What's she getting at? She's driving me crazy with her nonsense. First, she rejects me outright, then she writes a huge check to my family for the very reason that led me to betray her. She pushes me away when I kiss her, but then drags me into a passionate romp. Invites me to eat while scolding me… I have no clue what this woman wants right now. Should I leave? *Not a chance.* Or should I actually shower?

"I… don't know where the bathroom is." I attempt to decipher the situation.

With her back to me, she retorts, "Figure it out. You didn't want to leave when I asked you to, now you deal with it."

Okay… I guess I'll go for a power wash.

The house is spacious, with rustic decor and high-quality furniture. I like that she kept that rustic touch. The bathroom is at the end of the hallway. Very cozy, too. On the edge of the bathtub, two towels are neatly folded, emanating a floral scent.

I grin at the sight of Alizee's thoughtfulness. She didn't want me to leave… She's just incapable of owning up to her decisions. Yet it must have been a carefully considered gesture; you don't just write such a check to someone you hate.

As I step into the shower, something on the steamy glass disturbs my field of vision. I approach the corner, reading an inscription delicately traced with fingertips in the steam:

I love you, too.

I swallow, close my eyelids for a few seconds to savor those three words. It's impossible to suppress the warm sensation in my chest, compressed with pleasure.

Relief.

After a refreshing shower, I wrap a towel around my hips—a must for charming the ladies—and return to the living room, sporting a silly grin on my face.

Alizee is busy taking out the delicious-smelling pizzas from the oven. As soon as she sees me, I pass under her scrutinizing gaze. From the spark in her eyes, I can tell her appetite is redirected toward something else.

Yeah, you hit the jackpot with that one, kitten…

She remains frozen. She squints, understanding my satisfaction, shakes her head, and then abruptly closes the oven. "Let's eat."

She might say this with dryness, but I can sense a lot of discomfort behind her facade. A communicative awkwardness, because even I don't know how to react to avoid being kicked out, perpetually playing my eternal role as *persona non grata*.

This damn pizza is good. Or maybe the situation is altering its flavor?

Who knows? They say love makes you stupid. Well, I was already pretty dumb before falling for this lousy cook.

We eat in tense silence. I'm seated at the end of the table, and she's right next to me, avoiding my persistent gaze. We'll have to communicate eventually; sex is great, but it's not enough to heal the wounds.

"Thank you," I begin.

She glitches for a moment, then continues eating with her eyes lowered.

"You can't imagine what your gesture means to me. Whether it works out or not, this check is—"

"I suppose Alan never compensated you," she cuts in coldly.

I swallow hard. That's a subject that makes me uncomfortable. "He was banking on your next success to pay me."

She scoffs bitterly, hydrating her throat with a sip of water. "How did you meet him?" she asks.

"It's a long and boring story. Let's just say he was there for my mother when my father left. He's known me since I was young."

"Family friend, then," she mutters. "The way he used you speaks volumes about his integrity, in any case."

She doesn't know how right she is. That shark never inspired trust in me. "I was desperate."

"I know. Or at least I hope I know," she says, shaking her head. "I wouldn't have done it for just anyone, but I understand... I understand the reasons that drove you to go through with it. I remembered your warnings, your hesitation, your refusal to commit. Some lies are still painful, but I understand."

My chest tightens.

She takes a bite, offering me a profile of innocent beauty. Her hair is loose as I like it, her green eyes lightly made up, and her lips glistening with sauce.

"You may act tough, but you're a beautiful person, Alizee. Right now, I probably don't deserve you, but I'll do everything to be worthy of you."

Her cheeks blush. "You won't go far in a bath towel," she grumbles with a bored air that I know is feigned.

"Stop it, you secretly enjoy this testosterone display. I've read all your books, you know. You won't fool me."

She doesn't smile, damn it! I'm sure she's holding back.

Suddenly, something brushes against my calves. I startle, seized with fear, then curse that damned black cat as it flees with his tail in the air, his asshole on display. Damn Vampyr!

"Some things never change around here."

"There're things we'll never be able to do without," she murmurs, her mouth full and her gaze averted.

In that moment, the image I perceive transcends me. I know it begins now. Our story starts the moment she surrenders, when her lips curve into a subtle smile, though she remains on the defensive.

Happy, I slide my hand onto her thigh. "Tomorrow, I'll come back to make you chocolate chip pancakes."

EPILOGUE

Ervin was right. It wasn't that big of a deal, this TV show stint. Well, I must say, for now, I only agree to appear on late-night shows, watched by true literary enthusiasts who have nothing better to do with their evenings.

It took me a year to muster the courage. A year during which my boyfriend worked me over in every sense of the word. And there you have it: in reality, once the surprise that I'm not a man wears off, my fans couldn't care less about my appearance. Joy!

What's a bit more complicated for me is handling criticism without hurling curses at these failed writers. My books are best-sellers, so why nitpick? Readers are happy, they buy, read, love… Geez! These interviewers won't teach me how to do my job.

As I say goodbye to the last guests on the set, a figure moves behind the technical team. Marshall waves frantically, urging me to pick up the pace.

"You're just arriving? The show's over," I reprimand, once he reaches me.

"Sorry, I got held up in the lobby by an unexpected issue," he says, giving me two cheek kisses.

"An unexpected issue?"

"An unexpected issue waiting for you in your dressing room."

"Oh."

I have a pretty good idea about the nature of this obstacle, and he's going to hear about it.

I open the door to my dressing room and find Ervin pacing, his eyes locked on his watch. Wasn't he supposed to be sitting in the audience until the end of the show?

"Hey, you!"

He startles as if I caught him red-handed... whatever it may be. It's suspicious!

"It's about time. It took forever! You rocked it, kitten," he exclaims, enveloping me in his strong arms where I always feel so comfortable.

No! He won't charm me that easily! "Can I know what happened with Marshall?"

He steps back to scrutinize me better, a furrow forming on his forehead. "Does he have to show up at all your interviews? For support, I'm here; his presence isn't necessary."

I knew it! That stupid jealousy! "He's my publisher, Ervin."

"So what? He didn't write the book; we don't need him."

Disheartened, I shake my head, sighing. If I dare to declare that I like having my editor and friend close to me, Mr. In Love will sulk for days. He doesn't hold Marshall in high regard, only seeing him as the man whose tongue once scraped the back of my throat.

Moreover, he applies himself to it with dedication at this moment. Didn't he have an appointment after the recording of the show? He had warned me that once it was over, he would leave quickly.

"Babe?" he grumbles against my lips.

"Mm, yes?" The effect of the stress fading away and his palms sliding over my waist generates a flurry of tingles on my skin.

"Babe?"

"Mmm, yes, babe?" I repeat between his delicious kisses.

His excitement grows against my hips.

When he slips his hand into my pants, I flinch.

"Here?" I whisper, scandalized. What a naughty little rascal! Not that it surprises me coming from him, though.

He pauses, squinting at me oddly. "Alizee... what day are we?"

My mental calculations are faster than my response. "Oh!" I exclaim, wide-eyed. "*Ovulation!*"

He nods solemnly, relieved that I finally understand, and lets me take over.

"We have to be quick; I've got something after."

I push him onto the chair, block the door with another chair, and stand before him, lifting my skirt and removing my thong.

"Your elephant trunk and I are going to work wonders, my sex machine!"

***

Indeed, Ervin and I are trying to conceive. The love he has for me has awakened his paternal instinct. Since then, he has been trying to woo me with crap plans like cooking every day during my pregnancy, foot massages, chocolates galore, and all that jazz. Of course, I gave in. Besides, the idea of a mini-him doesn't repulse me as much as I imagined. The magic of love, I suppose.

Obviously, I'll make a bad mother. But he will be an exemplary father, which will balance things out. Armed with this certainty, the idea enchants me more and more, so we copulate to the max during my ovulation period. Well, it doesn't change much because ever since we moved in together, it's been a sausage fest every day! This man is insatiable. And I enjoy the orgasmic benefits his sexual appetite provides me.

Only Galati knows our intentions, and she's more than thrilled, eagerly awaiting a playmate for her Laura. Her little Gollum—a nickname that now sticks to her like glue—requires a lot of attention. So, she decided to resign from her job, dedicating herself more to writing her increasingly popular books. Also, she takes care of my donations to the Vanilla-Chocolate orphanage, since I now lead a hectic life. I learned that Vadim and Maeva, the most obedient ones at the institution, were able to be placed together in a foster home. That's the best I could have wished for them; separation would have shattered them. My best friend reported the news to me in an ecstatic state.

Milo and she recently married, crushed by the pressure from their respective parents. I think they're happy about it, but that's why I keep my plans secret. I have no desire for anyone to impose anything on me. My mother—happy that I'm in a relationship—is now focused on building my family.

We'll see once the seed is sown.

Speaking of family, while I'm getting along better and better with Charles, the relationship between Guillaume and me is still tense. I no longer hold any resentment, having understood my mother's pain regarding my father's infidelities. But years of rejection cannot be easily erased.

Meanwhile, Ervin is producing more and more interesting documentaries around the globe. He drags me along, sharing with me his love for exploration. My books thank him for it!

I imagined that our chaotic start would have strained our feelings, that despite my forgiveness, our relationship would suffer. Not at all! This scoundrel is the best boyfriend the world has ever seen. One might also think that he's making amends to make up for his betrayal, but his behavior with his family belies this hypothesis.

Speaking of his family, my check was not in vain; my future mother-in-law has been benefiting from the much-coveted treatment for the past few months. While its effectiveness was initially questioned, in recent weeks, the results have been evident. No remission, but a clear slowing down of the disease.

Hallelujah! I didn't suffer for nothing.

The relief and gratitude calming the face of my Adonis are worth all the gold in the world; I love him even more for it. Yes, I'm crazy about Ervin Shiro, even if I show it to him sarcastically. This seducer got under my skin. I'll be eternally grateful to him.

Another piece of good news: my romance novel has been a hit. I occasionally visit the set of its film adaptation and am delighted with the choice of actors. As soon as she met Ervin, the lousy director tried to snatch him up to play my male lead! The rascal wasn't against it, so I had to set the record straight. Every kiss exchanged with the heroine, however fake it might be, would be equivalent to a missed lovemaking session. That quickly discouraged my little womanizer.

These days, I slip into the skin of Liliana Fork and sketch imaginary worlds, much to the delight of my man, one of my most fervent fans. According to Delphine, my fantasy editor, although I still have work to do, she predicts a big success. Her predictions elevate my motivation to its peak.

Meanwhile, Alan seethes in silence. Well, not exactly silence. He, who used to praise me to everyone, now doesn't hesitate to tear me down whenever he gets the chance. His resentment is ugly. Nevertheless, I'm just waiting for the end of my contracts to reclaim my rights. Let him choke on his greed; it will serve him right!

The days... no, the years ahead look wonderfully bright. I'm happy, I have the best boyfriend on the planet—incidentally, the best walking sex toy that could exist—my curves no longer bother me in the least. I'm professionally fulfilled, and... fuck, I feel nauseous!

Other novels from
WARM PUBLISHING

Scan to easily acess all of Warm Publishing books:

Join also our Facebook Group, Book Warmers, to get the lastedt updates and talk about books and more!

Falling for the Voice
by *Mag Maury*

The sexiest of surprises... and the most unbearable!

My plan was simple: Find a job quickly in order to make rent. And I found one. A waitressing job at the hottest pub in town!

Everything was going smoothly until he arrived: Matt. Sexy. Arrogant. Six feet three of muscles that drive women into a hysterical frenzy at every single one of his concerts.

This guy is really comfortable on stage and oh, so enticing. We girls can try to put him out of our minds but we end up wanting him anyway. And he knows it.

Except me, Charlotte. I say no!

Well... Maybe! After all, I have never really been good at resisting temptation...

My HipsterNext Door
by *Mag Maury*

In Liverpool, the barbershop Hipster Maniac is an institution. Run by three bearded, tattooed friends, it is the place to listen to great rock, get a trim, and have a drink.

But for Line, it also spelled trouble. For starters, when she first got to the neighborhood, she rear-ended Jordan's car, who turned out to be one of the three barbers. Then she discovered that they were neighbors in business and residence! So no way can she escape this muscle-flaunting, smoldering man who is covered in tattoos and... completely insufferable!

He draws her near only to push her away. He toys with her shamelessly. But worst of all he hates Christmas whereas that is Line's very favorite time of year!

Beneath a backdrop of festive fairy lights, intoxicatingly passionate kisses, and blistering banter... It's on!

The Cocky Heir
by *Ana K. Anderson*

She is about to get married. But not to him.

Quinn MacFayden, an accomplished expat businessman in New York, is set to return to Scotland in extremis to protect the precious family legacy. His 91-year-old grandfather is about to marry a perfect stranger sixty-six years his junior... And that is out of the question! Quinn swears it. Over his dead body will Dawn Fleming ever be part of the family!

But Dawn is not a future bride like the others. She is nowhere near the gold digger he imagined and, above all, she knows just how to stand up to him. And so a game of cat and mouse begins between them. A war with no holds barred and where surrender has never been so tempting...

My Stepbrother: A Sexual Revelation
by *Sophie S. Pierucci*

Cassie is a highly intelligent young woman... Too much so for her own good!

And she is as daunting as she is intriguing. Carl, the son of his father's second wife, would hardly say otherwise!

Carl is the exact opposite of his steady father. He is a player and a slayer. Afraid of nothing and no one. Except for Cassie when she asks him to introduce her to the pleasures of the flesh.

And when the situation gets out of control, it is too late to turn back, and the two lovers find themselves ensnared in forbidden passion. Forbidden by everyone: society, their parents, their friends.

But how to resist the desire that consumes them?

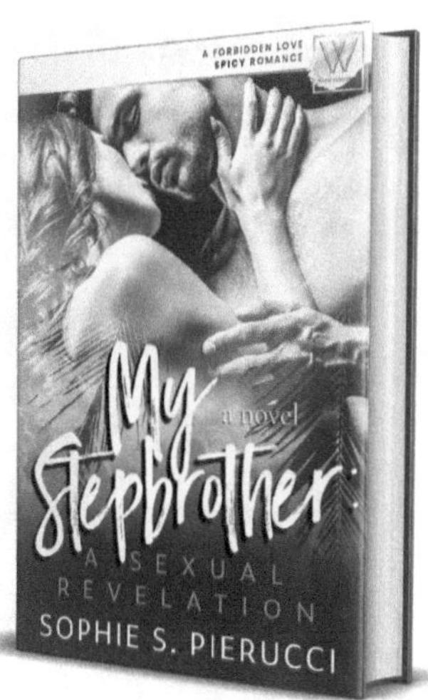

Roommate with my Boss
by *Erin Graham*

Boss, roommate, fake fiancé... real lover?

Étienne is cold, charismatic, and he never shies away from a challenge.

He masters everything down to the smallest detail... until a little accountant with an unlikely look and flowers in her hair inserts herself into his daily life.

She is whimsical, full of life, laughs at the rules and gets around them, talks all the time except about her past... and she drives him crazy. Yet, it's impossible to fire her.

She needs a job and a roof over her head; he needs a fake fiancée...

Is it a deal?

Your Power Over me
by *Missy Heart*

A family home heavy with secrets, a dangerously charismatic owner.

Will her arrival at Iron House be the end of her?

Ever since she was a teenager, Lovisa has known it: at Iron House, anything can happen, especially the worst.

However, when she is forced to return to the family home for her stepfather's funeral, her heart races: she is going to see him again, this "brother" who she never wanted and who yet turned her whole world upside down.

Now at the head of a drug cartel, authoritarian and brutal, Niklas is nothing like the teenager she knew nine years ago. At his side, Lovisa finds herself immersed in a harsh, ruthless—but fascinating—world.

Irremediably attracted to this man who wants her as much harm as good, will Lovisa manage to fight her unmentionable desires? Or will she give in to Niklas' magnetic darkness?

Touchdown
by *Sonia Birdy*

She's a runner, but the campus star quaterback runs faster than she does!

Rocky has had a chaotic life from which she concluded three fundamental things: life is a succession of problems to be solved, men are assholes to be avoided and promises are only binding on fools who want to believe in them. So, unlike the other girls on campus, boys are not a priority for her. Worse, she sees them as an obstacle to her success!

But during a student party, she meets Jude. Freshly transferred from Harvard to play on Brown's soccer team, Jude is the new star on campus. Handsome and inaccessible, he is the type not to get attached: the perfect candidate for a one-night stand.

But the chemistry is too strong. And though Rocky is determined to run away from him, he is determined to conquer her heart.

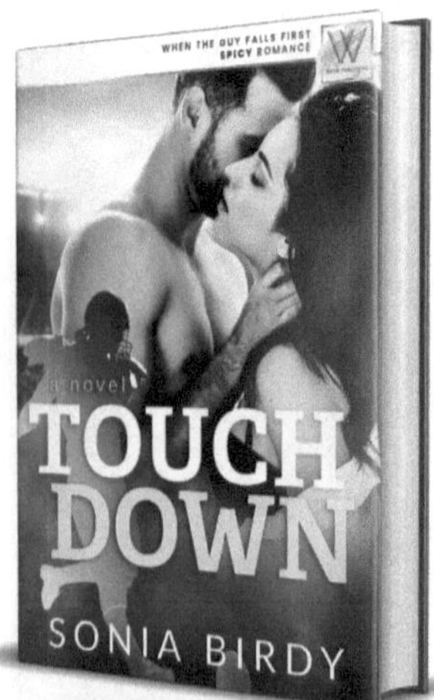

The Courtesan Queen
by *Anna Triss*

After centuries of peace, the four Elemental Clans of Symbiosis are at war with each other. Sylvan, the young King Fuegis, a cruel and ruthless warrior with the ability to control Fire magic, is enslaving the other three kingdoms of Symbiosis, spreading death and terror in his path.

I am Queen Alena of the Glace Clan, which is affiliated with Water magic. I was captured by my worst enemy during the siege of my city. I already know the fate that awaits me tonight. Like the princesses of the other two Elemental Clans that preceded me, I am destined to become the new wife of the tyrant Sylvan.

And tomorrow at dawn... I will be executed.

But queen or slave, I am first and foremost a Glace. I will honor our ancestral philosophy.

"Facing his enemy, a Glace sheds no tears, and never gives up wielding his weapons."

The Private Garden
by *Oly TL*

The most disturbing and transgressive of contracts...

Tiger Sexton seems to have it all. Charisma. Respect. Relentless business acumen. More fortune than he could spend in a life and a sublime wife, Sophia.

When Oceane is invited by Mrs. Sexton for a job interview in one of the restaurants that her husband gave her, the young French tourist knows nothing about this couple. Their name means

nothing to her, people are not her thing. She just wants a job, a place to live and to move on with her life... Sophia's proposal comes at the right time: the Sextons are looking for an *au pair*.

But by opening their doors to her, many other locks are likely to open. Is Oceane ready for this? And what about Sophia, and especially the Tiger lurking in this Secret Garden?

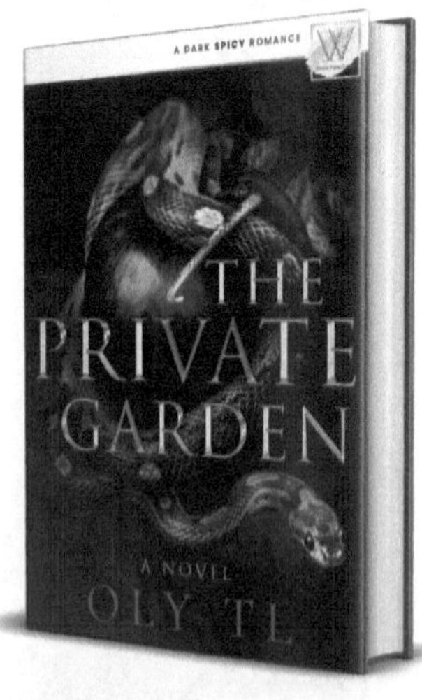

Keep in touch with Farah Anah

Join her on her social medai accounts!

Facebook:
https://www.facebook.com/farah.Anah.Auteure/?locale=-fr_FR

Instagram:
https://www.instagram.com/farah_anah_auteure/?hl=fr

Acknowledgments

Here I am, at the end of this story, or shall I say, at the end of my challenge! Indeed, I was eager to see if I was capable of writing a light romance... IN JUST ONE BOOK. I'm so thrilled to have succeeded.

Around this adventure, I would like to thank several people.

First and foremost, Sarah, the superb editor (a little reminiscent of Ludivine, perhaps?), thank you for trusting me once again. What a relief to have convinced you with *The Romance of My Life... No Way!* Especially in this genre. Ervin sends you lots of kisses!

Thanks to Emma who shared this challenge with me, followed me chapter by chapter, and reassured me about my uncertainties.

Thanks to Maya who inspired the hero's name, of whom I'm now particularly fond.

Let's talk about this hero! Like many authors, I draw inspiration from male models for both their physical appearance and the aura they exude. This time, it's someone I've seen with my own eyes during a trip abroad. I won't go into details, but I'll direct you to Club 281, a renowned dancers' club in Montreal, and if you happen to spot a certain *Owen* there, give him my regards! (Check out the website.) Thanks to him for fueling my imagination and giving nuances to Ervin!

Thanks to Haley and Marie for their proofreading. Thanks to the Black Ink team for all the editorial work, thanks to Léni for proofreading and for the little extra added at the end of the journey.

Thanks to Momo, my friends, my family for their

unwavering support.

Thanks to you, readers, for your feedback, your enthusiasm, your support—you have no idea how much it means to me! It's a real driving force, an additional motivation to make my dreams come true!

Thanks to the Black'Inkettes for always being there, for the fun, for the little family that makes this strength!

I'll see you in the next adventure!

About the Author

Farah is a 35-year-old Belgian novelist who has been crafting stories since childhood, using her imagination as a means of escape. Initially inspired by manga, she now explores a wide range of genres, always with romance at the heart of her work. After sharing her stories on an online platform, she caught the eye of a French publishing house and has since published around fifteen books. While she has a particular fondness for dark, emotionally charged romances, she also enjoys weaving sensitive topics into her lighter, fun, and sexy stories.